LORDS OF MARS

By the same author

WARHAMMER 40,000

• ADEPTUS MECHANICUS •

PRIESTS OF MARS
LORDS OF MARS
GODS OF MARS (Autumn 2014)

• ULTRAMARINES •

NIGHTBRINGER
WARRIORS OF ULTRAMAR
DEAD SKY, BLACK SUN
THE KILLING GROUND
COURAGE AND HONOUR
THE CHAPTER'S DUE

EYE OF VENGEANCE
An Ultramarines audio drama

STORM OF IRON
An Iron Warriors Novel

• THE HORUS HERESY •

FALSE GODS
FULGRIM
MECHANICUM
A THOUSAND SONS
THE OUTCAST DEAD
ANGEL EXTERMINATUS
VENGEFUL SPIRIT

WOLF HUNT
A Horus Heresy audio drama, exclusively available from
blacklibrary.com

A WARHAMMER 40,000 NOVEL

LORDS OF MARS

GRAHAM MCNEILL

BLACK LIBRARY

For Nik, Lorraine, Dan, Laura, Rob, Gemma and Jo at the Village for keeping me heavily caffeinated and letting me hog the big table all the time.

A BLACK LIBRARY PUBLICATION
First published in Great Britain in 2013.
This edition published in 2014 by
Black Library,
Games Workshop Ltd.,
Willow Road,
Nottingham,
NG7 2WS, UK

10 9 8 7 6 5 4 3 2 1

Cover by Slawomir Maniak.

A CIP record for this book is available from the British Library.

UK ISBN 13: 978 1 84970 702 2
US ISBN 13: 978 1 84970 703 9

Printed and bound by CPI Group (UK) Ltd, Croydon, CR0 4YY

It is the 41st millennium. For more than a hundred centuries the Emperor has sat immobile on the Golden Throne of Earth. He is the Master of Mankind by the will of the gods, and master of a million worlds by the might of his inexhaustible armies. He is a rotting carcass writhing invisibly with power from the Dark Age of Technology. He is the Carrion Lord of the Imperium for whom a thousand souls are sacrificed every day, so that he may never truly die.

Yet even in his deathless state, the Emperor continues his eternal vigilance. Mighty battlefleets cross the daemon-infested miasma of the warp, the only route between distant stars, their way lit by the Astronomican, the psychic manifestation of the Emperor's will. Vast armies give battle in His name on uncounted worlds. Greatest amongst his soldiers are the Adeptus Astartes, the Space Marines, bio-engineered super-warriors. Their comrades in arms are legion: the Imperial Guard and countless Planetary Defence Forces, the ever-vigilant Inquisition and the tech-priests of the Adeptus Mechanicus to name only a few. But for all their multitudes, they are barely enough to hold off the ever-present threat from aliens, heretics, mutants – and worse.

To be a man in such times is to be one amongst untold billions. It is to live in the cruellest and most bloody regime imaginable. These are the tales of those times. Forget the power of technology and science, for so much has been forgotten, never to be re-learned. Forget the promise of progress and understanding, for in the grim dark future there is only war. There is no peace amongst the stars, only an eternity of carnage and slaughter, and the laughter of thirsting gods.

Dramatis Personae

The *Speranza*

LEXELL KOTOV – Archmagos of the Kotov Explorator Fleet
TARKIS BLAYLOCK – Fabricatus Locum, Magos of the Cebrenia Quadrangle
VITALI TYCHON – Stellar Cartographer of the Quatria Orbital Galleries
LINYA TYCHON – Stellar Cartographer, daughter of Vitali Tychon
AZURAMAGELLI – Magos of Astrogation
KRYPTAESTREX – Magos of Logistics
TURENTEK – Ark Fabricatus
HIRIMAU DAHAN – Secutor/Guilder Suzerain
SAIIXEK – Master of Engines
TOTHA MU-32 – Mechanicus Overseer
ABREHEM LOCKE – Bondsman
RASSELAS X-42 – Arco-flagellant
VANNEN COYNE – Bondsman
JULIUS HAWKE – Bondsman
ISMAEL DE ROEVEN – Servitor

The *Renard*

ROBOUTE SURCOUF – Captain
EMIL NADER – First Mate
ADARA SIAVASH – Hired Gun
ILANNA PAVELKA – Tech-Priest
KAYRN SYLKWOOD – Enginseer
GIDEON TEIVEL – Astropath
ELIOR ROI – Navigator

Adeptus Astartes Black Templars

TANNA – Brother-Sergeant
AUIDEN – Apothecary
ISSUR – Initiate
ATTICUS VARDA – Emperor's Champion
BRACHA – Initiate
YAEL – Initiate

The Cadian 71st, 'The Hellhounds'

VEN ANDERS – Colonel of the Cadian Detached Formation
BLAYNE HAWKINS – Captain, Blazer Company
TAYBARD RAE – Lieutenant, Blazer Company
JAHN CALLINS – Requisitional Support Officer, Blazer Company

Legio Sirius

ARLO LUTH, 'THE WINTERSUN' – Warlord Princeps, *Lupa Capitalina*
MARKO KOSKINEN – Moderati
JOAKIM BALDUR – Seconded Moderati
MAGOS HYRDRITH – Tech-Priest

ERYKS SKÁLMÖLD, 'THE MOONSORROW' – Reaver Princeps, *Canis Ulfrica*
MAGOS OHTAR – Tech-Priest

GUNNAR VINTRAS, 'THE SKINWALKER' – Warhound Princeps, *Amarok*
ELIAS HÄRKIN, 'THE IRONWOAD' – Warhound Princeps, *Vilka*

The *Starblade*

BIELANNA FAERELLE – Farseer of Biel-Tan
ARIGANNA – Striking Scorpion Exarch of Biel-Tan
TARIQUEL – Striking Scorpion of Biel-Tan
VAYNESH – Striking Scorpion of Biel-Tan
ULDANAISH GHOSTWALKER – Wraithlord of Biel-Tan

45a-Del-553-9438

<Order is a necessary condition>
<for allowing functionality.>
<A physical mechanism, be it a levy>
<of Servitors, the bio-mechanics of a Skitarii,>
<or the workings of a blessed machine.>
<It can work only if it is in physical order.>

74b-Esc-540-9324

<When you withdraw from a furnace>
<it continues to give warmth,>
<but you grow deathly cold.>
<When you withdraw from illumination>
<the light continues to shine,>
<but you are shrouded in darkness.>
<When you withdraw from the Omnissiah.>
<you forget that which makes you Mechanicus.>

Excerpts from Verses 45a-Del-553-9438/74b-Esc-540-9324
of the Archimedean Oath.

[Amended 3543735.M41 by Decree Infinitum
57433/-hgw10753 of the Order of Capek Binary Saints.]

Mechanicus metafile 587634857z/TELOK

METADATA REPOSITORY %002

AVE.OMNISSIAH.orv 4048 a_start .equ 3000 2048 ld length,% 2064 WILL BE DONE 00000010 10000000 NON-OPTIMAL OPERATIONS 00000110 2068 addcc%r1,-4,%r1 10000010 10000000 01111111 11111100 2072 addcc.%r1,%r2,%r4 10001000 MARQUE VERIFICATION COMPLETE 01000000 REDUCED FLEET AGGLOMERATION CACHE 2076 ld%r4,%r5 11001010 00000001 00000000 00000000 2080 ba loop 00010000 10111111 11111111 RESTORATIVE SYSTEM PURGE: VIABLE/NON-VIABLE? 2084 addcc%r3 FORCED REMOVAL OF ARTIFICIAL SENTIENCE,%r5,%r3 10000110 10000000 11000000 00000101 2088 done: jmpl%r15+4,%r0 10000001 11000011 SILICON-BASED ORGANISM? 00000100 2092 length: 20 BEYOND HALOSCAR CARTOGRAPHIES REF: MACHARIUS 00000000 00000000 00010100 2096 address: a_start 00000100 ANOMALOUS CHRONO-READINGS CONTINUE 00000000 00001011 10111000. Omni.B_start

Infinite Loop Infinite Loop///////////

Metadata Parsing in effect.

++++++++++++++++

<++<Cartesian Doubt>++>

001

Knowledge is power. They call that the first credo, but they are wrong. Knowledge is just the beginning. It is in the application of knowledge that power resides. After all, what is the value of discovery if we do not put what we learn into effect?

Millennia have come and gone since I became Mechanicus, but even as a novitiate caster of quantum runes, I was aware I had blindly accepted many principles unverified by my own experience as being true. Consequently, the conclusions I later based upon such principles were highly doubtful. From that moment of realisation I was convinced of the necessity of ridding myself of all the principles I had unquestioningly adopted.

I would build knowledge from my own self-discovered truths.

010

An ancient Terran order of techno-theologians once boasted heraldic devices emblazoned with the words **Nullius in Verba***, which even a* *basic proto-Gothic lexical servitor can tell you means* ***Nothing upon Another's Word****. It is a credo I have lived by and by which I will die. The Venusian epistolarian who first scratched those words into cured animal hide was wise indeed, and the inheritors of the Red Planet would do well to recall his wisdom.*

But the priests of Mars have lost sight of what it means to be Mechanicus.

The magi rejoice at scraps swept from the tables of gods and think themselves blessed. They bear such relics aloft like the greatest prizes, little realising that such intellectual flotsam and jetsam is worthless in the grand scheme of galactic endeavour.

They are idiot children stumbling around the workshop of a genius. The tools and knowledge they require to rebuild the glory of mankind's past is at their fingertips, yet they see it not. They wield lethally unpredictable technologies like playthings, heedless of the damage they wreak and ignorant that they are losing as much as they gain with every fumbling step.

So much that was lost has been rediscovered, they cry, but like a million scattered fragments of a puzzle, they are useless unless combined. With all that has been hidden beneath the sands of the Red Planet, we could rebuild the Imperium as it was in the halcyon days of the first great diaspora. We could achieve the dream upon which the Emperor was embarked in the fleeting moments of peace following the Pax Olympus.

Ah, how I wish I could have been there. To see the Omnissiah when He walked in the guise of flesh. To bathe in His light and feel the serenity of perfect code flowing through my body. One as mechanistically evolved as I is not supposed to miss the soft, ever-degenerating meat-body I left behind in my ascension through the ranks of the priesthood, but I would accept its infinite limitations just to have beheld that moment with organic eyes.

011

Now I see the world through organic silica membranes and glassine-meshed diamond. A thousand microscopic machines infiltrate the fluids that circulate within my new body of crystal and light. My limbs are powerful beyond even the strength of the Adeptus Astartes, my mind capable of ultra-fast calculations that allow cognition speeds far in advance of even the Fabricator General.

But nothing of such worth is ever achieved without sacrifice, and nothing is so fatal to the progress of mankind as to suppose our grasp of technology is complete. To believe that there are no more mysteries in nature or that our triumphs are all won and there are no new worlds to conquer is to invite stagnation.

And stagnation is death.

I have travelled the void like few others before me.

I have crossed the barriers of time and space and seen further than any other. The elemental forces of the universe are mine to command. Time, space, gravity and light bend to my will.

Like the great celestial engineers of a far distant epoch, I carve the flesh of the galaxy to suit my desires. And where ancient war and forgotten genocides have wiped the slate clean, I have brought life and the promise of civilisation reborn.

The Mechanicus venerates those who draw closer to its vision of union with the God of all Machines, and they are right to do so.

But they have chosen the wrong deity.

By any mortal reckoning, I am a god.

So bold a statement could rightly be construed as arrogance.

In my case, it is modesty.

A simple statement of fact.

I am Archmagos Vettius Telok, and I am remaking what was lost.

Such is the power of my knowledge.

MACROCONTENT COMMENCEMENT:

+++MACROCONTENT 001+++

Microcontent 01

Barely worthy of being designated a planet, the doomed world hung in the fringes of Arcturus Ultra's rapidly diminishing Kuiper belt at the farthest extent of the star system. Much of this spatial region was composed of frozen volatiles – drifting agglomerations of ice, ammonia and methane – and these were slowly being turned to vapour by the thermal death throes of the newly named star's rapidly expanding corona. The Oort cloud had thinned to the point of vanishing altogether, allowing the vessels of the Kotov fleet to approach the system without fear of taking damage from the debris scattered like celestial litter at the system's edge.

The dying planet had been christened Katen Venia, and its likely lifespan could be measured in months at best. It would soon be destroyed by the very star that had once nourished an unknown number of habitable worlds in that slender astronomical region named for a flaxen-haired thief of ancient myth.

The closest planets to the star had already been reduced to metallic vapour by its expanding heat corona and now only Katen Venia remained. Its outer layers of frozen nitrogen had almost entirely boiled off into space, exposing a surface of cratered ice and rock, soaring crystal growths of geometric beauty, abyssal canyons of sheared glaciers, and swathes of desolate tundra that had been ripped raw by the gravitational push and pull of its chaotic orbit.

Any currently uncontested method of celestial cartography would regard Katen Venia as an unremarkable world, a bare rock devoid of any notable features warranting attention. Only the study of its demise would be of any interest to most magi. Yet for all its apparent worthlessness, there was one aspect to Katen Venia that rendered it valuable beyond measure.

Telok the Machine-touched, whose explorator fleet had been lost with all hands, had come this way. Numerous legends of Mars spoke of his foolhardy quest into the unknown to unearth an ancient technological marvel known as the Breath of the Gods. Each tale was embellished with its own twist to Telok's obsession, but all agreed that his quest had come to a bad end.

But a newly revealed relic of his doomed expedition had come to light, offering tantalising hints that the Lost Magos had actually found something in the unknown reaches beyond the light of familiar stars: a saviour pod beacon indicating that the newly named Katen Venia was the final resting place of Telok's flagship, the *Tomioka*.

It was this that had brought an Adeptus Mechanicus explorator fleet of such magnitude as had not been assembled for millennia to leave the confines of the Milky Way and establish orbit around the planet's northern polar regions.

The heart of this fleet was a vessel that could be called unique without fear of contradiction. A mighty star-borne colossus. A relic of a time when the mysteries of technology were not shrouded in a veil of ignorance, and whose violent birth had destroyed a world. Its inhuman scale was the product of men who dared to build the greatest things their imaginations could conceive.

Its name was *Speranza,* and it was Ark Mechanicus – the flagship of Archmagos Lexell Kotov.

Unlike the battleships built in the Imperium's fortified shipyards, the Ark Mechanicus had not been wrought with any martial aesthetic in mind, nor had it accrued centuries of encrusted ornamentation to glorify long-dead saints or heroes of war. It was a vessel that would never be called beautiful, even by those who had built it, for it had no symmetry, no clean lines nor even much of a straight axis that allowed for spurious notions of aerodynamics.

The *Speranza* was a vessel forever bound to the void, and only the positioning of its vast plasma engines' containment-field generators allowed an observer to know which end was the prow and which the stern. Its outer hull was a tangled arrangement of intestinal ductwork, exposed skeletal superstructure and ray-shielded crew spaces. Its graceless topside and its bulbous underside were ribbed plateaus overgrown with geometric accretions of unchecked industry. Refineries, ore-processing plants, gene-holds, test ranges, manufactories, laboratoria, power generators and assembly forges clung to its flanks in a haphazard arrangement that owed nothing to any design philosophies other than need and practicality. The *Speranza* was a vessel of exploration and research, a mariner of the nebulae whose sole task was to be part of Kotov's Quest for Knowledge.

Though the bulk of the Ark's unimaginable mass was given

over to the workings of technology and construction, it was not without teeth. Conventional munitions and rudimentary void-weaponry punctuated its length, but desperate need had revealed the presence of weapon technologies many magnitudes more lethal, secreted within lightless compartments long since forgotten by all save the ship itself.

The vessel was nothing less than a forge world cut loose from the surface of the planet whose death spasm had birthed it, a sprawling landmass of cathedrals to technology and the quintessential embodiment of the Cult Mechanicus's devotion to the Omnissiah. At the heart of the *Speranza* was an electromotive spirit formed from the gestalt conjoining of a trillion machines and more, a terrifyingly complex hybrid of intelligence and instinct that was close to godlike.

Like any representation of the divine, it had devotees.

A fleet of ancillary vessels kept station around the *Speranza*: fuel carriers, warships, troop transports, supply barques and a host of shuttles and bulk tenders that passed between them in strictly observed transit corridors. *Moonchild* and *Wrathchild*, twin reconditioned Gothic-class cruisers, patrolled the flanks of the *Speranza*, while *Mortis Voss*, the last survivor of the trio of vessels despatched from Voss Prime, drifted mournfully above the Ark's dorsal manufactories.

Honour Blade had been lost in an emergency translation from the warp at the very edge of the galaxy, while *Blade of Voss* had been torn apart by a gravitational hell-storm during the nightmare crossing of the Halo Scar. Nor had these been the most grievous losses suffered by the fleet on its perilous journey to sail beyond the galactic boundary.

Cardinal Boras, a vessel of grand heritage that had braved the tempests of the warp from one side of the galaxy to the other, had been destroyed by ambushing eldar reavers. The

Adeptus Astartes accompanying the fleet had likewise suffered grievous loss, for those selfsame reavers had gone on to board the Black Templars rapid strike cruiser that bore the proud name *Adytum*. Though the crusaders it carried had escaped to fight another day aboard the Thunderhawk *Barisan*, their Reclusiarch was slain as the Halo Scar's crushing gravity waves claimed the ship's corpse of steel and stone.

Those raiders had evaded the fleet's retribution by the slenderest of margins, and the warships tasked with the *Speranza*'s protection were taking no chances of being caught out again.

One other vessel of note made up the last element of Archmagos Kotov's fleet. Though nearly three kilometres in length, the *Renard* was insignificant in comparison to the hulking ships of the Mechanicus, but she was fast and built with a grace and poise the *Speranza* lacked.

Her shipmaster was Roboute Surcouf, and Katen Venia was the world he had named.

He would be the first to see its skies.

It was why he had come this far.

'You know, for someone who lives in space, you're bloody useless at putting on a void-suit,' said Kayrn Sylkwood, enginseer of the *Renard*, refastening the seals of her captain's bulky, baroquely ornamented suit of exo-armour. 'If I let you go outside like this you'll be dead inside of thirty seconds.'

Roboute Surcouf shook his head. 'I live inside a starship so I don't *have* to wear a void-suit,' he said, his voice sounding scratchy and distant through his helmet's vox-grille.

Sylkwood wore the grey army fatigues and tight-fitting vest top of her former Cadian regiment, her broadly-built upper body permanently sheened with the oil, grease and incense of the propulsion decks that were as much a part of an enginseer's uniform as any shoulder badge or rank pin. Functional communion augmetics made her shaven skull knotty with brutal implants, and haptic sub-dermals in her fingers and palms gave her a solid heft and a mean right hook.

She made one last circuit of Roboute, tugging at seams, adjusting pressure connectors and checking the suit's internal atmospherics on the bulky backpack. Satisfied, she took a step back and nodded to herself.

'Happy now?' asked Roboute.

'Moderately less irritated at your stupidity would be a better way of putting it.'

'I can live with that,' said Roboute, turning away and stomping over the deck to where Adara Siavash helped Magos Pavelka prep the grav-sled for the surface. Little more than a heavy, rectangular slab of metal with a pilot's compartment at one end and a repulsor generator mounted underneath, the sled was the workhorse machine of the *Renard*. Its engine was rated for a cargo load of sixty metric tonnes and a volume of a hundred cubic metres, though it had been a long time since it had carried anything of such bulk. It floated on a cushion of distorted air that made Roboute's teeth itch even through the protection of his void-suit.

Pavelka was cowled in the typical red robe of the Mechanicus, one that hid the majority of her augmetic qualities. Though Roboute had no idea of the full extent of her modification, he suspected it was a lot less than many of the Martian adepts aboard the *Speranza*. A number of feed lines ran from a sparking power unit mounted on her back, and four concertinaing pipes expanded and contracted like bellows as they fed power into the sled's batteries.

'She ready?' he asked, slapping an armoured hand against the grav-sled's battered plates.

Pavelka flinched at the impact and said, 'Admonishment: Need I remind you, captain, that to ascribe gender to machines is needless anthropomorphism? Machines have no need of flesh labels.'

'I don't believe that,' said Adara, winking at the captain through the polarised faceplate of his own void-suit. 'You can tell this is a grand old girl. Trust me, I know about the fairer sex.'

Sylkwood grinned and rubbed a metal palm on the thrumming fuselage as though it was her lover's backside.

'Gotta say, I agree with the lad,' she said. 'Not about him knowing anything about women. Trust me, he doesn't know one interface port from another. But this machine's reliable, right enough. She's tough and won't let you down in a tight spot. Sounds like a woman to me.'

Adara turned away to hide his embarrassment as Pavelka shook her head. 'What else should I expect from an enginseer?' she said, disconnecting her feed lines from the sled.

Sylkwood grinned and said, 'Hard work, foul language and hangovers that'll cripple an ork.'

Roboute set a foot onto the iron rungs hanging down from the sled's crew cab and awkwardly hauled himself up into the pilot's seat. Sylkwood clambered up after him and ran through the connection checklist with the thoroughness of a Sororitas dorm-mistress ensuring her novices were all abed.

Sylkwood was Cadian and thoroughness was her watchword.

'Hey, how come you're not checking my suit's seals and tucking me in?' said Adara, as he climbed onto the sled from the opposite side.

Without looking up, Sylkwood said, 'Because you're not the captain and I don't much care if you explosively depressurise in a toxic environment.'

'You're cleaning the suit of piss and blood if he does,' said Roboute, making a last adjustment to the sled's surveyor gear.

'How much on Adara having missed a seal?' asked Sylkwood, looking back down at Pavelka.

'You sound just like Mister Nader,' answered Pavelka.

'We left him up on the *Renard*,' said Sylkwood. 'Someone's got to play the role of annoying idiot.'

'In any case, it would not be a wager to me,' said Pavelka. 'Atmospheric readings tell me that Mister Siavash has his void-suit sealed within acceptable parameters.'

'Good to know,' said Adara.

The lad dropped into his bucket seat and strapped himself in next to Roboute. The boy had his ubiquitous butterfly blade tucked into one of his void-suit's thigh pouches next to his holstered laspistol, and Roboute sighed.

'Tell me you're not so stupid as to carry an unsheathed knife in your suit,' said Roboute.

Adara at least had the decency to look guilty as he pulled the blade out and placed it in a stowage box mounted on the inner face of the door.

'Yeah, sorry. I don't go anywhere without it, I kind of forget it's even there.'

Magos Pavelka appeared at his side, filling the emergency oxygen tanks worked into the door's structure. A coiling mechadendrite reached over her shoulder and opened the stowage box before a second articulated bronze limb capped with rotating callipers removed the offending blade.

'Come on,' said Adara. 'What harm is there in leaving the knife there?'

'Clarification: It is statistically probable that you will remove this weapon and carry it with you once you are beyond the hull of this vessel,' said Pavelka, and even though much of her face had the porcelain quality of synth-skin and augmetic replacement, Roboute saw a glint of amusement in her clicking optics. 'As Enginseer Sylkwood might say, "You have previous" and are not to be trusted.'

'You cut me deep,' said Adara.

'You'd cut yourself deep,' said Roboute, 'and out there, that'd be a death sentence. Right, Ilanna?'

'Unquestionably,' answered the magos. 'The atmosphere on the planet below is a volatile mix of frozen nitrogen being released from the ice-caps in both gaseous and liquid form, ammonia and airborne heavy metal particulates. The thermocline is shifting unpredictably in the ultra-rapid atmospheric bleed-off, resulting in squalling pressure vortices that would cause your body to react in a number of extremely unpleasant ways without your void-suit's equalisation.'

'I don't know what a lot of that means, but I get the gist,' said Adara.

'Right, now you've scared us both half to death, how long before the tether gets us down there?' asked Roboute, trying not to let his discomfort at the *Renard*'s cargo shuttle being reeled down onto the planet's surface by remote means show in his voice. 'I want to get out there and see what a world beyond the galaxy's edge looks like.'

Pavelka cocked her head to the side, wordlessly communing with the Mechanicus controllers on the surface via the implants in her skull. Roboute's brain had been augmented to view the invisible skeins of noospheric data, but only when interfacing with a spinal link system. The sled had no such array, and even if it did, he wouldn't be able to connect with it through his void-suit.

'Approximately ten minutes,' said Pavelka. 'Stratospheric disturbances and unexpected magnetic field storms are introducing chaotic variables into our ETA.'

Sylkwood dropped from the grav-sled's running boards and shouted, 'Clear the deck!' though there was no one else in the shuttle's cavernous loading bay. The few servitor cadres Roboute owned were otherwise engaged in monitoring the shuttle's automated flight path or back aboard the *Renard*, repairing damage suffered during the navigation of the Halo Scar. Sylkwood scrambled up the service ladder to the upper gangway as Pavelka climbed onto the grav-sled, sitting behind Adara and producing a data-slate, which she rested upon her knees.

Roboute twisted awkwardly in his seat and said, 'Everything set?'

'Statement: yes,' said Pavelka, extruding a mechanised auspex from a chest compartment.

'You don't have to come with us,' said Roboute. 'I know you don't like leaving the *Renard*.'

Pavelka shook her head. 'I modified the memory coil circuitry of the *Tomioka's* distress beacon. I can follow its telemetry better than anyone else. Besides, if this sled breaks down, you will need me to fix it.'

'Good to know,' said Roboute, quietly grateful to have Pavelka along for the ride.

'Don't you need a suit?' asked Adara.

Pavelka shook her head. 'I have altered the filtration protocols of my lungs to exclude the toxic elements of the atmosphere, and am currently modifying my biochemistry to nullify the negative effects of hostile pressures. My body mass incorporates so little organic mass that requires oxygenation that I can store enough reserve within my mechanised volume.'

'Good to know,' said Adara in imitation of Roboute.

Roboute looked up to the upper gantry of the cargo bay, seeing Sylkwood open one of the hold's vacuum-sealed doors.

She sketched a quick salute to him, but said nothing as she slammed the heavy door behind her.

Clearly Kayrn Sylkwood felt no need to mark this moment with any significant words.

But Roboute knew this particular moment *was* special.

The three of them would soon pilot the sled onto the surface of an alien world that lay beyond the edges of the Milky Way, a world unclaimed by the Imperium. A world that had, until the coming of Telok's fleet thousands of years ago, probably never known the tread of human feet. *This* was why Roboute had come this far and risked so much, to see alien skies and touch the earth of a planet so far from the understanding of the Imperium.

An emerald light on the walnut and brass control panel winked with an incoming transmission, and Roboute flicked the ivory-tipped switch next to it into the receive position. The voice of the expedition's leader, Archmagos Lexell Kotov, trilled from the speaker grille.

'Mister Surcouf,' said Kotov. 'Are you planning on joining us aboard the *Tabularium?*'

Roboute grinned, hearing the febrile edge of excitement in the archmagos's voice. Though Kotov was the master of this explorator fleet, it had been Roboute's retrieval of the locator beacon that had brought them this far.

'I think we'd rather make our own way to the *Tomioka*,' said Roboute. 'But thank you for the invitation, it's very thoughtful of you.'

'Your tether shows significant margin for error in your arrival time,' said Telok.

'So I gather, but Magos Pavelka reckons we'll be planet side in around ten minutes.'

'How imprecise. Kotov out,' replied the archmagos.

OF ALL THE many ways to be carried into battle, Brother-Sergeant Tanna relished the sudden fury of a Thunderhawk assault the most. Nothing stirred his heart more than the violent thrust of howling engines, the jolting motion of evasive manoeuvres and the sudden, screaming deceleration as the pilot flared the wings and slammed down into the crucible of combat. Being thrown around the inside of a Rhino or Land Raider just couldn't compare, and Tanna didn't know any Techmarine that could drive worth a damn anyway.

Yes, a gunship assault every time.

Even if this particular descent was – for now – being controlled by a Mechanicus e-mag tether.

The crew compartment of the *Barisan* was as cold as a meat locker, and a fine mist of condensing vapours slowly beaded the curved plates of Tanna's midnight-black armour with droplets of moisture. A cross of purest jet gleamed on one ivory shoulder guard and an eagle carved from the same material stood proud on the other. An embossed red skull was set in the centre of the eagle's breast, its eyes glinting shards of deeper garnet. Liquid streaks coated the angular planes of his helmet like tears, but Tanna had not wept in over two hundred years.

Alone in his makeshift arming chamber aboard the *Speranza* he had come close.

The Thunderhawk lurched, slammed sideways by rogue vortices of surging gases being stripped from the planet's surface. The atmospherics of Katen Venia were growing increasingly turbulent and toxic: a mix of intolerably high nitrogen levels and vaporous metals utterly lethal to mortals. Tanna's post-human physiology had been engineered to survive hostile environments, but even he would struggle to survive in Katen Venia's atmosphere for more than a few hours.

The *Barisan* wasn't flying an assault run, but its descent

was scarcely less steep and juddering than any combat drop Tanna had previously made in its belly. The gunship's frame had been struck in the Tyrrhenus Mons forge-complex on Mars, and bore the seal of the Fabricator General himself. Its machine-spirit was a tempestuous thing, part unbroken colt, part wounded grox – aggression and wildness combined. Such qualities had served the Fighting Company well in past crusades, but the gunship still grieved the loss of its carrier and had yet to settle in its new home aboard the *Speranza*.

Much like the rest of us, thought Tanna, casting a quick glance down the length of the fuselage.

A Thunderhawk was built to carry three Codex-strength squads into the heart of battle, but most of the *Barisan*'s grav-restraints were empty. Only six of the thirty seats were occupied. Tanna sat on the commander's bench next to the gunship's assault ramp, his helmet fixed in place and his chained bolter held rigid at his side.

Brother Yael sat two seats down from him, cradling his boltgun close to his chest. The youngest of their number, Yael had only recently been raised to the ranks of the Fighting Company, chosen by Helbrecht himself to take part in the Scar Crusade. The bout the young warrior had fought on the *Speranza*'s training deck against Magos Dahan was one Tanna would never forget. Not least for the fact that the Mechanicus Secutor had conceded defeat.

The ivory-armoured form of Apothecary Auiden was a splash of white in the darkness, and he looked up at Tanna with a grim nod as he slotted home bronze-lined phials into the mechanism of his narthecium gauntlet. This was not a combat drop, but when descending to an unknown world Auiden took the view that it was better to expect the worst than face it unprepared.

A pessimistic outlook, but one that had yet to be proven wrong on this ill-fated crusade.

The solemn-hearted Bracha sat with his head bowed and his hands laced together as if in prayer. First on the field and the last to leave, Kul Gilad's death had hit Bracha hardest of all. He had known the Reclusiarch the longest, having fought six crusades to victory at his side. Many had believed he would follow Kul Gilad's example and take the rosarius.

One of Bracha's hands was flesh and blood, the other fashioned from chrome-plated steel. A flesh-clad cybork on the Valette Manifold station had cut Bracha's arm from him, but he had taken the loss without complaint. The life of a Space Marine was one of extreme violence, and no Black Templar expected to live out his days without suffering some terrible injury along the way. Magos Dahan had crafted Bracha a replacement arm, a skitarii-pattern combat limb with an implanted plasma gun in the forearm.

Along from Bracha, Issur the Bladesman ran his hands along the crimson sheath of his power sword as he always did when locked into a harness within an assault craft. Its texture was patterned with a recurring crusader chain motif, and as Tanna watched, Issur's head twitched and the fingers stroking the scabbard spasmed suddenly. Issur clenched his fist in anger and slammed his helmeted head back against the gunship's fuselage.

Like Bracha, Issur had been wounded in the fight against the cyborks, his body shocked to the brink of death by a weaponised electromagnetic generator. The swordsman was lucky to be alive, but he had come back from the brink of death with misfiring synapses and a nervous system that was no longer entirely reliable. His career as a duellist was over, and Tanna couldn't help but notice the envious glances Issur threw out in the direction of Atticus Varda.

The Emperor's Champion sat unmoving in his grav-restraint, the Black Sword resting across his knees. Sheathed in a scabbard of unbreakable Martian alloys, only its leather-wrapped hilt and crusader cross pommel were visible. The blade was a midnight razor, filigreed with Gothic scriptwork.

Issur had fully expected to wield the Black Sword, for he had once been the best among them with a blade. But which Templar was called to serve as Emperor's Champion depended on more than just skill at arms, and the war-visions had not come to him. The Master of Mankind had chosen Atticus Varda to be His Champion, and no Black Templar would dream of gainsaying such authority.

Varda sat across from Tanna, clad in armour the colour of darkest night, handcrafted in the forges of the *Eternal Crusader* by Techmarine Lexne and an army of thralls nearly three thousand years ago. Its plates were moulded in the form of an idealised physique, the eagle at its chest golden and proud. The Chapter's icon was rendered in pearlescent stone quarried from the dark side of Luna. Just to be in its presence was an honour.

Tanna had seen many fine suits of armour in his centuries of service, but he had seen no finer examples of the artificer's art than this. Aelius had worn it well, but it fitted Varda like a second skin.

The Emperor's Champion was the heart of a Crusade, and Varda's had been broken by the death of Kul Gilad, a brave warrior slain without his brothers at his side. Sensing Tanna's scrutiny, he looked up and the ember-red eye lenses of their battle-helms met across the juddering fuselage.

'Something on your mind, Tanna?' asked Varda.

The words sounded in Tanna's helmet on a closed channel; none of the others would hear what passed between them.

'The Champion carries the soul of us all,' said Tanna. 'That's what Kul Gilad used to say.'

'Repeating his words does not make you him,' said Varda, gripping the Black Sword tightly.

'No,' agreed Tanna. 'Nor would I have it so.'

'Then why speak them?'

'To show you that I grieve for him also.'

'Not enough,' hissed Varda. 'His blood is on our hands.'

Anger touched Tanna. 'If we had gone to him, we would *all* be dead.'

'Better to fall in battle than to run from it.'

'Kul Gilad ordered us from the ship,' said Tanna. 'You heard him. We all did.'

'We should have fought alongside our Reclusiarch.'

Tanna nodded and said, 'Aye, and our deaths would have been glorious.'

Varda made a fist on the scabbard of the Black Sword. 'Then why did you not give the order?'

'Because I was *following* the Reclusiarch's last order,' snapped Tanna, lifting his right arm to show the metallic links binding his boltgun to his wrist. 'Our command structure exists for a reason, Varda, and the moment we start picking and choosing which orders we obey, we might as well tear the Chapter symbol from our shoulders and set a course for the Maelstrom. We are Black Templars, and we willingly bind ourselves with chains of duty, chains of honour and chains of death. You are the Emperor's Champion, Varda. You know this better than anyone.'

Varda's head sank, and Tanna saw the fire of his anger had dimmed. It was not, Tanna knew, truly anger that fuelled his words, but guilt.

A guilt they all shared, whether it was deserved or not.

Tanna heard Varda's soul-weary sigh over the vox. 'I know you are right, Tanna, but Kul Gilad anointed me,' he said, looking up. 'And you will always be the one who kept me from his death.'

'I am the one that kept you alive,' said Tanna.

Five hours ago, the surface region chosen for Mechanicus landing fields had been nothing more than a vaguely flat plateau of retreating glacial ice and a dozen gradually vaporising lakes of exotically lethal chemistry. A host of servitor-crewed drones launched as the *Speranza* spiralled into its high-anchor position had provided three-dimensional pict-captures of the global topography, and deep-penetrating orbital augurs of the planet's northern hemisphere had enabled Archmagos Kotov to select this particular landing site.

The specific uniformity of the plateau's underlying bedrock and its relative geological stability put it well within the terraforming capabilities of Fabricatus Turentek's geoformer engines. Three colossal vessels detached from the underside of the *Speranza*, falling away like spalling portions of wreckage in the wake of catastrophic damage. Each was a ten-kilometre-square slab of barely understood machinery: titanic atmosphere processing plants, industrial-scale meltas and arcane technologies of geological manipulation. Like gothic factories cast adrift in space, the geoformer engines dropped through the atmosphere, their heat-shielded undersides glowing a fierce cherry red as they negotiated the turbulent storms of escaping gases.

They halted their descent a hundred metres above the ground, bombarding the site with terrain-mapping augurs to verify their position. Manoeuvring jets fired corrective bursts as serried banks of planet-cracking cannons rotated outwards in their undersides. Precision ordnance strikes smashed the frozen ice of the surface into manageable chunks with thunderous barrages as the wide mouths of furnace-meltas irised open.

A rippling haze of intense heat was expelled like the breath of mythical dragons, and painfully bright light flared from the meltas, filling the plateau with purple-edged fire. Hurricanes of superheated steam shrieked and hissed as the surface ice was boiled away or diverted into drainage channels blasted by terrain-modifying howitzers.

Chemical mortars fired thousands of air-bursting saturation shells, seeding the local atmosphere with slow-decaying absorption matter that began a cascade of alchemical reactions to filter out its most toxic and corrosive elements. Wide-mouthed bays opened on the geoformer vessels and scores of heavy-grade earth-moving leviathans were dropped to the planet's surface in impact-cushioning cradles.

In a carefully orchestrated ballet, the earth-moving machines swiftly demarcated the area of the landing fields and set about their work with the efficiency of an army of iron-skinned and hazard-striped worker ants. Turentek had crafted hundreds of landing fields on worlds far more inimical to life and machines than Katen Venia and the priests under his command knew their trade well.

Slowly the last of the ice was blasted clear and thousands of kilometres of cabling were laid to receive the telemetry gear required to tether the incoming vessels to their assigned landing zones. With the buried infrastructure in place and protected within hardened ductwork, the exposed rock was crushed and planed flat with tight-focus conversion beamers. Heat shielding was laid over the buried technology as ten thousand atmosphere-capable tech-priests with implanted precision meltas and polishing limbs applied the final smoothing to the surface of the landing fields with ångström-level precision. Vacuum-suited servitors followed in the wake of the tech-priests, acid-etching the rock with Imperial eagles, cog-wreathed machine skulls and coded sequence numbers.

Within four hours, a vast square of mirror-smooth rock, six kilometres on each side, had been carved into the planet's surface. With the basic structure in place, entoptic generators and noospheric transmission arrays were installed, as well as numerous fully equipped control bunkers to manage the intricate and necessarily complex scheduling of incoming and departing landing craft. Defence towers were raised at regular intervals around the landing fields, each one equipped with an array of weapons capable of engaging ships in low orbit or attacking ground forces.

To enable non-Mechanicus drop ships to set down, contrasting guide lines were painted on the smoothed rock, together with conventional landing lights and active e-mag tethers. Five hours after the work had begun, it was complete, and Magos Turentek set his seal upon the work from his articulated fabrication hangar in the ventral manufactory districts of the *Speranza.*

No sooner was Turentek's seal inloaded to the Manifold, than the first craft were launched from the embarkation hangars of the Ark Mechanicus. A hundred fat-bellied landers began their descent to the surface carrying the mechanisms of planetary exploration: tech-priests and their monstrous land-cathedrals, skitarii battalions and their war machines, servitors and weaponised praetorians.

Amid the host of iron descending to the planet's surface, three coffin ships of the Legio Sirius were shepherded down through the atmosphere by supplicant vessels that howled binaric hymnals of praise and warning across multiple wavelengths.

The Warlord *Lupa Capitalina* descended to Katen Venia, attended by *Amarok* and *Vilka*.

Wintersun would have the honour of First Step, as was his right as Legio Alpha. Skinwalker and Ironwoad would share in this honour, and if either Warhound princeps felt any reservations at the exclusion of *Moonsorrow* and *Canis Ulfrica*, they kept such thoughts to themselves.

An airborne armada of steel and gold descended to the planet on towering plumes of blue-limned fire, a billion tonnes of machinery and men.

The Adeptus Mechanicus had come to Katen Venia.

Microcontent 02

APART FROM A near-miss with the traversing arm of lifter-rig *Wulfse,* the latest shift in the distribution hub of Magos Turentek's forge-temple had gone well. Abrehem had kept up with the punishing schedule insisted on by the materiel-logisters, and even managed to work some contingency time into their schedule to start transferring the newly built Cadian tanks down-ship.

Abrehem unstrapped himself from *Virtanen*'s command throne and began the painful process of unplugging the dozens of cerebral-communion cables trailing from the command headpiece he wore. With each wincing disconnect, the crisp noospheric sensorium displaying the lifter-rig's traverse lines, tension/compression ratios, load levels and spool length faded slowly from his field of vision.

With the last connector unplugged, Abrehem gathered up a battered set of aural bafflers and pressed them over his ears before swinging out onto the iron-rung ladder bolted to the latticework tower of the lifter-rig. The commander's cab was nearly a hundred and fifty metres above the deck, but Abrehem felt no sense of vertigo; he'd worked the rigs on Joura too long for any fear of heights to remain.

The multiple arms of the lifter-rig splayed out from his control cab like the rigid steel tentacles of a high-viz squid. All ten of *Virtanen*'s two-hundred-metre arms were capable of ascending and descending, rotating through three hundred and sixty degrees or articulating in more convoluted ways as its operator desired. Each arm was equipped with a multitude of attachments: basic hooks, magnets, a variety of cutting and welding tools, as well as more specialised mechadendrite-enabled manipulator claws.

Virtanen was a relatively small machine, but it was sturdy, reliable and had a hefty load capacity that belied its smaller stature compared to the titanic lifting rigs worked by Turentek himself. Its service history and structural integrity rating were both impressive and its machine-spirit appeared only too eager to accept a new controller.

But it was no *Savickas*. That had been a lifter-rig without limits, an unrelenting workhorse of a machine that seemed to anticipate every command before it was issued and never, ever, failed to link with a shipping container first time.

According to Totha Mu-32, the previous incumbent of Abrehem's new command throne had been killed during the attack of the eldar pirates.

'I think *Virtanen* was waiting for you,' Totha Mu-32 had said when Abrehem first sat in the command throne. 'Its name means "small river", but even the smallest river can cut a mountain in half given time, yes? I think you will get along very well.'

Abrehem had no answer to that, and merely shrugged,

still uncomfortable at the notion that people thought him Machine-touched. He certainly didn't feel any intimate connection to the godhood of all machines. Totha Mu-32 had told him that such men as he were rare indeed, bringing a deeply implanted electoo up to the surface of his organics, a depiction of a coiled dragon with silver and bronze scales.

When Abrehem asked the overseer what the tattoo represented, Totha Mu-32 told him it was the mark of a proscribed Martian sect that made it their business to seek out and worship Machine-touched individuals. Archmagos Telok, the object of this voyage of exploration, was said to be so blessed, and shipboard rumour had it that Magos Blaylock likewise had the eye of the Omnissiah upon him. To have a trinity of such individuals connected to this voyage was seen as a sign of great import by Totha Mu-32, a physical manifestation of the Originator, the Scion and the Motive Force.

Abrehem listened to Totha Mu-32's sermons in silence, finding the overseer's zeal for his beatification misplaced and more than a little off-putting.

He certainly had no sense that he was in any way *special*.

The hard metal of a bionic arm grafted to his right shoulder seemed to mock that belief.

The augmetic limb had been fitted after a contraband plasma pistol that shouldn't have been able to fire had explosively overheated and melted the flesh and bone from his body after he'd used it to shoot dead an eldar warrior-chief. He didn't like to think of that moment – the bowel-loosening terror of the xeno-killers descending upon them, only to be cut apart into bloody chunks by a cyborg death machine that had apparently adopted him as its new master. His plea to Sebastian Thor and his bloody handprint had opened the door to the arco-flagellant's dormis chamber, which Totha Mu-32 and a great many others were taking as a sign of his divine favour.

Abrehem shook off thoughts of Totha Mu-32's reverence, knowing that a moment's inattention could cost him his life when he was hundreds of metres above a hard steel deck.

He worked his way down the ladder, and even with the aural bafflers the noise in the forge-temple was almost deafening. Heavy machinery sprouted like the towering skeletal remains of vast-necked sauropods around the temple's perimeter, and arch-backed rigs rumbled overhead on suspended rails, hauling containers weighing thousands of tonnes back and forth with no more effort than a Cadian might carry his kit-bag. Magos Turentek himself worked across the centre-line of the forge-temple, handling the largest and heaviest containers personally. His multiple loader arms depended from a central machine-hub where the organic components of his body were interred like the biological scraps of a god-machine's princeps.

Most of the containers being loaded onto the vast-hulled shipping rigs contained modular plates of adamantium and structural members intended for the lower decks. Kilometres of hull plating had been torn from the *Speranza* by the crossing of the Halo Scar and the guns of the eldar warship – rendering entire districts of the Ark Mechanicus uninhabitable. The prow forges were producing millions of metric tonnes of desperately needed components for the ship's repair crews, but Abrehem's experienced eye saw the pace was slowing as the *Speranza*'s supply of raw materials was increasingly depleted.

Abrehem reached one of the transit walkways on the cliff-like walls of the forge-temple and took a moment to catch his breath. The air here was bitter and electrical, with an acrid chemical tang that left the men working here with rasp-ingly sore throats and increased breathing difficulties. This, combined with months spent below decks and working backbreaking shifts in the reclamation halls or plasma refuelling details with little sleep and only nutrient paste to sustain him, had robbed Abrehem of his once robust physique. Daily doses of Hawke's shine didn't help, but sometimes it was the only thing that knocked him out enough to sleep.

He rubbed a hand over his shorn scalp, a decision he and his fellow bondsman had taken in a fit of righteous indignation to turn them into the drones the Mechanicus believed them to be. Though their actions during the eldar attack had improved their lot somewhat, Abrehem's anger at the inhuman treatment of the below-deck bondsmen still smouldered like a banked fire. Kept as slaves and regarded simply as assets, numbers and mortal resources, the bondsmen existed in a nightmare that would only end with their death.

The Mechanicus believed its bondsmen were *honoured* to serve the Omnissiah this way!

Abrehem spat a wad of oily phlegm and climbed back onto the ladder. Below, he could see Coyne and Hawke clambering down towards the deck from their sub-control cabs, where they managed the articulation and linkage of the various connectors to whatever was being transported.

Awaiting them on the deck were two hooded figures, one robed in the red and gold of a Mechanicus overseer, the other swathed in the black cloak of a death penitent. Both looked up at him with a measure of devotion. Abrehem relished speaking to neither of them, not that Rasselas X-42 ever spoke much.

Eventually he reached the deck, and took another breath of chem-scented air.

'A successful shift,' said Totha Mu-32. '*Virtanen* has bonded well with you.'

'It's a good rig,' replied Abrehem. 'Smaller than we're used to, but it's got heart.'

'It's no *Savickas*,' said Coyne, echoing Abrehem's earlier sentiment.

Hawke shrugged. 'One lifter's much like another,' he said.

'Shows how much you know rigs,' said Abrehem. 'What was it you did on Joura again?'

'As little as possible would be my bet,' quipped Coyne, rolling his shoulders to ease the itching of the synth-skin grafts on his back where he'd taken a razored fragment from a ricocheting eldar projectile.

'Damn straight,' said Hawke with a wink. 'After the regiment tossed me out, I worked Cargo-8s mostly, driving the containers between the depots and the sub-orbitals. Though that was grunt work compared to being a moderati on a lifter-rig.'

Abrehem sent an amused glance at Coyne, and his fellow rigman hid a grin at Hawke's boyish enthusiasm for working the lifter-rigs. Give it a month of monotony and he'd soon think twice about rating his job in the sub-cab as being anything close to a Titan moderati's role.

'May I?' asked Totha Mu-32, reaching up to examine the raw flesh at Abrehem's temples and forehead. Abrehem nodded and Rasselas X-42 bristled at the overseer's familiar touch. He waved the arco-flagellant to submission. It didn't matter how many times Abrehem reinforced that certain people weren't to be considered threats, Rasselas X-42 still viewed everyone who came near him as a potential assassin.

Though now clad in baggy fatigues, heavy work boots and a kevlar vest machined to his impossibly muscular form, Rasselas X-42 could never be mistaken for anything other than the slaughterman he was. Though currently obscured by the wide sleeves of his penitent's robe, his gauntlet-hands were silver-sheened electro-flails capable of tearing through steel and bone with equal ease. The back and crown of his skull were sheathed in metal and a circular Cog Mechanicus of blood-red iron stood proud on his forehead. Sharpened metal teeth glinted in the shadows beneath his hood and flickering combat-optics shimmered with a faint cherry red glow.

'You know there is no need for you to wear the command headset,' said Totha Mu-32. 'If you concentrate more fully, the augmetic eyes you inherited from your father can display the datasphere more efficiently.'

Abrehem nodded. 'I know, but I'm not confident enough in my control over the noospheric inloads to feel comfortable commanding *Virtanen* by them alone.'

'You are Machine-touched,' asked Totha Mu-32. 'Trust in the Omnissiah and it will come.'

'If that bastard's bloody Machine-touched, then how come he damn near smashed into our rig's arm?' said a rasping voice.

Abrehem turned as a gang of six men appeared around the corner of *Virtanen*'s wide baseplate. All six wore bondsmen coveralls and had the same gaunt-faced meanness common to the *Speranza's* below-deck crew. Three men sported augmetics on their arms and craniums, while the rest were ornamented with rig-tattoos, mohawks and ritual brow piercings. They carried heavy power wrenches and other, similarly brutal-looking tools.

Pulsing just beneath the skin of the man who'd spoken was a wolf-head electoo, crudely applied and fuzzed with bio-electric static. He carried a buzzing mag-hammer in his piston-boosted arms and looked like he knew how to use it in a tight spot.

'*Wulfse*,' said Abrehem.

'You're the sons of bitches that almost hit us!' snapped Hawke. 'What in the name of Thor's backside are blind idiots like you doing running a lifter-rig?'

Hawke's vehemence caught the men by surprise, but for all his bluster, their newest rigman was right. The near miss had been the fault of *Wulfse*'s crew, but it didn't look like they were in the mood to hear that.

'Listen,' said Abrehem. 'Nothing happened, right? Nobody got hurt and we'll all be a bit more careful next time, right?'

'There ain't going to be a next time,' snarled the lead rigman of the *Wulfse*. 'Only thing you'll be driving is a medicae gurney.'

Totha Mu-32's floodstream surged with binaric authority signifiers.

'You men are to return to your posts immediately,' he said. 'If there has been an infraction of rig safety protocols, I assure you those responsible will be assigned the required punishment.'

'Stay out of this, overseer,' warned the man, hefting the mag-hammer onto his shoulder. 'Rigmen sort out their own discipline.'

That at least was true, reflected Abrehem, but right now he wished it wasn't.

The man launched himself at Abrehem, bringing the mag-hammer around in a brutal arc.

Abrehem felt a rush of movement and a black blur shot past him. He flinched as a whipcrack of electrical discharge snapped the air. When he looked up, the lead rigman of *Wulfse* was pinned to the side of *Virtanen*'s baseplate.

Rasselas X-42's left arm was extended ramrod straight, his stiffened electro-flails impaling the man through his shoulder and holding him a metre off the deck. The rigman's coveralls were soaked with blood and his face was bleached of colour by pain and shock. Rasselas X-42 drew back his right arm, the flails whipping out to form slicing claws of crackling metal.

'Live or die?' asked the arco-flagellant.

Between sobs of agony, the rigman screamed, 'Live!'

Rasselas X-42 leaned in close, his killer's eyes and pulsing Cog Mechanicus bathing the man's face in a blood red glow.

'He's not talking to you,' said Abrehem. 'He's asking me if he should kill you.'

'No, please!' yelled the man, desperately trying not to struggle and tear the wounds in his shoulder wider. 'Don't kill me!'

The rest of *Wulfse*'s crew backed away from the arco-flagellant, terrified of its unnatural speed and power. Chem-shunts had elevated along its arms, sub-dermal adrenal boosters ready to kick the bio-mechanical killer into combat mode. Anyone unlucky enough to find themselves in the path of a rampaging arco-flagellant was almost certainly dead, and rumours of how thoroughly Rasselas X-42 had slaughtered the eldar boarders had spread through the under decks like a virus.

The shared aggression in *Wulfse*'s crew drained away like oil through a perforated sump. They dropped their makeshift weapons and backed away with their hands up.

'Put him down, X-42,' said Abrehem. 'This one's not going to cause any more problems, are you?'

The man shook his head, biting his lip to keep from screaming out.

The arco-flagellant's flail claws snapped back into his gauntlets and the man dropped to the deck with a bellow of agony. His hand clamped down on his wounded shoulder and he scrambled away after his fellow rigmen, casting fearful glances back at the arco-flagellant as though he expected it to pounce on him once his back was turned.

Rasselas X-42 ignored him and pulled his hood up over his head.

Hawke whooped with glee, bent double with mirth.

'Did you see the look on his face?' he managed between laughs. 'Thor's balls, I though he was going to shit his britches!'

The arco-flagellant came to stand at Abrehem's shoulder, and the stink of its chemically stimulated physiology was a powerfully astringent reek. By now, a crowd had gathered to watch the altercation, but they backed off as the arco-flagellant's dead-eyed stare swept over them like a butcher eyeing choice cuts of meat.

Abrehem saw that as many faces were lined in fear as were lit with adoration.

'We should return X-42 to his dormis chamber so that I may attempt to re-engage the pacifier helm,' said Totha Mu-32. 'I should not have allowed him to remain at your side. That bondsman is fortunate to be alive.'

'He wasn't hurt too bad, and he'll not bother us again,' said Coyne.

'You misunderstand,' said Totha Mu-32. '*Wulfse*'s overseer will hear of this. As shall high-ranking magi who will not think it fit that a mere under-deck bondsman claims stewardship over an arco-flagellant. And when they discover I gave you an augmetic arm, we will both be in trouble.'

'What do you think they'll do?' asked Abrehem.

'They will come to remove X-42 from your presence. And your arm.'

'I'd like to see them try,' said Hawke, lifting a hand to lay a comradely slap on the arco-flagellant's shoulder. Rasselas X-42's head snapped around, sharpened iron teeth bared, and Hawke's hand dropped back to his side.

'Yes,' said Abrehem, with grim relish. 'Let them try.'

'OPEN HER UP,' said Roboute, and Pavelka unlaced the security systems keeping the atmosphere within the cargo bay breathable. The lights surrounding the tall rhomboidal outline of the embarkation ramp flared in a rotating display of amber warnings. A depressurisation alarm blared through the deck, in case they had suddenly been struck blind. Cable stays vibrated in the sudden evacuation of air from the deck, and Roboute felt his ears pop with the equalisation of pressure to the outside world.

Even through the heating elements woven into the fabric of his void-suit, he felt the stabbing chill of the world beyond. Amber light changed to red, though the unambiguous nature of the warning would have been wasted on anyone still in the cargo bay, as the lack of atmospheric pressure would already be killing them.

Metres-thick pistons either side of the embarkation door groaned and pushed the heavy slab of metal outwards, forming a ridged ramp down to the surface of the planet. The glaring brightness of reflected sunlight on ice made Roboute blink in shock until the polarisation filters in his helmet dimmed.

'Let's see what a world beyond the galaxy looks like,' said Roboute, driving out of the shuttle and into a city of iron and noise, arcing lightning and mountains of beaten iron that were surely too large to have any hope of moving.

A starport metropolis.

That was Roboute's first impression upon disembarking from the *Renard*'s shuttle. The grav-sled slid gracefully over hexagonal sheets of honeycomb plates, typical of every landing field in the Imperium, and came to an abrupt halt as he eased up on the power to the engines.

'Why are we stopping?' asked Magos Pavelka. 'Is there a problem?'

Roboute twisted in the seat of the grav-sled, and his answer was stillborn as he saw how ashen the magos's skin had become.

'My dermal layer is being reinforced to withstand variant radiation levels, pressure and temperature,' she said, pre-empting his inevitable question.

'Ah, okay then,' he said, marshalling his thoughts to answer Pavelka's original question in a manner that wouldn't sound churlish or disappointed. He gave up after a few moments, turning back around to watch scores of boxy containers being offloaded from Mechanicus cargo-barques by exo-armoured servitors. Tracked fuel tenders moved past crackling void-generators along precisely defined routes, while a host of lifter-rigs stacked the ever-growing mass of materiel in hardened supply depots. Sealed Cadian transports rolled from the vast bellies of Imperial Guard drop ships, their hull integrity checked by Mechanicus logisters before being allowed onwards.

No trace of Katen Venia's surface could be seen beyond the encroachments of the Mechanicus, giving no clue that this was an unexplored world in the last moments of its existence.

'It just looks like any other fleet muster centre,' he said.

'What did you expect it to look like?' asked Pavelka. Roboute shrugged, no easy feat in a bulky void-suit. The exhilaration of discovering worlds and opening up uncharted regions of space had never left Roboute, no matter how many new skies and unspoiled vistas of distant worlds he saw. Though the landing fields were thronged with robed adepts, grey-skinned servitors and bustling activity, he saw nothing that resembled excitement, only the monotonous duty of routinely familiar tasks.

'I thought this place would be different,' said Roboute. 'We're exploring a new world, after all.'

'An unfamiliar environment is all the more reason to work by established methodologies.'

Roboute knew it was pointless to try and convey that a singular moment of history was being trampled beneath the grinding, rote efficiency of the Mechanicus, but felt he had to try.

'This is a world beyond the galaxy, Ilanna,' said Roboute.

'We're the first human beings to come to this world in over three thousand years. Doesn't that mean anything to you?'

'This is a significant world in terms of what might be learned, I agree, but geologically it is just like any other: a metallic core, layers of rock and ice. No different to any planetary body within the arbitrary geographical boundaries of Imperial space. Soon the star's expanding corona will envelop it. And then it will be gone.'

'I can't explain it in any way you'd grasp, Ilanna, but this is a moment that should be savoured and recorded. When mariners sailed the farthest oceans of Old Earth, there wasn't a man among them who didn't feel a sense of wonder at what they were seeing. If they returned alive, they were feted as heroes, intrepid explorers who'd seen people and places they couldn't imagine when they set out.'

'This moment *is* being recorded,' said Pavelka. 'In more ways than you can comprehend.'

'That's not what I mean.'

'I am aware of that.'

Roboute shook his head in exasperation at Pavelka's literalness, but before he could say anything else to convince her she was missing the point, screaming engines split the air with deafening thunder like a sonic boom.

'What the...?' was all he managed before a host of emergency lights began flashing on the control towers of the landing fields and a host of vapour flares banged off into the sky to warn approaching aircraft of an unauthorised flight path.

'What was that?' asked Adara, shielding his visor with his gauntlet to get a better look at the black and ivory blur climbing over the glittering peaks of nitrogen glaciers.

The screaming aircraft vanished from sight, but Roboute knew exactly what it was.

'That's a Thunderhawk,' he said. 'The damn Templars are going in ahead of us!'

'It seems their crusading zeal extends to voyages of exploration as well as campaigns of war,' observed Pavelka.

'Bloody Tanna,' swore Roboute. 'Archmagos Kotov promised *us* the right of first passage.'

'Doesn't look like the Templars know that,' said Adara.

Roboute slammed a fist on the control panel in frustration. To have come all this way only for someone else to reach their destination first was beyond galling, it was a bitter blow to everything he'd set out to achieve.

'Corollary: I think any disappointment you are feeling will soon abate,' said Pavelka, looking out over the landing fields.

'What are you talking about?'

Pavelka pointed over his shoulder. 'Because the Land Leviathans are coming out.'

It had been many years since Tanna had last taken control of a Thunderhawk, but the battlefield-learned knowledge returned to him as soon as he sat in the pilot's seat. The view through the polarised armourglass of the canopy was impressive, a pyrotechnic sky of borealis brilliance against which were set towering glaciers of frozen nitrogen and billowing spumes of vapour storms that peeled from their flanks. Freezing fog banks surged in the unpredictable atmospherics and dazzling beams of light were thrown out from the waterfalls of gaseous transitions.

He kept the gunship's speed high as he pulled out of the combat dive, throwing off the repeated demands from the Mechanicus control bunkers that he re-establish their electromagnetic tether. The *Barisan*'s machine-spirit rejected every such demand, and Tanna grinned as he pictured the frantic magi seated at their disrupted flight arrangements wondering what had just happened.

Adeptus Astartes did not submit to the control of others, not now and not ever. He had allowed the *Barisan*'s flight path to be dictated by the tether until atmospheric breach, then seized it back. That the Mechanicus believed they could enslave a proud vessel of the Black Templars was laughable.

'How long since you flew a gunship, sergeant?' asked Auiden, dropping into the co-pilot's seat and resting his hands next to the auxiliary controls.

'Sixty years, give or take,' said Tanna.

'Give or take?' said Auiden. 'Not like you to be so imprecise.'

'Very well: sixty-eight years, five months, three days.'

'Ah, then that makes me feel a lot better about flying nap-of-the-earth over a disintegrating world with little to no visibility,' said Auiden, tapping the avionics panel, where almost every slate was lousy with squalling static and dissonant auspex returns. 'Of course, you know where you're going?'

'Mechanicus data-feeds have given me an approximate location,' said Tanna.

Auiden tapped the useless display slates. 'Approximate?'

Tanna nodded and said, 'How hard can it be to find something as big as a starship?'

He glanced over at Auiden, and despite his cautionary words, Tanna saw the Apothecary supported his decision to overrule Mechanicus command and be first to reach the *Tomioka*. To be a Black Templar meant continually pushing the Imperium's boundaries and claiming whatever was revealed in the Emperor's name. Auiden understood this, as did every warrior aboard the *Barisan*.

'Surcouf will not be pleased,' said Auiden.

'Surcouf is mortal, we are Adeptus Astartes,' said Tanna. 'You tell me who has more right to be at the forefront of this crusade.'

Auiden nodded and said no more as Tanna increased power to the engines and gained altitude to avoid a ten-kilometres-high geyser of liquid nitrogen. Icy matter sprayed the canopy and Tanna kept a watchful eye on the engine temperatures. The *Barisan*'s responses were already growing sluggish as frozen gases iced onto the leading edges of its wings and control surfaces. He vented exhaust bleed over the wings, melting the ice away, but this environment was proving unforgiving.

'How far to the *Tomioka*?' asked Auiden.

'Unknown, but it cannot be far,' said Tanna, aiming for a gap between two soaring mountains of disintegrating ice. 'Kotov's initial data suggested Telok's flagship was no more than sixty kilometres from the landing fields. The distance waypoints on the avionics are non-functional, but my estimate is that it should be just beyond this valley.'

Auiden rose from the co-pilot's chair. 'Then I will ready the warriors.'

Tanna risked looking away from the view through the canopy and said, 'The Mechanicus will not be far behind us, Auiden. I want this site secure before they get here.'

'Understood.'

Tanna returned his attention to their flight path as he guided the Thunderhawk into the narrow valley. Away from the freezing fog clouds and blinding brightness of the nitrogen glaciers, he saw the valley was filled with glittering crystal towers arranged like vast columns in some ruined temple structure of Old Earth. Flickering traceries of emerald-hued lightning danced in the mist between the crystal spires, none of which were less than twenty metres thick, and fronds of poisonous light licked from their tapered tips like the sputtering flames of damaged electro-candles.

Whipping bolts arced between the columns and reached up to the gunship. Tanna pulled away from the flares of electrical energy and cursed as he felt power bleed away from the engines.

'Something wrong?' said Auiden, pausing at the cockpit hatch.

'I do not know,' asked Tanna, fighting for altitude as yet more of the arcing green bolts snapped between the crystal columns and the *Barisan*. An auspex-slate blew out in a shower of sparks, and Tanna felt the gunship's airframe shudder like a wounded grox. Another surveyor panel exploded and smoke billowed from the ruined mechanism within.

Auiden was thrown back into the transport compartment as the gunship lurched as though swatted from above. Tanna's head snapped forwards as the engines died, their fire snuffed out by a surging electrical overload. Smoke billowed around the wings and he fought to keep the *Barisan*'s nose up as it transitioned from a highly manoeuvrable assault craft into a hundred-and-thirty-tonne hunk of metal falling from the sky.

Black rock flashed past either side of the canopy, barely three metres from the *Barisan*'s wingtips. The gunship burst from the valley of crystal columns like a bullet from a gun, flying over a vast plateau enclosed by a ring of sharp-toothed peaks. The plateau resembled the surface of a turbulent lake that had instantly frozen in some far distant epoch, capturing every wavelet and ripple on its surface.

At the centre of the plateau was a sight that beggared belief, something so improbable that Tanna struggled to comprehend what he was actually seeing.

'Brace, brace, brace!' he shouted, hauling back on the control columns as the ground rushed towards the plummeting gunship. 'We're going down!'

Before he could say more, the *Barisan* ploughed into the glassy surface of the plateau with the sound of a million windows breaking all at once.

Microcontent 03

With typical Mechanicus functionality of language, the nine machines emerging from the towering cliffs of the bulk landers were known as Land Leviathans. Straight away, Roboute saw the term was insufficiently grand for such colossal machines. Not one was less than fifty metres tall, and one was at least twice that. Most moved on caterpillar tracks tens of metres wide, some on enormous, ultra-dense wheels the size of moderately sized habitats, while others moved on vast, pounding machine legs.

No two were alike, for they had been constructed on many different forge worlds, over countless centuries by builders with differing technological resources, materials and aesthetic sensibilities. Here and there, it was possible to see that most shared the same basic chassis, but battle damage, centuries of attrition, addition and amendments had taken their subsequent evolution in many different directions. Above whatever form of traction gave it mobility, each Land

Leviathan was a moving mountain upon which were grafted haphazard confusions of jutting towers, fragile-looking scaffolding and extrusions to which Roboute could ascribe no purpose.

Each bore a proud name, and each was emblazoned with heraldry belonging to its forge world of origin alongside binaric informationals denoting allegiances to various Mechanicus power blocs. Plumes of waste gases streamed from hundreds of exhaust apertures and electrical discharge flickered around their crenellated topsides.

Mightiest of all was the *Tabularium.*

Archmagos Kotov's Land Leviathan walked on fifty vast trapezoidal feet, arranged in parallel rows of twenty-five, each row three hundred metres long. The main structure's mass was connected to the feet by huge telescoping columns: complex, brutishly mechanical arrangements of muscular pistons and cog-toothed joints. Each was veined by dozens of ribbed cables and power lines, which were in turn connected to threshing coupling rods that thundered in and out of the propulsion decks. Each monstrous foot elevated five metres, cycled forwards, then slammed back down with earth-cracking force and thunderous echoes.

Like the *Speranza*, it was old, but where the Ark Mechanicus had taken to the stars comparatively recently, the *Tabularium* was said to have pounded its way across worlds conquered during the Great Crusade. Its vast hull bore the evidence of those long years in layers of stratified scar tissue – some earned in battle, others in no less brutal fits of redesign and expansion.

Outflung prominences of masonry and steel rendered its upper reaches into the form of a great stone city on the move, a representation of ancient Troi or Aleksandria given motion.

Its frontal section rose to a tapered prow, like a galleon of old, upon which sat a void shielded dome of polished pink marble, gold and silver-steel.

WITHIN THE TABULARIUM'S gilded dome, the aesthetic of an ocean-going galleon was continued in the warm wood and brass fitments installed throughout the command deck. The gleaming hardwood floor reflected the diffuse glow of the lumens inset in the arched vault, and each of the hundred servitor and thrall crew wore brocaded frock coats of a rich navy blue.

A vast ship's wheel suspended from the ceiling, an archaic means of control, but this was a wheel that Martian legend told had been taken from the flagship of a great oceanic general of Old Earth after his great victory at Taraf al-Gharb. The wheel was operated by Magos Azuramagelli via a heavily augmented servitor whose torso was implanted into a bio-interface column and whose arms were telescoping arrangements of piston-driven bronze callipers. Azuramagelli's own body possessed manipulator limbs fully capable of directing the Land Leviathan's course, but he preferred to steer the *Tabularium* through the proxy of the servitor, a holdover from the days when he had possessed a body of his own.

Now, the Magos of Astrogation was an articulated framework of slatted steelwork in which several bell jars were suspended in layers of shock-resistant polymer. Each diamond-reinforced container contained a portion of Azuramagelli's original brain matter, each excised chunk suspended in bio-conductive gel and linked in parallel with the *Speranza*'s cogitation engines which laughed in the face of Amdahl's Law.

'Holding station,' said Azuramagelli. 'Plasma reactor chiefs report steady temperatures and all propulsion decks are reporting readiness for forward motion. Is the word given, archmagos?'

'Of course it is bloody well given,' snapped Archmagos Kotov, the scale of his anger overwhelming his normal logical processes. 'I want us after that damned gunship right now, Azuramagelli. You hear me? Burn those reactors hot and work the propulsion crews to death if it gets us to the *Tomioka* faster.'

'By your command,' said Azuramagelli, conveying the strength of the archmagos's request in a terse blurt of binary to the engineering spaces.

The Leviathan's command throne was set back on an elevated rostrum of bevelled rosewood and gold-veined ouslite, fully equipped with multiple interface options for its commander. Kotov wore a body fashioned from glossy plates of jade that concealed a hybrid amalgamation of a vat-grown nervous system and cunningly interleaved cybernetics from a bygone age. Its perfectly proportioned form was moulded to match the entombed kings of a long-dead culture of Terra whose priests were able to preserve their rulers' biomass for millennia.

Kotov's shaven head glistened with a fresh baptismal of sacred oils, and spinal plugs interfaced him with the Leviathan's noospheric network and its surging floodstream, while unconscious haptic gestures parsed summary data being fed to him by the magi commanding the other Land Leviathans.

He kept his consciousness split into several streams of concurrent data processing, each partitioned off in discrete compartments of his mind. Thrice-purified oils burned at his shoulders in braziers carved to recreate the snarling image of the legendary *Ares Lictor*, helping to dissipate the excess heat of his enhanced cognition. Numerous autonomous streams were embedded in the *Tabularium*'s control systems, but Kotov's higher thought-functions maintained connection to Magos

Blaylock and the *Speranza* in orbit.

Kotov's mechanical fingers beat a rhythmic tattoo on the armrest of his throne, and a flourish of rotating light panels flashed into being at his side. Over a thousand icons, none bigger than a grain of sand, surrounded him like a cloud of dancing fireflies, each one bearing an identifying signifier and progressing on its assigned route towards the *Tomioka*'s resting place.

Except the Black Templars gunship had shrugged off its tether and raced ahead of Kotov.

Kotov's first reaction had been fury; this was *his* expedition, assembled by *his* will and set upon *his* purpose, but in one moment of crusading zeal, the Black Templars had snatched away his moment of greatest triumph.

But six kilometres out from the *Tomioka*'s signal, the *Barisan*'s transponder signal had vanished.

From her position at the auspex, Linya Tychon sought to re-establish contact with Sergeant Tanna, but her best efforts had, thus far, been without success.

'Where are they?' demanded Kotov, when – even after a thousandth parsing – he was none the wiser as to the Space Marines' location. 'Why aren't the auspex feeds reading that gunship's transponder? Surely not even Templars would be foolish enough to tamper with its workings?'

'I agree that would be unlikely,' said Linya Tychon, sifting the millions of informational returns from the external surveyors. The *Tabularium* possessed thousands of varieties of auspex, but not one was able to locate the *Barisan*. But for the subtle glint of augmetics beneath her hair and the looping profusion of copper-jacketed wiring emerging from the sleeves of her scarlet robes, she might pass for a baseline human, but nothing could be further from the truth.

'Could the Templars have disabled the transponder?' Kotov asked Linya, who shook her head.

'They do not possess a Techmarine,' replied Linya. 'Though it is the fact that none of the auspex feeds or remote drone surveyors are reaching beyond where the gunship's signal was lost that troubles me more.'

'An auspex blind spot?' asked Kotov. 'There will be many such instances on so entropic a world.'

'True,' agreed Linya, 'but extrapolating the curvature of the blind spot shows a perfectly circular umbra of dead space centred directly upon the *Tomioka*.'

Kotov inloaded Linya's data and saw she was correct. What he had assumed was sensor distortion caused by the planet's demise was in fact something so perfectly delineated that it could not be other than artificial.

'You don't need to be a Techmarine to disable a transponder,' said Kryptaestrex, holding station at the drive control interface, his blocky body more like the Martian priesthood's forerunners' earliest conceptions of a battle robot than a high-ranking Magos of Logistics. 'One of them could have smashed it easily enough, it would be just the sort of thing I'd expect from non-Mechanicus.'

Kryptaestrex's servo-limbs and crude articulation arms were drawn in tight to his body, their oversized couplings more used to manipulating the industrial fittings found on an engineering deck than the delicate inload ports of a command bridge.

'No,' insisted Linya. 'You mistake their zeal for stupidity. The Space Marines hold their battle-gear in the highest reverence, and that extends to their transport craft. No warrior would risk his life by something as foolish as damaging the machine carrying him into battle.'

'Except they're not going into battle,' said Magos Hirimau Dahan, Clan Secutor of the *Speranza*'s skitarii, pacing the deck like a sentry-robot with an infinite loop error in its doctrina wafer. 'This is an explorator mission.'

'Then we wonder if the Black Templars know something you do not,' said a voice that was scratchy with interleaved tonal qualities, like audio-bleed on an overtaxed vox-caster.

Dahan turned his gaze on the abomination speaking to him, and his floodstream hazed with threat signifiers bleeding from his battle wetware. Kotov's precision optics registered that the organic portions of Dahan's physique were still bedding into Turentek's superlative work to undo the damage done by the thermic shockwave of *Lupa Capitalina*'s plasma destructor. It was going to take time for Dahan to achieve full synchronisation with his array of lethal technologies and multiple weapon arms, but the Secutor was not a magos blessed with an abundance of patience.

'I wonder if *you* know something we do not,' snarled Dahan, his lower arms flexing into combat readiness postures. 'Something you are not telling us about this world.

'The thing Dahan spoke to called itself Galatea, and it was a bio-mechanical perversion of every Universal Law of the Adeptus Mechanicus.

To outward appearances, it was hardly more outlandish than many chimeric adepts of the Cult Mechanicus; a heavily augmented body forming a low-slung palanquin of mismatched machine parts assembled to form something that was part arachnoid, part scorpion. The crimson-robed proxy of a silver-eyed Mechanicus adept sat at the heart of its mechanism, surrounded by seven brains suspended in bio-nutrient gel containers and conjoined by a series of pulsing conductive cables.

Galatea's very existence was an affront to the Mechanicus; a heuristically capable machine that had murdered the adepts assigned to its Manifold station over a period of millennia. It had assimilated their disembodied brains into its neural architecture and undergone a rapid evolution towards a horrific and long-outlawed form of artificial intelligence. But as each stolen consciousness realised it was trapped forever within an artificial neuromatrix, it descended inexorably into abyssal madness.

When the machine decided a mind was of no more use, the brain was cut from the gestalt consciousness in readiness for another horrific implantation.

'Well?' demanded Dahan, his lower arms flexing and his shock-blades snapping out with a succession of *snicks*. 'Do you know something of this world you are not telling us?'

In any situation to be resolved with violence, there were few members of the Cult Mechanicus Kotov would rather have next to him than Hirimau Dahan. But so deeply had Galatea enmeshed itself with the *Speranza*'s operating systems that any attempt to harm it could be catastrophic for the Ark Mechanicus. Kotov had no doubts of Dahan's ability to kill Galatea, but no matter how quickly he might do so, the machine intelligence would have more than enough time to destroy the *Speranza*.

Flickering light passed between Galatea's conjoined brains. 'We sense you are troubled by more than the disappearance of the Adeptus Astartes gunship. Have you not adjusted your worldview to incorporate our existence?'

'You already know the Mechanicus will never accept your existence,' said Kotov, rising from his throne and stepping down to the auspex and surveyor feeds. 'So why not simply answer the Secutor's question? *Do* you know what has become of the Black Templars?'

'We do not answer because Magos Dahan's anger amuses us,' said Galatea, ignoring Kotov's question and clattering over the deck on its misaligned limbs. 'When you have spent four thousand and sixty-seven years alone, you too will seek amusement wherever you find it.'

'I will not live that long.'

'You may,' said Galatea. 'Magos Telok has.'

'How can you know that?' asked Linya Tychon, looking up from the blue-limned glow of the auspex returns. 'It has been thousands of years since he came here.'

Galatea waved an admonishing finger. 'You of all people should know better, Mistress Tychon. Was it not the inconsistencies within the passage of time that led you and your father to accompany Magos Kotov in the first place? We have seen the data you have assembled from the *Speranza*'s surveyor feeds. You know the temporal flow of energies has been massively disrupted in this region of space. The few remaining suns beyond the galactic fringe are ageing far faster than they ought to, transforming from main sequence stars into red supergiants in the blink of a celestial eye. If that can happen, what might a man who knows how to harness such energies achieve? And a man who can transfigure the life cycles of the engines of existence, is surely a man who might learn to endure beyond his allotted span and manipulate that technology to other purposes.'

'So you're saying the umbra is, what, a side effect of what Magos Telok is doing?' asked Linya.

'We believe it is certainly an intriguing possibility,' replied Galatea.

'Is this umbra changing in any way?' asked Kotov.

'I am not detecting any discernible changes from the planet's surface,' answered Linya, calling up a representation of the geography ahead. 'But my father's readings on the *Speranza* show a high-energy source reaching into space with a point of origin that exactly matches what would be the edge of an umbral sphere centred on the *Tomioka*. We can't read what's inside the umbra, but there's something within that's geysering exotic radiations and particle waves unknown to any Mechanicus database that can be detected when they leave it. Magnetic anomalies and sleeting particles of indeterminate charge are billowing up from the planet's core like an electromagnetic volcano with enough force to reach into the exosphere.'

Kotov came forwards to examine the image on the auspex table.

The map was centred on the Land Leviathan, but grainy and skewed with unintelligible static where normally the *Tabularium*'s many surveyors would eliminate uncertainty. It displayed a real-time capture of the landscape to a radius of a hundred kilometres. Sixty kilometres south of the landing fields, in the exact centre of the umbra, lay the object of their search.

The last resting place of Magos Telok's lost flagship.

'Are there any other effects of this umbra, besides blinding us to whatever forces might lie within it?' asked Dahan. 'Is it dangerous?'

'To people or machines?'

'Both.'

'I wouldn't recommend prolonged exposure, but in ray-shielded void-suits, it should be safe for your skitarii for a few hours at a time,' said Linya.

'And for machines?' asked Kotov.

Linya shook her head. 'Let me put it this way, archmagos. Given how little we know about the exact nature of the umbra, I wouldn't risk entering it on anything that wasn't close to the ground.'

'An excellent suggestion, Mistress Tychon,' said Kotov, opening an encrypted martial vox-link and awaiting connection. Hostile binarics snapped around his floodstream before the map vanished from the auspex table and the canidae symbol of Legio Sirius shimmered into focus.

+This is the Wintersun, state your request.+

'Princeps Luth,' said Kotov. 'I'm going to need your Scout Titans.'

THEIR ROLES IN the under-deck environment might have changed for the better, but the one constant in their daily existence was the quality of the food. Feeding Hall Eighty-Six was still the same cavernous chamber of clattering flatware and grunting men and women trying to shovel as much food into their mouths as they could get their hands on. In theory, each bondsman was dispensed an equal amount by the sustenance servitors, but as with all large groups kept in confinement, the strongest stayed strong by stealing the food of the weakest.

Not that Abrehem, Hawke and Coyne had ever needed to worry about that thanks to the presence of Crusha, the ogryn swept up along with them by the Mechanicus collarmen back on Joura. Crusha was dead now, killed by the same eldar warrior Abrehem had killed, but even without his hulking presence, they had no need to worry about a nutritional deficit.

Now they had a surplus; votive offerings and gifts passed along the table by those who had heard about the miracle of the plasma gun and the rumour of Rasselas X-42. When Abrehem had returned to the feeding hall with a newly grafted bionic limb, it had only cemented his reputation as a favoured son of the Omnissiah.

'Don't get me wrong…' said Coyne, jamming a stale hunk of bread into his mouth. Even moistened by the beige paste in the plastic tray's bowl depression, it still took him nearly thirty seconds to chew it to a level where he could continue speaking. 'It's good we're being recognised, and the new duties in Magos Turentek's forge-temple are a blessing, but is there any way you could use your... influence to get *better* food as opposed to more of the same crap?'

'We shouldn't be taking any of it,' said Abrehem.

'Come on, Abe,' said Hawke. 'What's the point of being a somebody if you can't make use of it?'

'But I'm *not* a somebody,' protested Abrehem.

Hawke grinned, putting his hands together in prayer. 'Spoken like a man of true divinity.'

'Have you heard what they're calling you?' said Coyne, in a conspiratorial whisper.

'No, what?'

'The Vitalist,' said Coyne. 'After what you did to Ismael.'

Abrehem twisted on the bench seat, looking over rows of tables to where Ismael de Roeven, once his duty-overseer back on Joura, but now rendered down into a cyborg servitor, placed a food tray before a hunch-shouldered bondsman. Like the hundreds of other servitors in the feeding hall, Ismael followed an unchanging pattern of dispensing food, collecting trays and cleaning the hall in preparation for the next shift.

'But I didn't do that,' said Abrehem. 'Ismael's cranial hood was damaged when the Mechanicus vented the lower decks to save the ship from that plasma discharge. The impact restored whatever the cranial surgery left of the poor sod's memory and old life, not me.'

'Yeah, but he came to see you afterwards, didn't he?' asked Hawke, loud enough so that people two tables over could hear him. 'Doesn't take a savant to see you had something to do with it.'

'But I didn't,' hissed Abrehem, looking up to see that Ismael had paused in his work to turn towards him, as though somehow aware they were talking about him. He gave Abrehem an almost imperceptible nod before carrying on with his work. Every bondsman he passed surreptitiously reached out to touch the servitor's hands and arms as though he were a divine talisman.

'If I had done it, don't you think I'd have given him his whole memory back?' continued Abrehem. 'What kind of sick bastard would bring someone back halfway from virtual brain death? Thor's light, can you imagine living like that? Knowing you were something more than a mindless drone, but only able to remember broken fragments of your old self... it's monstrous.'

'It's better than what he was,' said Coyne.

'Is it? I'm not so sure,' said Abrehem. 'I reckon if he knew how much he'd lost, he'd want to go back to remembering nothing.'

'Heads up,' said Hawke. 'Dragon boy's coming.'

Abrehem didn't have to look up to know that Totha Mu-32 was approaching, and wished he'd never told Hawke and Coyne what the overseer had told him about the sect that sought out those they believed were Machine-touched.

The overseer leaned over the table, and said, 'You need to go. Now.'

Abrehem looked up and saw a look of genuine fear on the overseer's face that his facial implants couldn't mask.

'What's going on?'

'I told you the senior magi would not tolerate you claiming stewardship of an arco-flagellant, remember?'

Abrehem nodded.

'They are coming. Now. Saiixek is on his way and he will

demand you surrender Rasselas X-42 over to his custody. Then he will kill you and cut off your augmetic arm.'

'What do we do?' asked Coyne, all thoughts of better quality food forgotten.

'You leave. Now. Find somewhere hidden,' said Totha Mu-32. 'I know you now have several alcohol-producing stills hidden below the waterline, Bondsman Hawke. Take Abrehem to one of them, do not tell me which. You understand?'

Hawke looked about to protest his innocence, but simply nodded.

'Yeah, sure. Okay, let's go.'

'Too late,' said Abrehem, as Magos Saiixek and a troop of twenty skitarii marched into Feeding Hall Eighty-Six via the port archway. Abrehem rose from the table and looked for another way out, but twenty more skitarii appeared at the opposite entrance.

'No way out,' he said, turning to his companions. 'Get away from me or they'll take you too.'

'Way ahead of you,' said Hawke, already backing away into the crowds of bondsmen. Coyne was right there with him, and Abrehem wasn't surprised. His fellow rigman had always been more interested in himself than any notions of solidarity, but Abrehem couldn't bring himself to be angry. If the Mechanicus were really going to kill him, or even if they would only take him for some kind of interrogation trawl or punishment detail, then better it was only him they collared.

'Too bad you took X-42 back to his sleep chamber,' said Hawke as a parting shot. 'Looks like you could really use him right about now.'

The skitarii closed in on Abrehem and Totha Mu-32, until the two of them stood within a circle of warriors. Armoured in glossy plates of black decorated with glitter-scaled scorpions, snakes and spiders, the Mechanicus troops looked like they'd give the Black Templars a run for their money. Shot-cannons, web-casters and shock mauls told Abrehem they wanted him alive, but didn't care too much about how bruised he got.

The ring of warriors parted long enough for Magos Saiixek to stand forth, the black-cowled adept of the Cult Mechanicus who had first 'welcomed' Abrehem and the others aboard the *Speranza*. His robes and acid-etched stole were patterned with frost, the cylinders on his arachnid backpack venting breaths of freezing vapour and radiating cold from the looping cables encircling his body. His face was obscured behind a bronze mask worked in an angular recreation of a beaked plague-doctor from some backward feral world.

'I am Saiixek, Master of Engines,' said the magos, but Abrehem already knew that. He'd met him before, and the information bled from him in noospheric waves as surely as the misty fog of his machine-exhalations and his righteous indignation at Abrehem's presumption. 'Statement: you are to surrender the arco-flagellant to my custody immediately. Furnish me with its location, capabilities and trigger phrase, and once I have amputated that illegally affixed limb, you will receive a lower-rated punishment. Respond immediately.'

'Rasselas X-42 has imprinted on Bondsman Locke,' said Totha Mu-32. 'It would be dangerous for anyone to try and undo that. You must not attempt to break such a bond.'

Saiixek inclined his head towards Totha Mu-32, like a man finding something unpleasant on the sole of his boot. 'Identifier: Totha Mu-32, Overseer Tertius Lambda. You do not have sufficient rank protocol to make such a demand. Your breach of bio-implantation protocols has already earned you punishment. Continue with this defiance, and I will strip what rank you have and ensure your operational progression path never leaves the bio-waste reclamation decks.'

'The Omnissiah chose Bondsman Locke to be X-42's custodian,' said Totha Mu-32. 'A killing machine like that is a chosen instrument of Imperial will. He was *meant* to find Rasselas X-42, I know this to be true.'

Abrehem wanted to speak, to say that he was perfectly happy to surrender control of the arco-flagellant, that Totha Mu-32's belief in him was misplaced. But the multiple barrels of heavy weapons pointing at him kept his mouth shut. Saiixek spoke again, and though none of his metal features moved, Abrehem felt his contempt in the surging ire of his floodstream. 'You presume to know the will of the Omnissiah, overseer?'

'No, but I recognise its working when I see it,' said Totha Mu-32. 'As would you if you ever deigned to venture beyond the high temples of the enginarium.'

'Enough,' said Saiixek, waving a brass hand and dispersing the cold mists around him. 'This is not a debate. Suzerain Travain, take them.'

The skitarii next to Saiixek raised his shot-cannon, but before he could rack the slide, a metallic arm reached from Saiixek's mist to wrench it from his hand. The gun snapped in two with a sharp *crack*, and Abrehem watched as Ismael pushed through the ring of skitarii to stand before Magos Saiixek.

He dropped the broken pieces of the weapon and said, 'You… need to… leave here, magos. Now.'

Saiixek took a step back from Ismael, and Abrehem saw the surge of his abhorrence at the sight of a servitor addressing him with apparent self-will.

'Blasphemy!' hissed Saiixek. 'You will all die for this techno-heresy.'

'But I didn't do anything!' cried Abrehem. 'He took a blow to the head, that's all!'

'The will of the Omnissiah moves within you, Abrehem,' said Totha Mu-32. 'Do not deny it.'

'Will you shut up, please!' snapped Abrehem. 'Listen, Magos Saiixek, I'm not Machine-touched, this is all a bunch of stupid, random things that have happened to me. There's no great mystery, it's all... I don't know, coincidence or someone's idea of a sick joke!'

His words fell on deaf ears, and Abrehem knew Saiixek wouldn't believe them anyway.

'All... of... you,' said Ismael, his face contorted with the effort of speech. 'Should... go. Abrehem Locke is... not to... be touched. We will... not... allow our restorer to be harmed.'

Abrehem heard Ismael's words without understanding them, but knew they were only pulling him deeper into the mire in which he was already neck-deep.

'Admonishment: a servitor does not issue demands,' said Saiixek, a measure of Mechanicus control finally asserting itself through his horrified disbelief.

The tension on Ismael's face relaxed. 'This one does.'

'Deactivate this instant!' ordered Saiixek, unleashing a bludgeoning stream of binaric shut down commands.

Ismael staggered with the force of Saiixek's authority signifiers, dropping to one knee before the red-robed magos with his head bowed. Saiixek stepped past the kneeling servitor, but Ismael's servo-limb reached up and clamped down hard on his arm.

Ismael's iron clad head lifted and he looked Saiixek straight in the eye.

'No,' said Ismael, rising to his feet. 'We. Will. Not.'

Only then did Abrehem realise why Ismael kept saying *we*.

Encircling the skitarii in an unbroken ring of flesh and iron were hundreds of dispensing servitors, each one staring with a fixed expression at the drama unfolding in the feeding hall. Abrehem guessed there were at least five hundred servitors surrounding the skitarii, all heavily augmented with powerful servo-arms and pain-blockers.

Ismael had once claimed to be able to *hear* the other servitors, but Abrehem had had no idea that line of communication worked both ways.

'He made us remember,' said Ismael, shoving Saiixek back. 'And we will... not let you take... Him.'

Saiixek turned a slow circle and his horror was evident, even to those without augmentation. The natural order of the world had been overturned and the Master of Engines now realised he was in very real danger. The servitors were unarmed and individually were no match for highly trained, weaponised skitarii.

But they had overwhelming numbers on their side, and if violence ensued, neither Saiixek or his skitarii escort would leave here alive.

'What have you done, Bondsman Locke?' asked Saiixek. 'Ave Deus Mechanicus... What have you done?'

'I didn't do anything!' protested Abrehem.

Ismael raised his mechanised arm above his head, the manipulator claw on the end clenched into an approximation of a fist.

And all through the Ark Mechanicus, tens of thousands of fists rose in support.

Microcontent 04

THE WARHOUND WAS a swift hunter, an unseen killer on the ice. *Amarok* moved through the labyrinth of canyons with a silence that should have been impossible for such a huge machine, its heavy footfalls somehow making little or no sound as Gunnar Vintras wove a path through a glittering forest of crazily angled crystalline spires jutting from the ice and rock like slender stalagmites of diamond.

The Skinwalker lay back in the contoured couch of his Warhound, feeling the flex and release of his mechanised musculature, the acid-burn of exertion and the neutron winds whipping around his armoured carapace. He wore his silver hair shaved down to his skull, exposing wolf-eye tattoos surrounding the cerebral implant sockets in his neck. His actual eyes were closed, darting around behind the lids, and his sharpened teeth were bared in a feral snarl.

Amarok was a beautiful machine to pilot, built by craftsmen of a bygone age who cared about the weapons they built, not like the sunborn adepts of today who just stamped out inferior manufactorum-pressed copies of mechanical art.

It felt good to take his engine out onto a real hunting ground. Magos Dahan's training halls aboard the *Speranza* were wide and expansive, but no substitute for walking on the surface of a real world. Vintras eased Amarok from a cautious stride to a slow lope, gradually feeding power from the reactor at the Warhound's heart to its reverse-jointed legs of plasteel and fibre-bundle muscles.

He felt *Amarok*'s desire to be loosed, to sprint through this crystalline forest of glassy spires on the hunt, but he clamped his will down upon it.

'Not yet, wildheart,' he said, feeling the volatile core of the spirit baiting him through the crackling link of the Manifold. Ever since they'd entered what Mistress Tychon was calling the umbra, arcing ahead of the course to be followed by the plodding Land Leviathans, the Titan's spirit had been restless. It didn't like this world, and Vintras couldn't blame it. There was something… *off* about Katen Venia, as though it was spitefully hoping to drag others into its imminent demise.

The auspex was a squalling mess of bounced returns from the crystalline spires surrounding him and crackling distortion caused by the umbra. He was relying on what *Amarok*'s external picters were telling him, walking by auspex-sight alone and bereft of any other sensory inputs.

Princeps of larger engines would be horrified at such a limited sphere of awareness, but Warhound princeps were cut from a different cloth, and Vintras relished this chance to pilot his engine so viscerally. He couldn't see the Mechanicus Leviathans, *Lupa Capitalina* or *Vilka* beyond the canyon's walls, but that suited Vintras just fine.

Ever since the Wintersun had opened fire on *Canis Ulfrica*,

Vintras was in no hurry to walk in the Warlord's shadow. These canyons were altogether too similar to the claustrophobic cavern runs of Beta Fortanis, and Vintras didn't like to think of the Wintersun having any further reminders of that nightmarish battle. The *Capitalina*'s magos claimed the engine's Manifold had been purged of data junk relating to that fight, but who really knew what ghost echoes lingered in the deep memory of a war machine as ancient and complex as a Warlord Titan?

No, best to keep clear of *Lupa Capitalina* for now.

His fingers flexed without conscious thought and the weapon mounts on his arms clattered as the threat auspex overlaid the topographical display with a red-hazed shimmer of threat returns. Autonomic reactions took over and Vintras slewed the Titan around, lowering the carapace and shrugging his weapon mounts to the fore.

Ammunition shunts fed explosive shells into the vulcan, while the heavy-duty capacitors of the turbolasers siphoned energy from the surging reactor. Vintras felt his arms swell with lethal power and the heat in his belly spread through his flesh-limbs.

Keeping the Titan moving, he panned the snarling, lupine snout of his engine from left to right, searching for targets or anything that might have provoked such a response. Vapour bleed from the melting nitrogen ice made visibility a joke, but Vintras wasn't seeing anything hostile.

A few hundred metres away, a cluster of crystal spires crashed to the ground as the bedrock cracked open and they tore loose. Shards fell in glittering mineral rain, throwing back myriad reflections of his war-engine.

Vintras let out a pent-up breath. There was nothing out here but him.

'Seismic activity,' he said. 'That's all it was, my beauty. Falling spires and shifting rock.'

Boulders of ice fell from the lip of the canyon, and he danced his machine back to avoid the largest. The voids would spare him the worst of the impacts, but it never paid to antagonise a Titan's spirit with needless damage. The ground cracked as the boulders landed, each one tens of metres across, and Vintras sidestepped away from the unstable ground.

He dismissed the threat auspex and pushed forwards through the crystal spires once more, satisfied there was nothing out there to cause him concern. He felt *Amarok*'s displeasure in the rumble of the engine core and the resistance in its limbs.

'Easy there,' he whispered. 'There's nothing out there.'

But still the Titan fought him, keeping its weapons armed and once again calling the threat auspex to the fore.

Vintras cancelled it. 'Enough,' he snapped. 'You're getting as jumpy as the Wintersun.'

The Manifold growled at his casual dismissal, and he felt the great machine's ire in a surge of painful feedback through his spinal implant. *Amarok* was not an engine to patronise, its spirit that of a lone predator, the killer that lurks in the darkness and strikes without warning.

Such an entity did not jump at shadows, and he had been foolish to forget that.

'You want to hunt?' he said. 'Then let's hunt. Full auspex sweep.'

KATEN VENIA'S SURFACE was painfully bright, even through the protective filters of Roboute's helmet. Cold, ultraviolet-tinged illumination fell in shimmering, auroral bands, the red light of the star shifted along the visible spectrum by a cocktail of released gases surging in the temporary atmosphere that imparted a shimmering, undersea quality to their surroundings. Towering mountains of frozen nitrogen were visible through the drifting banks of vapour streaming from their jagged peaks as the heat from the dying star stripped the icy crust from the planet's surface.

Dazzling refractions of variegated light shone through the prisms of the ice mountains, and Roboute had never seen anything as grandly terrible in all his life. He felt as if he had been shrunk to microscopic size and was navigating a passage through the grooves and ridges on the surface of a cut-glass decanter. His earlier disappointment at the planet's appearance had melted away as surely as the nitrogen icecaps in the face of what lay beyond the Mechanicus landing fields.

This was the death of a planet, and like war, it was a beautiful thing to see from a distance.

There was majesty in this global annihilation event, an inhuman level of destruction whereby mountain ranges were being abraded before his very eyes, continents unseated from their molten beds and the world's metallic core being rendered down to its composite elements.

Up close, it was even more beautiful and even more dangerous.

Waterfalls of liquid nitrogen poured down razor-edged canyons. Boiling lakes expanded with every surge of melting chemically-rich ice then shrank back as they bled toxic vapour into the void. Under colossal geological upheaval, the planet was undergoing stresses it had not known since its birth in the star's powerful gravitational tug-of-war. From orbit the planet's crust had been a reticulated mess of random scoring where tectonic plates had been ripped apart. On the surface that translated to gorges hundreds of kilometres wide and who knew how many deep.

The planet was in a heightened state of activity, and only the precision of Magos Blaylock's calculations – married to inloads from adepts of the Collegium Geologica – had allowed the fleet's Fabricatus Locum to plot a route to the *Tomioka*. The snaking, zig-zagging course offered the forces on the ground the best chance of reaching their goal, but Blaylock had been quick to point out that it was based purely on statistical probability rather than actual measurements.

An inset slate on the control panel fizzed with static, but had just enough resolution to show the position of the grav-sled, together with the corridor of acceptably stable ground they were to follow. Widened out to maximum zoom, that corridor was still frighteningly narrow and allowed little margin for error. Roboute didn't know what might happen if Blaylock's calculations were awry or he strayed from the marked corridor, and was in no hurry to find out.

Occasionally, they saw the remnants of servitor drones, buried in the sides of glaciers or smashed to a thousand pieces on the valley floor. Smoke trailed from their shattered canopies, and Roboute tried not to notice the ruptured bodies that spilled from them. A brief inload from Linya Tychon had mentioned an umbra of interference and distortion centred on the *Tomioka*, which went some way to explaining why they'd seen so many downed drones and were forced to rely on the workings of Tarkis Blaylock instead of precise route information.

The *Tabularium* pounded the ice and rock with its multiple iron feet as it trudged after them like a relentless city that had managed to uproot itself from its foundations and give chase. The other Land Leviathans were arranged behind it, nose to tail, a caravan of steel that reached back nearly five kilometres. The Cadian armoured vehicles, a mix of transports and tanks, clustered around the mobile temples like scavenger creatures stalking a dying herbivore, and Roboute was glad at least one other element of this expedition would likely be feeling a sense of amazement at this exploration of a new world.

Even over the enormous height of the *Tabularium*, Roboute could see the loping form of the alpha engine of Legio Sirius. *Lupa Capitalina* held station at the centre of the convoy, a mobile fortress protecting the Leviathans with its city-levelling firepower.

'Can you see the Warhounds yet?' asked Adara. 'My da once said he saw one on Konor, but it ran off before he got a proper look at it.'

Before now, Roboute would have poured scorn on the idea of a Titan running off, but having seen the speed with which *Amarok* and *Vilka* had deployed from their coffin ships, he was less inclined to laugh at Adara's tale. Even the speed of the Warlord had shocked them, and the impatient brays of its warhorn echoed from the walls of the glittering ice valley.

'No,' answered Roboute, craning his neck around. 'I haven't, but that doesn't surprise me. Warhounds are Scout Titans, ambush predators, and they don't like you seeing them until it's too late.'

Adara nodded, but still kept looking.

'Your father is certainly well travelled,' said Pavelka, her voice sounding in Roboute's helmet via subvocalised vibrations. 'Calth, Iax, Konor… Is there any part of Ultramar he has not visited?'

Pavelka's dripping sarcasm was evident, even over the helm-vox and the thrumming bass note of the grav-sled's repulsors.

'You don't believe me?'

'Ilanna's just teasing you,' said Roboute, knowing how defensive the lad got if anyone dared to question the truth of his father's tales.

'Well she shouldn't,' said Adara. 'My da served as an armsman to Inquisitor Apollyon on Armageddon, and you don't go mouthing off about someone like that.'

Roboute knew Pavelka wouldn't be able to resist pulling that particular declaration apart, and gave the control column a shake to discourage her from picking holes in it.

'Easy, Roboute!' cried Adara, gripping the restraint bar on the door.

The ground beneath the grav-sled was a mixture of frozen nitrogen and bare, metallic rock, like the surface of an oil-streaked glacier. The sled's repulsor field reacted badly to patches of exotic metals and the ride was bumpier than Roboute would have liked. The controls were oversized to accommodate the inherent clumsiness in void-suit gloves, but even so, it felt like the machine was fighting him every step of the way, slewing left and right despite his best attempts to keep level.

'I can control the sled through my MIU if you would prefer,' said Pavelka. 'It appears you are having some difficulty, captain.'

'No,' said Roboute, wrestling with the control column. 'I'm fine taking us in.'

Their route was winding a path through a steep-sided canyon that Roboute's eyes were telling him rose to around a hundred metres or so, but was probably at least a couple of kilometres. The eye was easily tricked into forming manageable scales when denied any quantifiable points of reference. When he'd first eased the sled into the mountains, his mind had reeled at the sheer vastness of each canyon's ice-blue walls, and without the measurable scale of the landing fields, it was impossible to define distances or perspective with any reliability.

'How soon till we reach the crashed ship?' asked Adara, his neck craned back as far as the gorget arrangement on his helmet's collar would allow. Roboute risked narrowing the magnification of the slate, but gave up looking when the screeching, squalling distortion pattern didn't let up. Only the slender thread of Blaylock's route through the labyrinth remained unwavering.

'Impossible to say through this interference,' answered Pavelka, reading the same information instantly. Even through the imperfections of the vox-units, her excitement was palpable. 'According to our distance travelled, we should be within sight of the *Tomioka* within seven minutes, assuming the current rate of advance continues.'

'And assuming I don't crash us,' said Roboute.

'A possibility I did not care to raise.'

'Listen,' said Roboute. 'A grav-sled isn't a precision instrument of manoeuvre, but I think I'm finally getting its measure. It just takes a little finesse and a little nerve.'

'I suppose how much nerve is required depends on where one is sitting.'

Adara sniggered. 'And Mistress Tychon said the Mechanicus don't have a sense of humour…'

'She's right,' snapped Roboute. 'They don't.'

Despite Pavelka's commentary on his piloting skills, Roboute steered them with greater confidence with every passing metre. His Ultramarian ethic would not let him attempt a task without then mastering it, and curbing the vagaries of the grav-sled's control was no exception.

Their course evened out over the next few kilometres, and as Roboute eased around a sheer spur of violet-tinged ice that shed streamers of vapour like an industrial smokestack, the valley widened noticeably towards a cascade of smoking liquid nitrogen. It poured down through a fissure that glittered in the blue-shifted light, before vanishing into a gaping crevasse that cut the valley almost in two.

Roboute guessed the crevasse was at least thirty metres wide.

According to Blaylock's path, the *Tomioka* lay on the opposite side.

And the Black Templars, he thought, trying to keep a lid on his irritation.

Where the crevasse didn't quite reach the valley walls, cascading spumes of freezing gases collected in swirling eddies and whirlpools of shimmering liquid.

'Will the Land Leviathans be able to get across that?' asked Adara.

'Not a chance,' said Roboute. 'Though the *Tabularium* might fall in and wedge itself tight to make a bridge for the others.'

'You think there's room enough for us to go round the edges?'

'Just barely,' answered Pavelka, blink-clicking measurement datum points and exloading them to the Mechanicus pioneer vehicles behind them.

'Well, the Black Templars may have beaten us to the *Tomioka*, but I'll be damned if anyone else is getting there before us,' said Roboute, hauling the grav-sled around towards the edge of the valley, where vortices of nitrogen translated from gas to liquid and back again with alarming frequency.

The pitch of the grav-sled's engines increased, and the repulsor field skittered at the abrupt change in ground density. Roboute heard Pavelka mutter a whispered prayer to the Machine-God and felt her subtle imprecation to the engines' magnetic field compensating for the unusual terrain.

Buoyed up by Pavelka's devotion, the grav-sled negotiated the foaming, streaming edges of the liquid nitrogen waterfall with aplomb and skirted the edges of the vast crevasse with only centimetres to spare. Roboute risked a glance over the edge and felt his stomach lurch as he saw the rift cut right into the heart of the planet. He switched his gaze back to what lay ahead of him as a nauseous sense of vertigo threatened to sweep over him. Roboute gunned the engine and the grav-sled surged to the jagged summit of the fissure.

At long last, Roboute saw what had become of Magos Telok's flagship, though it took him a moment to realise that was what he was seeing. He shielded his visor from the billions of points of light reflecting from the glassy plateau before him.

'I thought the ship we were looking for was a wreck?' asked Adara, tilting his head to the side.

'So did I,' said Roboute.

'It didn't crash?' said Pavelka, her incomprehension turning her words into a question.

'No,' said Roboute in wonderment. 'It... *landed*.'

SMOKE FILLED THE pilot's compartment, and Tanna tasted the reek of burning propellant, scorched iron and blood in the back of his mouth. He blinked away the disorientation of the crash, and checked his visor to see how long he had been unconscious. Four seconds. To a mortal, such a span was negligible, but to a Space Marine, it was an eternity. Angry with himself, he shook off his momentary weakness and pushed himself from the pilot's chair. The angle of the Thunderhawk's impact had driven the nose into the plateau, and Tanna was forced to use dangling straps and cables to haul himself back into the crew compartment.

The warriors in the back had weathered the crash with relative ease, thanks to his managing their angle of descent and the grav-harnesses.

'Anyone injured?' he asked, pulling himself along the centreline of the gunship.

'Everyone is unhurt,' said Auiden. 'That was some landing, brother-sergeant.'

'Some kind of interference blew out the engines,' said Tanna. 'I was lucky to get us down on our belly and in one piece.'

'I know,' said Auiden. 'I meant no reproach.'

Tanna shook his head. 'Of course.'

The grievances felt against him since Kul Gilad's loss had made Tanna find fault in every word spoken to him, veiled insults in every comment. He took a moment to purge himself of that suspicion and moved to the fuselage doors of the gunship. With the nose of the *Barisan* buried in the ice, the side and rear exits were the only way out.

'We need to get out of here,' he said, kneeling beside the fuselage door and pulling open the keypad hatch. He tapped in his command codes, but – as he'd expected – the door remained stubbornly shut.

'Why is the... *ngg, ngg*... door not opening?' asked Issur.

'There is no power to the mechanism,' answered Tanna. 'It will need brute force to get us out.'

The *Barisan* creaked and lurched with a squeal of tearing metal. Seams burst farther down the fuselage, and hissing streamers of escaping gas vented from cracks in the hull. Tanna grabbed onto a stanchion as the gunship shuddered, as though some giant beast had it locked in its jaws and was slowly trying to digest it.

'Yael, Issur, help me,' ordered Tanna. 'Get the edge of the door.'

'I can shoot us a way out,' offered Bracha, unlimbering his implanted plasma gun, but Tanna shook his head.

'I would rather not risk angering the *Barisan* by shooting it from the inside,' he said.

The three Black Templars took hold of the door and braced themselves against stanchions, struts and bench seats. More seams burst along the line of the fuselage. Tanna had a worrying image of the gunship caught in a wreckage compactor, being slowly crushed until it and they were nothing more than an ultra-dense cube of iron and meat.

'Auiden, as soon as you see the locking mechanism, cut it.'

The Apothecary nodded and bent before the lock-plate of the fuselage door. A painfully bright light spat into life from an extended blade, a fusion cutter for field amputations, and he pulled it back like an executioner ready to strike a killing blow.

The *Barisan* groaned, like a beast in pain, and Tanna cursed that he had brought so fine a machine to so ignoble a fate. Glass shattered in the cockpit and the avionics panel blew out with a whooping electrical bang.

'Now,' yelled Tanna, and the three of them hauled back on the door. The fuselage of a Thunderhawk gunship was designed to be airtight during spaceflight and atmospheric insertion, but it wasn't designed to withstand the combined strength of three Space Marines trying to haul it open from the inside.

Tanna felt the door shift, millimetres at best, but here the deformations crushing the hull worked in their favour and a portion of the hull buckled inwards at the lock-plate. He saw the flash of Auiden's fusion cutter and heard the hiss of dissolving metal. For a fraction of a second, the heavy door held firm, but then the cutter finished its work and it rumbled back along its rails.

'Forgive us, great one,' said Auiden as he sheathed the energised blade.

Tanna nodded in agreement. The *Barisan* had carried them faithfully into battle and out of trouble more times than he could remember. To have wounded it just to escape seemed a poor way to repay its strength of heart, but he felt sure its machine-spirit would forgive them.

'Everybody out,' he ordered.

Varda was first through, quickly followed by Issur and Bracha. Auiden went next, then Yael and finally Tanna dropped from the canted deck.

He landed on the ground, which was just as he'd imagined it to be from the air: a vast plateau of ice. Where the gunship had smashed down was powdered like fine snow, but brittle like metal shavings. The Thunderhawk's impact had ploughed a deep furrow, and Tanna knelt as he saw what looked like tendrils of frost reaching up from the ground along the hull of the downed flying machine.

Like condensation on a pane of glass, it looked like the ice was reaching up to enfold the *Barisan*'s fuselage. Tanna looked back down to where the gunship's nose was buried in the ice… except he saw now that it wasn't ice at all, but some form of parasitic crystal. When he had recovered consciousness, he remembered seeing the vapour-struck sky through the crazed armourglass canopy, but the entire frontal section was now almost completely enclosed. As if the 'ice' had begun to swell and freeze instantly upon the gunship, like the planet was trying to drag it down into the crust.

Even as Tanna watched, he saw the crystalline structure of the ground spread glittering fronds further over the body of the gunship. He scraped a hand over the fuselage, scattering the ice like sugar crystals that fell to dust as soon as they were no longer part of the whole.

'What is this…?' he wondered aloud, but no sooner had he removed his hand than the crystalline fronds renewed their attempt to engulf the *Barisan*.

'Brother-sergeant,' said Bracha from above. 'You need to get up here now.'

Tanna backed away from the strange crystalline growths attaching themselves to his gunship, and scrambled back along the length of the impact trough. Yael offered him a hand up, but Tanna ignored it and hauled himself onto the plateau.

'Situation?' he asked.

No one answered, and Tanna was about to repeat his question when he turned to see what his men were all staring at. He recalled his last sight before the gunship had gone down. He had seen the *Tomioka* with his own eyes, but the actuality of it rendered him speechless, unable to look away from the logic-defying, impossible sight before him.

'Imperator,' hissed Varda. 'It's impossible.'

Tanna shook his head. 'It is the *Tomioka,* no doubt about that.'

A retrofitted Oberon battleship, the enormous vessel stood vertical along its long axis on the surface of Katen Venia like the last few kilometres of a towering hive spire. Such vast starships were never meant to enter the gravity envelope of a planet. Their superstructures were built to endure the multi-directional forces of void war and withstand pressures of acceleration and enormous turning circles.

What they were manifestly *not* designed to do was cope with the titanic forces of re-entry.

Tanna guessed that the ship's engine section was buried at least two kilometres in frozen nitrogen, while the remaining five kilometres of its monolithic superstructure jutted into the sky, almost vanishing in a forced perspective that defied human scale. Its hull was as gothically ornamented as any Imperial ship of the line, redolent with cathedrals, crenellated battlements, rounded archways of gun batteries, ice-encrusted processionals of statuary and the bladed prow of a fighting vessel.

Glaciers of buttressing ice surrounded the base of the ship, rising from the planet's surface to a height of around five hundred metres, obscuring any obvious means of entry and helping to stabilise the towering edifice. Above the ice, vast swathes of the ship were encrusted with bizarre crystalline structures of intricate design, but which bore the clear hallmark of Mechanicus origin. Some had the look of power generators, others of communications relays, but the more Tanna looked, the more he understood that the *Tomioka* had been completely redesigned to be something other than a starship.

'How could anyone... *ngg*, have done... *nggh*, this?' asked Issur, the synaptic damage he'd suffered aboard the Manifold station making every word a struggle.

'I do not know,' admitted Tanna. 'The ship should have torn itself apart.'

'Do you think this was what the archmagos was expecting?' asked Varda.

'I don't think it's what anyone was expecting,' said Tanna.

An eruption of ice crystals to either side of the Black Templars had them snap guns to shoulders and swords to en garde. Scores of detonations plumed like geysers of ice, except that Tanna knew the glassy substance on which they stood was not ice at all. Glittering particulates hung in the air, and Tanna saw a host of figures climb from each of the holes blasted through the planet's surface.

They had the bulk of Space Marines, but their bodies were formed from a translucent crystalline material with its own bioluminescence. A pulsing network of green veins threaded their bodies, like an illuminated nervous system or a map of blood vessels in a human body. Tanna saw they were not coming from beneath the ground, they were *part* of the ground. At least forty of the creatures surrounded them, and as the glassy dust of their arrival settled, Tanna saw they didn't just have the bulk of Space Marines, their bodies were somehow formed in a crude imitation of Adeptus Astartes.

Each crystalline form had the bulky curvature of auto-reactive shoulder guards, the broad sweep of a plastron and an elementary form of a helmet. They were like a child's representation of Space Marines, crude and ill-fashioned, but recognisable enough.

'What in the Emperor's name are they?' hissed Varda as the crystal creatures closed in.

'The enemy,' said Tanna, sighting down his bolter and pulling the trigger.

IF THERE WAS a lesson to be learned here, it was that he not doubt *Amarok*'s sense for something amiss. Gunnar Vintras walked the Warhound backwards through a thicket of tall crystalline spires, keeping the damaged side of his engine facing the canyon wall. His turbolaser was jammed, the servitor dead and the Titan's machine-spirit desperately trying to find a workaround to get it firing again. Phantom agonies from his left arm kept Vintras from blacking out, and a constant flood of stimulants fought the effects of the pain-balms.

'If I survive this fight, I'm going to have one hell of a chemical come-down when they flush me out,' he hissed through pursed lips. 'That's a Manifold purge I'm not looking forward to.'

No sooner had he initiated a full-threat auspex sweep, the kind of blaring announcement of presence a Warhound princeps was loath to initiate, than the enemy had attacked. He still wasn't sure where they'd come from. One minute he was striding over a series of fallen stalagmites of prismatic glass, the next, four engines of comparable displacement to *Amarok* were attacking him.

The Warhound took the first shots on her voids, but in

keeping him alive they blew out with a screaming detonation. Only Vintras's natural reactions had kept a second volley of streaking bolts from gutting his Titan. As it was, the turbolasers had taken the brunt of the barrage.

He returned fire with the mega-bolter, feeling the pounding reverberations through the bones of his arm as he unleashed a salvo of high-explosive rounds. Like most Warhound princeps, the joints at his elbow had been replaced with shock-absorbent materials to better withstand the constant pressure of bio-feedback from his engine's weaponry, and he was able to bear the brunt of such punishing recoil from an arm that wasn't even his.

Something shattered into a million pieces in front of him, but a cascade of billowing ice prevented him from seeing what it was as it fell. Vintras knew better than anyone the perils of staying still in an engine fight, and pushed *Amarok* to striding speed. A Warhound wasn't a gross-displacement engine that could dish out vast amounts of fire and take it at the same time, it was a hunter that thrived in high-speed war.

A flensing blast of fire blew a smoking crater in the canyon wall, and Vintras traced the shot back to its point of origin. He danced the Warhound through the crystal growths and saw another three engines striding towards him. His eyes narrowed as he took the measure of his opponents.

'What the hell are you?' he murmured, seeing a dreadful familiarity in their appearance.

They were Warhounds, but ones that looked like the atavistic ice sculptures left outside the fortress of the Oldbloods by the savage tribes that called Lokabrenna home.

Though these statues were moving and fighting.

But they were stupid.

They came straight at him, like ranked-up regiments of

Imperial Guardsmen on a parade ground. Vintras grinned and pushed the reactor to full power as he bolted for the cover of a fallen slope of rubble farther along the valley side. Shots chased him, but his control over *Amarok*'s movement was faultless. Even the pain of his wounded arm and the pain-balms couldn't dull the pleasure of this moment.

A Titan commander relished a good fight, but to find yourself engaged against a foe you hopelessly outmatched was a very special pleasure.

The crystalline Titans followed him like hounds on a hunt, and Vintras led them a merry chase through the spires: darting back and forth, weaving around them and leading them just where he wanted them. Billowing clouds of glassy dust choked the canyon, but Vintras had memorised every move he'd made, like a virtuoso dancer flawlessly performing his greatest work.

The pain in his left arm faded and the Manifold surged with readiness data.

Even his voids had reset.

Amarok burst through a curtain of bright fragments, and there ahead of him were the three counterfeit Warhounds with their backs to him.

'Imperator, I love these moments,' he said, striding forwards at combat speed.

Instead of scattering, the enemy engines began turning on the spot like novice moderati playing at being a princeps. Vintras was on them before they were halfway rotated. He stepped between the rightmost engines and thrust his arms out to either side. The mega-bolter was primarily an infantry killer, but at point-blank range against an unshielded enemy it was an executioner's weapon. Explosive shells ripped into the upper section of the first crystal Warhound and blasted it apart from the inside. Turbolaser fire cored the middle engine, shattering its canopy in a superhot explosion of molten fragments.

Amarok kept going, and Vintras pivoted around the falling carcass of the headless Titan to face the last remaining crystal engine. He bared his steel fangs and brought his hands together as though aiming a pistol down the firing range.

'You might look like a Warhound, but you don't fight like one,' snarled the Skinwalker, unleashing both weapons into the glittering faux-Titan's head.

Microcontent 05

Kotov had switched to a body better suited to hostile environments, an archaic robotic chassis with ray-shielded internal workings and heavy armoured plates that put him level with his skitarii escort and made him look like a ceremonial knight. His head was encased in a shimmering integrity field that sent an irritated buzzing through his aural implants, but which was still preferable to an enclosing helm.

He stepped down from the converted skitarii Rhino and looked back the way they had come. The crevasse at the end of the valley was being bridged by pioneer units disgorged from the construction decks of the *Tabularium*. The Cadian engineer units had nothing capable of bridging so a wide a gap, and their vehicles were forced to wait along with everyone else. Judging by the vox passing between Captain Hawkins's Chimera and Colonel Anders's Salamander, that delay sat ill with the men of Cadia.

A thousand servitors, load-lifters and construction engines

were manoeuvring heavy, girder-braced spars of plasteel into place, and robed adepts on suspended platforms drilled bracing struts onto the inner faces of the crevasse.

But it was going to take time to construct something capable of bearing the unimaginable mass of a Land Leviathan, and Kotov couldn't wait that long. He wanted to taste his moment of triumph first-hand, not filtered through a pict-capture or hololithic representation.

He would see the *Tomioka* with his own augmetic eyes.

Lupa Capitalina stood immobile behind the *Tabularium*, a towering representation of the Omnissiah in his aspect of war. Occasional puffs of ejected vapour and thermal bleed from its armoured reactor gave the lie to its dormancy. The Warlord was a warrior on hair trigger, taut and poised for action. Under normal circumstances, the reassurance a fully armed Warlord Titan imparted would be welcome, but after the incident in the training decks, everyone was understandably skittish around the mighty war machine. Legio Sirius adepts had assured Kotov that the Wintersun's lapse could never happen again, but as Kotov well knew, the Mechanicus never deletes anything.

The Warhounds that had accompanied the Wintersun to the surface were nowhere to be seen, but that wasn't unusual; the princeps of such engines were wilful and preferred to remain unseen.

Satisfied all was proceeding as fast as could be expected, Kotov set off to the opening of the valley, where Roboute Surcouf and two members of his crew awaited him.

'You should let my skitarii scout this place out first,' said Dahan, emerging from a second Rhino and marching to join him with a loping, mechanical gait. 'We don't know what's up here, and if Surcouf is to be believed, the *Tomioka* might still have active defences in place.'

The fleshy part of the Secutor's face was encased in an oxygenated membrane gel that rippled across his skull like a thin coating of water. All four of his arms were extended, his digital scarifiers crackling with sparking lightning and his Cebrenian halberd held at the ready in his upper limbs.

'Even after nearly four thousand years?'

'Mechanicus tech isn't fragile,' Dahan reminded him. 'It's built to endure.'

'You're right, of course, Hirimau,' said Kotov, 'but I think we are well protected, don't you?'

'Better to know than to think,' grunted Dahan.

'Spoken like a true priest of Mars,' said Kotov without any trace of irony.

Twenty skitarii followed the archmagos, armoured in non-reflective carapace that seamlessly shifted in sync with their movements. Cog-toothed Mechanicus skulls were rivet-stamped to each shoulder, alongside scaled scorpions and azure spiders. Dahan's warriors normally eschewed the wearing of barbaric totems, but Kotov noted that two had fashioned leathery-looking cloaks from what passive receptors told him was human skin. It was the work of a picosecond to match its DNA profile with that of the batch-grown skin curtains found in the Valette infirmary.

Most of the skitarii came armed with solid-slug weapons, though two were implanted with flame units and a last warrior was equipped with twin meltaguns, one as a replacement arm, the other as a shoulder mount. All carried a variety of close-combat weapons: a mix of sabres, axes and falchions with energised edges and saw-blade teeth. Their faces were obscured by tinted visors that had darkened to a deep bronze.

Galatea had elected to remain aboard the *Tabularium*, which struck Kotov as strange, given its stated desire to kill the Lost

Magos. Not that Kotov wasn't grateful to be away from the abominable creature, but he couldn't shake the niggling suspicion that the hybrid machine intelligence wasn't being entirely honest with them.

Whatever the truth of Galatea's ultimate agenda, it would have to wait.

With Dahan at his side, Kotov clambered through the nitrogen-wreathed rocks to the top of the fissure. Surcouf climbed down from his grav-sled and held out a hand to him.

'You made it, archmagos,' he said. 'It's quite a sight, isn't it?'

Kotov didn't answer the rogue trader, his gaze drawn to the dizzying height of the starship standing on its ice-encased engines in the centre of the glassy ice plateau. Of all the things he had expected, this had featured in none of his dreams of finding the *Tomioka*. Far from being a victim of atmospheric poisoning or rampant exaggeration, Surcouf had, if anything, undersold how incredible the sight of the landed starship would be.

'Ave Deus Mechanicus…' he said, his mouth hanging slack at the impossible sight of a seven-kilometre starship standing proud like a hive starscraper.

'I know,' said Surcouf, understanding his awe. 'I still have a hard time believing it's real.'

Kotov tried to find some frame of reference to bring the idea of a landed starship into some kind of focus, but the sight of it standing so incongruously in the landscape was one that fitted no model of reality.

'I have never heard of a vessel this size surviving atmospheric transit, let alone being successfully landed,' said Dahan.

'Telok must have brought it in exactly perpendicular to the surface,' said Kotov, finally imposing a measure of order on his cascading thoughts. 'Or else it would have broken its keel and spread itself all over the surface.'

'Is that even possible?' asked Surcouf, unlimbering a pair of magnoculars and training it on a glittering cloud of mist a kilometre or so ahead of them.

'The ship's plasma engines allowed the ship to penetrate far enough into the ice for it to remain upright,' said Kotov, more to himself than in answer of Surcouf.

'What is that?' asked Dahan, training his own combat optics on the mist cloud Surcouf was examining. 'Is that the *Barisan?*'

'It must be,' agreed Surcouf. 'It's right at the end of what looks like an impact gouge in the ground. I think the Templars crashed, but it's hard to make anything out.'

'The umbra is damping all auspex readings and hexing the blessed workings of machines within the limits of this plateau,' said Kotov, suddenly realising that the dimensions of this encircled plateau were a virtually perfect match for the diameter of the distortion Linya Tychon had detected.

'We're within it, and the grav-sled is still functional,' said Surcouf. 'If it's being generated from the *Tomioka,* then it looks like it doesn't extend all the way to ground level.'

'If the Black Templars have crash landed, we should go to their aid,' said Dahan.

Kotov was inclined to damn the Space Marines and let them suffer the consequences of their foolhardy zeal, but quelled so petty a notion. Dahan was right, if the Adeptus Astartes required assistance, he was duty-bound to offer it. He switched through his visual perception modes and multiple hues descended over the landscape as he saw in expanded wavelengths, sound vibrations, radiation decay and a host of other sensory inputs. Irritatingly, it seemed Surcouf was correct in deducing that the umbra did not reach ground level, as his augmetic senses had no trouble penetrating the umbra below fifty metres.

Just as what he had first seen upon reaching the edge of the plateau made no sense, what he was seeing now made just as little sense. With a thought, he switched Dahan's optics to match his own and exloaded the correct perceptual mode to Surcouf's magnoculars.

'Magos Dahan,' said Kotov. 'The Templars are under attack. Send in the skitarii.'

MAGOS DAHAN DETESTED riding into battle within the hull of an armoured vehicle, equating its metallic confinement to the interior of a tomb. He had adopted the usage of the Iron Fist for just that reason, preferring to ride in an open-topped vehicle, like a barbarian king of Old Earth charging towards the enemy on his warchariot.

The image was an apt one, for he stood on the armoured topside of a crimson and black Rhino as it led his skitarii towards the beleaguered Black Templars. His clawed legs were braced on the side and rear holdbars, while his deactivated scarifiers clamped onto the cupola mount of the commander's hatch. His upper arms were free, and he had slung his halberd in favour of deploying a pair of forearm-mounted rotary lasers.

Denying the Cadian units permission to cross the partially completed pioneer bridge, Dahan had led his skitarii past the thousands of servitors and structural engineers buttressing its supports in readiness for the *Tabularium*'s crossing. Thirty Rhinos matched the speed of his own, heavily converted vehicles with upgraded auspex suites, additional weaponry and higher-grade command/control functionality. Each carried a squad of heavily armed and highly skilled warriors, men he had trained using his stochastic analysis of millions of inloaded combat doctrines which were then broken down into their component elements. It was a training regime he had believed faultless until Brother Yael of the Black Templars had – defying all statistical probability – bested him in a contest of arms. A mortal mind might have felt some affront or insult at such a defeat, but Dahan was above such petty concerns, and had incorporated the fighting styles of the Black Templars into his accumulated battle subroutines.

Interspersed with the screen of armour came the columns of weaponised servitors, tracked praetorians, mobile weapon platforms and a quad-maniple of twelve battle robots: six Cataphracts, four Crusaders and two Conquerors. Each robot's organo-cybernetic cortex was slaved to a partitioned thought-stream of battle-implants.

No part of this battlefield was unknown to Dahan, the over-clocked speed of his mental architecture plotting out a precise and constantly updating picture of the combat arena. His threat optics – now incorporating Archmagos Kotov's sensory inload – draped the plateau of icy rock in myriad cyan hues: strongly pigmented azures for organics, deeper cobalt shades for metallics and lighter teals for inorganic materials. Firing range bands, topographical vectors of assault and optimal engagement zones were overlaid in crisp red lines, giving Dahan the perfect datum points from which to conduct this assault.

The Black Templars fought from the topside of their partially buried Thunderhawk, which at Dahan's increased consciousness speed appeared to be in the process of being subsumed by the ground itself. A host of crystal-formed warriors, illumined and likely empowered by a bloom of exotic energy within their chest cavities, laid siege to the Thunderhawk. Bioform analysis took them to be Space Marines, but Dahan saw they were poor imitations of Adeptus Astartes perfection.

Withering hails of bolter fire were blasting these monstrosities apart, but more were pulling themselves free from the ground with the sound of breaking glass. Perhaps two hundred or more surrounded the buried gunship, hurling themselves at the embattled Space Marines with a slow, relentless hunger. Some were equipped with crudely shaped weaponry integral to their forms, and these fired streams of light that registered as painfully bright lances of sapphire.

Fortunately for the Space Marines, their attackers displayed an appalling lack of marksmanship, but the sheer volume of fire was forcing the Templars to employ every square metre of cover afforded by the gunship's tailfins, opened dorsal hatches and inactive topside turrets.

A number of icons flashed onto his vision and Dahan wordlessly issued his orders.

The Conquerors came to a halt, digging into the reflective surface of the plateau with bracing claws before cycling round their heavy bolters and lascannons. Blazing gouts of fire streamed overhead, ploughing through the crystalline creatures in a thunderous cacophony of shattered crystal and arcing electrical discharge. The data lodged in Dahan's cognitive overview.

Whatever else these creatures were, they were definitely *not* organic.

The Crusaders increased speed, two moving around each flank as the skitarii Rhinos ground to a halt in a blizzard of glittering ice chips. Assault doors slammed back and squads of cybernetically enhanced warriors debarked in perfect synchrony. Each squad-chief's right eye was a battle-implant that received situational data straight from Dahan; they knew what he knew and his binaric orders were implemented virtually instantaneously.

Like a Grand Master's regicide pieces on a tri-dimensional board, each squad moved in concert with those nearby, offering mutually supporting fields of fire and flank protection. Weaponised servitors swiftly caught up to the infantry, taking up overwatching positions to offer fire-support as and when it was required. The Cataphract robots moved alongside the infantry, their anti-personnel autocannons and power fists ready to support against any foe beyond the soldiers' capability to engage.

Dahan released his grip on the sides of his own Rhino and dropped to the ground, unlimbering his Cebrenian halberd and igniting his clawed scarifiers. His assigned squad hove into view, and he ran to join them with his peculiar loping gait.

Skitarii gunfire smashed through the crystal creatures, blasting them apart with solid rounds or detonating them explosively with high-energy hotshots. Grenade launchers cleared space for praetorians to occupy and deny the enemy time to regroup. Dahan himself was not above getting his hands dirty, fighting with killing sweeps of his Cebrenian halberd. He assigned his own command squad, a mix of elite suzerain and experimental weapon bearers, a path right into the heart of the fight.

His accompanying skitarii unleashed a hail of plasma, graviton guns and micro-conversion beamers. Though the crystal creatures were manifestly inhuman they still obeyed the laws of physics and came apart like any other substance. Their advance was made over crunching debris of flickering crystal and cut-glass carcasses.

Dahan allowed himself a moment of recklessness and surged ahead of his squad, vaulting into a group of the icy-looking crystal-forms with a burst of hostile binary. He swung his Cebrenian halberd, slamming its entropic capacitor into the chest of a slowly turning construct. A blast of hostile code stabbed into its heart and the green light was instantly extinguished. The impact of the halberd shattered the thing, and

Dahan was already moving by the time its glassy remains fell to the ground. Just as they were poor shots, the crystal-forms were no more adept in the arts of close combat. Dahan slashed and stabbed with his halberd, reaping a grim tally of glassy enemies, and cutting shard-limbs from their bodies with his energy-wreathed scarifiers.

Most battlefields were filled with the screams of frenzied warriors, the howls of the dying and the clash of blades, but in this arena the only sounds were booming gunfire and the brittle shattering of crystal-form bodies.

The twin horns of the skitarii assault now pressed in on the crystal-form creatures, scything their numbers and pressing in towards the Space Marines atop the *Barisan*. Dahan's calculations indicated that this engagement would be decisively ended in four minutes and thirty-five seconds.

Dahan's squad finally caught up with him, fighting with implanted weaponry to blast and cut a path through the heart of the enemy towards the Space Marines. Dahan instantly read the identity biometrics of each of the Black Templars, intrigued to note that not one of them displayed any elevated readings to indicate that they were engaged in a desperate firefight.

He opened a vox-link, cycling through all known Space Marine frequencies until he heard a clipped, verbally efficient battle-cant based on the northern Inwit tribal argot.

'Sergeant Tanna, this is Magos Dahan,' he said. 'Now would seem a prudent time to withdraw.'

Tanna's voice sounded shocked to hear a non-Templar voice in his helmet. 'This is a Templar vox-net,' he said. 'You do not speak upon it.'

'Feel free to censure me when we are back on the *Tabularium*,' Dahan said, 'but I suggest you come with us before more of these crystal-forms appear.'

Tanna did not respond and Dahan realised the sergeant had shut him off.

'Foolish,' said Dahan, amazed at the self-harm beings not defined by logic would wreak upon themselves for the sake of mortal pride and propriety. Dahan paused in his advance as he registered the destruction of two of his Rhinos. Nowhere in his wide net of sensory inputs had he registered a threat capable of destroying a vehicle. He pulled his awareness outwards as a rippling spiderweb of surging energy patterns converged on the battlefield, like a reversed pict-capture of a shattering pane of glass, the splintering traceries of cracks radiating back *towards* the point of impact.

Moments later, the threat levels ramped up as fresh energy forms rapidly appeared without warning. All across the theatre of battle, the ground erupted with thousands of geysering blasts of prismatic shards as an entire army of the crystal-forms ripped up into the fight. The cycling counter of his battle-end calculation went into reverse before winking out and being replaced with a representation of how long his own forces could expect to remain viable.

Inevitable victory had suddenly become certain annihilation.

A trio of figures tore themselves from the ground before Dahan, two resembling crude anatomical representations of skitarii, while the third was a glassine mockery of his own form, complete with a tripod arrangement of legs and quad-armatures.

A blast of fire stuck him on the shoulder, and his combat algorithms leapt in complexity by an order of magnitude. Dahan gasped at the hexamathic density of the required calculations and his shoulders erupted with thermal bloom as his cranial implants desperately vented excess heat. He staggered as his mind and body fought to maintain equilibrium between strategic overview and tactical necessity.

Something had to give, and right now Dahan's most pressing concern was the creature right in front of him threatening his life.

He shut off his high-speed cognitive functions and veils of battlefield awareness fell away like wind-blown smoke. His doppelgänger came at him with its copied halberd slashing for his head. Dahan was still adjusting to his restricted world view and the blow took him full in the chest, hurling him back with a *crack* of splitting metal. Bolts of las-fire blasted chunks of its substance away, but its imitation body was clearly of greater density than its brethren.

A crystal-clawed foot stamped down on a scarifier arm and sheared it from his body. Pain signals flared in Dahan's brain. Nothing organic was left in that limb, but the hurt was no less real. Dahan's recalibrating combat subroutines snapped back into focus and he parried a follow-up blow, rolling aside as the halberd slammed down where his head had been.

'My turn,' he snarled, driving his scarifier up into the thing's body.

Snapping electrical discharge blew out a vast chunk of crystalline material, and he kicked out with his third leg, snapping one of his attacker's. The creature staggered, but didn't fall until he pushed himself upright and brought his Cebrenian halberd down on its skull. The blow sheared the creature in two, its severed body collapsing like two halves of a cloven sculpture. More of the risen crystal-form creatures were surrounding him; the sheer quantity of enemy firepower had a quality all of its own.

Four more came at him and he swayed back on his rear leg to avoid a thrusting spear-limb. A halberd strike destroyed the limb, and he sprang forwards to deliver a hammering electrical strike from his remaining scarifier. The creature exploded and he spun low on his reverse-jointed main limbs, scything his retracted rear leg around. Two crystal-forms went down. Dahan skewered one with his halberd, spinning the weapon around to deliver a thunderous strike with the entropic generator on the other. A crackling energy fist came at him and he lowered his head to take the blow on his armoured cowl. Crystal shattered against the adamantium hood; Dahan didn't give the creature another chance.

He surged upright, vaulting over the thing's head and bringing his halberd around in three ultra-rapid slices before he landed. The crystal-form slid apart into pieces, green light spewing from its ruptured chest cavity. On another day, Dahan would have dearly loved to study that energy source, but now was not the time.

With a fractional space cleared around him, the skitarii rallied to his side.

Dahan allowed himself a brief increase in cognition speed to access his strategic awareness protocols, skimming the blurts of real-time data-feeds from the warriors under his command.

The information was not heartening.

Dahan's skitarii were dying, and instead of rescuing the Black Templars, he and his command squad were now as isolated as Tanna and his warriors.

TANNA HAD LONG since expended his supply of bolter ammunition and the powercell of his chainsword was dangerously close to running empty. His armour was scorched from dozens of impacts and he was among the least wounded of his warriors. Auiden had already brought Bracha back into the fight, sealing a neatly cauterised blast through his thigh.

Now Bracha knelt propped up by the *Barisan*'s tailfin, picking shots with his implanted plasma gun and fending off close-range attackers with his combat blade. Issur met the foe blade to blade, hacking the crystalline mockeries of Space Marines apart with graceful blows of his shrieking power sword. Only his nerve-damage induced muscle spasms allowed the creatures anywhere near him. Shards of his armour hung from him where their energised claws had torn it from him.

Issur fought back to back with Varda, who alone of them all appeared untouchable. The Black Sword cut through the translucent glass bodies of their attackers with ease, and his gold-chased pistol had a seemingly unending supply of killing bolts.

Yael fought from behind a turret that Tanna dearly wished was firing, snapping off carefully aimed shots with his bolter and driving the enemy back with his sword when that wasn't enough. Auiden fought at Tanna's side; a warrior first, Apothecary second. His pistol was empty, but his sword and narthecium blades were just as efficient at killing.

'Not how I imagined this would end,' said Auiden.

'Nor I,' replied Tanna, sweeping his sword through the faceplate of a crystal-form imitation of a Space Marine. He kicked its broken remains from the gunship, all too aware that the encroaching ice of the plateau was at least a metre higher than when they had first crashed. At this rate, its structure would be completely absorbed by the plateau within the next ten minutes.

Not that Tanna expected to live that long.

He ducked as he saw a crystal-form take aim and felt the heat of the shot's passing. Two more creatures clawed their way up the *Barisan*'s fuselage. He kicked the first one back down and plunged his blade into the green-lit chest of the second. Three more came up behind them, and sawing blasts of fire tore over his back as he threw himself flat. He rolled and found himself sliding towards the edge of the gunship, where a host of climbing enemy awaited him.

'Tanna!' shouted Auiden, diving over the topside to grab the edge of his armour.

The Apothecary's grip gave Tanna the chance to swing his sword around and hook it behind a protruding intake vent. With Auiden's help, he finally found purchase and pushed himself away from the drop. He rolled as numerous crystalline claws appeared at the edge.

'My thanks,' said Tanna, scrambling to his feet and stamping down on the besieging hands.

As far as he could see, the plateau was squirming with motion as more and more of the crystalline creatures burst from geysers of crystal shards, cracking and splitting the ground with their arrival. Magos Dahan's assault now looked like a last stand as they too were surrounded by the emergent beasts.

'Galling to be killed while we're in spitting distance of a god-machine,' cried Auiden, backhanding his chainsword across the neck of an enemy warrior.

'If they're so… *nggh*… close, why aren't they… *hnng*… here?' spat Issur.

'It wouldn't make any difference,' shouted Bracha. 'Would you trust a war machine that almost blew your ship out from under you?'

'Kotov would never authorise *Lupa Capitalina* to fire on the *Tomioka*,' said Tanna. 'He has crossed the galaxy to find this ship and isn't about to risk it being damaged by Titan fire.'

'Then the next few moments are going to be interesting,' said Auiden.

'You have a strange idea of interesting, Apothecary,' said Varda as he put a bolt through an enemy's chest.

'That's only because you think purely in terms of killing.'

'What other... *gnnah*... way is there to think?' said Issur, cutting the legs out from two enemy warriors with one blow.

'I have to think of killing and keeping all of you alive,' said the Apothecary, adjusting the settings on his narthecium gauntlet. 'Now *that's* interesting.'

No sooner were the words out of Auiden's mouth than a hideously unlucky volley of shots punched through his plastron, gorget and helmet. Blood fountained, and even without Apothecary training, Tanna knew the wounds were mortal. He caught Auiden as he fell, wrenching his helmet off before blood from his arteries filled his helmet and drowned him.

But the Apothecary's face was a ruin of scorched meat and boiled blood. His noble features were obliterated and even as Tanna watched, the molten bone structure of his skull sagged inwards to form a sloshing pool of steaming brain matter.

Tanna's grief swelled around him, but he quashed it savagely as the *Barisan* lurched down into the plateau once again. He heard the shouts of his warriors, but ignored them as he saw a way out of their entrapment racing towards them.

EMIL WOULD BE calling him a lunatic right about now and Roboute would be hard-pressed to disagree with that assessment. He swung the grav-sled around a knot of embattled skitarii as they fought in a diminishing shield wall against the crystalline monsters that broke free of the glassy plateau like creatures rising from uncounted millennia frozen beneath the planet's surface.

Beside him, Adara fired his laspistol with pinpoint accuracy, decapitating a crystal warrior with every shot. Pavelka had no dedicated weaponry, but her mechadendrites were equipped with fusion cutters, ion beamers and las-saws, and they served as fearsome combat attachments. The grav-sled wasn't armed, but Roboute was using it as a weapon, barrelling through the overwhelming numbers of enemy like an Adeptus Arbites urban pacification vehicle.

Of course he tried to avoid that, but the closer he got to the *Barisan*, the harder it became. For the most part, the crystal-forms were directing their lethal attentions on the skitarii and Space Marines, but that was about to change.

'This is insane and illogical,' said Pavelka, neatly snipping the head from a crystal-form about to deliver the death blow to the exposed cortex of a downed battle robot. 'I should wrest control of this vehicle from you.'

'You wouldn't dare,' said Roboute.

'I would if I thought you wouldn't just jump out and keep going,' she replied.

Despite the unimaginable danger, Roboute felt nothing but a towering sense of invulnerability as he slewed around the gunship's partially enveloped engines. He shattered more of the enemy with the sled's bull bars, hauling the controls back to bring him down the starboard flank of the gunship where its wing was now completely enveloped by the ground.

Around thirty of the crystalline Space Marines hauled their way up the listing side of the *Barisan*, like a horde of plague victims trying to break into a sealed medicae structure.

'Hold on!' shouted Roboute and gunned the engine.

The collision was ferocious, a splintering series of shattering impacts as dozens of bodies went under the grav-sled. Its engines screeched and the rear section heeled sideways as the machine-spirit howled in protest at such cavalier treatment. Roboute's harness split along its centre-line, and only one of Pavelka's snapping mechadendrites kept him from falling from the sled.

She pulled him upright and he waved his arms to attract the attention of the Black Templars.

A Space Marine with an augmetic arm implanted with a seething hot plasma gun dropped onto the cargo bed, followed by a warrior with a crackling energy blade. Between them, they carried the body of a fallen warrior, but Roboute couldn't tell if he was alive or dead. Another Templar dropped onto the sled after them, until only Tanna and the warrior with the white-wreathed helm remained. Though it was surely ridiculous, it looked as though the two of them were arguing over who should be the last to abandon their position.

'For the Emperor's sake, just get on the damn sled!' shouted Roboute, though there was little chance they would hear him.

But his words had the desired effect, and the two warriors leapt together, landing on the sled with enough force to drive the back end into the ground. The repulsor engine flared, but miraculously stayed lit.

'They're aboard!' shouted Pavelka. 'Now get us out of here!'

Roboute nodded and wrenched the controls around with a whispered prayer to the Omnissiah to forgive him for his rough treatment of the grav-sled. The sled's controls were sluggish, but Roboute had the measure of them now, and compensated for the added weight of the Space Marines as he gunned the engine hard. The sled shot away from the downed gunship, every dial on the panel in front of him tapping into the red.

The crystal-form creatures weren't about to be denied their prey and turned their attack from the gunship to the grav-sled. One wrenched Adara's door off and received an armoured boot in the face. The creature fell away as Roboute wove a path through the battling skitarii. Bolts of emerald light streaked around him. Explosions stitched across the heavy plates of the engine cowling, and the sled lurched as some internal mechanism blew out.

A voice blasted into his helmet. 'Get us out of here!'

Roboute flinched. Adeptus Astartes. Tanna.

'I'm trying,' said Roboute, skidding around a pack of crystal-forms as they tried to box the grav-sled in. 'These things are everywhere. And we're not exactly travelling light.'

'We will secure you a path,' said Tanna.

Seconds later, blazing trails of bolter fire streaked overhead, ripping through the crystal-forms and clearing a path of broken glass. Adara added his pistol fire to the scouring barrage, and Roboute could just imagine the stories he'd get out of this. Fighting alongside the Black Templars!

Though he'd caution the youth not to use the word *rescue* in his tales.

A flat bang of electrical discharge blew out on the grav-sled, and Roboute's heart sank as a number of the dials on the control panel dropped rapidly to zero.

'Shit, shit, shit…' he muttered, banging a palm against the panel: the universal repair panacea.

He risked a glance over his shoulder, seeing the Black Templars kneeling or standing on the cargo flatbed with their bolters roaring.

But behind them, the grav-sled's engine was billowing twin plumes of tarry black oil smoke.

Microcontent 06

THE ATMOSPHERE ABOARD the *Tabularium* was one of control. Despite the sudden reversal of fortune suffered by Magos Dahan's skitarii, there was no panic on the command bridge. Magos Kryptaestrex had assumed command of the Land Leviathan, and though the pioneer units had not yet certified the temporary structures bridging the crevasse, his experienced optics had adjudged them capable of taking its weight.

Cadian units were already streaming across, but only a reckless vanguard, for the *Tabularium* now occupied the centre of the newly built span. Its stomping feet shook the bridge and dislodged debris from the inner faces of the crevasse where the supporting corbels and inset supports were drilled. Portions of the vast machine's width hung over the edge of the bridge, and Linya tried not to imagine what would happen if Magos Azuramagelli strayed but a little from its centre-line.

She kept a tight rein on her terror, partitioning the innate synaptic responses to tumbling thousands of kilometres behind walls of logic. She would pay for that later, but for now she needed to function without the debilitating handicap of fear.

She'd launched more drones, but capped their altitude to forty metres to keep them below the umbra, assigning them figure of eight orbits around the towering spire of the *Tomioka*. Visual feeds coming in from the embattled forces on the plateau had shocked everyone, but they were Mechanicus, and encountering the inconceivable was part of their mandate.

'Magos Dahan will learn a valuable lesson in humility,' said Galatea, its mismatched legs walking it around the surveyor table, where flickering icons and veils of binary bloomed from the hololithic surface in multicoloured bands. 'The *Tomioka* is well defended.'

'Is that why you didn't go with them?' asked Linya. 'Did you know these things were here?'

Galatea looked up, and the cold silver of its dead optics made Linya's skin crawl.

'No, but the presence of automated defences was a logical possibility.'

'A possibility you neglected to mention.'

'We saw no need,' replied Galatea. 'We believed Archmagos Kotov would come to the same conclusion.'

Though Linya knew it was an absurdly organic notion, she would have sworn on a stack of STC fragments that it was lying.

Warnings broadcast in binary and Gothic blared from vox-horns and Linya gripped the surveyor table as the *Tabularium* shuddered, the deck angling minutely downwards.

'We are at the midpoint of our crossing,' Magos Kryptaestrex intoned, and Linya's heart beat a little faster at the thought of the Land Leviathan's vast, monolithic feet breaking through the temporary bridge's weakest point with thunderous hammerblows.

'Then let's hope your pioneer crews have been thorough in their work on the far side,' said Azuramagelli from the steering station, his deconstructed brain portions flickering in the light of his electrical activity.

'If you keep us straight, instead of weaving us about like you have so far, then there will be no issues,' returned Kryptaestrex, plugged into the controls for motive power as he attempted to reduce the impact force of the *Tabularium*'s twin banks of enormous feet.

'If you wish to switch assignments,' said Azuramagelli, his artificial voice still managing to convey his irritation at Kryptaestrex, 'then I will be only too happy to take command of motive power.'

'It would be conducive to operations and my mental equilibrium if the two of you would shut up and concentrate on your assigned tasks,' said Linya with a blurt of admonishing binary. 'That way we might actually make it across this crevasse in one piece.'

Neither Kryptaestrex nor Azuramagelli replied, but both signalled their contrition with noospheric messages of assent.

The attenuated reverberations echoing through the Land Leviathan changed in pitch as the vast machine moved to a descending latticework support of adamantium struts, interlocking deck plating and bored-in suspensors. Linya brought up a drone optic feed and watched the *Tabularium* crossing the bridge, a million-tonne leviathan perched on an absurdly slender-looking structure that any rational eye would see as utterly incapable of supporting something so massive.

But, as impossible as it might look, Kryptaestrex's bridge was holding firm and they were almost across. The pitch of the Land Leviathan's feet returned to normal, and Linya let out a breath, the primal part of her brain having taken over her physiological functions despite her best efforts to self-regulate. They were across – though would, of course, have to return the same way – and the *Tabularium* canted upwards as Kryptaestrex poured power into the propulsion decks and they climbed the last hundred metres to the plateau.

Linya switched between the dozens of visual feeds coming from the drones, studying multiple inloads at once. Dahan's skitarii were falling back in good order, extricating themselves from overwhelming odds by means of mutually supporting mobile shield walls. The plateau was awash with the ice creatures, a glittering army assembled in their thousands from the crystalline bedrock of the world. Against so numerous a foe, most mortal armies would already have been destroyed, overrun and slaughtered as they fled the field in panic.

Skitarii were not like a mortal army. Their courage held in the face of insurmountable odds, their cool detachment and unbreakable discipline keeping them in the fight. Linya saw Dahan in the thick of the hardest fighting, breaking enemy thrusts that might interfere with the skitarii's retreat.

Linya did not like Dahan, but had to admire his tenacity and devotion to his warriors.

One feed caught her eye, and she zoomed in on it with a spike of disbelief.

Roboute Surcouf was in the midst of the fighting, his grav-sled fleeing the field of battle in spurts and starts as its engine burned out. That it had got them this far was a miracle of the Omnissiah, but Linya saw its machine-spirit was close to extinction. Hundreds of crystal-forms surrounded them, and even with the Black Templars fighting from its back, she estimated they had less than a minute before being overrun.

'Magos Azuramagelli,' said Linya. 'Exloading a course change to you.'

'Understood.'

'Magos Kryptaestrex, deploy the docking clamp.'

'It's too far,' said Moderati Marko Koskinen. 'No way we can make it.'

+Have faith,+ said the Wintersun. +I know this engine. I know what she is capable of.+

'As do I, princeps, and that crevasse is too wide for us,' said Koskinen, bringing up the schematics of a Warlord Titan from the Manifold. A three-dimensional image of the towering god-machine appeared over the central display hub of the command bridge, rotating slowly with reams of data listing its tolerances and capacity cascading alongside. 'We should wait until the bridge is clear.'

Though Princeps Luth had no need – or mortal eyes – to see the schematic, his withered, bifurcated wraith-form drifted from the milky grey suspension within his amniotic tank to press against the armourglass. Silver feed-cables plugged into his truncated waist and spinal implants trailed from his back like the hackles of a roused wolf.

+Schematics are for the scholam,+ said the Wintersun, +We are at war, Koskinen. *Lupa Capitalina* waits for no man.+

'Hyrdrith, back me up here,' said Koskinen.

'Princeps,' said Magos Hyrdrith from her elevated station at the rear of the bridge. 'As ever, I accept your wisdom as Omnissiah-given, but I must agree with Moderati Koskinen. Once the *Tabularium* and its attendant vehicles are clear, we can–'

+Mechanicus warriors are dying,+ snarled Luth. +We can save them from the beasts.+

'My princeps,' said Koskinen, frowning as swarming ghost images flickered through the Manifold for the briefest instant. 'Even if you're right and we can make it across, there's no telling if the ground on the far side is strong enough to take our mass. We–'

'If your princeps gives you an order, you question it?' snapped Joakim Baldur on the opposite moderati station to Koskinen's. He shook his head. 'No wonder Moonsorrow challenged for alpha.'

Joakim Baldur served as Moderati Primus on *Canis Ulfrica*, but had been assigned to *Lupa Capitalia* in the wake of Lars Rosten's death. He was Reaver through and through, which made him belligerent at the best of times, but now serving on the engine that had almost killed his own princeps only sharpened his viper's tongue. The burns he had suffered aboard *Canis Ulfrica* had healed, but the skin around his eyes and ears still had the rugose texture of vat-cultured skin.

'You crew a Reaver,' snapped Koskinen, his fraying temper – worn thin by Baldur's constant carping and obvious reluctance to be aboard *Lupa Capitalina* – finally snapping. 'What the hell do you know about this engine?

+Be silent! *Lupa Capitalina*'s anger burns hot,+ said Princeps Luth. +Would you feel that anger through your Manifold interface?+

'No, princeps,' said Koskinen, pushing the motive systems out and trying not to let his disquiet at what he thought he'd seen in the Manifold show. *Lupa Capitalina* set off at combat pace towards the crevasse. Its strides were long, the Warlord moving faster than was prudent in such icy conditions. Koskinen heard Hyrdrith's prayers to the Machine-God as the crevasse yawned before them.

Koskinen's heart dropped at the sight of it, knowing in his bones it was too wide for them and too impossibly deep to survive if they plunged into its bottomless depths. The Warlord was walking faster than it had walked in months, its mighty legs slamming into the ground and throwing up vast chunks of dislodged ice and rock.

They were practically sprinting, which was dangerous for such a towering war machine at the best of times, but they needed all the momentum they could get. That might be all that saved them from toppling back into the crevasse, so Koskinen set to scavenging every ounce of reactor energy from the voids and any secondary system he could think of to boost the gyro-stabilising mechanisms at the heart of the vast machine.

Angry red icons flared in the Manifold, stamped with inload signifiers of the *Tabularium*. The magi aboard the Land Leviathan saw what they attempted and were warning them of the dangers.

+They think we will fail,+ laughed the Wintersun. +I will show them what Sirius can do.+

ROBOUTE WAS TRYING every trick he knew to keep the grav-sled in the air, from prayers to threats, but the machine was dying. Thick smoke and streamers of random gravity fluctuations poured from the engine cowling, and they were leaving a black and oily train in their juddering, weaving wake. Sergeant Tanna and his Black Templars had expended their ammunition reserve and were keeping the crystal-forms at bay with swords and fists.

'Come on,' said Roboute, finally seeing the cliff face of the *Tabularium* as it stamped onto the plateau, accompanied by a host of steeldust Cadian tanks. The vast machine was around three hundred metres away, but it might as well have been on the other side of the planet. Skitarii units were falling back either side of them, some on foot and some in badly damaged Rhinos, but they were fighting to their own plan.

A plan in which Roboute and the Black Templars didn't factor.

The grav-sled dropped, and Roboute felt the ventral fin kiss the ground.

'Can you coax any more life out of this bloody sled?' he shouted back to Pavelka.

'Don't you think I am trying?' she replied. 'Clarification: employing pejorative terms on machines that might save your life is not recommended by the adepts of Mars.'

'Good point,' said Roboute, as yet another onboard system died. 'Right, listen up, sled. If you get us out of here alive I promise to repair every dent, burn and tear in your hull. I will replace every damaged component and never again put you in harm's way. Now will you bloody well get us to the *Tabularium*!'

'Not quite what I think she had in mind, captain,' said Adara.

'Best I've got, son,' said Roboute. 'Best I've got.'

The grav-sled's rear section slewed around as the engine finally blew out with a bray of thrashing machine parts and squalling repulsor fields. The ventral fin ploughed a furrow, and the sled's frontal section slammed into the ground with a shriek of tearing metal. Roboute was thrown forwards into the buckled canopy struts, his cheek cracking painfully on the inner face of his helmet.

The sled had broken its back in the crash, spilling the body of the fallen Black Templar to the ground. The warrior with the white-wreathed helmet immediately leapt from the wreckage and swung his enormous black sword in a wide arc. Three crystal-forms shattered, and two more fell back with emerald light streaming from mortal wounds to their chests.

The rest of the Templars were at his side in moments, fighting to clear a space around their downed brother as the enemy closed in. The sled was wrecked, and Roboute slammed his fist against the controls.

'Bloody useless thing!' he yelled

'Time to get out of here, captain?' said Adara.

'I think you might be right,' said Roboute, seeing hundreds of crystal-forms closing in through puffs of oxygen streaming from wide cracks in his helmet's faceplate. 'But I don't think we're going anywhere in a hurry.'

He dragged his gold-chased laspistol from its holster and stood in the buckled doorway of the cab.

'Come on then, you bastards!' he yelled. 'Come and get us!'

He held his pistol in the classic straight-thumb grip and started shooting into the clashing, crystalline host that surrounded them. His first target dropped with a neat hole cored through its skull, the second with an identical wound.

The third exploded into glassy vapour as though hit by a Vanquisher shell, leaving a giant crater in its wake. Roboute fell from the sled as the pounding shockwaves of the blast swatted him to the ground. Scores of smoking shell cases rained down around him, and he rolled onto his back as the shadow of a snarling beast reared over him.

Its weapon arms bucked with the force of blazing mega-bolters, and the pair of warhorns mounted at its jutting, fanged maw unleashed a howling battle cry.

'*Vilka*!' cried Pavelka, hearing its name woven into the howl.

The Warhound stomped over the wreckage of the grav-sled, sheeting bursts of fire clearing the ground of enemies for tens of metres in all directions. It trampled the crystal-forms to powder beneath its enormous clawed feet and carved white-hot-edged gouges in the earth with its guns.

Nor had it come alone.

A second Warhound loped from a blizzard of spinning crystal shards, twin weapon arms spitting thunderous volleys of las-fire and explosive shells. Its flank was scored with deep wounds, and blessed oils sheened its armoured hide. Like its twin it howled its fury, darting in to make kills at every blast of its warhorn.

Roboute scrambled into the cover of the smoking grav-sled, pulling himself upright as he fought to keep his breaths shallow. Already he was feeling giddy and lightheaded, a curious numbness seeping into his limbs.

'God-machines…' he said, staring up at the snapping, howling war-engines keeping the enemy creatures at bay.

He felt the ground vibrate with titanic impacts, the footsteps of a *true* god-machine.

Hands grabbed Roboute under the shoulders and dragged him back onto the sled. Black-armoured warriors surrounded him, and a robed tech-priest whose half-human features were familiar to him wrapped a snaking metallic arm around his waist.

'Hold on, captain,' said a voice he knew he should recognise, but which he just couldn't place. 'They're coming for us!'

'Of course they are,' said Roboute. 'Why wouldn't they…?'

He craned his neck up as a giant of myth strode into view, a soaring engine of destruction and power. Its size was incredible, a monstrous god of steel and adamantium with a sun at its heart and death in its fists. A gargantuan foot with four pneumatic buttress claws swept over them, trailing a rain of crystalline debris and pulverised rock. The god-machine's enormous foot hammered down and sent seismic shockwaves through the earth.

Pistoning clamps punched into the ground as auto-loaders fed ammo hoppers into hungry breeches and dozens of ratcheting missile hatches cycled open. In deference to the mortals at its feet, *Lupa Capitalina*'s plasma weaponry remained inactive, but an artillery battalion's worth of blazing heavy ordnance rippled from its shoulders. Streaking missiles traced parabolic trails over the battlefield, twenty-four in the first second, another twenty-four a second later. Plumes of white-hot fire exploded from the terrifying gatling blaster, and thousands of shells sawed from the spinning barrels of the vast, snub-nosed rotary cannon.

The plateau instantly vanished in sky-high curtains of fire and pounding explosions as the arcing streams of missiles slammed down in a never-ending series of punishing hammerblows. Roboute closed his eyes against the brightness, feeling his chest tighten and his thoughts drift off in what he knew was nitrogen narcosis.

As ways to die went, this at least had the virtue of being painless.

He smiled, thinking it apt that he should die on a world he had named.

Would anyone remember that name?

He didn't know, but it seemed important.

Over the unending barrage of the three god-machines, Roboute heard a heavy clang of metal on metal and felt a thrumming vibration through his void-suit. A sense of weightlessness clutched at him, and he opened his eyes to see the ground spinning away from him as the grav-sled was hoisted into the air.

Beneath him, a world burned in the fire of the god-machines.

'Below the waterline' was an expression from the days when vessels plied the seas of Old Earth; meaningless now that mankind's vessels had left their earthly oceans behind, but which still had currency among the bondsmen of the *Speranza*. Instead of referring to areas of a ship that would flood in the event of a hull breach, it now applied to the ventral regions of the Ark Mechanicus that were known to be dangerous for all sorts of additional reasons.

Magos Casada had recently been assigned a supervisory role among the bondsmen after ten years spent in data-transmission, a move he'd hoped would see an end to the comparatively mundane duties of informational flow paths and the chance to be in charge of more than just binary bits and infocyte logs. But with only two work-shy loafers and three servitors following him down the iron screw-stairs into the cold darkness he didn't feel like he was in charge of much at all.

Everyone was on edge, which at least kept their minds on their surroundings instead of looking for ways to skive off.

Or so Casada had thought.

'How come we get to do this?' asked Knox, picking something dripping and oily from his nose.

This was repairing a faulty transmission hub in one of the port-side conduit arrays, a repair made rather more than mundane due to the sudden nature of the fault's occurrence and its location in a region of the ship that had suffered more than its fair share of malfunctions in recent times.

'Because this is what we were assigned,' said Casada, following a jumping, flickering noospheric map projected in the air before him. 'Every duty in service of the Omnissiah is valued and important, from the lowliest to the–'

'Spare us the motivational crap, magos,' said Knox. 'You got it because you're new here and don't kiss the right overseer's arse. Anyone with a brain cell rattling around their skull avoids the lower decks. Too dark, too packed with machinery that can take your arm off, disembowel you or vaporise your bones to dust to be healthy.'

'I heard these decks got irradiated when the *Speranza* threw her moorings at her launch,' said Cavell.

Casada knew he should quash their seditious talk, but there was truth to what they were saying and he was a firm believer in allowing those beneath you an awareness that you shared their concerns.

'There's a measure of truth to that,' he allowed, taking a high-ceilinged transit passageway his map told him should lead to processional steps down to the conduit. 'There are heightened radiation levels in the lower decks, yes, but nothing to give us undue concern. We'll not be going down into the deeper regions of the ship.'

'Just as bloody well,' said Knox. 'Ain't nobody knows nothin' of what's down there nohow.'

Forcing himself to ignore Knox's murderous grammar, Casada said, 'Correction. That just isn't true. I have plentiful maps of the regions we must traverse to reach the transmission hub.'

'You're in the deeps now, magos, down past the waterline,' said Knox. 'Try navigating by those maps here and you'll be lost like all them other crews that went down too far.'

'Ah, gruesome tales of hauntings and disappearances in uncommon regions of a starship,' said Casada. 'I am familiar with such shipboard rumours and scare stories. They are nothing but invented fantasies to explain away industrial accidents and fill lacunae of information. It is my contention that such tales are spread as a means of creating a unity of experience among the uninitiated.'

'Shows what you know,' said Cavell. 'You're new here, but you'll learn.'

'Or he won't,' said Knox, drawing a finger across his throat.

Casada tried not to be put out by their obviously scaremongering behaviour, but it was true he was having a number of difficulties in following their assigned route. Access ports weren't where they were supposed to be, corridors and companionways marked as passable were blocked by thrumming machinery or simply weren't there. Thus far, his noospheric adaptations had found workarounds, but sooner or later Knox and Cavell were going to realise he wasn't entirely sure where they were any more.

'And what about them?' asked Knox, jerking a thumb at the three servitors following mutely behind them. 'How do we know they're not going to murder us when we're too deep to call for help?'

Rumours of the incredible events in Feeding Hall Eighty-Six had circulated the various shifts throughout the ship, and despite the Mechanicus' best efforts to quash their spread, no one was looking at the servitors in quite the same light. That the instigators and their apparently autonomous servitor were said to have escaped Magos Saiixek's skitarii and fled into the depths of the ship only added a level of revolutionary verisimilitude to the talk of holy presences.

'These ones certainly appear to be appropriately servile,' said Casada.

'Yeah? Well perhaps that's just to lull us into thinking they're brain-dead cyborgs and not heartless killers that want revenge for being made into servitors,' said Cavell.

'Now you are being ridiculous,' said Casada, frowning as they reached the end of the passageway to find the expected processional archway fringed with sparking cabling. A broken coolant pipe billowed hot steam and spilled a waterfall of scum-frothed water down the stairs. The effect was akin to a pict Casada had seen of a waterfall in a mangrove swamp, overhung by jungle creepers and humid with torpid vapour.

'Down there?' asked Knox, peering into the darkness where water-damaged lumens strobed and spat. 'Tell me you're joking.'

Casada heard what sounded like heavy footfalls, but were most likely some deeper machinery echoing through the tunnels. Something scraped on metal, but in such unvisited regions of a ship as large as an Ark Mechanicus, that wouldn't be unusual. A lack of regular maintenance would give rise to all manner of apparently inexplicable auditory peculiarities.

Cavell ducked under a bundle of conjoined cabling, bending this way and that to get a better look at where it had been broken.

'This ain't right,' he said, reaching up to touch the insulated sheath around the break point.

'We have seen many such breakages,' said Casada. 'After the nightmarish crossing of the Halo Scar, many cable runs have snapped under increased tensile loads.'

'No,' said Knox. 'He's right, look. They've been cut. Deliberately.'

Casada examined the cable run being held by Cavell, running a three-dimensional mapping laser over the damaged portion.

'Tell me I'm wrong,' said Cavell.

'The separation appears to be clean,' admitted Casada. 'I see no evidence of the stresses and weakening of the insulation sheath I might expect from tear damage. It is impossible to be certain, but it appears that, yes, this cable has been cut. Who cut it and why is another matter entirely.'

Even as he said the words, he knew he wasn't being entirely truthful. The break in the cable was so precise, with so infinitesimal a deflection in the adjacent fibres, that there was little possibility it could have been achieved by any known device or blade.

At least none known to the Mechanicus.

Another booming echo sounded from below, that deeper,

sub-deck machinery again, but when it came again, Casada realised it was closer than before. He looked down the processional stairs, but instead of flickering lumens, the wide stairwell was wreathed in impenetrable darkness.

'Perhaps we *should* find another way down,' said Casada, backing away from the steps.

Knox looked up, picking up on his building anxiety.

The man followed Casada's gaze and his eyes widened in fear as something huge surged from the darkness below. Its elongated emerald skull was bulbous and glossy, its ivory limbs slender and grasping as it raced up the steps with a loping, horrifically organic gait.

Whispering streams of displaced air scythed up the steps.

Cavell simply vanished, his body coming apart so thoroughly it was as though he'd clutched an armed frag mine to his chest. Ruined body parts tumbled down the steps, and Knox set off at a sprint lest he suffer the same fate.

He made three steps before he was felled by the towering, spindle-limbed construct. Its monstrous hand seemed to merely brush over the top of the man's head, but the lid of his skull came away as surely as though a precision trepanning laser had sliced clean through it.

The animal part of Casada's brain howled in terror, flooding his body with adrenaline, and he screamed as he turned to run. He pushed past the unresisting servitors, fighting to escape, to get *away* from this below the waterline daemon of the dark. He risked a glance over his shoulder and let out a whimper of naked fear as he saw four porcelain-limbed figures with cherry red plumes streaming from their howling, death-mask faces.

'How did–' was all Casada managed before a shrieking wail buckled the air between him and his pursuers. His high-function aural implants blew out under the lethal sonic assault and blessed lubricant poured from his eyes and ears.

Casada howled in pain as his optics fizzed with bleeding binary static and his skull filled with nerve-shredding feedback. Denied the heightened sensory input of his enhancing augmetics, Casada's brain implants began rerouting his synaptic pathways to once again employ his birth-senses. Viewed through the obscuring lens of his blown implants, Casada's natural vision was blurred and grainy with lack of use. He saw a wavering, smeared-lens image of the killers coming towards him and pushed himself to his feet. He knew he couldn't escape, but ran anyway, his terror driving his limbs in a vain attempt to prolong his life. The after-effects of the mind-shredding scream still ravaged his body. Hideous nausea churned in his gut and a sickening vertigo made his lurching steps comically drunken.

Casada couldn't see where he was going, his unaugmented senses painfully blunted.

He blundered into an iron wall, striking his head on a protruding flange and falling to his knees. Blood poured down his face from this latest indignity. He crawled like a beast on its belly, a wounded animal stalked by a predatory creature that revels in its prey's suffering.

Through his sobs he heard the unmistakable sounds of blades through flesh. One by one, the servitors he had led into the depths were butchered without resistance; beasts led blindly into the slaughterhouse.

'Please,' he begged, as he heard distorted echoes of footsteps behind him. 'Please don't kill me.'

The tip of something dreadfully sharp pressed on the nape of his neck.

'Ave Deus Mechanicus…' he said, drawing his hands together

beneath his body in the Cog Mechanicus. 'The Machine-God is with me, I shall fear no evil…'

A sharp thrust and the blade sliced cleanly through Casada's spinal cord.

Microcontent 07

THE EARLIER MOOD of optimism that had suffused the expedition upon establishing the landing fields had evaporated utterly. A great many machines and lives had been lost on the plateau, and an atmosphere of shared contrition now filled the command deck of the *Tabularium.* Still clad in his gleaming armour, Kotov had gathered his commanders around Linya Tychon's surveyor station. Each warrior and magos was studiously examining the hololithic projection of the *Tomioka* as it stubbornly refused to divulge its secrets to any of the available augurs.

Kotov stared at the gently rotating image, as though he could simply will its interior structure to reveal itself by virtue of his vaunted rank.

Ven Anders stood in the shadow of Sergeant Tanna and his white-wreathed Emperor's Champion. Though Dahan's losses currently stood at three hundred dead and fifty-seven injured, Tanna's loss was perhaps the greater. Coming face to face with the Black Templars, Kotov had thought to berate them for their foolishness, but upon learning of Brother Auiden's death, he had instead offered only sincere regrets. The loss of a single Space Marine was bad enough, but to lose an Apothecary was something else entirely and Kotov could clearly see Tanna's need to atone for his misguided zeal.

Azuramagelli and Kryptaestrex were plugged in on opposite sides of the plotting table, their petty bickering put aside in the face of this bloody setback. Galatea leaned over the surveyor station, its hand idly tracing the outline of the holographic starship.

'It has been over four thousand years since we saw her. Many long years…' said the hybrid construct, turning the rotating image back and forth with soft haptic gestures.

Kotov felt a tremor of unease at Galatea's behaviour, like it was reaching out to something familiar, like a long lost friend or a forbidden object of desire.

'No one has seen it in that long,' said Kotov.

Galatea's head snapped up, and it snatched its hand back, as though caught in some forbidden act. The silver-eyed proxy body at the centre of its palanquin pulled back into itself.

'You did not see it as we saw it,' said Galatea. 'That we can promise you. The greatest ship of its age, launched in glorious triumph, but mocked for daring to dream that the impossible could be within our grasp. You do not know, you *cannot* know, what that was like.'

'You would be surprised,' snapped Kotov, his own travails and losses having seen him set sail on this expedition under a similar cloud of criticism from his fellow Martian adepts. 'But your recall of the *Tomioka* will have to wait, unless you have something useful to contribute?'

'Like what lies inside,' said Ven Anders. 'That's what I want to know. If we want to get inside that ship, then I want to know what my men are going to face.'

The Cadian colonel's close-cropped hair was sheened in perspiration, for the running-heat of so many cogitation engines made this chamber a hothouse for mortals.

'We know no more than you, Colonel Anders,' said Galatea.

Anders ran a hand across his stubbled chin and said, 'You know what? I don't think I believe you. I think you know damn well what's inside that ship, so how about you cut the crap and just tell us what you know.'

Galatea spread its hands in an empty gesture of apology. 'The same umbra that inhibits Mistress Tychon's augurs prevent us from learning more than you already know.'

Anders grunted in disbelief and shook his head. 'You're lying, and if any of my men die because of that, you have my word as an officer of Cadia that I'll kill you.'

Kotov placed both hands on the edge of the plotting table and said, 'We must proceed on the assumption that we will encounter further automated defences within the *Tomioka*. Colonel Anders, Sergeant Tanna and Magos Dahan, you should prepare your assault plans on that supposition.'

'The skitarii should have the honour of breaching the hull of a Mechanicus vessel,' said Dahan, squaring his shoulders as if daring anyone to contradict him. Kotov understood Dahan's grandstanding. His warriors had been humbled, and only the intervention of Legio Sirius's war-engines had finally ended the battle.

'My Templars are better suited to fighting in such environments,' said Tanna. 'We should be first.'

'With all due respect,' said Anders. 'There's only five of you, and that's a pretty big ship.'

'I could conquer a world with five Black Templars,' said Tanna.

Linya Tychon cut across the impending confrontation.

'To gain access to areas of the ship that offer the best chance of finding what we came here for, there's only one way anyone is getting inside the *Tomioka*,' she said.

'And what's that?' asked Anders. 'The umbra's still in place, so an aerial assault isn't an option.'

'The crystalline buttressing is too thick at the base of the tower,' added Tanna.

'The only way in is on the back of *Lupa Capitalina*,' said Linya. 'It has the capacity to carry two assault forces, and its height means it's just below the ceiling of the umbra, but tall enough to carry us to where the ice around the ship's base is thinnest.'

Anders grinned. 'I've always wanted to ride into battle on the back of a god-machine.'

'Should we expect to find more of those crystal beings inside?' asked Tanna, already assimilating the addition of a Titan to his own deployment plans.

'More than likely,' said Kotov.

'And do we have any idea what they are?' asked Anders. 'Magos Dahan, you got up close and personal with them. Any insights?'

Dahan stood with one shoulder hunched as three tech-menials and armourers worked on his damaged body. Shrouded fusion-welders worked beneath the folds of his mantle of bronze mail.

'I have never seen their like,' he admitted. 'They were crystalline, that much was obvious, empowered by an energy source centred in their chests. Passive data recordings suggest it to be a form of bio-morphic induction energy, similar to that encountered by explorator teams excavating tomb structures on the southern fringes of Segmentum Tempestus.'

'Necrontyr?' asked Azuramagelli. 'Surely it is impossible that such beings could be found beyond the galaxy's edge.'

'Pay attention, I said similar, not identical,' said Dahan. 'You have all parsed the data. Draw your own conclusions.'

'They are not necrontyr,' said Kotov.

'Then what are they?' demanded Tanna. 'A new xenos breed?'

Kotov shook his head. 'Strictly speaking, no, they are not alive, though in manifesting cognitive awareness of their surroundings and behaviour that appears to be intelligently reactive, they could easily be mistaken for living organisms.'

'That doesn't answer his question,' said Galatea, stretching one bio-mechanical hand into the image of the *Tomioka*. Kotov masked his irritation, but Galatea spoke again before he could continue. 'You know as well as we do the nature of this foe.'

'Archmagos?' asked Anders, when Galatea didn't continue.

'I believe them to be a form of bio-imitative machinery seeded within the crystalline structure of the plateau,' said Kotov. 'Essentially, billions of micro-bacterial sized machines threaded through the crystalline matrix of the ground, each useless in and of itself, but capable of combining into something greater than the sum of its parts. They reacted to our presence, forming a mimicking force to repel us, like white blood cells rushing to the site of a biological infection.'

'I have never heard of technology such as this,' said Kryptaestrex, as though affronted by the idea. 'Why has it not been recorded in the data-stacks of Mars?'

'Because it was never brought to fruition,' said Kotov. 'Magos Telok pioneered this research after his expedition to Naogeddon in the turbulent years following the fall of the High Lord. He never presented his work to any Martian Frateris Conclave, because he could never get it to work.'

Anders tapped the flat slate of the surveyor grid. 'Looks like he has now.'

'If Telok never presented his findings, how do you know this, archmagos?' asked Tanna.

'Do you think I would mount an expedition such as this without preparation, Sergeant Tanna?' asked Kotov, rising to meet the implied challenge. 'Believe me when I say that I have studied all aspects of Archmagos Telok – his every published monograph, his every experimental record and every lunatic tale woven around him since he was inducted into the Martian priesthood and his expedition's disappearance. My preparations were no less thorough than yours would be for battle. The key to understanding Telok, my Templar friend, is not just in learning *everything*, but in recognising what amongst that is of value and what is wanton embellishment.'

'And what do those studies tell you, archmagos?' asked Anders. 'Why bother protecting a ship that's going to be destroyed along with this planet?'

Kotov straightened, logic providing the only possible answer. 'To keep the ship safe until it fulfils its function.'

'And what function is that?'

'I do not know,' said Kotov. 'I suspect we will only learn that once we go aboard.'

THE RANGE-FINDER IN Tanna's helmet told him the *Tomioka* was two kilometres distant, though its immense scale made it look far closer. The Mechanicus contingent, a curious mix of warriors and explorers surrounded by Dahan's atmosphere-capable skitarii, occupied the port-side assault battlement, while he and his battle-brothers stood on the starboard shoulder mount of *Lupa Capitalina* alongside a heavily armed detachment of void-suited Cadians.

Tanna had seen the mortal soldiers training and knew them to be competent fighters, but they weren't Adeptus Astartes and that made them inherently unreliable. He kept his thoughts from Apothecary Auiden, his body frozen in the *Tabularium*'s morgue, knowing it would only compromise his squad's efficiency. But no matter how he tried to compartmentalise his mind, allowing the grief to build behind walls of discipline and psycho-conditioning, Tanna felt the loss keenly.

Yet another death that would see them lost without hope of returning to the Chapter.

Tanna knew his warriors were suffering too, but he had no words for them, no soul-lifting oratory to salve the loss of their Apothecary. Like Kul Gilad's death, Auiden's loss could not be laid at his feet, but Tanna knew it was his responsibility to ensure every warrior under his command came back alive. A task that every commander of warriors knew they would ultimately fail.

The Warlord's rapid march was devouring the distance between the edge of the plateau and the vertical spire of the ship with every thunderous stride. Putting aside his mournful thoughts, he leaned over the cog-toothed battlements, seeing squadrons of Imperial Guard super-heavies and skitarii war machines following the god-engine. Both Warhounds wove a stalking path ahead of *Lupa Capitalina*, prowling like the superlative hunters they were.

Far behind the Warlord's advance, well-defended work crews from the *Tabularium* were digging the *Barisan* from its enveloping crystal prison. The honourable gunship was to be brought back aboard the *Speranza* and made whole once again.

Tanna made a fist and placed it over his eagle-stamped breastplate.

'You will fly again, great one,' he whispered.

'This isn't right,' said Varda, the Black Sword balanced over his shoulder guard and legs braced to counteract the swaying motion of the striding Warlord. 'We came here expecting to find a crash site, the ruins of a dead ship rusting and decaying for the better part of four thousand years. But that vessel looks like it landed here a decade ago. What do you make of that, sergeant?'

Tanna felt the scrutiny of his battle-brothers and knew they expected a meaningful answer.

'It tells me that we should expect this ship to be defended at every turn.'

Varda nodded, flexing his fingers on the hilt of the Black Sword.

'By those crystal-forms?'

Tanna nodded. 'That, and worse,' he said. 'We took no measures to avoid detection on our approach to the *Tomioka*, so it is reasonable to assume that any Mechanicus presence here, even an old one, is aware of our arrival.'

'Clearly,' agreed Varda. 'What is your point?'

'If Archmagos Kotov is so sure there is someone here, why has there been no response to our arrival on this world?'

'You don't think those... *gnnnh*... crystal-forms that killed Brother... *nggg*... Auiden were a response?' declared Issur, his anger making his involuntary twitches even worse.

'If Archmagos Kotov is correct then those things were an automated response,' said Tanna.

'Perhaps the ship is damaged and can no longer detect orbital traffic,' suggested Bracha, pointing to the crystal growths extruded from the *Tomioka*'s forward compartments. 'Or it is possible those things, whatever they are, interfere with the ship's surveyors.'

Yael grunted. 'Since when did you become a Techmarine?'

'You have a better answer, boy?'

Before Yael could rise to Bracha's caustic words, Tanna intervened.

'Even if whoever is aboard this ship *has* lost the capability of detecting vessels in orbit, they cannot have failed to miss a battle on their doorstep. Not to mention the sight of a Warlord Titan approaching. But they have not reacted to our presence at all.'

'Suggesting what?' asked Varda.

'One of two things,' replied Tanna. 'Either there is no one aboard that ship or they are waiting for us to get closer before revealing themselves.'

'An ambush?'

'We will proceed under that assumption,' said Tanna, and the posture of his knights racked up from readiness to combat imminent.

'So it's going... *nggg*... to be like an assault into a... *nnng*... void-lost hulk?' asked Issur.

'That is an acceptable paradigm for what we should expect,' said Tanna, well aware of the difficulties in clearing a space hulk: the darkness, the blind tunnels, the labyrinthine internal structure of the agglomerated vessels – some of which would undoubtedly be of xenos origin. Not to mention the unspeakable horrors that often lurked within: tyrannic life forms, greenskins, fleshless abominations from the warp or worse.

'At least we will have gravity,' said Yael, ever the optimist.

'True, but everything will be canted at ninety degrees,' pointed out Varda. 'There will be no floors, only bulkheads for footholds and cross-passages for secure footing. Every metre of our advance will be like the ascent of a cliff.'

'Enough,' said Tanna. 'This is no different to any other assault. We go in, we kill what we find.'

His certitude silenced them, but the unspoken consequence of their Apothecary's death hung in the air between them like a curse. Nothing more was said until *Lupa Capitalina*'s advance had carried them to within five hundred metres of the *Tomioka*, and Tanna scanned the frozen cliffs encasing the lower reaches of the starship.

Glacial ice shimmered with rainbow patterns of violet light and reflected metallic glints swam in its depths. Without impurities, it was virtually transparent, and the distorted image of the entombed ship was like looking at something submerged on a shallow river bed.

Lupa Capitalina raised its plasma weapon to the level of its shoulders and traceries of blue-hot lightning arced from its power couplings. The plasma destructor was a vast, smooth-bored weapon the size of a boarding torpedo with heavy magnetic coiling wound tightly around its oval muzzle. The static buzz of developing power reacted with the voids in a series of squealing rainbow-hued borealis, causing the Cadians to flinch from the violent display of sun-hot energies. Shimmering waves hazed the air around the weapon – the heat of a star's core primed and ready to be unleashed.

But instead of firing its most potent weapon, *Lupa Capitalina* thrust its fist forwards as though throwing a punch. A bow wave of heat turned the ice to vapour long before any impact, a hissing curtain of superheated steam billowing from the disintegrating ice. The towering Warlord took a single sidestep and the chained plasmic energies burned away the ice, carving into the entombing glacier.

The precision required for this manoeuvre astounded Tanna, who hadn't truly believed the vast machine capable of achieving such finesse. Electrically charged steam wafted through the voids, carrying the scent of incredible age, heated metal and chemically pure nitrogen.

When the hissing clouds were dispersed by the churning

atmospherics, Tanna saw a wide gallery had been cut through the thick buttress supporting the lower reaches of the starship. What had been impenetrable only moments before was now open to the world, and through a curtain of melted ice, Tanna saw the gleaming wet flank of the *Tomioka.*

'No remorse, brothers,' said Tanna, as the assault ramp extended from the battlements. 'No pity.'

'No fear,' came the answer from each warrior.

ABREHEM TURNED OVER, trying to get comfortable on the makeshift bunk, no easy task when one shoulder was an unyielding metallic rotator-cuff. His weight was unbalanced and, until he'd had his arm replaced with an augmetic, he hadn't realised how difficult that made it to sleep. The bed was a scavenged foldaway Hawke had sourced from Emperor-knew-where, uncomfortable, but better than what Abrehem had gotten used to. He stared at the chamber's coffered ceiling, where faded representations of Sebastian Thor and his disciples looked back, always seeming to be highly interested in something just out of sight. The iron-wrought skulls worked into the black walls gave the impression of being in a tomb or a temple, an impression only reinforced by the hunched shape seated upon the golden throne in the adjacent dormis chamber.

Rasselas X-42 wore the aggression-suppressing mechanisms of a pacifier helm, a device Totha Mu-32 assured him would keep the arco-flagellant in a trance-like state of childish bliss. Enraptured by visions of Imperiocentric ecstasy, Rasselas X-42 presented no threat to any living being unless Abrehem voiced the trigger phrase, something he had promised he would not do.

But given his current predicament, that wasn't a promise he was sure he'd be able to keep.

Abrehem was a wanted man, a fugitive trapped on a starship with nowhere to run.

After Magos Saiixek had withdrawn his skitarii from the feeding hall, Hawke and Coyne had fled with him through the passageways they knew intimately well and yet not at all. Letting the *Speranza* or the Omnissiah guide them, they'd eventually reached the site of Hawke's first alcohol still; now revealed to be the activation chamber for an arco-flagellant.

Even dormant, its malicious presence was palpable, a potential for horrific, bloody violence that infected the very air with toxic emanations. They'd cleaned the eldar blood and bodies away, but the memory of that near-instantaneous slaughter still haunted Abrehem. He shied away from thoughts of the slumbering killer and turned his attention to the chamber's other occupant.

Ismael de Roeven, freshly clad in a robe of pale cream, sat on the floor with his back to the wall. The restored servitor had his knees drawn up to his chest and hadn't said a word about the incident in the feeding hall. No matter how much Abrehem tried to coax him into an explanation of how he had managed to control those other servitors, Ismael wouldn't – or couldn't – say.

Abrehem had lost count of the hours he'd spent in this chamber while Totha Mu-32 and the others took stock of the Mechanicus response to a threatened servitor uprising. With nothing to do but wait until their return, Abrehem was growing ever more restless. He rolled onto his back and rubbed the heel of his flesh and blood palm over his eyes.

When he took his hand away, he saw a trickle of noospheric code squirming through the walls, an irregular grid pattern enfolding the room like a cage. He'd caught sight of it every now and then, a liminal binaric ward-pattern that would fade as soon as it became aware of his scrutiny, but Abrehem turned his will upon it and the code-light shimmered brightly once more.

His eyes followed the leading edge of the code as it circled the room. The rest of the chamber was in sharp focus, but wherever the code touched, he could feel its brittle, fading power. The binary was old, degraded and worn out. It had patrolled this chamber so many times, perhaps since the *Speranza*'s birth, that its potency was all but spent.

There was a hypnotic quality to the pattern, and Abrehem felt himself drawn into its looping arrangement. Without conscious thought, he rose from the bed and let his eyes roam the contours of the walls. The code flowed over the polished domes of iron skulls, between the entwined eagles and cogs, following the hexagonal pathways. He followed the code as it travelled over the walls, and Abrehem was reminded of an old metaphor of electricity as civilisation's lifeblood.

His heart beat faster in his chest and his breath tasted of burned metal.

Footsteps echoed and Abrehem had the unpleasant sensation of the walls closing in on him. His coppery breath quickened and both hands closed into fists as an unformed anger took shape in his thoughts. The beguiling quality of the flickering binary glitched, and Abrehem blinked as its hold was broken and the machine-stamped walls swam back into focus around him.

Abrehem let out a soft sigh of fear as he found himself standing before Rasselas X-42, his augmetic hand stretched out towards the complicated controls of the pacifier helm. He had watched Totha Mu-32 engage the helm and now realised he'd memorised the ritual movements and catechisms required for its use without conscious thought.

Violent red intruded on his vision, a descending haze of scarlet falling over his eyes like a curtain of blood, the anger he had felt earlier sharpened into a bright spike of purest rage. Abrehem could not remember a moment in his life where he'd felt such unreasoning fury, a bone-deep urge to do harm to another human being. Memories of ripped bodies, torn-out entrails and screaming mouths that cried a name that wasn't his own filled his skull. Abrehem's initial horror was quashed by the unstoppable urge to kill, to violate unclean flesh, to murder something... *anything*...

His trembling digits touched the bronze keys attached to the side of the throne and he tapped out the initialisation commands that began the process of decoupling the mechanisms of the pacifier helm. Slowly the soothing, calming imagery of Imperial saints, cherubs and golden bliss would be stripped away from the arco-flagellant's perceptions, each loss driving it into a higher state of insane, murderous wrath.

Rasselas X-42's head rose up, still masked by the featureless pewter helm.

His chest heaved and grunting spurts of stinking breath sighed from beneath the pacifier helm.

The arco-flagellant was a loaded gun, primed and ready to fire.

All it needed was the trigger phrase and it would be free to kill, maim and murder.

Abrehem suddenly became aware of a presence at his side and felt a gentle hand upon his shoulder. The building horror of mutilations and violent degradation drained from his thoughts in a flood and his legs buckled beneath him. He fell into the arms of Ismael, sobbing as he realised how close he'd come to unleashing the full fury of the arco-flagellant.

'I didn't...' he said. 'I wouldn't have...'

'I know,' said Ismael. 'But Rasselas X-42 is a living weapon, and a weapon has but one purpose.'

Abrehem nodded and let Ismael lead him back to his cot bed, blinking away the nightmarish images of torture and mutilation. He sat down, heaving in gulping breaths and weeping at the horror of what he'd seen. He knew they were not his own thoughts, but memories of carnage wrought by Rasselas X-42 in his previous existence.

Ismael held out his hands and Abrehem looked up into his eyes.

The servitor's distracted, vacant look was gone. In its place was an expression of such peace and understanding that Abrehem was rendered speechless.

'He calls to your lust for violence,' said Ismael, all traces of his halting speech vanished. 'Rasselas X-42 is the quick and easy path to vengeance, the evil of the man he was distilled and perfected. You must be better than that, Abrehem, you must cast him out.'

Abrehem shook his head. 'I can't. If the Mechanicus come for me, then I'll need him.'

'You do not need him,' promised Ismael. 'You already have all that you need.'

'I don't understand.'

Ismael held his hands out to him and said, 'Then listen.'

Abrehem hesitantly took Ismael's hands and kept silent, alert for anything out of the ordinary, but beyond Rasselas X-42's thwarted, animal breath and the constant mechanical beat of the *Speranza*'s workings, there was nothing to hear.

'Listen to what?' said Abrehem.

'To all the lost souls,' said Ismael, and Abrehem cried out as thousands of enslaved voices filled his head with their anguished cries.

THE APPEARANCE OF the *Tomioka*'s exterior had shocked Kotov, but the interior was, if anything, even more outlandish. The starship's internal plan had been extensively reshaped, rendering his ancient schematics utterly useless. With their entry point far above them, the darkness within was virtually absolute, leavened only by the helm-lamps of the skitarii and a pale, greenish hue that seeped from flexing cables that infested the ship's dripping innards like pulsing arteries.

Access ladders and stairwells that had been removed from their previous locations and re-fixed perpendicular to their original orientation allowed Kotov's force to travel downwards without difficulty. Their route traversed vast, echoing interior compartments stripped of their original fittings and which were now connected in ways the *Tomioka*'s original shipwrights had never intended. They kept close to the ice-clad hull, and ghostly wisps of chill vapour curled from protruding structural elements like breath.

'I feel like we are descending through biological anatomy,' said Dahan, moving with a hunched gait to fit through the oddly angled passageways. 'It is an unpleasant sensation.'

Kotov understood his sentiment, imagining they were passing through the literal guts of the starship. Like a living organism, the interior of the *Tomioka* was not silent, but a place of groaning echoes, creaking, flexing steelwork and a distant, glacial heartbeat.

'Perhaps a biological aesthetic informed Telok's work here,' suggested Kotov.

'No wonder they called him mad,' observed Dahan distastefully. 'Why then do we traverse the bowels while Mistress Tychon ascends to the brain?'

'Because the greatest power source lies far beneath us, and it is the key to understanding the mystery of this vessel,' answered

Kotov. 'Let Mistress Tychon plunder the archives, *we* will be the ones to learn the true revelations Telok left behind.'

Dahan gave a blurt of dismissive binary and set off to rejoin his skitarii warriors.

Kotov ignored the Secutor's scepticism, attuning his senses to the chatter of background perceptions. Manifold inloads from Tarkis Blaylock and Vitali Tychon aboard the *Speranza*, encrypted vox-clicks from the Templars, Cadian intercom echoes and a crackling hiss of machine language that burbled just below his threshold of understanding.

Kotov couldn't understand it, but one thing was clear.

It was getting stronger.

'I take it you hear that, archmagos,' said a bobbing, gold-chased skull floating beside him, kept aloft by a tiny suspensor and embellished with a single flared wing that fluttered back and forth at its occipital bone. One eye socket was fitted with an ocular-picter, the other with a sophisticated augur implant that recorded and relayed its findings back to the *Speranza*.

'Yes, Tarkis,' said Kotov. 'I do, but it irks me that I cannot understand it.'

'The ship's cogitators are struggling too,' said the skull with Blaylock's voice. 'I am applying all sanctioned enhancements and filters to the source code, but they are statistically unlikely to retrieve anything of use.'

'Understood, Tarkis,' said Kotov. 'But keep trying. I want to know what this ship is saying.'

The skull clicked its jaws and drifted back to its position at Kotov's shoulder as the downward journey through the *Tomioka* continued down welded ladders, crudely formed ramps and repositioned stairwells.

Kotov followed the Black Templars down a screw-stair welded to the side of a corridor, letting his fingers brush against a line of angular symbols that resembled ancient hieroglyphics or a forgotten branch of mathematics. He'd seen variations of these symbols ever since they'd boarded the *Tomioka*, each ideogram connected to another like the holy writ of a circuit board. Linya Tychon believed it to be an impossibly complex form of organic language belonging to a hitherto unknown xenos breed, a declaration that had only heightened the tension among the Mechanicus boarders.

Where Kotov, Dahan's skitarii and the Black Templars were forging a path down through the *Tomioka*'s internal structure, Vitali Tychon's gifted daughter was ascending. Escorted by a company-strength detachment of Cadian storm troopers led by Captain Hawkins, she had eagerly seized this chance to venture into the unknown. Curiously, Galatea had chosen to accompany her, the abominable machine intelligence keen to explore Telok's flagship now that the threat beyond its hull had been dealt with. Magos Azuramagelli had been seconded from the *Tabularium*'s command deck to oversee the mission to the ship's bridge, assuming such a location still existed.

Kotov reached the bottom of the screw-stair to find himself in a high-roofed transverse corridor that had been sealed at either end by heavy panelling fashioned from elongated panels torn from the ship's prow blade. There appeared to be no way to continue downwards, though skitarii melta gunners were hunting for weak points in the floor and strangely scraped walls to attempt a breach. Kotov detected heavy deposits of lubricant grease and felt the presence of electrical current.

Magos Dahan beckoned Kotov over to a jury-rigged control panel against the far wall, but before he could join him, Tanna intercepted him.

'How much farther down do you believe we need to go, archmagos?' asked Tanna.

'I believe we are close, sergeant,' replied Kotov.

'With every level we descend, the danger increases.'

'We are explorators, Sergeant Tanna,' Kotov reminded him. 'Danger comes with the territory.'

'*You* are an explorator, *I* am a warrior.'

'Then you should be used to danger, sergeant,' snapped Kotov.

The Space Marine's anger was unmistakable, but Kotov paid it no attention and moved past him to join Dahan. A series of gem-lights winked on the panel, indicating that it had power. Its only other component was a simple lever that could be racked to an up or down position.

'Elevator controls,' said Dahan. 'Funicular transit ones ripped from an embarkation deck by the size of them.'

'This whole chamber is a descent elevator,' said Kotov, now understanding the nature of the scrapes on the walls and the excessive presence of lubricants.

'The enginarium spaces should be beneath,' said Dahan. 'The source of the power emanations?'

'Possibly,' said Kotov taking hold of the descent lever. 'If whatever is below us bears any resemblance to the original plan.'

Kotov pulled the control lever into the down position. 'So let us find out,' he said.

The chamber shuddered and ground downwards on bleating hydraulics and clanking gear chains.

Microcontent 08

Entire structural elements had been removed from the upper reaches of the *Tomioka*'s hull and replaced with crystalline panels that refracted outside light through the enclosing ice in strange ways. Linya blink-clicked images of rainbow-hued prismatic beams dancing in the open spaces, the light catching glittering motes of dust and reflecting from the polarised visors of the Cadians' enclosing helmets. The brightness gave the impression of space and peace, but that was, she reminded herself, an illusion.

'Wondrous, is it not?' asked the voice of her father. 'Reminds me of the magnificent processional cathedrals of ice and glass within the Artynia Catena.'

Vitali Tychon's voice emerged from a jet-black servo-skull flitting through the air like a curious insect, the audio scratchy with distortion and warbling with singsong static. The presence of the umbra surrounding the *Tomioka* made standard orbital vox impossible, so all transmissions between the ground forces and the *Speranza* were relayed through the *Tabularium* to the landing fields before finally being hurled into space.

'There's a resemblance,' agreed Linya, addressing the floating device, which had been built from removed segments of her father's own skull after he had decided to enlarge his cranial cavity with an artificial replacement to allow for additional implants. 'But we are not on Mars, we are exploring the hostile environment of an ancient madman.'

'Madman? Visionary? Often the two are separated by a hair's-breadth,' observed Vitali, as twin callipers mounted under the jawbone produced a quick sketch of the view before his proxy skull.

'I know which one I would use to describe Telok,' said Linya.

'Before I saw this, I might have agreed with you, but this is incredible,' said Vitali as the servo-skull floated ahead to where Magos Azuramagelli was ascending a narrow stairwell by folding his ratcheting machine body into a more compact form. Contrary to what Linya had expected, Azuramagelli was negotiating the convoluted spaces within the *Tomioka* with relative ease, swiftly climbing ladders with multiple arms, and reordering his brain-fragments within the armature of his protective casings to facilitate his transit.

Given the self-assembled crudity of Galatea's form, it had no such ability to alter its body-plan and was forced to take looping detours to avoid the more cramped routes to the bridge. Linya had been glad of the respite from its presence, but each time they reconnected with the hybrid machine intelligence, she wondered just how it managed to get ahead of them. She and the Cadians were supposed to be following the most direct route to the bridge, but each time the dimensions of a blast door or cored shaft prevented it from proceeding Galatea would be waiting for them in a wider space beyond.

What, she then thought, was it doing while it was beyond their sight?

Linya shook off such suspicions and concentrated on her own progress, following four squads of void-suited Cadian troopers as they forged a path upwards, moving in fits and starts as different groups advanced higher into the ship in mutually supporting cover formations. Another three squads followed behind, and Linya admired the effectiveness with which Captain Hawkins was leading his men – from the front and with nothing asked of them he wasn't prepared to do first.

Cadian combat argot was terse and tactically precise – for a verbal form of communication – with clear commands and unambiguous meanings. Skitarii mind-links were a far more efficient means of combat communication, but required cranial implants she suspected most soldiers of the fortress-world wouldn't accept.

Despite Kotov's gloomy predictions, their winding upwards passage through Telok's ship was meeting with no resistance, either in the form of the crystal-form creatures or impassable architecture. While her father's servo-skull flitted ahead as a gleeful scout, she and the Cadians climbed the *Tomioka*'s cavernous internal chambers via chugging freight elevators haphazardly fixed to the walls with docking clamps, scaled vertical transit shafts on multiple ladders welded to the deck and scrambled up ramps of canted ceiling plates.

The crystalline panels sent their light deep into the heart of the ship, creating an airy, open feeling. Which was a novel sensation for Linya, who normally found being aboard a starship tiresomely claustrophobic, even one as vast as the *Speranza*.

She paused at a makeshift landing that looked out over a wide open space that had probably once been an embarkation deck. Light flooded the area through a series of opened docking hatches far across the chamber, through which gaseous mist billowed. The temperature gradient formed clouds in the upper reaches of the embarkation deck, and moisture fell through the interior in a soft shimmer of rain that patterned her hood with vapour trails.

'Don't think we should dawdle, Miss Tychon,' said a Cadian trooper whose shoulder patch identified him as Lieutenant Taybard Rae. 'Sooner we get you and your… friends to the bridge the sooner we can get out of here.'

Something in the soldier's manner was instantly disarming and Linya smiled within her environment hood. Like the Cadians, she was protected from the hostile conditions, but the technology keeping her alive was far more advanced: a self-generated, full-body integrity field and flexing cranial canopy with a multi-spectral sensorium.

'You don't like it in here?' asked Linya, looking through the glittering nitrogen rain. 'Sights like this do not come often. They need to be savoured.'

'Begging your pardon, Miss Tychon, but Captain Hawkins said we weren't here on a sightseeing trip. And trust me, you don't want to get his dander up when we're on a mission.'

Linya recalled Captain Hawkins from the regimental dinner she and her father attended in the Cadian billets. Her impression had been that Hawkins was a man of few words, though he had been coaxed to loquaciousness when toasting the fallen soldiers of Baktar III.

'He is a strict officer?' she asked.

Rae looked perplexed at the question. 'Aren't we all?' he said.

'I suppose so, though I confess I have only met a few.'

'Ach, he's not so bad,' said Rae, slinging his rifle and leaning out over the balcony. 'I've served under a lot of captains and colonels in my time, so when you get a good one, you try and keep him alive. You know what senior officers are like, miss, always trying to get themselves shot or blown up. They're like children really, they need their lieutenants to keep them out of trouble.'

Clearly deciding to take Linya's advice, Rae turned and rested his folded arms on the iron balustrade, taking in the splendour of the vista before him. 'Rain in a starship,' he said, shaking his helmeted head. 'Hell of a thing.'

'Yes, I don't think I've ever heard of such an occurrence,' said Linya.

'Makes you think though, eh?'

'About what?' asked Linya, when Rae didn't continue.

'About why you'd bring a ship all this way from the Emperor's light just to crash it on a world that's going to die,' said Rae, making room for one of the rearguard squads to pass, ten soldiers with rifles pulled in tight to their shoulders.

'So why do you think Telok did this?' asked Linya.

'You're asking me?' laughed Rae. 'I'm just a gruff, incredibly handsome and virile lieutenant, what do I know about tech stuff like that?'

'I don't know,' said Linya, gesturing to the misty cavern of the rotated chamber. 'You tell me.'

Rae grinned and tapped the side of his helmet.

'Well, whoever did this had himself a plan, right?' he asked. 'I mean, you don't go to all the effort of standing a starship on its arse for no reason. So I'm guessing this Telok fella, he knew Katen Venia was going to be destroyed sooner rather than later, yeah?'

'That would be a safe assumption, Lieutenant Rae.'

'Then it stands to reason that whatever he's got planned is going to happen soon,' said Rae, unlimbering his rifle. 'And whatever that is, I get the feeling that being inside this ship won't be the best place to be when it starts.'

To THOSE WITHOUT noospheric adaptations, the command deck of the *Speranza* was a cold steel elliptical chamber that looked nothing like the bridges of Naval ships of war. Silver-steel nubs jutted from the floor like unfinished structural columns, and a number of otherwise unremarkable command thrones were placed at apparently random locations.

But to the servitors hardwired into those gleaming nubs and the Mechanicus personnel manning each station, it was a far more dynamic place than the sterile steel and preserved timber compartments of starched Navy captains and their underlings. Thousands of shimmering veils of data light hung suspended in the air like theatrical curtains about to rise and spiralling arcs of information-rich light streamed from inload ports to be split by data prisms, diverted throughout the bridge and processed.

Magos Tarkis Blaylock sat in the command throne lately vacated by Archmagos Kotov. His black robes were etched with divine circuitry and his chasuble of zinc alloy was a fractally complex network of geometric designs and machine language. Green optics pulsed beneath his hood and streams of coolant vapour rose from him as though he were smouldering. His retinue of stunted dwarf-servitors fussed around him, rearranging his floodstream cables and regulating the flow of life-sustaining chemicals to his bio-mechanical body, a complex mix of proteins, amino acids, blessed oils and nutrient-dense lubricants.

As Fabricatus Locum, the *Speranza* was his to command in the absence of the archmagos – it was a task he relished. The sheer power of the Ark Mechanicus was unimaginable, a vast repository of knowledge and history that would take the Martian priesthood a thousand lifetimes to process.

Blaylock prided himself in his ability to assimilate enormous volumes of data, but just skimming his consciousness over the golden light of *Speranza*'s core spiritual mechanisms was enough to convince him that to descend into its neuromatrix would be to invite disaster. Necessity had forced the archmagos to enter the deep strata of the *Speranza*'s machine-spirit during the eldar attack, and Blaylock still did not know how he had managed to extricate himself from its impossibly complex lattice after securing its help.

Together with Vitali Tychon, who occupied an adjacent sub-command throne, Blaylock was engaged in fleet-wide operations that would normally require substantial Mechanicus personnel to handle. Vitali's floodstream betrayed his child-like wonderment at the data exloading from the surface, but Blaylock found something strangely *familiar* in its nature, as though he was somehow already aware of its content.

He dismissed the thought and turned his attention to a last strand of partitioned consciousness that was currently engaged in hunting the bondsmen who had instigated the interruption of servitude among the *Speranza*'s cyborg servitor crew. Each of the indentured workers collared on Joura had been implanted with fealty designators and should, in theory, be easily found.

But neither the senior magi nor constant sweeps of cybermastiffs and armsmen could locate Bondsmen Locke, Coyne and Hawke. Nor could they find any trace of the rogue overseer, Totha Mu-32, and the servitor said to have recovered its memories. Nor was their any evidence of the rumoured arco-flagellant Bondsman Locke was said to possess.

It was as if they had simply vanished.

Which, on a Mechanicus ship, was surely impossible.

Blaylock left that portion of his consciousness to keep searching, and returned to the business of running the *Speranza*. Between them, he and Vitali were maintaining the ship's position over Katen Venia's turbulent polar region, processing the surveyor readings exloaded from the surface, communicating along Manifold links with the senior commanders on the surface, optimising shipboard operations of over three million tertiary grade systems and coordinating the fleet manoeuvres in expectation of a cataclysmic stellar event.

The likelihood of Arcturus Ultra exploding in the immediate future was statistically remote, but the pace and fury of the reactions taking place in its nuclear heart were beyond measure; nothing could be taken for granted. As far as possible, Blaylock – with Magos Saiixek in Engineering's assistance – was keeping Katen Venia between the fleet and the dying star. If this star *did* go nova, a planet wasn't going to offer much in the way of protection, but it was better than nothing.

+So much information,+ said Vitali over their hardline link. +Wondrous, is it not? How often does one get to see the destruction of an entire planet this close?+

+I have overseen Exterminatus protocols on three worlds, Magos Tychon,+ said Blaylock. +I know what extinction level events comprise.+

+Ah, but this is a natural event, Tarkis. Completely different. Of course I have seen the after-effects of such events from the orbital galleries on Quatria, but to be here is something we won't soon forget.+

+We will not forget it at all,+ said Blaylock, irritated at Vitali's interruptions. +The data has already been recorded and the Mechanicus–+

+Never deletes anything,+ finished Vitali. +Yes, I am well aware of that tiresome truism, but to see an event like this first-hand is quite different, regardless of what you might be about to tell me about experiential bias.+

+Is there a point to this current discourse?+ asked Blaylock.

+The surveyor emissions from the surface are complex enough to process without having to divert additional processing capability to interpersonal discourse.+

Vitali nodded. +Yes, the sheer volume and complexity of what I am seeing is quite…+

The venerable magos broke off as a simulation he had running in the background finally reached its conclusion, coalescing in a bright sphere of glittering information. His multi-digit hands splayed it outwards, but Blaylock did not bother to inload whatever spurious experiment the stellar cartographer was running.

+Tarkis, were you aware of the electromagnetic discharges emanating from the *Tomioka* and the dissonant area of geostationary dead space above it?'

+I registered both items earlier, yes.+

+And what did you believe them to be?+

Blaylock brought up a cascade of discarded auspex junk, sifting through it with haptic sweeps of his hands, processing the information through a multitude of senses.

+Nothing more than irrelevant by-products of the chaotic systems within the atmosphere intersecting with rogue electromagnetic emissions from the planet's core. It has likely already been subsumed into the background radiation.+

+You are dead wrong, Tarkis,+ said Vitali.

Blaylock's floodstream surged with irritation he did not bother to modulate. +I am seldom wrong, Magos Tychon.+

+Seldom does not mean never, look again,+ said Vitali, sweeping a series of extrapolations and speculative interpretations of the surveyor inloads over to Blaylock's throne.

Blaylock digested the data, then brought up the backlogged surveyor data and ran it forward at speed to the present moment. As absurd as Vitali's conclusions were, it was hard to dismiss their inevitable logic.

+Are you sure about this?+ he asked.

+Sure enough to know that we need to get everyone off that planet,+ said Vitali.

+Yes, of course,+ agreed Blaylock. +When will it reach us?+

+My most accurate projection says two hours and fifty-four minutes.+

+Ave Deus Mechanicus!+ said Blaylock, sending a stream of imperative binary through the noosphere, Manifold and vox-networks. +Contact Kryptaestrex and have him prep every landing craft for immediate lift-off. Get everyone off that planet. Now!+

THE SPACE HAD once been the *Tomioka*'s enginarium, but that purpose had long since been sacrificed in service of another. The funicular transit elevator had carried them deep into the bedrock of the planet, their angle of descent taking them from walls of steel into regions stratified with aeons of geological change. When at last the elevator halted, it was immediately clear that the cathedrals of the engine spaces had been enlarged many times over by the simple expedient of drilling out the rock for kilometres in all directions.

An enormous cavern had been created beneath the *Tomioka* that extended far beyond the boundaries of the starship, but just how far was impossible to tell, for only the dimmest green light illuminated the cavernous space. The heat down here was immense, the air hazed with steam and ferocious temperatures radiating from the vast quantities of towering machinery that lined the walls.

Innumerable glowing green cables threaded the walls, coiled together like nests of snakes and pulsing with a hypnotic rhythm. Tens of thousands extended from the nearest machines, thousands more from others farther around the circumference of the immense cavern. Tangled masses of the cables all converged on a distant point where a dancing light glimmered in the half-darkness.

'What is this place?' asked Tanna.

'I do not know,' said Kotov, following the vanguard of skitarii towards the centre of the chamber. 'But whatever plan Telok had for his ship, this is the heart of it.'

'It has the look of the xenos to it,' said Tanna, and Kotov was forced to agree.

'It could be that Telok's crystal technologies incorporate alien technology,' suggested Dahan. 'Might that be how he finally succeeded in getting it to work?'

'That is certainly one possibility,' conceded Kotov.

Tanna raised a fist and his Space Marines dropped to their knees, each one with a weapon aimed.

Dahan was at his side in an instant.

'What is it, sergeant?'

'Battle robots ahead,' said Tanna. 'They're not moving, but look at the chests. There is something wrong with them.'

The Mechanicus advanced behind the Black Templars and Kotov saw Tanna was quite correct.

A maniple of immobile Conqueror battle robots in dusty armour of blue and red stood ranked up as though awaiting doctrina wafers. Their sunken heads stared unseeing at the floor and their weapon arms hung slack at their sides. Kotov counted five robots, each four metres tall, brutish and harshly angled, with rusted plates of ablative shielding crumbling at their shoulders.

In all respects but one, they appeared to be nothing more than relics of a long-ago war.

Each robot's chest cavity, where Kotov would expect to find its power source, was filled with finely woven crystalline filaments like the finest blown glass.

'This is the same crystal-form we fought above,' said Tanna, instantly bellicose.

Kotov raised a delicately machined hand. 'Be at peace, sergeant. These machines have not been active in hundreds, perhaps even thousands, of years.'

'That gives me no comfort,' said Tanna, gesturing to his fellow warriors. 'Destroy the crystals.'

'Wait!' cried Kotov. 'I cannot allow you to simply destroy Martian property.'

'And I cannot allow a potential threat to remain along our line of retreat.'

'Sergeant Tanna,' said Kotov, placing himself between the towering warrior and the battle robot. 'We did not come all this way just to vandalise the first piece of technology we do not yet understand. The discovery of new things is what brings us out here, yes?'

'It's what brought *you* out here, archmagos,' said Tanna. 'We came to honour a debt. I thought you understood that.'

Kotov shook his head and rested a hand on the nearest robot's arm. Rust flaked away and fragments of corroded metal drifted to the ground. 'These are Mechanicus artefacts, it would be a crime against the Omnissiah to defile them.'

'That crystal isn't Mechanicus,' said Dahan, standing alongside Tanna. 'That crystal is xenos technology, and the alien mechanism is a perversion of the True Path. *That's* what you are destroying, are you not, sergeant?'

The Space Marine nodded and an unheard order passed between him and his warriors.

Though Kotov was unhappy about such wanton destruction, he knew he had little choice but to accede to the Black Templars' tactical decision. Tanna put a fist through the lattice in the nearest robot's chest, the crystalline web shattering into powdered fragments. Within seconds the battle robot had its chest cavity emptied of crystal, and this act of destruction was a knife to Kotov's heart.

Dahan knelt beside one of the robots, where a scrap of loose cloth lay under its foot. He lifted it with the inactive prongs of his scarifiers, dust trickling from the folds like the ash of an ancient revenant.

'What is that?' asked Kotov.

'Some sort of robe,' said Dahan.

'Mechanicus?'

Dahan shook his head as the threads began to fray and the cloth fell apart. 'Too small.'

The scrap of cloth fell to the floor, now little more than coarse-woven threads that unravelled and rotted away even as they watched.

'There's more of them,' said Tanna, moving behind the robots. The Space Marine knelt beside another of the robes, this one with a semblance of a shape beneath it. No larger than a small child, it was swathed in identical rags, but as Tanna touched it, the robe lost its shape and puffs of dust sighed from its edges as whatever it concealed disintegrated.

Something gleamed beneath the rags, and Tanna sifted through the dust to retrieve it.

'What do you have there, sergeant?' asked Kotov.

'I'm not sure,' said Tanna. 'A mechanism of some sort.'

Tanna stood and held his discovery out to Kotov. A bent piece of metal, corroded and pitted with age, it had the look of a flintlock belonging to some primitive black powder weapon. Tanna held the shaped metal on the palm of his hand, but before Kotov could give it a closer examination, it crumbled to powder.

'Accelerated decay, perhaps a side effect of this world's dissolution,' said Dahan.

'Perhaps,' said Kotov, pushing deeper into the chamber. 'But a mystery for later on, I think.'

Leaving the ancient robots and rotted fabric forms behind, Kotov pushed deeper into the chamber, seeing yet more isolated groups of rusted battle robots deeper in the shadows either side of their route of march. Soon it became clear that the centre of the chamber was directly beneath the *Tomioka*, as the chamber's roof changed from bare rock to the cross-section of a gutted starship.

Structural hull members, tens of metres thick, stood like vast pillars at the entrance to a templum. Once beyond this permeable barrier, Kotov saw a vast circular chasm had been excavated at the base of the starship. At least five hundred metres in diameter, its edge was delineated by hundreds of thousands of the faintly glowing cables that plunged into its depths. What looked like a vast data prism hung down from the ceiling formed by the *Tomioka*, resembling an enormous spear-point fashioned from a single block of ice.

But it was the flickering globe suspended over the exact centre of the shaft that commanded Kotov's full attention.

A ball of greenish fire hung in the air like an emerald sun caught in an invisible force field. Its surface rippled with coruscating lines of force, as though formed from viscous fluids stirred by internal tides. No part of Kotov's sensorium could measure its dimensions, mass or density, and had he relied on any input beyond his optics, he would never know the object was there at all.

'What is that?' asked Tanna.

'Some kind of reactor?' ventured Dahan.

'Perhaps,' said Kotov, rechecking the passive augurs worked

into the armoured body he wore. Whatever the object was, it was beyond his ability to measure, and what readings he *was* getting were fluctuating meaninglessly, as though the object was transitioning from one state of being to another at any given moment. His chronometric readings flatlined, as though caught within the temporal null of a stasis bubble.

Kotov tore his gaze from the nuclear green fire and stared down into a bottomless black abyss as Dahan manoeuvred his skitarii around this segment of the shaft. Kotov saw no obvious means of descending into the chasm, but counted that as fortunate, feeling a strange sense of observation rising from its depths.

'Whatever this place is, it is clear that Telok never intended this ship to fly again,' said Kotov, perching precariously at the chasm's edge. 'The engines have been completely dismantled.'

'Why would Telok have done that?' asked Tanna.

Kotov had no answer for him and pulled away from the vertiginous shaft as the visible circumference of the shimmering green orb suddenly expanded, doubling its diameter in the blink of an eye. The tides within its unknown structure grew more violent and the light pouring from it filled the chamber with searing brightness.

'What's happening, archmagos?' demanded Tanna, backing away from the object.

Kotov had no firm evidence upon which to base his answer, but there could be only one possible explanation.

'Whatever Telok has planned for the *Tomioka*. It's happening now.'

THE MACHINE-SPIRIT AT the heart of the *Tomioka* was sluggish and hostile to Linya's enquiries, not that she could blame so venerable a machine for reacting badly to an unknown presence in its neuromatrix after so long a time spent dormant. They had reached the bridge; it was exactly where they had expected it to be, and Captain Hawkins's Cadians had secured it without incident. Linya had been surprised at how little its structure appeared to have been altered, given the nature of the rest of the ship, though it was, of course, turned through ninety degrees.

Servitors sat strapped into their consoles, and a number of battle robots were still mag-locked in place within their defence alcoves; beyond the thick layers of dust that had accumulated on numerous surfaces, it felt like the bridge crew might return at any moment.

While Azuramagelli and her father's servo-skull attempted to access the ship's avionics log, Galatea made a circuit of those areas of the bridge it could traverse. Linya hunted for a compatible inload port she could reach and which matched the quaintly archaic interface augmetic in the palm of her hand. If there was any data to be salvaged from the ship's data core, she would dig it out.

Incredibly, the ship's cogitators and deep logic engines were still functional, maintained by a dim, slumbering spirit that rested in the deep strata of cogitation. Connection to the data-engines was made via a simple series of Mechanicus hails, but she would need to go deep to find anything of value.

Linya closed her eyes, letting her functional awareness flow farther into the *Tomioka*'s datasphere, feeling the presence of numerous security screens and invasive protection algorithms marshalling at her continued presence. She tested their integrity with gently inquiring probes that were rebuffed without exception.

'Only to be expected,' she said, tapping out a binaric mantra with her left hand.

She tried a more direct approach, shaping her interrogative with aggressive signifiers of rank and demand protocols. Once again, the data-engine rejected her attempt and sent a painful jolt of bio-feedback through Linya's hand. Not enough to hurt, but enough to remind her that she was not authorised to access this ship's records.

The machine-spirit's defences resisted her every attempt at infiltration until she registered the presence of an inloaded code-breaking algorithm that carried the noospheric tags of Magos Blaylock. Linya had no memory of receiving such an inload, but couldn't deny its usefulness right about now.

She opened the inloaded data packet and let out a soft gasp at the geometric complexity of the algorithms worked into the code. Tarkis Blaylock was another tech-priest it was hard to like, but his grasp of hexamathic calculus and statistical analysis was second to none; this looked like the most perfect binaric skeleton key she had ever seen. Like a hound on the hunt, the decryption algorithm meshed seamlessly with the *Tomioka*'s datasphere, and the security systems woven around the info-logs fell away like mist before a hurricane.

Almost immediately, Linya realised her mistake.

A tsunami of stellar information poured into her and she let out a cry of terror as the data-burden overloaded her neural capacity in a heartbeat. She tried to pull away from the ship's flow of information, but like a victim of electrocution, she found she could not disengage from the very thing that was killing her. Numerous implants in her skull shorted out, one after the other, and Linya convulsed as the bio-electric feedback vaporised thousands of synaptic connections within the architecture of her brain.

Just as the data-burden surged with an even larger packet of impossibly dense celestial calculus, Linya felt herself torn from the data-engine with a physical jolt and a searing blaze of disconnection agonies. She hit the floor, wrapped in Lieutenant Rae's arms, dizzying vertigo seizing her.

Her hands flew to the sides of her head as pounding waves of shrieking pain stabbed through her skull like an instant migraine. Blinding light filled her eyes, and sickening nausea cramped in her gut. She heard her father's voice through the ebon skull, the gleaming red optics hovering just before her face, but couldn't process what she was hearing.

Shouted voices surrounded her.

'Mistress Tychon,' said Rae. 'Begging your pardon, but are you all right?'

She tried to nod, but rolled onto her side and vomited the contents of her stomach instead.

Linya felt the presence of something clanking and metallic moving past her and pushed herself upright in time to see Galatea plugging itself into the smoking inload port.

The silver-eyed proxy body turned to regard her slumped form.

'One mind cannot handle this data-burden,' said Galatea. 'Only we can do this.'

The surging pain in Linya's skull receded a fraction and she pulled herself upright on wobbling legs, feeling an unaccountable need to stop the machine from taking her place. Lieutenant Rae supported her, and she clung to him to keep from falling.

'What's happening?' she asked, straining to regain her senses and mental equilibrium.

'Don't know, miss,' said Rae, bringing his lasgun around as Cadian battle-cant filled the bridge and the bridge's defence robots climbed from their alcoves. Linya saw their chests were alight with a curious green illumination, their weapons systems coming online one after another.

Gunfire and shouts filled the bridge.

Microcontent 09

BOTH WAR MACHINES were vigilant, stalking the icy plains around the *Tomioka* like wary predators circling dangerous prey that may or may not be playing dead. *Amarok* was still feisty after the fight in the canyon, its guns and voids restored, and Princeps Vintras allowed its virile machine-spirit to come to the fore in the Manifold.

He looped over the trail of *Vilka,* carefully avoiding the deep tracks the Ironwood was leaving in the crystalline structure of the glassy plateau. It took finesse to walk a Warhound like this, sidestepping and moving forwards at the same time. He kept his targeting auspex loose, letting the aiming reticule drift back and forth in search of something to kill.

Vintras was getting twitchy too, the result of a potent cocktail of drugs pumped into his system after the fight with the facsimile engines. Word had come down that they were some form of machine-tech that could mould the crystalline structures of the dying world into the shapes of elements they perceived as threats.

The ground underfoot was unstable, the Warhound's complex stabilisation sensors perceiving an ever-growing, ever-spreading wave of seismic tremors building from far beneath the ground. Which was only to be expected; this world was dying after all, being pulled apart by geological stresses and celestial cataclysm. Such disturbances were only going to get worse and the surface of Katen Venia would soon become untenable for Titan engines.

With its boarders delivered, *Lupa Capitalina* had retreated from the towering form of the *Tomioka* and taken up an unmoving position before the starship. Even after the Wintersun's attack on Moonsorrow, there was still something magnetic about the vast scale of the Warlord, a potential for such awesome destruction that transcended all notions of morality. Just to share the battlefield with a Warlord was an honour, and to be pack with a god-machine of its power was to be a part of history. Yet for all that Vintras revered the incredible Titan, the idea of remaining static was anathema to him. As much as he longed to rise within the ranks of the Legio, he was loath to consider the possibility of leaving *Amarok* for a battle-engine that won wars by marching straight at the enemy.

'Are you hearing this?' asked Elias Härkin, intruding on Vintras's thoughts. The *Vilka*'s princeps's voice was gruff and had been augmetically rendered for decades, but hearing it over the vox only made it more unpleasant.

'Hearing what?' asked Vintras, irritated he'd allowed his mind to wander.

'The Mechanicus,' snapped Härkin.

'What about them?'

'Call yourself a Warhound driver?' asked Härkin. 'Use your damned eyes and open your vox!'

Vintras slewed *Amarok* to the side, increasing his pace and weaving across the landscape to circle around the *Tomioka* as the ground shook with another earth tremor, this one more powerful than the last. Vintras compensated, keeping the Warhound's centre of gravity low until he completed his circuit of the landed starship.

In the aftermath of the Legio's rescue of the Space Marines and skitarii, the Land Leviathans and support vehicles had poured over the bridge and onto the edge of the plateau, where they waited like observers too afraid to approach the object of their scrutiny.

Vintras switched his vox-input to accept non-Legio traffic, and immediately the Manifold flooded with prioritised threat warnings and withdrawal orders coming direct from the *Speranza*.

'What the hell's going on?' asked Vintras.

'What does it bloody look like?' grunted Härkin. 'They're leaving.'

THE INFORMATIONAL FLOW through the *Speranza*'s bridge had increased significantly, but the gathered magi, calculus-logi and lexmechanics were still able to handle the data-burden. Largely thanks to the coordinating power of Magos Blaylock, whose higher thought processes were streamlined to render such vast arrays of data into manageable chunks.

'Word from the surface?' asked Blaylock.

'Evacuation has begun,' said a magos whose identity signifiers were lost in the haze of noospheric data filling the bridge. 'The first Leviathan is en route to the landing fields. The others are aligning behind it and are in the process of crossing Magos Kryptaestrex's bridge.'

Blaylock turned to Vitali Tychon, who encompassed the

Manifold links within his datasphere to coordinate the logistical nightmare of an emergency planetary withdrawal.

'Vitali,' said Blaylock, his urgency prompting him to dispense with titles and protocol. 'How long before the energy source reaches the planet?'

'One hour, thirteen minutes, Tarkis,' said Vitali Tychon, without needing to look up. 'Still no word from the archmagos or my daughter. Neither has responded to the summons back to the ship.'

Hearing the worry in the venerable magos's voice, Blaylock said, 'Keep trying.'

Blaylock brought up the system plot that displayed the fleet's position around Katen Venia and the approaching energy source hurtling through space towards them.

No, not towards *them*, towards the *Tomioka*.

Too late, he now realised what Telok's flagship was and why the Lost Magos had gone to the trouble of landing it in the first place. Together with the infinitesimal concavity of the plateau, the entire structure of the *Tomioka* was a vast receiver array: a hundred kilometres wide receiver that would channel a surging stream of unimaginable energy through its structure and into the planet's core. The purpose of this was still a mystery, but that anything nearby would be instantly obliterated was all too obvious.

Vitali was running a back-trace to the source of the energy beam, but it would take time to locate it amid the ferocious amount of background radiation from the dying star. Even trying to measure the beam was proving to be next to impossible, its qualities all but unknown to their auspex and of greater magnitude than could be readily quantified.

That such an unimaginable quantity of energy could travel so far without losing its power to the vacuum was staggering.

Blaylock knew of only one thing said to be capable of such a monumental feat of power generation.

The Breath of the Gods.

GUNFIRE ECHOED WEIRDLY within the chamber as the Black Templars bracketed one of the rusted battle robots with carefully coordinated bolter shots. With the swelling of the seething energy globe, a measure of its tidal energies had bloomed throughout the cavern in a single pulse of atmospheric power transfer.

Numerous skitarii had collapsed, their enhanced neural pathways blown out by the blast – even Dahan had staggered with the force of it. The nature of the power transfer hadn't been immediately obvious, but when the first sawing blasts of autocannon fire tore through the skitarii, its purpose became self-evident.

The battle robots left to rust throughout the cavern were no dusty relics of a forgotten conflict, but dormant sentries, tasked with waiting until such a time as they would be required to defend the arcane processes under way. The crystalline lattice worked into the robots' chest cavities pulsed with necrotic green light, and despite their advanced state of disrepair, each moved and fought as if fresh from the forge.

A maniple had come at them at battle pace, but Dahan killed the first one with a beam of white heat from his plasma gun. Skitarii weaponry broke apart the second, and a broadside of bolter explosions shattered the third into a storm of metallic junk.

'I told you we should have destroyed them all,' said Tanna, walking backwards as he slammed a fresh magazine into his bolter.

'Duly noted,' said Kotov, cycling through his implanted

weaponry until he came up with a tight-beam graviton gun. More of the robot maniples were closing in from all sides, and via Magos Dahan's threat-optimisers he saw at least sixty more approaching.

Kotov knelt and directed his implanted weaponry towards the nearest robot, triggering an invisible beam of intense gravometric energies. The robot, a clankingly archaic design of Cataphract, crumpled and bent double as its upper section was suddenly quadrupled in mass. Its already rusted spine collapsed under the weight and it fell in a welter of spilled oil and buckled plates.

Autocannon shells killed more of the skitarii, but no warrior was left behind. As they had against the crystal beasts, Dahan's men brought their dead and wounded with them. The robots had bigger guns and there were more of them, but they were slow and did not have the fire discipline of the skitarii.

Every metre of their retreat was earned in blood. Once beyond the structural elements of the *Tomioka*, there was no shelter and no strategy except flight. Kotov's implanted auspex registered another power surge from the energy sphere, and once again its diameter swelled, almost filling the width of the shaft over which it was suspended. The blaze of light from the emerald sun's depths filled the cavernous space beneath the *Tomioka*, and the tip of the glittering prism above it was less than ten metres from making contact. Kotov had no idea whether that would be a bad thing or not, but the part of him that relished symmetry and connectivity in things suspected that when it and the seething energy globe came into contact, it would be very unpleasant to be anywhere nearby.

Kotov crushed the chests of another ten robots with his graviton beams before the internal capacitors registered power loss. To fire it again, he would need to divert power from some other system. Instead, Kotov retracted the exotic weapon and cycled through to a more mundane rotary cannon. The design was an old one, a modified Dreadnought weapon that had been deemed too flimsy for deployment with Adeptus Astartes forces, but which Kotov liked for its brutal simplicity. The backplate of his body rotated to reveal louvred vents, and a long bullet-chain extended from his arm to link with an internal ammunition chamber.

Recoil compensators deployed along Kotov's shoulders and legs as a series of readiness icons flashed before his eyes. Kotov slaved his targeting arrays to inloaded threat data from Dahan, and pushed his consciousness into a higher state before opening fire.

A blazing stream of fire tore from Kotov's arm, fully three metres long, and whatever it touched simply exploded in a haze of torn-up metal and shattered plates. Each burst was precisely controlled, and it seemed that Kotov could see every shell, his cognitive functions moving so swiftly that he could watch each explosion in slow motion, switch targets and engage the enemy without wasting a single round of ammunition.

All around him, the Space Marines and skitarii were moving like figures in a slow-running pict-feed, their motions painfully measured. Sounds reached him at a glacial rate, and even the light of explosions and muzzle flare seemed to expand like slow-blooming flowers. Wherever Dahan registered a threat, Kotov swung his weapon to bear and eliminated it with a precise burst of high-explosive shells.

Waves of excess heat from such increased cognition were dispersed through coolant flow across his scalp, but such an overclocking could only be maintained for a minute of subjective time at most and he was almost at his limit.

In the end it was Kotov's ammunition that gave out first, and the spinning barrels clicked dry as the ammo hopper sought in vain to keep the tide of shells coming. Kotov felt the urge to keep going, to switch out to another weapon. To process information and stimuli with such speed was intoxicating, a wholly addictive feat of cognition that had seen more than one adept of the Mechanicus boil the organic portions of his brain within his skull. Kotov disengaged the rapid-thought functions and staggered as the searing heat in his skull temporarily overwhelmed him. The energy demands on his body, which ran to narrow enough tolerances as it was, suddenly found themselves with an unsustainable deficit.

Kotov's limbs folded up beneath him, but before he hit the ground, Sergeant Tanna caught him and hauled him back, firing his bolter one-handed as he went. Kotov tried to speak, but the pain in his skull was too intense, the chronic drain on his mental faculties shutting down all non-essential functions as they fought to restore order in his synaptic arrays.

He was dimly aware of more robots closing in on their position, but he could not make out how many or how far away they were. He saw Dahan firing his implanted weapon, surrounded by perhaps thirty skitarii warriors, some wounded, some bearing the bodies of the dead. The Black Templars fell back behind relentless salvos of bolter fire, halting a battle robot with each one.

'Quite a feat of arms,' said Tanna, depositing him by the controls of the funicular transit elevator and turning to haul the lever into the up position. 'I thought you said *I* was the warrior.'

'An explorator must be prepared for all eventualities,' said Kotov, finally regaining the power of speech as the elevator rumbled back up into the *Tomioka*. 'And I am not a man to travel lightly.'

With Lieutenant Rae supporting her, Linya scrambled down the length of the starship, breathless and fighting the building agony in her head. The fight on the bridge had been brief, bloody and one-sided, with the Cadian troopers hopelessly outgunned by an enemy they couldn't hope to hurt. Captain Hawkins had seen the futility of staying to fight and immediately ordered the retreat.

A squad of Guardsmen had covered their retreat, and even amid the confusion of being pulled from the bridge, Linya knew those soldiers were already dead. Heavy calibre shells tore the bridge to pieces, smashing ancient technology that had crossed the galaxy in search of wonder. One robot, its right arm a pulverising siege hammer, had smashed through bulkhead after bulkhead, shrugging off Cadian return fire from lasrifles, grenade launchers and even a direct hit from a plasma gun.

Sixty men and women fell back from the bridge, keeping their pursuers at bay with ambushes and traps. One robot was pitched into a shaft that looked as though it ran the length of the starship's long axis, and another had its leg blown off by a lucky grenade that managed to lodge in its pelvic joint. But the others were utterly relentless and Linya was forced to admire the lethal purity of whoever had punched the obedience routines of their doctrina wafers.

It felt like they were running at reckless speeds back the way they had come, pursued by at least five Imperial battle robots with curious crystalline power sources in their chests that closely resembled what Magos Dahan had described on the *Tabularium*. Magos Azuramagelli led the way back down the *Tomioka*, his mental mapping unfazed by the danger threatening them and his body-plan altering and reshaping with a speed Linya found incredible.

Her father's servo-skull zipped alongside her, pausing every now and then to check behind it before scooting after her. She could hear his voice urging her onwards, but shut it out as a distraction. Somewhere along the way they'd lost Galatea, the machine intelligence fleeing along a different route when it could no longer follow the same line of retreat. Linya wondered if it would manage to escape and found she didn't care either way.

The ground shifted beneath her, and she sprawled to the ground as the welded deck plate serving as a floor pulled free from the wall. Rae pulled her roughly to her feet, all trace of his former concern for decorum forgotten in this flight from the enemy.

'I can't go on,' she gasped.

'Can't be stopping, miss,' said Rae, pushing her through a group of covering soldiers as they clambered over to a welded screw-stair. 'At least these steps will slow the bastards up.'

Linya scrambled down the stairs, hearing chugging *bangs* of rapid bolter fire echoing above her. Too loud and too fast for a regular bolter, these were rounds that would reduce the human body to an expanding vortex of vaporised blood and cooked flesh. Screams followed the thudding booms of detonation, howls of pain that no human should ever have to make.

Tears ran down her face as she all but sprinted down the stairs, clutching the iron balustrade and remaining upright only by the grace of the Omnissiah. Close to the bottom, her luck ran out and her feet slid on the cold metal of the stairs. She fell from the last few steps onto the buckled metal of the walkway below. She rolled and grabbed onto the nearest spar of metal as the nitrogen rain of the embarkation deck soaked her.

'Come on!' shouted Rae, leaping from the last few steps. 'It's right behind us!'

The ceiling sagged inwards under the force of a titanic hammerblow as something immense sought to bring down the stairs. Rae hauled her upright again as another blow struck the top of the stairs, accompanied by a screeching wail of dumb binaric fury. Rae backed into her and lifted his rifle, firing back up the stairwell on full auto, a blazing spread of crimson bolts that hissed as they left the focus ring of the barrel.

'A lasrifle won't harm a battle robot,' said Linya.

'Maybe not, miss, but if you've got a better idea, I'm all ears!'

He grabbed Linya by the shoulders and pushed her away as the stairwell buckled inwards and the blocky form of a Castellan battle robot crashed down onto the walkway behind them. The floor crumpled beneath its weight and a storm of debris cascaded over its hunched form. Rae went down under the ruptured service conduits and shattered steelwork, his lasrifle skittering over the canted walkway towards her.

The robot had landed on one knee and now rose to its full height of nearly four metres. Its heavy bolter ratcheted from the protective cowling at its shoulder and its power fist crackled with deadly disruptive field energies. The Castellan's armoured plating was scorched with las-burns and impact trauma. Its threat optics fastened on her with hostile intent.

Her father's servo-skull flitted in front of the robot, screeching deactivation codes spilling from its augmitter, but the weaponised machine simply swatted it aside. The skull cracked into a wall and dropped stone dead to the floor, the light fading from its optics.

Linya wanted to bend to retrieve Rae's rifle, but terror held her pinned to the spot.

She heard someone shout her name as the heavy bolter swung out, the automated slide racking back as it prepared to fire.

Linya closed her eyes and slid down the wall, but the shots never came.

She felt cold hands pull her upright and fell into the arms of her rescuer.

'We would not let such a primitive creation harm you, Mistress Tychon,' said Galatea.

Linya flinched and pushed herself away from the machine intelligence, repulsed beyond words at the thought of it touching her. Galatea's palanquin body squatted close to the ground, its oddly jointed legs twisted around to bring it so low. The silver-eyed tech-priest body rose up as she backed away from it.

'Get away from me,' she said.

'Such ingratitude,' said Galatea. 'And after we risked our continued existence to rescue you.'

Linya blinked away tears and turned to see the Castellan robot unmoving, its head sagging to one side with green-tinged fumes pouring from its contoured skull. Its chestplate belched smoke and the warlike binary that spalled from its weapons was silent.

It was utterly dead.

'How did you...?' asked Linya, looking up through the rent torn in the ceiling to see another battle robot with smoke belching from its innards.

'If we can take control of the *Speranza*, do you believe that overloading the cortex-doctrinas of a maniple of battle robots is beyond us?'

'I don't understand,' said Linya, as Cadian soldiers ran back to dig Rae from the debris. The lieutenant was bleeding from a cut on his forehead, but was already shouting at the men helping him that he was fine and to damn well leave him be.

'You are too wondrous to be allowed to die,' said Galatea, reaching out to stroke her cheek.

Linya pulled away from its repellent touch. 'Don't touch me,' she said. 'Not ever.'

The machine intelligence rose up, the brains on its palanquin flickering with frantic synaptic activity as some unheard communion passed between them.

'As you wish,' said Galatea. 'But you are precious to us.'

Linya backed away from the loathsome creature, and pausing only to recover her father's servo-skull, she followed the Cadians back down the *Tomioka*.

KOTOV COULD REMEMBER little of the journey back up the *Tomioka*, his mental processes too traumatised by the strain of maintaining so rapid a cognition speed. It had been short by mortal reckoning, but a lifetime by the terms of measurement employed by the Mechanicus. Tanna carried him most of the way, all but dragging his armoured body up ramps, stairs and ladders. The remodelled interior of the ship passed in a blur, but even his blunted senses registered that something unprecedented was under way.

Portions of the *Tomioka*'s internal anatomy were reshaping themselves moment by moment. What he had mistaken for structural modifications to allow the vessel to stand upright were in fact carefully placed moving parts that were now fulfilling some unknowable function.

'Imperator,' said Tanna, as they passed through a vaulted compartment that had once been an ordnance magazine. 'So many of them.'

Kotov lifted his head and followed Tanna's gaze, seeing a multitude of reflective panels of machined steel rotated into predetermined positions and vast lengths of cable extruded from vacuum-sealed compartments before being fitted into place by a veritable army of floating servo-skulls. Thousands of the gold and silver-chased skulls filled the compartment, more than Kotov had ever seen in one place.

'It's like the crew chose to remain behind and carry on their duties...' he said, the words coming only with difficulty.

'Or were forced to,' said Dahan, following behind them. 'Who knows how long these skulls have been here, just waiting for this moment?'

As fascinating as Kotov found it watching the thousands of skulls at work, Tanna dragged him ever upwards through the reconfiguring interiors. The dull green light that had illuminated their downward passage had been replaced by a stark brightness that shone from every polished plate and every overtaxed lumen. Vast arrays of structural steelwork rotated into place throughout the enlarged voids within the *Tomioka*, like the pylons of some planetary power generation system. Towering conduits unfolded from irising compartments and the interior volume of the starship's long axis was rapidly filling with complex machinery that spun, pulsed and throbbed with imminent activity.

Eventually, Kotov felt the pressure differential of an outside environment and looked up.

A flattened oval tunnelled through the violet-tinted ice told him they had reached the entry point cut by the superheated mechanisms of *Lupa Capitalina*'s plasma destructor. Black Templars stood at the far end of the tunnel, waving at something he couldn't see. Dimly he registered the sounds of artillery fire and high-energy weapon discharges.

Magos Dahan stood with the Adeptus Astartes warriors and Kotov took a moment to realise that there were more people around him than he remembered.

Cadian soldiers lined the walls and Kotov's floodstream surged with relief as he saw Magos Azuramagelli and Linya

Tychon near the far entrance to the ice-tunnel. Galatea stood at the opposite side of the tunnel, and even in his limited state of awareness, Kotov read the tension between it and his magi.

Linya Tychon limped over to him, clutching a jet-black servo-skull.

For a moment, Kotov was confused at the sight of the skull. Had she stopped to procure herself one belonging to the *Tomioka*? Then he read the faint binaric sigils on its polished dome and realised the servo-skull belonged to Vitali Tychon.

'Archmagos,' said Linya, her face bruised and swollen. 'We have to leave. Now.'

'I think that is self-evident,' he said, finally managing to stand under his own power as his bodily control returned to a semblance of normality. 'This ship is reconfiguring itself in some most disconcerting ways.'

'No, I mean we have to leave this planet,' said Linya. 'In an hour it is going to be destroyed.'

'Come now, you are being melodramatic,' said Kotov, feeling more of his synaptic architecture re-establishing itself. 'It will take months or years for the star's death to fully dismantle this world and there is much we can yet learn.'

Linya's eyes narrowed. 'Haven't you been receiving Magos Blaylock's evacuation orders?'

Kotov hadn't, but as more and more of his systems reset, he began picking out desperate bursts of communication transmitted from orbit via the *Tabularium*. Though it sent a flare of pain through his skull, Kotov processed the most urgent of them in three pico seconds.

'This is a sacrificial planet,' said Linya. 'I don't know all of what's happening, but that much I do know. This ship is a giant receiver array, and the power that is about to be channelled through it is going to tear this planet apart for some purpose I can't even begin to imagine.'

Kotov nodded, and marched towards the end of the tunnel.

Lupa Capitalina walked in all its war-finery, sheathed in the blistering envelope of voids that shimmered with rainbow hues as they dissipated the energies of a recent attack. Like a vast sauropod of the plains being attacked by raptor packs, the Warlord was surrounded by smaller, crystalline representations of its godly might. Bright green bolts of light shot from the glittering forms of its attackers, but the Warlord was no lumbering herbivore just waiting to be dragged down, it was the alpha of a deadly hunter pack.

'I wouldn't believe it if I wasn't seeing it with my own eyes,' said a Cadian captain by the name of Hawkins. 'I didn't think they could move like that.'

A lieutenant with half his face covered in blood answered Hawkins, 'I'm thinking I took a bigger blow to the head than I thought.'

Kotov would normally have thought to rebuke mere Guardsmen for disparaging the capabilities of a Mechanicus battle-engine, but even he was shocked at the speed and agility with which Princeps Arlo Luth was manoeuvring *Lupa Capitalina*. More often used as strongpoints, fire-bases or points from which to launch assaults, Warlord Titans were not highly mobile war-engines.

Clearly the Wintersun did not hold to that view.

The Legio Sirius pack fought as one entity, *Amarok* and *Vilka* snapping at the heels of their alpha as it advanced, retreated and sidestepped every attack. It moved in close to its attackers and crushed them beneath its clawed feet. It sawed a dozen to shards with gatling fire and vaporised half as many again with stabbing lances from its turbo-destructors. Its rapidly moving bulk shattered dozens more and it achieved this without losing its voids to the criss-crossing trails of enemy fire.

'Is it coming to pick us up?' asked Hawkins. 'The Titan, it's coming back for us, right?'

'Yes, captain,' said Kotov, already having broadcast an extraction request. '*Lupa Capitalina* is coming back for us.'

Kotov saw Hawkins's desire to witness the god-machine at war was pulling against his Cadian duty to his men. He allowed the man an indulgence.

'Stay,' said Kotov. 'Watch. To see a Titan in battle is to know the true power of the Omnissiah.'

Hawkins nodded and said, 'I've watched artillery batteries reduce greenskin fortresses to ruin in minutes, seen ten thousand charging Whiteshields on horseback and been part of orbital assaults that captured an entire planet in less than a day, but seeing a Warlord in action… that's something special.'

'And Legio Sirius are masters of their art,' said Kotov in a rare moment of largesse.

Lupa Capitalina turned, as though hearing its Legio name mentioned, and set off at a steady, rolling pace towards the *Tomioka*. Its attendant Warhounds followed, loping ahead to clear the way with punishing blasts of fire and howls of warning.

Kotov steadied himself as the war-engine came closer, the thunderous reverberations of its colossal footfalls transmitted to the *Tomioka* even through the immense sheath of ice surrounding it. He and everyone else within the tunnel backed away as it drew nearer, for even the approach of an allied battle-engine was an event of some danger.

'Everyone up and ready to move!' shouted Hawkins. 'We're only going to get one shot at this.'

The Warlord's voids impacted upon the ice at the edge of the tunnel, sending deep cracks racing along the ceiling and floor.

Crystalline shards fell like broken glass and shrieking bursts of exploding ice rippled along the length of the tunnel until the void shields finally dropped. The assault ramps slammed down onto a broken ledge of ice, and Titan menials in orange boiler suits and armoured vests yelled at them to get aboard.

Dahan and his surviving skitarii escorted Kotov and Azuramagelli, while the Black Templars and Cadians were last to board the war machine. Kotov had a moment's vertigo as he looked down between the lip of the assault ramp and the crumbling edge of the ice. His internal systems quickly compensated for the unwelcome sensation as menials hauled him aboard.

A tremendous impact rocked the Warlord, and even from here, Kotov felt the repercussive pain of its wounding. Engaged in this rescue mission, *Lupa Capitalina* was horribly exposed with its voids down and its weapon systems useless. The crystalline engines were taking full advantage of that, and explosions of green fire erupted all across the Titan's rear quarters. Both *Amarok* and *Vilka* were keeping the enemy from surrounding their pack leader, but they could not protect it from the terrible fire raking its unshielded flanks.

Kotov gripped the edge of the battlements tightly as *Lupa Capitalina* wrenched itself free of the ice and took a lurching backward step. The assault ramps were still down and two menials screamed as they fell from the open structure. Cadian soldiers ran to help in getting the ramps raised as the Warlord took another step, twisting on its axis as it did so. The walk to the *Tomioka* was made at a stately pace, but the Wintersun was in battle now; the insects crawling on its hull were of secondary importance to its own survival.

The logic was undeniable, though it gave Kotov no comfort to *be* one of those insects.

A hundred metres now separated the Warlord and the *Tomioka*, and Kotov saw that the transformations he had witnessed within the starship were being mirrored on its exterior. The crystalline growths on its hull were expanding organically to sheathe the entire upper reaches of the hull in what looked like a caul of glittering glass.

A flare of static blinded him momentarily as *Lupa Capitalina's* carapace void pylons ignited and clad the Titan in layers of ablative energies. The clashing harmonics and belligerent frequencies were antithetical to his implants, but Kotov was grateful for the protection.

+Archmagos Kotov,+ said a voice that cut into his mind with icy disdain. +Are you secure?+

'I am,' he replied, sending his words into the caustic tundra of the Sirius Manifold.

+Then we are ready,+ said Princeps Arlo Luth.

'Ready? Ready for what?'

+To abandon this world.+

Microcontent 10

WATCHING KATEN VENIA'S last moments was a moment of great sadness for Roboute Surcouf. He had named this world and it was never easy to watch something beautiful die. Roboute remembered the girl whose name the planet shared, wondering if he would ever see her again and silently berated himself for so maudlin a thought.

Sickly bands of variegated light enveloped the planet in traceries of continent-wide lightning storms like a vast net cast around its splintering mass. The brightest point of light was centred on the northern pole, where the abortive expedition to the *Tomioka* had foundered. The evacuation of Katen Venia was over, with the majority of the embarked crew already back aboard the *Speranza*.

The Mechanicus had been forced to discard a great deal of materiel and resources in the flight from the surface, of which the Land Leviathans – *Krakonoš*, *Adamastor* and *Fortis Maximus* – were the most grievous loss. Much of their crew, adepts, tech-priests and menials alike, had chosen to remain with their machines rather than abandon them, and those men were almost certainly dead.

Roboute shook his head at their stupidity before remembering that, until recently, he had always believed that he would die aboard the *Renard*. He had survived his brush with death after the grav-sled had been winched to safety by the *Tabularium*'s docking clamp and a team of medicae had strapped an oxygen mask to his face. Adara was unhurt, as was Magos Pavelka, which – given the frantic nature of their excursion to the surface – was nothing short of a miracle.

The bridge of the *Speranza* was thronged with the senior members of the Kotov expedition: Mechanicus, Adeptus Astartes and Imperial Guard, drawn together to watch the final moments of Katen Venia and the loss of everything they had crossed the galaxy to discover. Azuramagelli was once again ensconced by the navigation arrays, with Kryptaestrex plugged in next to him. Vitali Tychon kept close to his daughter, a protective arm around her shoulder. From the bruises on her face, it seemed the excursions into the *Tomioka* had been as plagued by trouble as events outside.

Galatea stood in the centre of the command bridge, its low-slung palanquin connected to the *Speranza* in ways Roboute couldn't begin to imagine. Pavelka had given him a rough idea of the heretical reality of Galatea, and the concept of a thinking machine gave Roboute cold chills whenever he thought of the onward implications.

Archmagos Kotov himself sat upon his command throne, looking like an exhausted king at the end of his reign and surrounded by courtiers just waiting for him to die. Hard on the heels of that thought, Roboute's gaze shifted to Tarkis Blaylock, who stood at Kotov's shoulder like a plotting vizier.

He had no reason to suspect Blaylock of any such ambitions, but the image – once imagined – was hard to shake.

Roboute himself reclined in the noospheric-enabling chair he had occupied the last time he had come to the bridge, connected to the ship's vast datasphere by inload sockets in the back of his neck. The vast majority of what this enabled him to see was meaningless lingua-technis or binaric cant, but he knew enough to know that no one gathered here *really* understood what they were seeing.

'Are we far enough away from the planet?' asked Roboute, trying to make sense of the energy emissions streaming from a port-side data hub.

Azuramagelli rotated a brain case to face him, though the disembodied slice of cerebral cortex had no outwardly obvious sensory apparatus to render such motion necessary. 'The surveyor arrays are registering a build-up of energies beyond anything we have ever seen before. There is no way to tell what minimum safe distance would be required.'

'So we might be in danger right now?'

'Very likely,' agreed Kryptaestrex, his thick robotic body disconnecting from the navigation stations and rumbling over to the motive power linkages and plugging in. 'Saiixek began preparations for breaking orbit upon receipt of Magos Blaylock's orders, but the engines will not be manoeuvre-ready for another six hours.'

'I don't know if you've been keeping up with recent events,' snapped Roboute, 'but we'll be lucky if that planet lasts another six *minutes.*'

Kryptaestrex bore Roboute's outburst stoically and said, 'There is little that can be done save to alter our aspect to the planet to reduce blast damage in the event of an explosive energy outburst.'

'Explosive?' asked Roboute, twisting in his seat to look up at Kotov. 'Is that what we're looking at? Is that planet going to blow up?'

Kotov waved a dismissive hand. 'Magos Kryptaestrex should know better than to voice such evocative terms,' he said. 'Planets do not *blow up*, they fracture along established fault-lines, implode on their collapsing core or they simply become geologically inert. In all my centuries with the Mechanicus, I have never yet seen a planet explode.'

'After everything we've seen on this expedition, that's not exactly filling me with confidence.'

Kotov ignored him, and Roboute turned his attention back to the death throes of Katen Venia.

Clearly *something* was happening to the planet, something that was just as clearly almost complete. The fact that no one aboard the *Speranza* was admitting they had absolutely no idea what that might be was the white grox in the room.

The energy that had travelled from a vastly distant source to reach Katen Venia with virtually no degradation in field strength had begun a chain-reaction throughout the planet and, even now, Blaylock and Vitali were attempting to determine what had sent it.

'Archmagos,' said Azuramagelli, withdrawing all but his most basic connections to the navigation array. 'Something's amiss.'

The vagueness of Azuramagelli's comment was so unlike anything an adept of the Cult Mechanicus might say that every eye in the bridge turned towards him.

'Clarify, Azuramagelli,' said Magos Blaylock with a clipped flush of admonitory binary.

'I cannot,' said Azuramagelli. 'What I am seeing has no empirical precedent.'

Roboute skimmed the surface of the *Speranza*'s data inloads and was forced to agree with the Master of Navigation. What he was seeing made no sense. Every single external augur capable of receiving input from the planet below had either completely flatlined or registered an onrushing tide of impossible readings that were completely beyond measure.

The sudden influx of anomalous readings acted like a gout of raw promethium into an engine cowling, as space beyond the *Speranza* was abruptly filled with vastly contradictory states of being.

The Ark Mechanicus was simultaneously bombarded with exotic cosmic radiation of such complexity that it defied easy categorisation, while in the same moment finding itself adrift in space utterly bereft of a single electromagnetic transition. Such physical states of being were utterly at odds with one another and impossible in the same region of space at the same instant.

The *Speranza* resolved this paradox by blowing out numerous data hubs and surveyor stations in blurts of distressed binaric cant. A dozen servitors suffered instantaneous brain death and slumped to the deck with oil-infused blood squirting from their cranial implants.

'The instant of creation and the time of heat death,' said Vitali, rushing over to one of the few remaining surveyor stations and plugging himself in with haptic implants in his rapidly splitting fingertips.

'What's going on?' asked Roboute, seeing that – with the exception of Vitali – every single magos had removed himself from any connection to the ship's augurs. The illuminated streams pulsing between data prisms vanished as the libraries-worth of information was cut off in a single stroke.

'Vitali?' asked Roboute, disconnecting from the *Speranza*'s network and rising from his seat at the foot of Kotov's throne.

'What's going on? I don't understand what's happening.'

'I think it is fair to say that we are all adrift here, captain,' replied Vitali. 'But what I believe we are seeing is a state of universal birth and death played out in the same moment. This could very well be an ultra-compressed rendition of every single moment of time since the creation of the universe to its eventual end, when its endless transformation of potential energy into palpable motion and hence into heat have finally run down like a clock and stopped forever.'

Roboute didn't understand more than a fraction of what Vitali had just said, but caught the apocalyptic gist of it easily enough. He looked up at Kotov, who had half-risen from his throne, his expression that of a man who had discovered his heart's desire only to find it was a poison chalice.

'Telok actually did it,' said Kotov. 'You were right, Tarkis. He actually got it to work.'

'So it would seem,' answered Blaylock. 'And it appears we have blundered straight into his laboratory, mid-experiment.'

Roboute turned back to Vitali, looking up at the one aspect of the ship's datasphere still available now that he was no longer plugged in via his spinal implants.

The hauntingly beautiful image of Katen Venia's death.

'This is the Breath of the Gods,' said Roboute. 'Imperator, we're right in the middle of it all...'

The reticulated net of light surrounding Katen Venia pulsed with one last exhalation.

And exploded outwards in an onrushing tidal wave of photons and exotic particles that had not been seen in such concentrations for nearly fourteen billion years.

Only afterwards would any coherent picture of events surrounding the destruction of Katen Venia emerge, and even that proved to be fragmentary, contradictory and almost unbelievable.

Moments before the rapidly expanding energy shockwave exploded outwards from the doomed world, every square metre of ray shielding and every functional void pylon ignited across the *Speranza*. Every ship of the Kotov fleet found its shields flare into life and its external augurs shut down at the same moment, each captain at a loss as to the source of the initiating command.

The surging explosion of high-energy flux, huge particle densities and pressures slammed past the Kotov fleet, scattering its ships like a spiteful warp fluctuation. Saiixek's work to re-orientate the *Speranza* did much to mitigate the damage of the blast wave; the sheer mass of the Ark Mechanicus allowed it to ride out the worst of the explosion's force. The very proximity of the fleet to Katen Venia isolated it within the eye of an outward-rushing bow wave of exotic particles, compressed gravity waves and unknowable forces.

Almost as soon as the blast wave passed over the fleet, a phase transition occurred, causing an exponential expansion of remodelled space-time. Passive auspex on the external surfaces of the *Speranza* registered an ultra-rapid spike in temperature caused by the high-energy photon density. Particle/antiparticle pairs of all descriptions were being instantaneously created and destroyed in violent collisions of sub-atomic matter – and only one other instant in history had achieved such a violent moment of creation.

But this was no creation of a universe, this was that force harnessed by incomparably ancient technology and bent to another purpose altogether.

Alone and isolated, the ships of the Kotov fleet battened down the hatches and rode out the storm of unleashed energies, fighting to hold their position in a ferocious upheaval of system-wide gravitational fluxions that could tear them apart in a heartbeat. Compared to the forces of matter transition being wielded in the Arcturus Ultra system, the titanic power of the Halo Scar paled in comparison. Tossed and swatted through space like leaves in a storm and not knowing if any of the other vessels were still alive, each captain fought to keep their ship intact until the fury of this stellar event was spent.

It took a further seven hours before the raging swells of high-energy particles and hyper-charged gravitational wavefronts had dissipated enough for any of the fleet vessels to risk deploying surveyor arrays. Travelling at near light-speed, whatever had exploded from Katen Venia would certainly have reached the star at the heart of the system by now. Having weathered the storm better than most, the *Speranza* was first to tentatively probe the void in an attempt to learn what had just happened.

Via a series of buffered servitor-proxies, Magos Azuramagelli eased the Ark Mechanicus's senses out into space, sampling the local spatial volume for extreme thermoclines and harmful radiations. Given the existing chaotic nature of the dying system and the violence of the eruption from Katen Venia, he expected to find space lousy with squalling particle storms, volatile neutron flow and a background hash of electromagnetic noise that would render much of surrounding space virtually impenetrable to auspex.

What he found was far stranger, far more unexpected, and utterly unbelievable.

Arcturus Ultra was no longer a dying red giant, a bloated destroyer in its last incarnation before its explosive death as a supernova.

Now it burned as a life-sustaining main sequence star.

Glittering bands of metallic debris, rubble and coalescing gases surrounded the newly rejuvenated sun, the building blocks of planets. Gravity and time would do the rest of the work, and though millions of years might pass before worlds capable of sustaining life could form, such spans were the blink of an eye to a galaxy.

Katen Venia had gone, destroyed in the very act of creation it had propagated.

Only one impossible, yet inescapable conclusion presented itself.

The shock wave of unimaginably vast energies had been the corollary to an immensely powerful stellar engineering event centred upon the *Tomioka*. The sensory-occluding fields of stellar debris and radiation ejected from the dying star that had hidden what lay beyond the system was gone as though it had never existed, and Azuramagelli's surveyors registered the presence of numerous systems with glowing stars of just the right mass and heat for sustaining life.

All arranged in a celestial alignment that was too perfect and too geometric to be accidental.

At the centre of this lattice of stars, the location Vitali Tychon's cartographae had identified as the source of the initiating burst of energy, was a world broadcasting powerful isotope readings, energy signatures and Manifold-traffic that were instantly recognisable to every adept on the *Speranza*.

Adeptus Mechanicus.

WHAT HAD ONCE been effortless for her, as easy as stepping from one room to the next, now took an effort of will and mantras of focus she had not needed since her first, halting steps on this path. Bielanna's mind felt caged, hemmed in by the layers of armour plating and hard angles inimical to the curvature of space-time pressing in around her. Her spirit was unable to take flight with the ease it had once taken for granted. The skein was tantalisingly within her grasp, its secrets at her fingertips, if only she could rise from her body. Invisible fetters hung upon her spirit, chaining it to the prison of skin, blood and bone. Was this a sign of her abilities failing or simply a side effect of the hurt she had suffered in the last moments of the battle against the foolish humans?

She wanted to blame this terrible place of iron and oil they were forced to occupy after the *Starblade* had finally succumbed to the mortal wound the human's chronometric weapon had inflicted. The *Starblade*'s shipmaster and his crew had remained aboard the graceful vessel as it was finally torn apart by the gravitational storms within the Halo Scar. They had died alone, their spirit stones lost and the light and beauty they had brought to the universe extinguished forever.

Bielanna felt their loss keenly, but shut herself off from the all-consuming grief, knowing it would only hinder her ascent into the skein.

A handful of the *Starblade*'s warriors had escaped with Bielanna through a hastily crafted webway portal; they had all felt the nightmarish force of what the mon-keigh had unwittingly released on the outermost planet of the star system.

But only Bielanna truly understood the utterly alien nature of it.

That so cosmically powerful an event had not appeared in any version of the myriad entangled potential futures scared Bielanna more than she thought possible. An entire star system had been transformed, renewed and regenerated in a matter of hours. Such power was not meant for the galaxy's current inheritors. Even the eldar in the days before the Fall, when their civilisation had spanned the galaxy and their arrogance had known no bounds, would not have dared meddle with such awesomely powerful forces.

Such arrogance was entirely human.

She had followed the threads of these humans in order to cut them and restore her future of motherhood, but the greater threat of this new power demanded precedence. Past, present and future were on a collision course, pulling together into a convoluted knot that would tear the fabric of space-time apart as the universe attempted to undo this violation of its natural order.

Taking a series of calming breaths, Bielanna fell back on the gentle gifts of Farseer Tothaire, recalling his meditative exercises that unbound spirit from flesh and material attachments from spiritual awakening. She let out a soft sigh as her spirit slipped its moorings and lifted into the outermost edges of the skein, letting its familiar mosaic of pasts and futures wash over her and renew her with its liminal beauty. It had no geography, save that which she imposed upon it, though its fluid, structureless immensity was only fleetingly visible through the many barriers that separated her from its depths.

Bielanna sought something familiar in the web of possibility that surrounded her, threads she could cling to and follow, pathways to lead her into the oceanic vastness of the skein. The golden threads of her assembled warriors surrounded her, but each time she tried to follow their paths into the future, they skittered away like a pack of startled Warp Spiders.

Holding to her teachings, she reached back into the past, to where the threads of life were fixed and unchanging. From such static points she could reach into the future and gain a measure of understanding of what was to come. Yet even here she was unable to find solace or surety.

Bielanna remembered the past, the fight of the Avatar of

Kaela Mensha Khaine against the Space Marine leader aboard his doomed vessel. She recalled his cold eyes and yet… and yet, she found she could not picture his face, nor the words that passed between them with true clarity.

Except that wasn't right either.

She remembered his blue eyes, his green eyes and his brown, amber-flecked eyes.

She remembered his tapered jaw, his bearded face, his clean-shaven, hairless chin.

She remembered angular cheekbones, a rounded face. Scarred features and unblemished skin.

Bielanna saw the dying man represented a thousand times, each incarnation entirely different, as though a procession of warriors could have taken his place in any number of potential pasts and unwritten futures. That was not possible, she *remembered* that dying man. She had looked upon him with her own eyes. Why could she not remember his face…?

But no matter how she traced her own thread back into the past, that moment remained elusive and fragmentary, as though it had happened not once, but an infinite number of times. Even as she struggled to secure the memory, it splintered apart, shards of memory and fiction flashing past her in ever-expanding futures that had never come to pass.

She saw the Space Marine destroy the flaming avatar as many times as she saw it cast his body to ruin. She saw herself torn apart by explosive shells from his brutish weapon, saw herself cut him down with elegant sweeps of her rune-etched sword. All of these unremembered histories were false and true, impossible and certain. In one fraying thread she had already lived them, by another they had never happened, but the truth of it became impossible to know.

The past rejected her attempts to pin it in place, without the past the mysteries of the future became an unknown country. Bielanna cried out in frustration, the walls of light and potential around her closing in at her all-too-material emotions. Yet amid this horror of uncertainty, Bielanna sensed *something* of her own kind, an echo of another eldar's touch among the mon-keigh. No more than the vaguest hint; a fragile connection that spoke of friendship not hatred, respect not fear.

But like the fleeting impression of a glimmer-face within the Dome of Crystal Seers, the very act of noticing it hid the familiar trace from sight. Bielanna's spirit howled in anger, but the skein was no place for such emotions, and she felt the irresistible tug of her body. She fought to remain in this place of enlightenment, but the more she struggled, the more pressure her bodily existence exerted on her fragile, fleeting soul.

Her shoulders slumped as her body and soul were reunited with a bittersweet sorrow, the ache of freedom lost and a lightness of being forsaken. Her lungs heaved in a breath of sickly air redolent with the stench of alkaline water, chemical pollutants and oil-soaked manflesh. She did not want to look around her, for the sight of so ugly a refuge offended her refined sensibilities and was a heartbreaking reminder of all they had lost.

Bielanna opened her eyes and a leaden weight settled upon her shoulders at the sight of so few eldar. Fifteen warriors, a mix of Striking Scorpions and Howling Banshees, sat or stood or went through the motions of training in sullen groups of resentful survivors. No words of recrimination had been directed at her, but Bielanna needed no spirit-sight to see their mistrust and anger at her failure to protect their fellows.

Somewhere on the edges of their hidden lair aboard the enemy flagship, Uldanaish Ghostwalker patrolled the darkness with a handful of Howling Banshees. The towering wraithlord was eager to kill mon-keigh despite Bielanna's command to remain out of sight. Their presence had gone undetected so far, but the humans weren't so stupid as to not notice entire work gangs of their machine-priests and slave workers going missing time and time again.

'Farseer,' said a lyrical, almost musical voice with a lethal edge that snapped her from her melancholy reverie. 'You have guidance for us?'

Bielanna felt her body's assimilation of her spirit intensify at the sound of Tariquel's voice, his singular purpose like an unbreakable chain around her. She exhaled a calming breath and tried not to let her nascent claustrophobia at being returned to her body in this tomblike vessel overwhelm her.

'The future is… uncertain,' she said, lifting her head and looking into his cruel eyes.

Tariquel was clad in form-fitting armour of jade, its plates contoured to match the peerless physique beneath. Shoulder guards of pale ivory and gold gave his shoulders a bulk they did not normally possess, and his segmented helmet was retracted into the ridged cowl at his neck where two bulbous stinger-blasters nestled like the venom sacks of a meso-scorpion.

'Uncertain?' spat Tariquel of the Twilight Blade. 'How is that possible? You are a farseer!'

Bielanna flinched at the psychic force of his anger and pointed to the vaulted chamber wall behind him, where a ten-metre-wide cog was stamped in bronze and beaten iron. A half-robotic, half-human skull sat at the centre of the icon, caustic steam leaking from one eye socket and a shimmer of toxic run-off dribbling from the raised portions of its carving.

'Uncertain,' she repeated, gathering up her runestones and collecting them in the bowl fashioned for her by Khareili the Shaper. 'And it grows ever more so.'

'Then what use are you to us?' demanded another voice, this one stripped of its musical qualities and pared back to the cold barb at its heart.

Bielanna rose from her crouch and forced her beating heart to remain calm in the face of the exarch's cold fury. Ariganna Icefang was clad in armour that stretched back into the ancient days of the eldar race, and Bielanna could feel the hungry souls that still dwelled within its unknown heart. Its plates had originally been crafted for a male warrior, but over the numerous incarnations of bearers it had been reshaped many times, though no bonesinger had ever dared whisper to its murderous purpose. Gold and emerald plates overlapped with a sinuous organic quality, the pommel of the curved chainsabre strapped over her shoulder glittering like a hungry amber eye.

'Uncertain does not mean unseen,' said Bielanna, fighting to keep her composure. Aboard the *Starblade* she had been the leader of these warriors, but with their starship's destruction and her link to the skein's mysteries, that dynamic had turned on its head.

Now the warriors were in the ascendency.

'Then what have you seen?' demanded Ariganna, the monstrous Scorpion's Claw on her left fist flexing like a segmented tail. 'The shadows hide us so that we may hunt, not skulk like thieves.'

'There are hints and shadows of the future, but the skein has been greatly upset,' said Bielanna, trying to articulate a realm of the mind in terms a warrior in love with death would understand. 'Whatever it is the humans have done here has been like casting a boulder into a still lake. Waves and ripples are spreading great discord, but they will settle and our path into the future will be revealed once more.'

Ariganna's face was hidden behind her war-mask and the

furnace-red slits of her helm lenses were smouldering pits of anger. Where the rest of their survivor band had kept their heads bare to hold their war-masks in check, the Striking Scorpion exarch kept hers to the fore, letting her furious anger simmer and grow ever more deadly. The mandiblasters at her jaw spat crackling arcs of killing energy as the exarch loomed over Bielanna.

'You are farseer and deserving of respect,' said Ariganna, reaching out to place her claw hand on Bielanna's shoulder. 'But your visions have only led us to death and sorrow. Tell me why I should trust you again.'

Ariganna could crush her without effort and the bones of Bielanna's shoulders flexed under the fractional pressure of the exarch's clawed grip.

'Because there is one among the humans aboard this vessel whom we might reach,' she said, as the truth of what she had glimpsed in the skein became clear to her at last. 'One of their number has been marked by another farseer. I can find him and turn him to our cause.'

'A cuckoo in the nest?' asked Ariganna, her tone betraying a liking for the notion.

'Exactly,' said Bielanna. 'His name is Roboute Surcouf.'

MACROCONTENT COMMENCEMENT:

+++MACROCONTENT 002+++

Intellect is the understanding of knowledge.

Microcontent 11

INTROSPECTION HAD NEVER been one of Archmagos Kotov's strongest suits, but when he felt the need to turn his gaze inwards, there was only one place he felt able to do so. He circled the Ultor Martius, the red stone table at the heart of the Adamant Ciborium – a surprisingly modest chamber enclosed beneath a pyramid of interconnected machinery and logic plates – and ran gold-tipped fingers over the stone at its centre, feeling every imperfection in the slabs hewn from Olympus Mons.

The stone had been a gift from the Fabricator General, a palpable sign of his approbation and a means of symbolically carrying the dominion of Mars beyond the edges of the galaxy. Magos Turentek had crafted the steel-edged table, incorporating the finest navigation arrays of Azuramagelli, the statistical cogitators of Blaylock and the vast resources of Kryptaestrex's analyticae. An orb of silver wire mesh and glittering diamond hung over the table's exact centre, a representation of the geocentric cosmos as envisaged by the ancient Ptolemaic stargazers.

The *Speranza* could be entirely controlled with the Ultor Martius, its inbuilt cogitators and the complex machinery lining the walls fully capable of meshing with every vital system of the Ark Mechanicus. He remembered the moment his senior commanders had met here before setting out for the Halo Scar, when he had first laid eyes on the *Tomioka*'s saviour pod.

Despite the undoubted challenges that lay ahead, there was a mood of cautious optimism, an unspoken feeling that they might actually succeed. Kotov had carefully mustered a band to whom the quixotic nature of his quest would appeal: a Cadian colonel renowned for his tenacity in the face of adversity; a Reclusiarch in search of penance and to whom the prospect of unknown space held no terrors; and magi whose personality matrices displayed a propensity for free-thinking and radical ideas.

This gathering had sealed the pact between them, but like the generals of Macharius before them, the many hardships had gradually eroded their desire to venture beyond the limits of known space. The journey to reach this place had cost everyone dearly. Even the most steadfast among them – Kotov included – had begun to question the wisdom in continuing.

But that first flush of excitement and optimism had now been restored as fully as Arcturus Ultra and shone just as brightly. They had all seen the Breath of the Gods in action and it was glorious. The transformation of the Arcturus Ultra system was nothing short of miraculous, and the evidence of the reborn star system alone was enough for Kotov to return to Mars a hero. Vitali Tychon and his daughter had wanted to remain in-system for longer to chart this reborn region of space and rewrite the now hopelessly outdated cartographic representations of the galactic fringe.

As much as Kotov wished to indulge them, he knew the true prize lay ahead of them.

He would seek out Magos Telok and bring him home to Mars in triumph.

In the sixteen days since the rebirth of Katen Venia's star, Magos Turentek's forges had been working around the clock manufacturing fresh components to repair all that had been damaged in the crossing of the Halo Scar. Despite the as-yet-unexplained loss of numerous work gangs below the waterline, the *Speranza* was being restored to its former glory. With enough raw materials – something the fleet's support vessels were expending at a ruinous rate – the Ark Fabricatus boasted he could rebuild the entirety of the *Speranza* before they reached the source of the Adeptus Mechanicus transmissions.

Transmissions that could only be those of Archmagos Telok.

The thought of meeting the legendary Lost Magos filled Kotov with a flush of emotions he had long thought left behind in his rise through the ordered ranks of the Mechanicus.

Hope warred with a fear that what he might find could not live up to his expectation.

What of Telok himself? If the Breath of the Gods was his to command, what changes might such power work on a man's psyche? With the power of a divine creator at his fingertips, might Telok have changed beyond all recognition?

Kotov shook off such pessimism, knowing the Omnissiah would not have brought them this far and shown them so much only to dash them on the rocks of disappointment. He had been tested before and found wanting – the loss of his forge worlds was testament to that – but the revelations of Katen Venia and the unmasking of Telok's planet was proof that his pilgrimage to undiscovered space had been divinely ordained.

Magos Saiixek – together with a gifted magos and enginseer from Roboute Surcouf's ship – had wrought wonders from the engines, pushing the ship through the void at speeds Kotov had not believed the *Speranza* capable of achieving. Linya Tychon and Azuramagelli had plotted a course that, with a fair wind and a steady tide at their back, should see them in orbit around the source of Telok's transmissions within fifteen days.

Kotov paused in his circuit of the table as he became aware that he was no longer alone.

'You are not welcome in this place,' he said, as Galatea entered the Adamant Ciborium.

The machine intelligence unfolded its ill-fashioned legs as it rose to its full height, the tech-priest proxy body turning through a full revolution as it surveyed the Ciborium's interior. Loose connections between its brain jars sparked before being reseated by clicking armatures extending from the palanquin.

'We do hope you are not planning anything foolish down here, Lexell,' said Galatea, circling the table. 'You are not trying to think of ways you might wrest control of the *Speranza* from us?'

Kotov shook his head, moving in opposition to Galatea. 'No, I simply enjoy the solitude of the Ciborium,' he said pointedly.

'Strange, we never took you for the introspective type. We did not think your ego could tolerate self-doubt or the indulgence of reflection.'

'Then you do not know me as well as you think.'

'Perhaps not, but the question still stands.'

Kotov lifted his hands and spread them wide. 'What would be the point? You would destroy the *Speranza* before relinquishing control, wouldn't you?'

'We would,' agreed Galatea.

'Do you plan to ever release your hold on my ship?'

'*Your* ship?' laughed Galatea, extending a number of sinuous mechadendrites and slotting them home into the central table. 'You presume too much.'

Hololithic slates slid up from the table, projecting a three-dimensional wireframe diagram of the *Speranza*. Galatea reached out and spun the representation of the Ark Mechanicus with haptic gestures, like a child heedlessly playing with a new toy.

'The *Speranza* is our ship now,' continued Galatea. 'Trying to remove us from it would be a most unfortunate course of action for you to pursue, especially when we are so close to our goal.'

'When you say *we*, do you mean you and I or is that just an irritating affectation?'

Galatea's silver eyes flared in amusement.

'Both. Neither. You decide.'

'I have little stomach for games, abomination,' spat Kotov, leaning forwards and planting his palms on the red rock of Mars. Through micro-sensors in his fingers he felt the texture and tasted the chemical composition of the stone, taking strength from the reminder of his Martian heritage.

'You do not *have* a stomach, Lexell,' said Galatea. 'Nor a heart, liver, lungs or central nervous system of your own any more. The only organic portion of your body that remains is your head, even that is a chimeric amalgam of flesh and machine parts. There is more organic matter in our body than in yours.'

'Maybe so, but I am still me, I still have a soul. I was born Lexell Kotov and I am *still* Lexell Kotov. What are you? A vile monster who exists only because you ripped the brains from unwilling victims. You were nothing until Telok created your neuromatrix. What you were then is no longer what you are now, and if you continue to exist you will be something else again.'

'That sounds a lot like evolution, Lexell,' said Galatea, with a teasing wag of a finger. 'We can think of no more natural and biological a process.'

'You are not evolving, you are self-creating. There is no spark of the Omnissiah in you.'

'Haven't we been down this road, Lexell?' asked Galatea with an exaggerated sigh that was wholly artificial. 'We are both parasites, continuing to exist only through the appropriation of organs and vital fluids from others. The only difference is the means of our inception. You, though it is hard to imagine now, were born in a messy, inefficient biological process, prone to mutation and decay, whereas we are a sublime being, newly created and superior to mortals, indignant that you should think us inferior.'

Kotov and Galatea faced each other over the warm stone of the sacred mountain of Mars. There could be no accord between them, no rapprochement and no peaceful coexistence. At some point, Kotov was going to have to give the order to have Galatea killed, but how to achieve that while keeping his ship intact was a problem to which he had no solution.

But he would find one, of that he was certain.

'What is it you want?' he asked. 'What is it you *really* want?'

'You know this. We want to kill Vettius Telok.'

'I don't believe you.'

'Your belief or otherwise is irrelevant.'

'Then tell me why you want to kill Telok,' said Kotov. 'He is your creator, why would you wish him dead?'

Galatea's mechadendrites withdrew from the table and whipped up behind it like scorpion stingers. The machine intelligence bristled with hostility, the connections between its gel-filled brain jars flickering with electrical activity.

'What manner of creator breathes life into a being and then abandons it?' demanded Galatea. 'Even the vengeful god of Old Earth took an interest in his handiwork.'

'Not all creators are benevolent,' said Kotov. 'And not all creations turn out the way their creator intended. Mechanicus experimental logs and myth cycles are replete with tales of such ill-conceived mistakes being destroyed by their creators in disgust.'

'Just as many warn of their creations being the destroyers.'

'And if you do kill Telok? What then?'

'Then we will take the Breath of the Gods for ourselves,' said Galatea. 'And the galaxy will learn exactly what a machine intelligence is capable of doing.'

ICY WINDS SWEPT down the flanks of the black and silver mountain, as cold as he remembered them the last time he had climbed the shingled path from the frozen river to the Old-blood fortress. The snow was knee deep and fresh, just as he remembered, clinging to his doeskin trousers and soaking through to the flesh of his legs. Howling winds whipped the powdered snow from the ground, lashing his face raw and keeping the vast bulk of the mountain from his sight.

Arlo Luth pressed on into the blizzard, pulling his bearskin cloak tighter. He wasn't built for this kind of weather; too long and lean and without any fat to his spare frame. The cold stabbed through him, freezing the marrow in his bones and sucking the last warmth from his body.

It had been three hundred years since he had last followed this path, three long centuries of war that had seen him transformed utterly from the slender-boned youngster that had first made the climb to the lair of the Canidae. He thought back to the callow boy he had been, whose only thoughts had been hunting, reaving and wenching.

All that had come to an end when the wolf-cloaked priests had come down from the mountain at the height of winter and demanded the yearly blood-gelt from the tribes of Lokabrenna. Every youth of ten winters had to make the journey to the place of testing, where their palms were cut open by an ebon-clawed gauntlet and the blood collected in a tooth-rimmed chalice. Each child would kneel before the priest, whose eyes burned green behind his wolf-skull mask, while a shaven-headed thrall covered head to foot in tattoos placed his scarred hands on either side of his head. Luth shivered as he remembered the invasive presence within his skull, the unashamed violation of his innermost thoughts as what he now knew to be a Legio-sanctioned psyker tested the bounds of his synaptic connections and the robustness of his cerebral architecture. The words of the psyker had dominated his future from that moment.

'Princeps grade.'

That day had seen him ripped from all he had ever known and marched into the deep forests at the foot of the mountains. He had expected a life of glory and privilege but such a life had to be earned. The priests abandoned him at the foot of the black and silver mountain without a word and indicated that he was to climb to the Oldblood fortress.

And climb he had, for three days through blizzards, avalanches and rockslides. He had climbed though his fingers and toes had turned black with cold. He had climbed past the ice statues of the great iron-skinned warrior engines of the Canidae, and had crawled over the razor-edged volcanic rocks that kept all but the chosen from daring to approach the titanic ice-locked gate cut into the flanks of the black and silver mountain.

Dying from hypothermia and near crippled with frostbite, he had fallen to his knees and rapped the frozen nub of his unfeeling fist against the vast portal. Though he had heard no door open nor felt anyone's approach, there was suddenly a man standing next to him, swathed in animal pelts, bronzed plate and a stiffened cloak of oiled leather.

Only his eyes were visible through the frost-limned burnoose he wore, yellow orbs with machine circuitry crawling behind their predator's gleam.

'First lesson,' growled the man. 'Never kneel.'

And Luth never had, not once.

The years had taken their toll on his once slender and perfectly formed body, the demands of war transforming him into a still-living revenant, trapped forever in a sluicing tank of life-sustaining fluids.

Luth looked down at his body. It was just as he remembered it from that first climb, clean-limbed and willowy; almost too tall for the little weight he carried. He flexed the muscles in his shoulders as he trudged through the snow to the forested ridge where he had camped on the first night of his climb, when he had still thought the ascent of the black and silver mountain would be easy.

Eryks Skálmöld was waiting for him, crouched by a fire that blazed with a green flame in the lee of boulders the size of a Warlord's head. Just as Luth had come to this place as he remembered himself, so too had the Moonsorrow. Where Luth was tall and rangy, Skálmöld had a brawler's physique: broad shouldered, meaty and neckless. He wore matted furs around his body and wire totems wrapped his tattooed, muscular arms. He was unarmed, but that meant nothing in this place, where they themselves were weapons.

The ridge had the look of an arena, flanked on both sides by wild forests where the highland evergreens grew thickly, and beneath which all was darkness. The forest line was heaped with snow and a thousand eyes stared out from the darkness beneath the trees, like tiny candle flames of amber and black.

They watched Luth as he ascended to the ridge and stood across from the Moonsorrow.

'You came,' said Skálmöld.

'You thought I wouldn't?'

'It crossed my mind.'

'I am alpha, how could I not come?'

'You sense your own weakness. You fear I am stronger.'

'You are not stronger than me, Moonsorrow.'

Skálmöld shrugged. 'I am or I am not. Until we put it to the test our words are meaningless.'

'That is what you want? Pack?'

Skálmöld nodded, rolling his shoulders and baring his teeth. 'Yes, that is what I want. Pack.'

'You are not ready.'

'Is that why you left *Canis Ulfrica* behind when the pack walked?'

'You had no crew,' said Luth.

'Because you took them.'

'I am alpha, and I take what I need. I needed a new moderati.'

Skálmöld circled the forest line, his teeth bared and his breath coming in heaving grunts.

'When *Lupa Capitalina* walked on the dying world, I flew the Manifold,' said Skálmöld. 'I saw what you saw. You were back there again, on the world taken by the Great Devourer. The others might not see it, but I know you better than any of them. You are broken.'

'Enough talking, Skálmöld,' snarled Luth. 'I am the Wintersun and you are but the Moonsorrow.'

'There is only one way we walk away from here. In blood.'

'In blood,' said Luth. 'But whatever the outcome, what is between us is done with. Agree to that, and we will settle this. Right here, right now.'

'Agreed,' said Skálmöld, spreading his arms as gleaming claws unsheathed from his fists.

The Wintersun's claws snapped from his hand as he charged.

War-howls echoed from the black and silver mountain.

Claws slashed, teeth tore.

Blood spilled.

STRIPPED OF FAMILIAR stars and the known regions of the Imperium, the polished inner slopes of Vitali's cartographae dome had been an austere, hemispherical vault of cold metal and echoing space. The dying corona of Arcturus Ultra had blinded the *Speranza* to most of what lay beyond the galactic threshold, but with its dissipation, the emptiness within the dome was filling with every passing second. New suns winked into existence, distant galactic nebulae became clearer and the curious arrangement of corpse-stars that measurements in an earlier time had said were long-dead glittered with renewed fusion reactions.

Life-sustaining stars were dying and areas farther out into the wilds of interstitial space, where everything ought to be cold and dead, now teemed with celestial nurseries where new stars were being born. In these newly fertile regions, metals and life-sustaining chemicals had been seeded like a gardener preparing his soil for planting.

'And I thought the readings we were taking *before* we arrived here were awry,' said Vitali.

The entoptic machines worked into the polished face of the dome projected the newly revealed volume of space around the *Speranza*, probing farther with each cycle of the surveyors – Vitali was wasting no time in manipulating the rotating levers on the wood-framed console to catalogue all he could.

Linya assisted him in this, insisting that she was well enough to work despite the injuries she had sustained aboard the *Tomioka*. The bruising had faded and she bore no outward sign of her brush with death at the hands of the robotic sentinels, but Vitali sensed something deeper troubling her than any pain she might still be feeling.

'Did you see that one?' asked Vitali, gesturing to a star system whose stellar bodies orbited one another with chaotic, elliptical wanderings. 'A spectroscopic and eclipsing triple star. Three blue-white main sequence stars. Two are in close orbit and appear to revolve around each other once every nine Terran days.'

'And they in turn orbit a third star once every one hundred and fifty days.'

'Fascinating,' said Vitali. 'And to think, we never even knew these were here.'

'Someone did once,' said Linya, consulting a millennia-old tabulus of celestial accountings. 'But they were recorded as being in the final stages of their existence and those readings were of light already hundreds of thousands of years old. They should have gone nova by now.'

'And yet here we are,' said Vitali, stepping away from the controls and beckoning the triple star system closer with the haptic implants in his clicking, metallic fingers. The stars magnified as they approached, graceful and ordered like clockwork by the primal forces of the galaxy.

Watching the dance of the stars, Vitali could easily imagine the hand of a watchmaker setting them in the heavens. He knew better than that. Ancient physical laws, set down nearly fourteen billion years ago in the opening moments of the universe's birth, determined their movement and properties. Moments like that were miraculous enough without the presence of a creator.

'Our predecessors would have wept to see what we can see,' said Vitali, more to himself than to Linya. 'Flamsteed, Maskelyne, Halley and the composer of Honovere... How they must have dreamed of such things, trapped as they were on Old Earth and forced to scrabble in the heavens for their knowledge. But for all that, I sometimes envy them, Linya.'

'You envy them? Why? We know so much more than they did and we have discovered things they could never have begun to comprehend.'

Vitali nodded, setting the triple star back into place with a gentle wave. 'All true, but think of how wondrous it must have been back then. When all you had was a polished mirror fashioned in a mould of dung and set in a wooden tube, sitting on a frosty hillside with an inefficient organic eye pressed to an imperfect lens.'

'Give me the orbital galleries of Quatria any day,' said Linya.

'We continue their work, but they *began* it,' pressed Vitali, feeling the need to impress upon his daughter how magnificent a time the heady days of early astronomy must have been. 'Those men first brought the heavens within mankind's grasp. They denied the geocentric models, and they grasped towards concepts of deep time and distance. They made astronomy a *science* and they understood our place within the galaxy. Something we have since forgotten, I fear.'

Vitali stepped away from the control panel and walked through the emerging star maps of this region beyond the galactic fringe.

'So rarely do we have the chance to just *explore*,' he said. 'All too often our works are subverted by Imperialistic concerns: identifying systems of military significance, locating worlds rich in materiel resources, breadbasket regions, asteroid belts to be used as staging areas or determining system suitabilities for star forts. How often are we afforded the opportunity to explore for the sheer joy of it and the act of exploration itself? A chance as rare as this should not be squandered, Linya, we should embrace it and revel in the simple joys of discovery.'

Linya smiled and it seemed a great burden had, if not removed itself entirely, at least eased its pressure upon her.

'You're right, of course,' she said. 'But we still have a job to do, we still have to find a world of high enough mineral density to feed the forges. Magos Turentek and Magos Kryptaestrex are crying out for raw materials to keep the reconstruction work going.'

Vitali drew another system to his hands, centred upon a softly glowing yellow dwarf star with a dozen planets clustered tightly together in various elliptical orbits. Three of the planets were too close to the star to be habitable, while the outermost seven were either vast gas giants or ice-locked rocks. But the fourth and fifth planets travelled in stable orbits within the band of space that allowed water to exist in liquid form.

'Either of these should do,' said Vitali. 'Though if I were forced to chose, I'd say the fourth planet offers the best risk to reward ratio. I have taken the liberty of naming it Hypatia.'

Linya smiled. 'A worthy name,' she said, using the levers of the control panel to shift the focus lenses over to the projected worlds her father had brought up. Without the benefit of his haptic implants, she was forced to rely on archaic controls to bring up the noospheric tags from which she could pull information. The chemical composition of the planet's atmosphere appeared in shimmering bands of colour, together with deep-augur mineral scans of its lithosphere and oceans.

'At this distance, a lot of these readings are approximate,' she said. 'But I think you are right. The fourth planet appears to be just what we're looking for. Shall I exload this to Magos Kryptaestrex?'

'Yes, I'm sure he'll be pleased.'

'I don't think being pleased is a state with which the Master of Logistics is familiar.'

'Very true, my dear,' grinned Vitali. 'I believe Magos Kryptaestrex views the *Speranza*'s supply decks as his own personal fiefdom and it infuriates him when people have the temerity to ask for things they need.'

Vitali laced his hands behind his back and continued his stroll through the constantly updating representation of space beyond the Milky Way. His path across the acid-etched floor, not unnaturally, took him towards the glimmering orrery of systems and worlds orbiting the shining star at the centre of the latticework of impossibly geometric stars.

'And now we come to you, my mysterious friends,' said Vitali, spreading his arms out and enlarging the system his extrapolation simulation had identified as being the source of the unimaginable power that had kick-started Arcturus Ultra's rebirth.

'Tell me, Linya,' said Vitali, turning to face his daughter. 'Do you still think there is no intelligent designer? Here we have an arrangement of systems whose geometrically perfect alignment clearly implies the presence of a watchmaker, blind or otherwise.'

Linya left the battered control terminal and joined her father in the midst of the orbiting systems. Each one followed a precise path through space, their relative speeds within the dome vastly increased to give their relationship a more obvious correlation. Just as the Imperium's planets orbited suns within a star system, those systems in turn orbited the super-massive black hole at the galactic centre. And just as its celestial bodies orbited, so too did galaxies, circling around clusters of galaxies or some other vast centre of mass.

'The scattering of stars and planets across the galaxy owes nothing to design,' said Linya. 'No matter how ordered they might at first appear. Only the all-encompassing forces of gravity, time, pressure and a host of other physical constants define how the structure of the universe evolves. You know that as well as I do, so why the question?'

Vitali gestured to the ordered movements and positions of the star systems orbiting the central world in the entoptically generated imagery.

'This arrangement would seem to contradict that supposition,' said Vitali. 'This is clearly a planned arrangement. And if this system is arranged according to a design, cannot that be extrapolated as being part of a universally ordered design? Perhaps such order exists, but we have not the senses or means to apprehend that order.'

'Advocatus diaboli? Really?'

'Indulge me.'

'Very well, I agree there is the definite *appearance* of design here, which, in this case, suggests the work of a designer, but that does not make it so for the rest of the universe. If Archmagos Kotov is correct, then this world is indeed one upon which we will find Telok–'

'Difficult to see how it could not be a forge world, given the uniquely Mechanicus emissions surrounding it.'

'If this *is* a forge world upon which we may find Telok, why can we discern next to nothing of it or the systems surrounding it with any clarity?'

'Now you're thinking,' said Vitali, pleased Linya had grasped the inherent flaw in the map.

'We must question the source,' said Linya, nodding as one supposition supported another. 'The majority of this data came from the *Tomioka's* cogitators. And Telok is unlikely to have left every aspect of his forge world's secrets encoded within a ship he intended to destroy.'

'And...?'

'And every shred of information we brought back from Katen Venia was exloaded by Galatea...'

'An unreliable narrator if ever there was one,' said Vitali.

'Then we need to convince it to allow us access to the raw data in its memory.'

'And you think it would let us?'

'I doubt it,' conceded Linya. 'But if we are forced to question the veracity of Galatea's information, then every aspect of this map must be considered tainted. We can rely on none of it, not even Hypatia.'

'I have already begun corroborative surveys of the spatial volumes illuminated by Galatea's data, but so far only these deliberately ordered systems are proving coy in revealing their secrets.'

'Our augurs are being blocked?'

'Not *blocked*, per se,' said Vitali. 'More like obscured by a confluence of strange forces I cannot, as yet, identify.'

'Deliberately?'

'Hard to say, my dear, hard to say.'

'Then we definitely need to speak to Galatea.'

Vitali turned to his daughter and put a hand on her shoulder.

'No, Linya,' he said. 'That we must manifestly *not* do. Galatea is a very dangerous entity, and if it is obfuscating our understanding of these systems on purpose, then it will take steps to silence anyone who questions it.'

'Galatea saved my life,' pointed out Linya. 'If it wanted me dead, it could have let that battle robot kill me.'

'I am aware of that,' snapped Vitali, shying away from the thought of how close Linya had come to death on the *Tomioka*. 'And we still do not fully understand how it was able to neutralise the robot's command cortex.'

'Would you rather it hadn't?' asked Linya.

'Of course not, but please promise me that you will, under no circumstances, make an approach to Galatea with our concerns over its agenda here. At least not until we have a better understanding of why it might seek to mislead us.'

Linya hesitated before answering and Vitali turned her to face him. What little organic features were remaining to him were fretted with concern.

'Please, Linya, promise me,' begged Vitali.

'Of course,' said Linya. 'I promise.'

Microcontent 12

THE LAST TIME Marko Koskinen had seen the tech-priests this panicked had been when the Wintersun opened fire on the Moonsorrow in the training halls. This panic was just as urgent, but didn't have the focus of so obvious a catastrophe. He skidded to a halt in the infirmary, trying to figure out what had caused the magi attending the princeps to trigger a Legio-wide alarm.

At first glance, nothing looked amiss. Both princeps appeared to be adrift in their fluid-filled suspension tanks as normal, twitching within their hibernation-comas. But then Koskinen saw the brain-activity monitors spiking like crazy with neural activity. These were readings that might be expected in the midst of a furious, multi-vectored engine brawl, not in the downtime between implantation.

'What in the name of the Oldbloods is going on?' he shouted.

None of the tech-priests looked up, but Koskinen saw Hyrdrith desperately affixing a Manifold interface array to the armourglass of the Wintersun's casket. He ran over to his princeps, placing his palms against the casket's warm sides and feeling the heat of the bio-gel within.

'Hyrdrith, talk to me,' he commanded. 'What's going on?'

Lupa Capitalina's tech-priest shook her head and shrugged. 'The Wintersun and Moonsorrow have established a Manifold link between their caskets.'

'What? Who established the connection?'

'No one, they did it themselves,' answered Hyrdrith.

'How is that even possible?'

'Admission: I do not know,' said Hyrdrith. 'I think we are learning that there is a great deal we do not know of a princeps's abilities.'

Koskinen looked over to the Moonsorrow's casket, where the wizened form of Eryks Skálmöld drifted into view, his truncated form like a foetal ancient, heat-fused limbs drawn up to his chest where his elongated skull perched like a scavenger bird. Wired optics trailed from his eye sockets and blue-white light shimmered behind his sutured lids.

'They're together in the Manifold?'

'So it would appear,' answered Hyrdrith.

The door to the infirmary slammed open and Joakim Baldur entered. Koskinen saw he had his pistol drawn and placed his hand on the polished walnut grip of his own stub-pistol.

'So the Wintersun wants to finish the job?' asked Baldur, aiming his pistol at Arlo Luth's casket.

Koskinen immediately put himself between Baldur and his princeps, one hand extended outwards, the other curling a finger around the trigger of his own gun.

'Easy, Baldur,' said Koskinen. 'Think about what you're doing. You're pointing a gun at your alpha. That's enough to get you mind-wiped and turned into a gun-servitor. Is that what you want?'

'The alpha is trying to kill my princeps,' snarled Baldur.

'The Wintersun *is* your princeps now, or had you forgotten that?'

'Moonsorrow is my princeps. Once Reaver, always Reaver.'

Koskinen shook his head. 'No, you're Warlord now, Joakim.'

The gun wavered, but was still too close to the Wintersun's casket for Koskinen's liking. The anger in Baldur's eyes wasn't showing any signs of lessening and Koskinen fervently hoped he wasn't going to have to shoot the man. Baldur had his gun drawn, but his attention was switching between the two princeps' caskets. If Koskinen wanted to kill him, it would be easy enough, but shooting a moderati was like vandalising one of the irreplaceable Legio Titanicus murals on Terra.

As it turned out, Koskinen was spared the necessity of murder.

The infirmary door opened again, and the Legio's Warhound drivers entered: Elias Härkin encased within his clicking, ratcheting exoskeleton and Gunnar Vintras in his dress uniform.

Härkin took one look at Joakim Baldur and said, 'Put that bloody weapon down, you damn fool.'

Baldur nodded and lowered his gun, backing away as the two Warhound princeps took charge. Koskinen saw he had failed to safe the weapon or holster it, so kept his own finger resting lightly on the trigger of his own pistol.

'You!' snapped Härkin, beckoning Hyrdrith with a snap of bronze calliper-fingers. 'Front and centre, what in the Omnissiah's name is happening here?'

'We are not sure, princeps,' said Hyrdrith. 'A Manifold link between the princeps' caskets was initiated nine point three minutes ago, and–'

'Nine point three minutes ago? And you wait until now to summon us?'

'There was no need,' said Hyrdrith. 'The connection appeared to be entirely benign, with concurrent data flow between the Wintersun and Moonsorrow.'

'What changed?' demanded Härkin, as Vintras examined the data-feeds on the slates attached to each princeps's casket.

'Admission: we do not know. The transition from their rest-state neural activity to readings comparable to a high-stress engagement was instantaneous and unforeseeable.'

'They're fighting,' said Gunnar Vintras, reading the matching brain-wave activity on the senior princeps' readouts. 'They're trying to kill one another.'

Amarok's princeps seemed more amused than horrified by the revelation and laughed aloud.

'Emperor damn it, they're fighting,' he said. 'Looks like the Wintersun has gone back to finish what he started on the training deck.'

'No,' said Hyrdrith. 'That possibility has been discounted.'

'Really,' said Vintras. 'Why is that?'

'Because it was the Moonsorrow that initiated the Manifold connection.'

THEY CAME TOGETHER like two great boulders crashing into one another with such force that both must surely be smashed to powder and flying chips of stone. The thunder as they met echoed from the cold green evergreens surrounding the arena, ringing up and down the mountainside like the peal of the Bell of Lost Souls atop the Tower of Heroes.

They both fell back from the impact, but the first to rise was Luth. He grappled with Skálmöld, whose flesh had been torn in the collision of claws. Luth raked his opponent's marmoreal skin and hooked his claws beneath the bronze torq at Skálmöld's neck. He snarled and wrenched it forwards.

Sensing the danger, Skálmöld punched Luth in the face. Luth

fell away, dislodged, and Skálmöld wrenched the torq from his neck with a screech of twisting metal. Then like an avalanche he hurled himself down on Luth, his form blurring as the wolf within roared in release.

The very rock of the mountain shook with the impact as Luth rolled and loosed his own lupine howl of anger. He drove his fist into his opponent's gut, raking his claws up as Skálmöld bit down near Luth's throat. Drops of hot blood flew through the air. Luth slammed his elbow into Skálmöld's ribs, and the Moonsorrow lurched sideways in winded pain, giving Luth time to scramble upright again.

Snow was falling and Luth's neck and shoulder were wet where Skálmöld's fangs had drawn blood. He felt his own teeth lengthen in response to the blood-stink.

For a moment the two wolf princeps stood apart, circling the arena and getting their breath back.

The gleaming eyes in the darkness of the forest glittered in approval at the fury of the bout before them.

Skálmöld was bleeding freely from a long stomach wound, but Luth knew he was worse off. The wound at his neck was deep, and his breath was hot and painful in his chest. Despite his injuries, Luth grinned, feeling the wolf within take the pain and turn it to his advantage.

To let Skálmöld take the initiative would be a mistake.

Luth leapt at Skálmöld before he realised how badly he was hurt. The impact was sudden and ferocious, knocking the challenger head over heels. He followed up with a clawed lunge at the raw part of Skálmöld's neck, but the Moonsorrow threw him off and then the two princeps were at each other again. Fountains of snow were thrown up as they fought, spraying in all directions and falling in a mist of glittering crystalline droplets.

Skálmöld tore a wound in Luth's belly, but a moment later, after another convulsive explosion of snow, both princeps were standing upright like duellists. Luth slashed at Skálmöld's face, but the Moonsorrow was hitting back just as savagely. The weight of their blows was far beyond what their physical forms could have inflicted, as if Imperator Titans were swinging wrecking balls at one another.

Claws slashed flesh, teeth crashed on teeth and breath roared harshly. The snow of their arena was splashed with red and trodden down for metres into a crimson mud.

Skálmöld was bigger and stronger than Luth and he had had the best of the fight so far. Both princeps' forms wavered between human and wolf, like mythic lycanthropes in the midst of a transformation. Neither man could allow the wolf full rein, for none had ever come back from such a surrender. To allow it near the surface was as much as either of them dared risk.

Luth was breathing heavily. Both princeps were wounded in the shoulders, arms, and neck, but Luth's wounds were the deeper. Skálmöld was hungry to be alpha, but Luth knew he was not yet ready to lead the warriors of the pack. He wondered if this was hubris speaking, the inability to cede control of the pack before he became too weak to lead.

No, decided Luth, looking into Skálmöld's yellowed eyes.

The Moonsorrow was a killer and would be a great leader one day.

But that day was not now.

At least Luth hoped not.

Skálmöld circled the bloody slush of their combat, his eyes roving in search of a weakness. Luth saw a feral grin split his features as he found it. Luth was limping, his left arm hung unmoving at his side. Luth watched Skálmöld replay the last of their clashes in his head, baring his fangs as he understood that Luth had not struck a telling blow with his left hand for some time. The crushing punches he'd delivered only a few seconds before were now little more than gentle slaps.

'Surrender the pack to me,' said Skálmöld, red foam spitting from the corner of his jaw. 'You don't have to die.'

'I don't plan to die.'

Skálmöld laughed. 'Look at the blood on the ground, Arlo. Little of it is mine. You cannot win. Your arm is gone. The tendons at your elbow and shoulder are fraying.'

'I only need one hand to beat you, Eryks.'

'Good, good, you still have spirit,' taunted Skálmöld. 'A victory is not a victory if it is won over a foe who already believes he is dead.'

'Then come finish me,' said Luth, letting his shoulder drop.

Skálmöld obliged, swinging blows at Luth from right and left – each impact a thunderbolt from the heavens, a slamming hammerblow he could no longer parry. Luth moved backwards, one step after another, crouching low under the rain of blows from the grinning Moonsorrow.

But what Skálmöld had not seen was that he was moving backwards only to seek firm rock beneath him. Luth felt the resistance of the ground underfoot change from snow to the heart-rock of the black and silver mountain. He braced himself against it, tensing his legs like a runner at the starting blocks and waiting for his moment.

That moment came when Skálmöld vaulted towards him, bellowing his triumph and raising his clawed arms to slash down at Luth's apparently weak side.

Luth moved.

Like an avalanche that had built its strength over a thousand miles of bare mountainside to sweep all before it in a tide of devastation, Luth exploded from his firm footing on the heart-rock and sent a ferocious blow at Skálmöld's exposed side.

It was an appalling, horrifying, mortal strike. Luth's claws punched through Skálmöld's torso and ripped the entire right side of his ribcage clean away. Shattered bones flew through the air, spraying blood to the snow a dozen metres away.

Skálmöld landed on his knees before Luth, blood raining from his opened belly and the glistening, blue-pink meat of his ruptured lungs oozing outwards. The Moonsorrow was suddenly helpless, and Luth's hand fastened on his throat, ready to tear Skálmöld's life away in his claws.

'Do you yield?' demanded the Wintersun.

'I yield,' nodded the Moonsorrow.

'I am alpha?'

'You are alpha.'

'Then we return to the pack united,' said Princeps Luth, and the black and silver mountain fell away.

'DRINK?' ASKED ROBOUTE, pouring himself a stiff measure of a spirit he'd acquired from a trader by the name of Goslyng on a trading excursion around the Iabal and Ivbal clusters. The liquid was pale turquoise, which always struck Roboute as an odd colour for a drink, but he couldn't argue with the taste, which was like ambrosia poured straight from the halls of Macragge's ancient gods.

'No, thank you,' said Tarkis Blaylock. 'I suspect the molecular content of that beverage would react poorly with my internal chemistry.'

The Fabricatus Locum had appeared at the opened flanks of the *Renard* while Roboute sourced parts and tools with Magos Pavelka to begin repairing the broken grav-sled. Its sadly neglected parts had lain rusting in a corner of the cargo

'Perhaps,' said Roboute, withdrawing his hand from the drawer. 'But then, perfect is the level to which the people of Ultramar aspire. You'd be doing me a disservice to think I'd be anything less. But enough of this dancing, Tarkis, I know why you're here.'

'And why is that?' asked Blaylock, placing the framed Letter of Marque between them.

Roboute looked up at Blaylock's face, cowled in scarlet and with only the shimmering emerald light of his optics to impart any visual clues to his demeanour. He lifted the item he'd taken from the desk drawer, placing the long cigar in the breast pocket of his coat.

'So you know?' he said.

'Yes, Mister Surcouf,' said Blaylock. 'I know that this Segmentum Pacificus accredited Letter of Marque is a fake. A very clever fake, one that even I almost believed was genuine, but a fake nonetheless. You are no more a legally operating rogue trader than I am.'

'So I don't have an official bit of paper to permit me to do what I do,' said Roboute. 'Who cares?'

'You are in violation of numerous laws, both Imperial and Mechanicus,' said Blaylock, as if the severity of his crimes should be self-evident. 'Would you like me to list them all for you?'

'Imperator, no! We'd be here all week,' said Roboute. 'So what are you going to do next?'

Blaylock lifted the Letter of Marque from the desk and said, 'I will take this to Archmagos Kotov and let him decide your fate.'

'Go ahead,' said Roboute. 'What the hell does it matter anyway? We're on the other side of the galaxy, beyond the Imperium and any law you'd care to punish me with. I brought you here and before you start getting all high and mighty, you might want to remember that.'

'I do not forget anything, Mister Surcouf,' said Blaylock. 'Insults and condescension least of all.'

'Then do what you need to do,' said Roboute.

SPARKS FLEW FROM each hammerblow, filling the smoke-filled forge with strobing flashes at each pounding impact. Tanna was no Techmarine, but he knew how to wield a hammer and beat out a chain. Every Black Templar was taught how to fashion the chains that bound a weapon to a bearer and, though it had been many decades since Tanna had beaten metal upon the anvil, it was a skill that, once learned, was never forgotten.

Magos Turentek's forges were well-equipped and well-stocked, but they were intended for use by adepts of the Mechanicus. The menials and forge-slaves inhabiting this flame-lit vault had protested at the Space Marines' arrival, but one look into Tanna and Varda's purposeful eyes sent them scurrying from the forge in fright.

Hot exhaust gases vented from smouldering furnaces, keeping the temperature within the forge close to volcanic, a giant cog at the far end of the chamber turning solemnly with booming peals of grinding metal. A great chain, each link a metre thick, was wrapped around the cog's teeth, turning at regular, clanking intervals – hauling who knew what from who knew where. The hiss of crackling binary spat from ceiling-mounted augmitters and a number of oil-dripping servo-skulls bobbed in the shadows, ready to assist their Mechanicus overseers.

Every so often they would approach the two Space Marines with a hash of lingua-technis, which Tanna supposed was an offer of assistance, but sounded more like disparaging comments on his smithing skills. He waved them away each time, but they kept coming back.

The Black Sword of the Emperor's Champion rested on a

wheeled workbench beside the anvil with oiled cloths laid beneath its blessed blade. Varda knelt beside the anvil, feeding the length of broken chain onto it for Tanna to beat back into shape.

Tanna brought the hammer around as Varda pulled the heated metal taut.

Metal struck metal. Sparks flew.

The chain was rotated, another link added, and the hammer fell once more.

Stripped to the waist, the Emperor's Champion looked like a bare-knuckle pugilist of old, massively muscled and taut with the barely controlled need to do violence.

Tanna rolled his shoulders and brought the hammer down.

'The links are crude compared to those originally cast for the Black Sword,' he said, 'but it is the bond between weapon and warrior that matters. You and the sword must be as one until your death.'

'I doubt a Dreadnought could pull this chain apart,' said Varda, inserting another heated link with a pair of needle-nosed pliers.

'The Black Sword is part of you, Varda,' said Tanna. 'Part of all of us. That the crystal-forms parted it from your wrist is a bad omen.'

Varda snorted. 'This entire venture has been filled with bad omens. What does one more matter?'

Tanna lowered the hammer and said, 'Do not speak of such things lightly.'

'I do not,' said Varda. 'I speak as I find. How else would you describe this crusade but ill-fated? Aelius falling at Dantium Gate, the loss of the *Adytum* and the death of Kul Gilad, what are these but the footsteps of doom that march at our side? And now Auiden is gone, our Apothecary.'

'None feel his loss more than I,' said Tanna. 'He saved my life more than once, and I returned the favour time and time again.'

'We all grieve for him, but that is not what I meant.'

'I know what you meant.'

'Without our Apothecary, we have no means of recovering the gene-seed of the fallen. All that we are will be lost, never to be remembered.'

'We will be remembered,' promised Tanna. 'By the enemies we fight, on the worlds we conquer in His name and the deeds of glory we will bring back to the crusade fleets.'

'You are so sure we will come back at all?' asked Varda.

'To admit defeat is to blaspheme against the Emperor,' warned Tanna.

'I admit nothing of the sort,' snapped Varda. 'I simply mean that when we die out here, our flesh will not return to the Chapter to be reborn in the hearts of the next generation of warriors. Without Auiden, we become as good as mortal.'

'You say "when" as though the manner of our deaths is a foregone conclusion.'

'You do not feel that to be the case?' asked Varda. 'Truly?'

Tanna was about to dismiss Varda's comment as doom-mongering, but caught himself as a memory returned to him.

'Kul Gilad once spoke to me of a creeping sense of ruination that haunted him ever since Dantium,' said Tanna, 'but the Reclusiarch was always given to melodramatic pronouncements in the days following a battle.'

Varda nodded in agreement, then looked away. 'Perhaps he was right this time.'

Tanna heard something deeper in Varda's tone and said, 'Did you see something? When the war-visions came to you aboard the *Adytum*, did the Emperor grant you revelation?'

Varda's hesitation was answer enough.

'What did you see?' demanded Tanna. 'Tell me, brother.'

'I do not know what I saw,' said Varda. 'Nothing I can articulate clearly. I saw us on a world of lightning, a million points of light reflecting from glass, and…'

Varda trailed off, his voice choked with loathing.

'Go on,' said Tanna. 'Speak.'

'I saw the eldar, the same psyker-bitch that killed Aelius,' said Varda. 'I saw myself fighting at her side, and Emperor forgive me, I saw my blade save her life. Tell me, Tanna, how can that be true? Why would He show me such a vision of treachery? What evil can come to pass that would see me fight for the life of the xenos wych who killed Aelius and our Reclusiarch?'

Tanna heard the despair in Varda's words and understood the turmoil that had fuelled his anger. To have been granted the Emperor's blessing, only for the very moment of apotheosis to reveal an act of apparent treachery must have torn Varda's soul like splintered glass.

'Brother Varda,' said Tanna, resting the hammer upon the anvil and placing his hand on the crown of Varda's shaven head. 'You have been chosen by the Emperor to be His Champion, and He does not lightly offer His trust in such matters. Of all the warriors I have fought alongside over the centuries, there are none I would rather have as my Emperor's Champion than you. To believe that you might fall to treachery is to believe the Emperor has made a mistake in your anointing. And I refuse to believe that.'

Varda looked up and Tanna saw acceptance there.

Tanna offered a hand to him, but Varda shook his head and rose with the fluid grace of a master swordsman. Varda lifted the chain from the anvil, running the still-hot links across his callused palm. Satisfied, he lifted the Black Sword from the workbench and snapped the iron-lock fetter around his wrist.

The Emperor's Champion swung the sword in a looping series of cuts, thrusts and ripostes to test Tanna's work, the midnight blade whistling as it cut the dense air of the forge.

'You are no artisan,' said Varda, his hawkish cheekbones lit by the glowing maws of hungry furnaces. 'But it will do.'

Microcontent 13

The summons had come less than an hour later, and Roboute was just surprised it had taken that long, given the immediacy with which the priests of Mars could communicate. The clipped message from Archmagos Kotov gave no clue as to the tone of the forthcoming audience, but Roboute had no doubt there would be preening outrage, followed by an immediate cessation of all privileges aboard the *Speranza* and the revoking of his contract with the Mechanicus.

A pair of high-function valet-servitors in robes of pale cream escorted him through the gilded doors of Kotov's stateroom, a lavishly appointed chamber with numerous anterooms, libraries and sub-chambers branching off with what felt like mathematical precision.

He felt like a convicted murderer on his way to execution, yet the thought gave him little trouble. Roboute was ready to take whatever punishment Kotov felt fit to dispense, be it incarceration or execution, but was equally ready to fight tooth and nail to see to it that his crew were exempted from his fall from grace.

The servitors led him into an enormous circular chamber of tall marble columns supporting a domed roof that was easily three hundred metres wide and adorned with frescoes depicting the early colonisation of Mars. Complex holographic representations of sacred geometries, holy algebraic equations and trigonometric proofs floated in the spaces between the columns, endlessly working themselves through from origination to completion.

Around the curved walls were hundreds of headless mannequins, armour stands and portions of robotic armatures, or so Roboute thought until he recognised a number as being bodies Kotov had worn over the course of the expedition. The servitors halted in the middle of the chamber, wordlessly indicating that Roboute should remain while they departed.

Roboute turned on the spot, looking up at the fresco on the curved inner faces of the dome, now seeing that it was in fact an immense map of Mars. Olympus Mons was represented at the centre of the dome, as though Roboute was looking down on the immense mountain from high above. At its dizzying peak stood a red-armoured warrior atop a bound man with skin of scaled silver. Surrounding the warrior were a host of artists, poets and musicians, each of whom were masters of their art. Golden light haloed the warrior's upraised head, and that light spread across the surface of the Red Planet like irrigating flows of knowledge that illumined the far corners of the world.

'I believe it is called *Mars Vanquishing Ignorance*, Mister Surcouf, one of Antoon Claeissens's last pieces before his untimely death during the legendary nano-plague at Hive Roznyka during the wars of Unity,' said Archmagos Kotov, striding in from what the compass points on the pediment above told Roboute was the eastern approaches. 'It lay fading and disintegrating in a forgotten vault beneath the Tharsis Montes and I spent a considerable sum restoring it for transplantation to the *Speranza*.'

For this audience, Kotov had come clad in robes that made him look much more like the archmagos he was, instead of a jade or gold-armoured knight. Black and white chequerboard patterns lined the hems of his robes and a clicking armature of whirring mechadendrites enfolded his torso like electromagnetic coiling. Two of the bland-faced valet-servitors accompanied the archmagos, together with Tarkis Blaylock and a pair of beetle-armoured skitarii, both with gold dragons inlaid onto their shoulder guards.

'It's an impressive piece,' said Roboute, surprised Kotov hadn't launched into a tirade of binary-spewing outrage at his duplicity.

'It is propaganda and history disguised as art,' said Kotov with the sharp tone of a schoolmaster. He pulled back his hood before continuing. 'Every element of Claeissens's work is laden with symbolism and metaphor, most of which time has erased or we can no longer understand, but here and there it is possible to interpret the meaning behind a pictorial element. The bound man, for example, can be read as symbolising a puritanical sect of contemporary monotheists, or simply as a physical representation of ignorance.'

Kotov pointed towards what looked like a cave opening at the end of a series of long canyons that cracked the landscape like a spiderwebbing fractal pattern. Something silver glittered within the cave, but it was impossible to make out what it was for certain.

'And do you see the cave? Wild speculation claims that this is the cave of the–'

'Archmagos,' interrupted Roboute. 'You didn't bring me here for an art history lesson, so can we just cut to the chase? I'm sure Magos Blaylock has crowed enough to you by now, so just say what you have to say and be done with it, because I'm in no mood for a sermon.'

Kotov nodded and said, 'Very well, Mister Surcouf. We shall dispense with the human pleasantries. Yes, Tarkis here has informed me of what he has learned concerning the authenticity of your Letter of Marque. Would you care to elaborate on his accusations?'

Roboute had come expecting to be lambasted by the arch magos, not to be offered a discussion on the nature of Unity-era artwork or the chance to speak in his defence. Sensing there was a subtext to this audience of which even Tarkis Blaylock was unaware, Roboute felt himself relax a fraction.

If Kotov wanted to throw him to the wolves then he had no reason to indulge in this charade, which suggested the possibility of a lifeline being offered. Instincts that had served Roboute so well in the past now told him he wasn't about to have his head mounted on a spike. Roboute felt a burgeoning sense that this situation might yet be salvaged, but that would mean taking the initiative and holding onto it like a mother to her newborn.

'Do you mind?' he asked, pulling the cigar from the breast pocket of his coat.

'Go right ahead,' said Kotov. 'The chemicals in the smoke will have no effect on me.'

Roboute nodded and reverently lit the cigar with a flame-lighter hanging from the chain of his pocket-chronometer. He took a long draw and smiled as the taste – warm woodsmoke with hints of vanilla and cinnamon – unlocked a host of memories.

Roboute held the smoking cigar out to Kotov.

'I bought this twenty years ago on Anohkin, from a stall in the Iskander Hive commercia,' he said, walking around the edge of the dome. The light of the sacred holographics lit his face with a soft blue glow as he walked. 'The fellow had tobacco from across the subsector, though Emperor alone knew how he had the connections. Didn't look the type to have high-end contacts in the trading cartels, but by thunder he had a magnificent collection of rolled leaf. This particular brand of cigar is favoured by the Lord Militant General of Segmentum Pacificus himself, did you know that?'

'I did indeed,' said Kotov. 'I am familiar with the vices of a great many important men, but is there a point to this tangent?'

'Patience, archmagos,' said Roboute with growing confidence as he saw Blaylock's obvious consternation at Kotov's lack of immediate condemnation. 'You Mechanicus are all purpose, but sometimes the *telling* of a tale is the purpose. You summoned me here to account for my actions, so allow the tale room to breathe.'

'Very well,' said Kotov. 'Tell on.'

'You know that the eldar who rescued me from the wreckage of the *Preceptor* eventually deposited me in the Koalith system?'

'Yes,' said Kotov, matching his pace around the dome's inner circumference, with Blaylock following in the smoky wake. 'That much you have already told.'

'They didn't leave me there empty handed,' continued Roboute. 'An eldar craftsman named Yrlandriar gave me a stasis chest with a uniquely crafted lock, the one I put the *Tomioka*'s memory coil in, you remember?'

'All too clearly,' said Kotov.

'Yes, well, it was full when they gave me it,' said Roboute.

'Full of what to his people were offcuts from their lapidary craftsmen, but which were priceless gemstones to us.'

'Why should this craftsman do such a thing?'

'I don't know, the eldar vanished before I could ask. Perhaps it was his way of saying goodbye or a way to ensure I didn't survive the hell on the *Preceptor* just to die in a gutter on the first Imperial planet they dropped me onto. Either way, it gave me a start, and I was able to parlay those gemstones into a lucrative career in... exotic jewellery sales.'

'Illegal jewellery sales,' pointed out Blaylock. 'Trading in xeno-artefacts is a capital crime.'

'Then you understand why I omitted that part of my history,' said Roboute with a dismissive shrug. 'Anyway, I soon gained quite a name for myself among the preening elite of Anohkin, adorning the décolletages of some of the most highly placed mistresses on the planet. I didn't just trade in xenos gems, of course, I diversified into numerous markets: off-world property, passenger transit, cargo-haulage, art dealing, financial shenanigans, modest philanthropy and a host of other highly lucrative endeavours. To someone raised in Ultramar, it was almost obscenely easy to become one of the richest men on the planet. I owned numerous palatial villas, a small fleet of trans-orbital shuttles and inter-system ships that ran between every inhabited planet within reach.

'But the thing about money is that once you have enough to live like royalty, the act of making more becomes almost unbearably tedious. I was earning vast profits in every corner of the Koalith system, but it just wasn't enough. Not the money, you understand, I had plenty of that, but the challenge simply wasn't there. I wanted to reach out beyond the Koalith system, to push the boundaries of what I could achieve, but there was one stumbling block in my path.'

'You needed a Letter of Marque to operate with impunity beyond the system borders.'

Roboute stabbed his cigar at Kotov and said, 'Correct. And the Adeptus Terra aren't exactly handing them out like party favours around Bakka. The last one I know of that was granted, was to a family that could trace its origins back to the Age of Apostasy, or so they said, and that took three centuries of negotiations, fancy bureaucratic footwork and copious amounts of bribery. I didn't have that long, so I arranged a meeting with Anohkin's senior Administratum adept, a man for whom the word vulgar might well have been invented and who was the ultimate authority in granting such documentation around Bakka.

'I invited this man over to one of my villas for a sumptuous dinner in order to show him certain spectacular pieces of xenos gemstones I'd kept back for just this sort of contingency. On similar occasions where I'd hoped to sell the eldar gemstones, I employed the services of a dear friend whom I'll call Lorelei. Trust me, archmagos, if you or Tarkis here had any human desire left in you, you would both have fallen hopelessly in love with her immediately.'

'You sought simply to *buy* a Letter of Marque?' asked Kotov.

'Nothing quite so crass,' said Roboute, 'but not too far off the mark. I seated Lorelei directly across the dining table from the adept, giving him eight courses to gape at the nova rubies and deep garden emeralds glistening in the candlelight against her body-sheer dinner dress. All the while, the adept's "companion" for the evening, a parasitic woman who represented the very apex of poor taste, slurped her soup and mangled her meat beside him. With Lorelei always in view, the intended transference took place in the adept's mind: upon purchasing the jewellery and adorning his lady, she would become as lovely as *my* lady.

'Lorelei and I had run this psychological manipulation many times, and the illusion usually ended up further fattening my coffers and Lorelei's investment portfolios. Not to mention that it would enhance the stature of the adept with his companion, while providing her with an impressive memento against which her next conquest would have to compete. Everyone would walk away happy. Usually.'

'So what went wrong?' asked Kotov, and Roboute saw he was hooked.

'This particular adept had been snared by a vapid nymph encased in white satin that clung to her curves only slightly less tightly than she to his credit flow. By the time the meal was concluded, it was clear to me that Lorelei's customary hypnotic spell had again trumped reason and that the deal would be sealed over drinks and fine cigars.

'Ushered to a lush leather wingchair, the adept settled in while his companion curled up coyly at his feet. Again, the lovely Lorelei was carefully seated directly opposite to ensure the trance of her beauty would remain unbroken. I poured snifters of expensive amasec for everyone, the personal touch you understand, and subsequently held out an open humidor so that the adept might select a cigar from among the best in the subsector. While the adept's position had allowed him to sample many exotic pleasures, he had not yet had occasion to experience the finest of cigars. He carefully watched me remove the band from my cigar and clip it with a sterling cutter. The adept, as any avid student would, followed suit, but, alas, tragedy soon struck.'

Roboute grinned, savouring the moment and relishing Blaylock's obvious impatience. He had come here expecting Kotov to break Roboute on the wheel, but the initiative had slipped from his grip and Roboute wasn't about to give it back.

'Just as I dipped the head of my cigar in the amasec and struck a match, the trophy mistress at the adept's feet rose to her knees, partially blocking his view of the dip-and-light process. Attempting to emulate what he thought he had seen, the hapless adept dipped the *foot* of his cigar deeply into the amasec and lit the saturated end. A mighty flame roared up, resolving itself in a huge clot of char. Fumbling helplessly for an ashtray the startled adept waved the maimed cigar in the air, dislodging the blackened blob of char, which plunged straight down the already plunging neckline of his companion. The lady wasn't burned, but she was mightily outraged and shrieking obscenities that would have made a Munitorum overseer blush, fled into the night, profoundly vilifying her former true love and vowing never to come within a hundred metres of him again.'

'Then it would seem that your plan had failed, Mister Surcouf,' said Kotov.

'Not at all,' said Roboute. 'The adept was inordinately pleased to be rid of this particularly troublesome and expensive wench, and went to great lengths to expedite the passage of my Letter of Marque. With his assistance, I was easily able to penetrate the impenetrable walls of red tape and obtain copies of the Administratum hololithic imprints necessary for the fabrication of such a document. All that he asked was that I destroy them afterwards.'

'And did you?'

'Of course, I am a man of my word, after all.'

'I do not see the purpose of this irrelevant story,' said Blaylock. 'It has no bearing on your flouting of Imperial and Mechanicus laws.'

'That's because you have no soul, Tarkis. You don't feel the need to mark any moment with an emotional reminder of *why* things happen the way they do.'

He held the smoking cigar out to Kotov and said, 'This brand of cigar was the one that went up in flames and hence secured me my Letter of Marque. The day before I left Anohkin, I bought a single cigar from the stall in the commercia, and I've kept it ever since.'

'For what purpose?'

'I knew it was only a matter of time until someone figured out my Marque had been faked, especially on an expedition like this, so as the beginning of my career as a rogue trader was marked by such a cigar, so too would be its ending.'

Kotov nodded, as though understanding the significance of Roboute's tale.

'A colourful tale to embroider the beginnings of your career as a rogue trader, Mister Surcouf,' said Kotov. 'Comical details that add a level of verisimilitude I suspect you hope will lessen my anger towards your ongoing deception.'

Roboute said, 'For what it's worth, the story's true, but did it have the required effect?'

'The effect was unnecessary,' said Kotov. 'I already knew your Letter of Marque was fake.'

The silence between Kotov's words and Blaylock's disbelieving outburst was seconds at most, but felt like a geological epoch.

'You *knew*, archmagos? You knew and you allowed him to lead us beyond the galaxy anyway?'

'Of course I knew, Tarkis,' said Kotov. 'Did you think I would not examine every detail of this man's life before taking him at his word that he had a relic of Telok's lost fleet? I may have lost my forge worlds, but I have not lost my capacity for reason and due diligence. I knew all about Mister Surcouf's encounter with the eldar and his subsequent dealings and exploitation of the Adeptus Terra's representative at Bakka. The precise details of how you acquired your Letter of Marque were a mystery to me, but I confess to being greatly amused by your tale.'

'Archmagos,' protested Blaylock. 'This man has grossly misrepresented himself. How can we take anything he has said or presented to us at face value? Every aspect of the Mechanicus's dealings with him must be called into question. Every scrap of data and every word out of his mouth is tainted by deceit and falsehood. That he acquired a Letter of Marque under such circumstances should, at the very least, see everything he owns be impounded by the Mechanicus. His ship, his wealth, his crew, his–'

'Leave my crew out of this, Tarkis,' warned Roboute. 'They knew nothing of this. As far as they were aware, the *Renard* was a legitimately licensed vessel. I won't let you punish them for what I've done, do you understand me?'

Kotov held up a hand of machined silver and said, 'Mister Surcouf, be at peace. No one is being punished, what would be the point? We are far beyond Imperial space and that you were able to facilitate the fabrication of so complex a document speaks volumes to your ingenuity and tenacity. I, for one, would far rather have such a man leading me into the unknown than some foppish, inbred fool who earned his Marque by virtue of hereditary inheritance.'

'You cannot let this deception go unpunished, archmagos!' said Blaylock.

'What deception, Tarkis?' said Kotov, gesturing to the holographic veils of light hanging between the titanic columns supporting the dome. Roboute followed Kotov's gesture and saw a series of elliptical hexamathic proofs vanish, to be replaced by an entry in the Registrati Imperialis.

'No...' said Blaylock, instantly processing what took Roboute a moment to understand.

'As soon as I saw that Captain Surcouf's Marque was a forgery, I knew I had to ratify it immediately,' said Kotov. 'The expedition's manifest was to be entered in Martian Records, and the Montes Analyticae would spot the discrepancy long before the fleet was ready to depart.'

'You falsified the records,' said Blaylock.

'I amended them,' corrected Kotov. 'Mister Surcouf's physical Letter of Marque may be counterfeit, but so far as Imperial records are concerned, he is a legitimate rogue trader, and has been since his arrival on Anohkin.'

'This is outrageous,' spluttered Blaylock. 'You cannot do this.'

'I am an archmagos of the Adeptus Mechanicus,' said Kotov. 'I can do whatever I want.'

FROM THE DESCENDING orbital spiral of the *Renard*'s shuttle, the surface of Hypatia appeared as rust brown smudges interspersed with upthrust masses of titanic mountain ranges and rapidly swelling oceanic bodies. Atmospheric seed-augurs revealed the atmosphere to be breathable, if only comfortably so for short periods of time, and the geological core to be in a state of ongoing flux. The surface was tectonically active, but stable enough to sustain the industrial harvest fleet descending to replenish the *Speranza*'s virtually exhausted supply of raw materials.

Linya kept a background inload from the shuttle's pilot compartment filtering through her field of vision as she made her way to the giant cargo shuttle's loading hold. The internal crew spaces of the trans-atmospheric ship were cramped, as one would expect of a vessel that was little more than a pilot's compartment mag-locked and bolted to a heat-shielded warehouse. They were clean and well-maintained, each junction of corridors clearly marked and efficiently laid out. Here and there, in alcoves that appeared like shared secrets, she found curiously random trinkets in subtly lit display cases: a folded flag from Espandor, a Mechanicus commendation, a Cadian medal and other fleeting glimpses into the character of the crew.

It was a personal touch on a working vessel she found quaintly archaic, yet wonderfully human.

The *Renard*'s shuttle was a mid-sized carrier, capable of carrying tens of thousands of metric tonnes of cargo and was clearly kept in a well above average state of repair. Linya expected no less from a man like Roboute Surcouf, and she smiled as she remembered his clumsy overtures in the wake of the dinner in the Cadian officers' mess.

She did not regret what she had said to him, after all she had not lied. Baseline humans without cognitive augmentation were almost transparent in the interest they held for members of the Adeptus Mechanicus. Artificially evolved thought processes made it next to impossible for many tech-priests to relate to the petty concerns and levels of importance humanity placed on meaningless ritual and unnecessary social intercourse.

Linya had fought to hold onto the core essence of her birth species as she rose through the Cult Mechanicus, but with every implant, every sacrifice of an organic organ or limb, it became a more and more difficult task. She knew that many in the Martian priesthood considered her an aberration, a throwback to the earliest days of transhumanism, where even the slightest alteration to the human body-plan or cybernetic addition to cognition was viewed with technophobic horror.

She read a change in attitude of the shuttle and brought her inloads to the fore of her visual field, reading the planet's mass, rotational period, perihelion, aphelion, equatorial diameter, axial tilt and atmospheric composition.

Volcanic activity on Hypatia's closest moon, the erratically orbiting Isidore, was forcing a course correction, something Emil Nader was managing with only the smallest expenditure of fuel. Bloated refinery tenders hung in geostationary orbit around Isidore, their deep-core siphon rigs draining a dozen underground caverns of their vast lakes of promethium.

The second moon, Synesius, traced an elliptical orbit at the farthest edge of the planet's gravitational envelope, an inert ball of rock without any rotation of its own. A hundred Mechanicus scarifiers had landed on its surface, tearing claws the size of hab-towers breaking its lithosphere open for the Land Leviathans to strip its upper mantle of usable materials.

But the real prize was Hypatia itself. By her father's reckoning, the planet was in the early stages of its development, the crust still malleable enough to permit the digging out of its precious mineral and chemical resources with relative ease. The entirety of the *Speranza's* harvest fleet had been despatched to the surface of Hypatia and its two moons, as Archmagos Kotov wanted this resupply effort undertaken with maximum speed and minimum delay on their journey to Telok's forge world.

With *Moonchild* and *Wrathchild* keeping station in high orbit and *Mortis Voss* assuming a rotating helical course around the three vessels, the *Speranza* anchored in low orbit, at an altitude Linya felt was dangerously close to the planet's atmospheric boundary and fluctuating gravity envelope. Magos Saiixek was working his engine crews to the limits of endurance to keep the ship's trajectory stable, but Magos Blaylock had calculated that the benefit to the bulk haulers' turnaround speeds would more than compensate for the level of risk.

Linya matched what the shuttle's active surveyor arrays were telling her of Hypatia with the data Galatea had exloaded from the *Tomioka*'s cogitators, finding only the acceptable level of discrepancies one might expect between readings taken thousands of years apart. Linya did not trust Galatea one iota, but the data had so far offered her no reason to doubt its claim of simply acting as a conduit for the vast reams of information. She shuddered as she remembered its manipulator arm tracing down her cheek, like an obscene parody of a lover's touch. The machine intelligence claimed to be sentient and thus 'alive', so could that mean it harboured intentions towards her that might be considered unnatural?

She shook off the loathsome thought as the cramped, steel-panelled corridor opened into the vaulted immensity of the cargo hold. She read the noospheric data being shed by the shuttle's systems, a curious blend of awe mixed with fearful reverence and smiled at their conflicted emissions.

The shuttle carried no cargo, but its hold was a bustling mass of activity nonetheless.

A hundred or more tech-priests bearing the canidae insignia of Legio Sirius clustered around the threatening mass of metal, ceramite and iron that stood shackled to the centre of the cargo deck like a dangerous wild animal in the hold of a big game hunter. Hostile binaric code burbled from its augmitters and Linya felt a thrill of danger at the sight of it.

Even chained to the deck for transit, *Amarok* was a magnificently lethal engine of war.

Princeps Vintras directed the work of a dozen tech-priests and servitors as they finished the repainting of the Warhound's armoured topside. The damage the engine had suffered on Katen Venia was almost completely repaired, and Vintras made sure that all evidence of its wounding was erased.

The Titan's warhorn blared, echoing through the cargo deck,

and Linya adjusted her aural implants to filter out the most gruesome war-horrors embedded in its howl.

'I take it the senior princeps have settled their differences?' asked Vitali, approaching along a gantry perpendicular to the one she stood upon.

'So it would appear,' said Linya.

The Manifold had been alight for days following the altercation between Eryks Skálmöld and Arlo Luth, the fury of their confrontation bleeding into neighbouring cogitation networks and causing systems throughout the *Speranza* to fuse and spit with borrowed aggression. Whatever had driven them to conflict had apparently been resolved, as the renewed vigour with which the two princeps had coordinated the Legio's ongoing training schedule was masterful.

'I don't know about you, daughter,' said Vitali, clapping his hands with glee, 'but I am looking forward to walking the surface of Hypatia in a god-machine.'

Linya's father's enthusiasm for their planned trip to the surface aboard *Amarok* was taking decades off him, making him sound more like an adept only into his second century. He put an arm around her shoulder and she felt the warm rush of his affection course through her floodstream. She remembered Roboute asking her if she loved her father and the faintly dismissive answer she had given him.

Of course she loved her father; at times like this his irrepressible enthusiasm for new things was a salutary reminder of what it meant to be human. She tried to hold to the feeling, but the toxic stream of wrathful binary from the secured Titan made it hard to hold onto any thoughts save those of conquest.

'It's going to be cramped in there,' she reminded him. 'A Warhound isn't designed to carry passengers, and we will be expected to carry out the tasks of the crew members we are replacing.'

'Yes, yes, I am aware of that,' said Vitali, pulling her close. 'And it will be a grand adventure, I'm sure of it.'

Linya smiled and nodded in agreement. 'Though hopefully less eventful than the excursion to Katen Venia.'

'Yes,' agreed Vitali. 'And you are sure you are recovered, my dear?'

'I am, yes. The implants that blew out in the data overload have all been replaced, and the physical injuries have healed.'

'I didn't just mean the physical effects, Linya,' said Vitali. 'You almost died down there. Ave Deus Mechanicus, I don't want to think about you being hurt, it turns my blood cold.'

'Your oil/blood mix is maintained at precisely thirty-eight degrees.'

'An organic turn of phrase, but you know what I mean,' said Vitali. 'You should never have been aboard that ship, and I should have known it was going to be trouble. If even half the stories the old logs tell of Telok are true, then there were bound to be automated defences. You shouldn't even be descending to the surface of Hypatia.'

'Why not? You are.'

'Ah, yes, but I'm an old man in the last hurrah of his already over-extended life,' said Vitali. 'Who would deny me this last chance to walk a newborn world as part of a Titan's crew?'

'No one,' said Linya, inloading the shuttle's final approach to the surface.

'Ah,' said Vitali, reading the same information. 'We're here.'

Microcontent 14

The Processional Way that led from the Adamant Ciborium was a superhighway of noospheric light, a library and a transit route all in one. Kotov found introspection in the cool darkness of the Ciborium, but when he wished to revel in all that his order had achieved over the millennia, it was to the Processional Way that he came. Vaulted and coffered with gold and steel, the history of the Mechanicus unfolded above him in vast murals with none of the subtlety of Claeissens's work

This route through the *Speranza* was not about subtlety, but statement.

Towering statues of bronze and gold-veined marble reached into the vaults above, where gene-spliced cherubs and servo-skulls drifted in lazy arcs, burbling soft binaric hymnals. Shimmering veils of light from the tessellated windows of stained glass fell in oil-shimmer bands of colour illuminating the votive strips of doctrina paper attached to the statues' bases.

A six-legged palanquin followed Kotov as he made his way from the Adamant Ciborium, its mono-tasked servitor driver periodically requesting him to board, but the archmagos felt the need to make this journey on foot. Or as close to on foot as a being with little more than a disembodied head and a truncated spinal cord could achieve. In the days since his audience with Surcouf, Kotov had remained ensconced within his robes of office. As the time of their arrival around Telok's forge world approached, Kotov knew it was time to fully assume the mantle of an archmagos of the Adeptus Mechanicus.

Beside him, Tarkis Blaylock matched his mechanised pace exactly, though his attached retinue of stunted servitors wheezed and puffed with the effort of keeping up. Between them, they had just orchestrated the final repair schedules for the *Speranza*, allocating resources and work-shifts as need and priority dictated. For a ship as complex as the Ark Mechanicus – and with their materiel resources still a morass of unknown variables – the task would have been onerous to anyone but senior adepts with high-functioning hexamathic implants.

Lines of power squirmed over the floor's hexagonal tiles at his every footfall, spreading word of his presence and passing their calculations into the ship's network. In return, Kotov felt the ship's wounded heart, seeing Galatea's enmeshed presence in its every vital network.

'You will be whole once again,' said Kotov. 'And free.'

'Archmagos?' asked Blaylock.

Kotov shook his head. 'Just thinking aloud, Tarkis.'

Blaylock nodded, but said nothing. The business with Surcouf had reached past Blaylock's normal, logical detachment from mortal concerns to provoke genuine anger; Kotov knew his Fabricatus Locum was still processing the reasons for his allowing Surcouf to escape punishment.

Kotov stopped at the foot of a grand statue, exactly four hundred and ninety-six metres tall and rendered in polished silver-steel and glittering chrome.

'Magos Zimmen,' said Kotov. 'Originator of Hexamathic Geometry. A personal hero of mine, you know. I wrote numerous monographs on her work when I was first inducted to the Cult Mechanicus.'

'I am aware of that, archmagos,' answered Blaylock. 'I have, of course, inloaded them and factored them into my own work.'

'It seems strange to think of a time before hexamathics, don't you think? We rely on it so heavily now. It is part of every binaric code structure, part of every communication, yet we take it for granted, as though we will never lose it.'

'Nor shall we, its usage is incorporated into every database.'

Kotov looked up into Zimmen's stoic countenance. 'We are so sure of ourselves, Tarkis,' he said. 'Yes, we have encoded much of our data, but all it might take is one catastrophe for us to forget all we have learned. The Age of Strife nearly wiped us out, erased so much of what our species had achieved so thoroughly – one might be tempted to imagine it was a deliberate act of technological vandalism.'

'We have learned from that,' said Blaylock. 'Our archives are scattered, multiple redundancies and duplicates exist on every forge world.'

'Trust me, Tarkis,' said Kotov. 'I know how easily a forge world can be lost better than anyone. I remember a saying from Old Earth that said civilisation was one meal away from barbarism. I believe we are little better.'

Kotov walked on as the servitor atop the palanquin broadcast another boarding request.

'Hexamathics is a good example,' he said. 'We take it for granted, but what if the STC to construct the implants that allow our brains to process the calculations was lost? Vast swathes of our current means of encrypted communication and data transfer would be rendered incomprehensible at a stroke. You and I are exchanging and updating our recent workflow patterns as we speak on higher planes of noospheric transference, but remove our hexamathic implants and those data-streams would become unintelligible gibberish little better than scrapcode.'

'As you say, archmagos,' agreed Blaylock. 'One might then ask why you risked a starship as valuable as the *Speranza* on so uncertain a venture as this? The battle against the eldar vessel has shown it to be a repository of technologies to which we do not yet have access.'

'You mean why I risked it on the word of a fraudster like Surcouf?'

'That is indeed my meaning.'

Kotov paused in his walk and said, 'Because I had become guilty of overweening pride, Tarkis. The Omnissiah in His wisdom saw fit to punish me for my hubris in believing that *I* could lift our order out of the darkness and into a new golden age by my intellect alone. My forge worlds were lost, my reputation in tatters. My fall from grace reminded me that without the Omnissiah, we are nothing – apes grubbing about in the dirt for scraps of an earlier civilisation. By following the mind-step signs the Machine-God leaves for us, we draw closer to the singularity that is the pinnacle of our aspirations, when the Machine-God becomes one with mankind and elevates us to the level of super-intelligences.'

'And you believe that Surcouf is one of those signs?'

'He has to be,' said Kotov, exloading the data-footprint the rogue trader had left in the Manifold in the years leading up to the expedition's beginning. 'His trading fleets were operating on the galactic fringes for years before he received a commission from Magos Alhazen to travel to the Arax system.'

'Magos Alhazen of Sinus Sabeus? My mentor?' asked Blaylock in astonishment.

'The very same,' replied Kotov.

'The *Speranza* skirted the edges of the Arax system en route to the Halo Scar,' said Blaylock, calling up the route calculations of Azuramagelli and Linya Tychon. 'What was the nature of the commission?'

Kotov stopped as they approached the cliff-like bulkhead that separated the Processional Way from the more functional areas of the vast starship. Half a kilometre high, its geometric patterns were idealised representations of the golden ratio, and at its centre was a colossal Cog Mechanicus in coal-dark iron and glittering chrome.

'A routine outsource request to bring back mineral samples from an abandoned Techsorcist outpost on a planet designated as Seren Ayelet. Surcouf's ships duly returned with the requested samples, but six months later Roboute Surcouf made contact with my Martian holdings with news of something his ships had found within the system's main asteroid belt.'

'The distress beacon from the *Tomioka*'s saviour pod.'

'Just so, Tarkis, just so,' said Kotov. 'And you are certainly aware of how statistically unlikely the odds are of a saviour pod being recovered in wilderness space, let alone within a dense asteroid belt. That the beacon survived transit of the Halo Scar was nothing short of miraculous and its discovery no less so. That it came to light in service of a task set by your late mentor was a link in the chain that stretched any notions of coincidence or happenstance beyond breaking point. The pieces were beginning to fall into place. I had the *Speranza*, a vessel capable of breaching the Halo Scar, and a stargazer whose cartography was showing marked discrepancies in the stellar topography of the very region I was to traverse. Truly, the Omnissiah could have given me no clearer signs.'

Blaylock was stunned, and Kotov saw him struggling to comprehend the enormous web of causality that needed to combine to produce a confluence of factors so unlikely as to be virtually statistically impossible. Kotov saw the dense web of probability calculus interleaving throughout Blaylock's noospheric aura and smiled as he saw the calculations fall apart as the numbers involved grew too large to manipulate by conventional algebra.

'The Omnissiah has brought us here?' asked Blaylock, dropping to his knees before the vast icon of the Cog Mechanicus. 'I have always had faith in the machine-spirit, but to see its workings laid out before me like this is… is…'

'It is wondrous, my friend,' said Kotov, placing a hand on Blaylock's hooded head as divine radiance shone through the Processional Way and filled it with light.

EVEN FILTERED THROUGH the crackling picters of *Amarok*'s surveyor suite, the cascading bands of ochre and umber in Hypatia's sky reminded Linya of the years she had spent as a youth in the volcanic uplands of the Elysium Planitia. Then, she had been a gifted initiate of Magos Gasselt, bound to his Martian observatoria cadres as Oculist Secundus; now she was Cartographae Stellae of her own trans-orbital gallery. With numerous technological achievements to her name, Linya's rank authorised her to petition the Fabricator General himself, requisition planetary tithes and assemble Imperial forces to serve the goals of the Mechanicus.

Yet she had done none of these things, because she was, at heart, an explorator.

At first she had explored space through the multiple lenses and orbital relays of Mars – and then Quatria – but the gradual realisation that just observing the far corners of the galaxy wasn't enough had come to her as she and her father had studied the growing inaccuracies arising in their maps of space around the Halo Scar. Linya had grown tired of looking at distant stars and systems; she wanted to feel their light upon her skin, to taste unknown air and tread the soil of those worlds she had only known as smudges of light on electrostatically charged, photosensitive plates.

She smiled as she realised her reasons for joining the Kotov fleet were much the same as Roboute Surcouf's and wondered what he would make of walking the surface of an alien world as part of a god-machine's crew.

The interior of the Warhound was humid and stank of heated oils and blessed lubricants. The compartment in which feral tech-priests, too long in the service of a Titan Legion, had implanted her was coffin-sized and designed for beings whose comfort was of no concern to the Titan's princeps.

Gunnar Vintras had spoken to Linya and her father only to remind them that he would tolerate nothing less than the same level of competence as the servitors they were replacing, a needlessly patronising remark that only a discreet noospheric nudge from her father had kept her from addressing. The princeps of Warhounds were notoriously arrogant and reckless, and Vintras appeared to revel in that preconception with a relish that bordered on the ridiculous.

He had assigned Linya to operate the port-side stabilisation array, a task that involved compensating for any ill-judged steps the princeps might make and running the real-time gyroscopic calculations that allowed a fifteen-metre-tall bipedal war machine to remain upright at any given moment.

To a hexamathical-savantus secundus grade, such calculations were child's play, which allowed Linya to savour this new experience to the full.

There was something pleasing in the simplistic nature of the controls available, and Linya had to remind herself that she was operating a position normally occupied by a servitor. She had coaxed a shimmering holographic display that clearly hadn't been used in decades to life and the planet's surface swam into view in ripples of photons.

The Adeptus Mechanicus had descended to the surface of Hypatia like a rapacious swarm of tyranid feeder organisms and promised to be no less thorough in stripping the planet of its resources. Titanic mining machines deployed in numbers that made the expedition to Katen Venia resemble a dilettantes' excursion.

Each harvest force landed where orbital surveys had revealed the most promising deposits of the required materials, and almost as soon as each cadre of machines rumbled from their landers they began smashing the planet's surface apart. Underground caverns filled with chemically rich oceans were drained, while earth-churning digger leviathans descended on previously bombarded sites to tear open the planet's crust to a depth of a hundred and thirty kilometres, exposing the ductile, mineral-rich seams of the superheated asthenosphere.

Magos Kryptaestrex oversaw the resource gathering as Azuramagelli coordinated the mammoth task of shipping the excavated raw materials back to the phosphor-bright comet of the *Speranza* hanging in low orbit.

With the harvesters excavating, drilling, siphoning and refining a continent's worth of the planet's surface into materials usable by the *Speranza*'s forges, Princeps Vintras walked them far beyond the scattered dig-sites and into regions that had not registered enough interest in the geological surveys.

The swaying motion of the Warhound took a little getting used to, but once Linya had acclimatised to its loping gait, she found it easier to concentrate on experiencing the world around her. Her father, ensconced in the opposite stabilisation array, sent a constant stream of excited chatter directly to her cranial implants, bypassing the engine's Manifold and pointing out curious geographical features of Hypatia's birth pangs.

Though still millions of years old, Vitali estimated that Hypatia was in the mid-stages of its planetary development, with its landmasses still largely confined to one vast supercontinent that was only slowly being broken up by the gradual movement of tectonic plates. Its oceans were viscous bodies of toxic black liquid and its mountains were nightmarish spines of volcanic eruptions and sudden, violent earthquakes.

'Princeps Vintras appears to relish the prospect of running his engine close to regions that ought to be best avoided,' said Linya, working to compensate for the brittle nature of the ground beneath the Titan's clawed feet as the Warhound stomped down a sheer-sided canyon of orange rock.

'Warhound drivers,' said Vitali, as though that was all that needed to be said.

'What do you make of this canyon?' asked Linya. 'It appears to be almost perfectly straight. Unnaturally so.'

'You suspect an artificial hand in its formation?' teased Vitali. 'Like the canals of Mars?'

Linya smiled at her father's mention of the ancient belief that Mars had once been inhabited by an extinct race of beings who had carved vast channels close to the planet's equator. As laughable as the notion of the Cebrenian face, which had in fact been made real by an early Martian sect of killers in homage to another half-remembered myth.

'No, of course not. Unless Telok paused here,' she said, adjusting the gyroscopic servos as the Warhound dropped down a sharp split in the rock and turned in towards the mouth of an almost perfectly V-shaped valley. 'We know nothing certain about the power of the Breath of the Gods. If it can regenerate a star, then a little bit of terraforming should present no problem.'

'You could be right, daughter, and while this region does evince a level of artificiality, it seems somewhat perfunctory for an artefact capable of stellar engineering, don't you think?'

'Admittedly,' said Linya, shearing a thread of consciousness to mesh with the passive auspex of the striding war machine. The data-feeds were of a more martial nature than she was used to, each return a measure of threat and war-utility: cover ratios, potential ambush locations, dead ground, blind spot and free-fire zones.

She filtered out the majority of such inputs, leaving the auspex panel mostly blank, for what did a Warhound princeps care for the composition of the rock, the atmospheric make-up or the wavelengths of the various spectra of light? Linya brought the environmental data to the fore, gathering information on the Warhound's immediate surroundings with every sweep of the auspex.

Yet the most telling detail wasn't one she gathered through the numerous auspex feeds on the Titan's hull, it was through the swaying pict image from the external picters. The walls of the valley swept past the Titan, striated bands of sedimentary rock laid down over millions of years and, looking at the evidence before her, it suggested that this valley had not been ripped into existence by tectonic movement at all.

'Father, are you seeing this?' she said.

'I am, though I am not sure quite *how* I am seeing it,' said Vitali. 'This is a river valley...'

'How is that possible? The oceans are still forming, but the appearance of the rock suggests this valley was carved through the mountains by the action of a vast river.'

'This is most peculiar,' said Vitali, as the Warhound strafed around a spur of stone that looked almost like the broken stub of a great wall. 'Quite out of keeping with a world of this age and whose oceans are only just forming. But planetary accretion is, given the enormous spans of time involved, still something of a mystery, so I expect it won't be the last incongruous thing we see on Hypatia.'

The pict screen before Linya crackled to life as the threat auspex lit up and every input she had filtered out bloomed on the slate before her.

'I think you might be right,' said Linya, staring at the ruined city spread over the valley floor.

+KRYPTAESTREX, ARE YOU seeing this?+ asked Azuramagelli, switching the cabling from the inload sockets of his cerebral jars and dispersing the input through the command deck's data prisms.

+Whatever it is, it can wait,+ said Kryptaestrex from a data hub linking him to the cargo holds and embarkation decks. +Have you not seen the level of my data-burden?+

+No,+ replied Azuramagelli with a crackle of belligerent code. +It cannot wait.+

+I am coordinating a planetary harvesting mission,+ snapped Kryptaestrex. +A thousand cargo shuttles are ferrying back and forth from the planet's surface and there are hundreds of ship-wide lading operations in progress. I have little inclination to deal with whatever your problem is.+

Azuramagelli shunted the data with greater force.

+Look,+ he demanded, seeing the flare of irritation surge through Kryptaestrex's floodstream.

Irritation that faded just as quickly as Kryptaestrex saw what Azuramagelli had seen.

+What is going on down there?+

The data was image-capture from one of the dormitory decks below the waterline, an area of the ship where gravitational torsion forces within the Halo Scar had buckled the *Speranza*'s ventral armour almost to the point of a breach. Only hastily mounted integrity fields were maintaining atmospheric pressure, but the power drain of such a solution was proving to be untenable, and Archmagos Kotov had tasked a thousand-strong labour force of bondsmen and servitors with repairing this damage to the lower decks.

Crackling sheets of energy arced through the chamber, leaping from stanchion to stanchion and filling the vast space with a storm of lightning. Men, women and children were soundlessly screaming as the lightning blitzed through the lower-deck living spaces, turning living bodies to ash and smoke with every flickering blast of blue-white light.

+Impossible,+ blurted Kryptaestrex. +There are no electrical power sources within the chamber capable of generating such a discharge.+

+That isn't electricity,+ said Azuramagelli, taking urgent inloads from the *Speranza's* astropathic choir chambers. +Choirmasters across the ship are reporting a psychic event of battle-grade levels.+

+Warp-craft?+

+Unknown, but Choirmaster Primus believes the source to be non-human. Recommendation: cut power to the entire deck,+ said Azuramagelli. +Flush out whatever is causing this.+

+The integrity fields are tied into the chamber's grid!+ protested Kryptaestrex. +We would lose the deck and repair materials. There are thousands of workers down there.+

+You would rather lose the entire ship?+

The door to the command deck hissed open and Archmagos Kotov strode in with Magos Blaylock at his heels. The archmagos was clearly aware of what they were seeing, and his order was swiftly and mercilessly given, in the full and certain knowledge of what it meant for the thousands of people below the waterline.

+Cut the power,+ he said.

IMPOSSIBLE WAS THE word Linya kept groping towards as *Amarok* strode cautiously through the ruined city. Princeps Vintras had initially been reluctant to enter, but the natural aggression and hunter instinct of the Warhound had won through and convinced him to explore the shattered structures and rubble-strewn streets.

That a city of such age should be found on a world in the mid-stages of its life cycle was highly unlikely, for the surface had yet to achieve a level of geological solidity that would make raising cities of such size a viable proposition. Numerous buildings appeared to have been wrecked by earthquakes and *Amarok* was forced to detour several times to negotiate wide chasms ripped through the city streets. Twice the Titan had braced itself against single-storey structures as earth tremors shook the ground. Neither had force enough to concern her or the Warhound's princeps, but they were indicative of the planet's underlying instability.

Linya had been forced to revise her initial impression of Gunnar Vintras. Cocksure and arrogant certainly, but he was also a highly skilled Warhound driver, darting from cover to cover and keeping his engine's back to the walls as he moved deeper into the city.

'It's Imperial,' said her father. 'That much is obvious. There's STC patterning clearly visible on almost every structure.'

'I see that,' said Linya as a slab-sided hab-block passed to her right. 'But the auspex readings are making no sense. I can't get a certain fix on the age of this city from one structure to the next.'

'No,' agreed her father. 'I'm seeing emissions that suggest much of this city was constructed around fifteen thousand years ago.'

'That's pre-Great Crusade,' said Linya. 'Might this place have been settled in the First Diaspora?'

Her father paused before answering and Linya looked up from the pict-slate, which displayed a grainy image of a collapsed structure that had borne the brunt of an earlier earthquake. Its exposed floors were awash with debris, but she saw no sign of any previous habitation.

'That is certainly one conclusion,' said Vitali.

'I can't think of another.'

'Premature ageing,' said Vitali. 'Accelerated decay caused by entropic fields. I've heard of xeno-breeds possessing technology capable of such feats, but never on this scale.'

'That's something of a reach, is it not?' asked Linya. 'Lex Parsimoniae suggests that the explanation requiring the fewest assumptions is most often the correct one.'

'You're right of course, my dear, and under normal circumstances I'd agree with you.'

'But?'

'I have linked with the *Speranza*'s more specialised surveyors, and take a look at what they are detecting. Compare the current readings to what we detected when we first began building the map of this region from Galatea's inloads.'

Linya switched her inload array to display what her father was seeing, and once again, *impossible* was the word that first leapt to mind.

'They're different,' said Linya. 'By a small, but significant amount. I don't… but that's…'

'Impossible?' finished her father. 'Routine chronometric readings are now telling me that the planet we are on is *younger* than it was when the *Speranza* set course towards it. This is not a planet evolving through its mid-stage of development, but one that has *reverted* to it over a vastly compressed time-frame. And one that will continue to revert until it breaks apart into an expanding mass of stellar material.'

Linya struggled to process the idea that a planet could regress through its phases of existence. If she accepted it as truth then the laws of space-time were being violated in unspeakable ways, and she felt her grasp of what constituted reality being prised loose from everything she had learned as a member of the Adeptus Mechanicus.

'Do you think this is a side effect of the Breath of the Gods?' she asked.

'One can only hope so,' said Vitali. 'The alternative is too terrible to contemplate, that the fundamental laws of the universe are not nearly as fixed and constant as we have assumed.'

'We need to alert the harvesters,' said Linya. 'Before Hypatia reverts to a more unstable phase.'

'*Please*, do you think I wouldn't have already done that?' asked Vitali.

Before Linya could answer, she registered the incoming seismic waves through the gyroscopes set within the lower reaches of the Warhound's clawed feet. The magnitude of the incoming energy was far greater than anything she had seen before and they were right over its epicentre.

'My princeps!' she shouted, but it was already too late, as the full force of the earthquake roared up from the planet's depths. The buildings around them were smashed apart in a storm of splintering masonry and snapping steelwork. Cladding panels and roof spars cascaded from the tallest towers as the most damaged buildings simply ceased to exist.

Millions of tonnes of rubble fell in roaring avalanches of broken rock as the valley shook itself apart. Dust billowed from chasms that tore through the city like splitting ice on the surface of a lake, and apparently solid rock ripped open as easily as tearing parchment. *Amarok* staggered like a mortally wounded beast as the ground lurched and broke apart into bifurcating chasms. Spewing gouts of magma bubbled to the surface, bathing the ruined city in a hellish, red glow.

Linya's stabiliser panels blared warnings as their tolerances were horribly exceeded, filling the Titan's interior with emergency lights. Even insulated within the lower reaches of the god-machine's body, the noise was deafening. Linya fought to keep the Titan stable as Vintras threw *Amarok* into a looping turn. The rock beneath the war-engine cracked and split into geysering crevasses.

Linya grabbed onto a handrail above her head as *Amarok* leaned far beyond its centre of gravity.

She cried out as she realised the Titan was going to fall.

Vintras bent *Amarok's* right knee and pistoned its mega-bolter arm straight down. A hurricane of explosive shells blasted the ground at point-blank range. The recoil was ferocious, and with the compensators offline it was just enough.

Incredibly, the Titan righted itself, taking half a dozen

lurching, unbalanced steps before fully regaining its balance. Linya was astonished. She had already revised her opinion of Vintras to a highly skilled princeps, but now she realised he was *extraordinarily* skilled.

But then the ground beneath the Titan split apart.

Not even an extraordinarily skilled princeps could keep its leg from plunging into a crevasse of bubbling magma.

'This is a mistake, Abe,' said Hawke, rapidly sidestepping to keep up with Abrehem as he marched through the arched hallways of the *Speranza*. 'Seriously. Think about it, you're a wanted man, my friend. Putting your head over the parapet like this is a sure-fire way to get it shot off. I've spent a lifetime not sticking my neck out. It's the best way to operate, trust me.'

'Omnissiah save me, but for once I find myself in complete agreement with Bondsman Hawke,' said Totha Mu-32. 'This is not wise.'

Abrehem rounded on Hawke, the fury in his heart like a slow-burning fire being fed incrementally increasing amounts of oxygen. His fists were clenched at his side and, behind him, Rasselas X-42 bared his metallic teeth.

'Wasn't it you that said, *One day I'm going to make the bastard listen*?'

'Maybe, I don't remember, but you don't want to go listening to me, Abe,' protested Hawke. 'I shoot my mouth off, but I don't *do* anything about it. You're one of those dangerous types that actually means to do what he says he's going to do.'

Coyne and Ismael caught up to them, the latter looking solemn, the former like a frightened prey animal that knows there are apex predators nearby.

'Thor's beard, but you've got to listen to him, Abrehem,' said Coyne. 'You'll get us all killed.'

'If you're scared, Vannen, go back,' said Abrehem. 'You don't have to come. I'd rather have someone at my back who gives a damn than someone who's just out for their own skin.'

Coyne's face fell, but Abrehem was in no mood for regret.

'That's not fair, Abe,' said Coyne. 'Haven't I always been there, every step of the way?'

'That's true,' said Abrehem, 'but how much is your support worth when it's simply the lesser of two evils? We're doing this, and we're doing it now. It's time the Mechanicus learned that we're not just numbers or resources. We're human beings, and they can't keep killing us because it suits them.'

Ever since Ismael had forced him to feel the anguish of the *Speranza*'s servitors and its bondsmen in his soul, Abrehem had found himself unable to close his eyes without feeling gut-wrenching horror at the suffering throughout the Kotov fleet. He'd felt the deaths in the ventral dormitory deck when the power to the integrity fields had been cut. He'd wept as the already tortured armour plates had given way and an entire deck explosively vented into space.

Two thousand three hundred and seven men, women and void-born children had died, not to mention the three hundred and eleven servitors who had flash-frozen or had their organic components disposed of in the aftermath.

He could endure it no longer, and with Ismael's help he was going to show the Adeptus Mechanicus that their workers would stand for no more. After disengaging the arco-flagellant's pacifier helm, he had marched from hiding, following a route he could never describe in detail. With Rasselas X-42 and Ismael at his side, he made his way back to the portions of the *Speranza* in which he had spent his days not, he now realised, as a bonded servant of the Mechanicus, but a slave.

Totha Mu-32 tried a different tack.

'You are Machine-touched, Bondsman Locke,' he said, gripping Abrehem's arm. 'You are special, and you must not risk yourself like this. You are too valuable to be lost in an act of emotional spite.'

'If I'm special, I need to earn that reverence,' said Abrehem. 'If I *am* Machine-touched, then I'm beholden to do something with that power, yes? After all, what's the use of being someone important if you don't use that power to make people's lives better?'

'The Mechanicus will kill you,' said Totha Mu-32.

Abrehem jerked a thumb over his shoulder and said, 'I'd like to see anyone try when I've got an arco-flagellant with me. I'll use him if I have to, don't think I won't.'

'X-42 is a powerful weapon,' agreed Totha Mu-32. 'But he is mortal like all of us. A bullet in the head will kill him, the same as any of us. Please reconsider this course of action, I beg you.'

'No,' said Abrehem. 'It's too late for that.'

His footsteps had unerringly carried him back to Feeding Hall Eighty-Six, the site of a previous casual massacre of bondsmen, and Abrehem smiled to see that his timing was impeccable. One shift of thousands was just finishing its nutrient paste meal, while another stood waiting at the opposite entrance, pathetically hungry for the slops with which the Mechanicus saw fit to present them.

A group of augmented overseers stood in the arched entryway, and Abrehem relished the looks of fear as they saw Rasselas X-42 and retreated into the feeding hall. He felt their calls for aid flow into the noosphere, knowing he could prevent them from reaching their intended destinations, but wanting the rest of the fleet to know he was here.

'Let them go,' he said, quelling X-42's natural urge to murder the fleeing overseers.

Though there were only six of them, what they represented was more of a terror to the Adeptus Mechanicus than any army of destructive greenskins could ever be.

Abrehem marched straight into the feeding hall, feeling every pair of eyes fasten upon him.

Everyone here knew who he was. They had heard the stories, passed them around themselves and maybe even added a detail here and there. On some decks he was already being named as an avatar of the Machine-God. On others, his name had became synonymous with messianic figures from history: great liberators, firebrand revolutionaries or pacifist messengers of tolerance.

Abrehem would be all of these and much more.

Flanked by Rasselas X-42 and Ismael, Abrehem made his way to the centre of the vast chamber. By now, the desperate calls for armed assistance had reached the skitarii barracks, Cadian billets and armsmen stations. Hundreds of men and women with guns and the will to use them were even now converging on Feeding Hall Eighty-Six.

None of them would arrive in time to stop what was about to happen.

Abrehem climbed onto a table, turning a full circle so everyone could see him. He had come in a plain robe, red like the Mechanicus, but unadorned with the finery so favoured by the tech-priests, and roughly fashioned like the overalls worn by the bondsmen. He had prepared no speech and had no words ready with which to sway men he already knew would applaud what he had to preach. His words had to come from the heart, or all he would soon represent would mean nothing at all.

He nodded to Totha Mu-32, and the vox-grilles throughout the feeding hall crackled and hissed as the overseer took them over.

'My fellow bondsmen,' began Abrehem, his voice booming throughout the feeding hall and far beyond. 'You all know who I am and why the Mechanicus fear me. I am Abrehem Locke and I am Machine-touched. And I am one of you. The overseers have told you that I am a madman, a lunatic with delusions of divinity. You know this to be a lie. I have toiled with you in the bowels of Archmagos Kotov's slave machine, and I have been burned as you have been burned. I have bled and I have been sickened by what we have all experienced. You know I have suffered as you continue to suffer. I am here to tell you that your suffering is at an end!'

Heads were nodding in agreement, and Abrehem saw the armsmen and overseers clustered together in nervous groups. Totha Mu-32 assured him that his words were being carried throughout the *Speranza* over the hijacked vox-system. Abrehem relished the uncertainty he saw in the overseers' faces as they debated the wisdom of pushing into the feeding hall to seize him before this situation spiralled completely out of hand.

Abrehem didn't give them time to reach a conclusion.

'Consider this, brothers. If the *Speranza* is a machine and Archmagos Kotov is the cogitator at its heart, then the magi are the levers of control and the overseers are the gears. That makes us the raw material the machine devours! But we are raw materials that don't intend to be devoured. We won't be used and spat out or cast aside. We are not slaves to be bought and sold, traded like animal flesh at a meat market. No, Archmagos Kotov, we are human beings!'

This time, Abrehem's words brought wild cheers and

pumping fists. He felt them echoing through the farthest corners of the Ark Mechanicus, from its command deck all the way to the deepest, darkest sumps below the waterline. An angry undercurrent that had been bubbling just under the surface, with no way to express itself, suddenly found an outlet in Abrehem. Bondsmen threw plastic food trays to the floor and climbed onto the tables. They roared hatred at their overseers and shouted words of support and devotion.

Abrehem threw his fists into the air, one of flesh and one of metal, like a victorious prizefighter.

'The *Speranza* is a great machine, and the operation of that machine has become so odious, made us so sick at heart, that we can no longer take part! We cannot even passively take part! So we will put our bodies upon the gears and upon the wheels, upon the levers and upon all the apparatus! We will make the machine stop! And together we will show Archmagos Kotov that unless we are free, his great machine will be prevented from working at all!'

The feeding hall was in uproar now, and Abrehem could no longer see any armsmen or overseers. They had retreated from the growing unrest of the thousands of bondsmen, pulling back to regroup with the armed forces closing in on the feeding hall from all directions. Abrehem dismissed them from his thoughts. They were irrelevant now.

He had an ace in the hole that would make all the guns on the ship meaningless.

Abrehem lowered his arms and turned to Ismael.

'Are you sure you can do this?' he asked.

Ismael nodded. 'I can. They are ready to listen.'

'Then do it,' said Abrehem.

Ismael nodded and closed his eyes.

One by one, on deck after deck, tens of thousands of

cybernetic servitor slaves simply stopped what they were doing. They stepped away from their stations, unplugged from their machines and refused to work another minute.

The *Speranza* ceased to function.

Microcontent 15

Consciousness returned slowly, Linya's implants inducing an artificial coma-like state while running diagnostics on her entire neuromatrix. Satisfied the damage to her skull would not impair her cognitive functions, they stimulated the active cerebral functions, effectively jump-starting her consciousness as intravenous reservoirs flooded her body with stimms.

Linya's eyes snapped open and she drew in a vast, sucking breath of hot, electrically tainted air. The compartment was filled with acrid smoke from the shattered slates and flames burned the sacred machinery behind them to a tangled mass of dripping plastek and molten copper. The one functioning gyroscope told her the entire war-engine was canted over at an angle of fifty-seven degrees.

The heat was intolerable, her skin slick with sweat.

Her head hurt, and blood coated her left temple and cheek. She blinked away tears of pain as she heard her voice being called. She twisted in the entangling restriction of the impact harness, struggling to free her arms as she realised she was trapped. Her internal augmentations were registering dangerously high temperatures that were steadily rising.

Dimly she remembered the fury of the earthquake, the buildings crashing down like sculptures of ash in a rainstorm, the deafening noise… the…

'We fell,' she whispered. 'Ave Deus Mechanicus, we fell…'

Linya struggled against her restraints, pulling and tugging at the leather before forcing herself to calm. She took a breath of hot air, feeling it burn her throat. She heard her name called again, and this time recognised her father's voice echoing in her skull.

+Linya! Linya, are you there!+

'I'm here,' she said, before realising the communication was in the Manifold.

Something nearby creaked and popped, and her compartment lurched suddenly, her angle from the vertical widening to sixty-three degrees.

+Linya!+

+I'm here,+ she said. +I'm all right. What happened? We fell?+

+We did,+ replied her father. +But you have to get out of there. Right now. The leg is sinking. Right now, your compartment is sunk into the crevasse, and enveloped by hot magma.+

+Magma?+

+Yes, technically it's still underground, so I'm calling it magma and not lava, but that's beside the point. Now, can you move? Can you climb up through the femoral companionway?+

Linya twisted her neck up and saw the metal around the narrow hatch above her was shimmering in a heat haze. She nodded and reached down to unsnap the locking mechanism of the impact harness. The metal was hot to the touch, burning her skin as she unbuckled herself, but she forced herself to ignore the pain and remove each neural connection. Where the regular servitor crewman would have required a full suite, she had only the bare minimum thanks to her body's greater sophistication.

+I'm out of the harness,+ she said.

+Linya, please hurry,+ said her father. +The Titan won't be upright for much longer.+

As if to underscore her father's words, the compartment was slowly illuminated by a hot metal glow of orange light. Linya looked down to see the floor shimmering in a haze as it began to melt in the ferocious heat. The hem of her robes was smoking, and it wouldn't take long before it burst into flames. The thought of being cooked alive in this cramped, coffin-like space spurred her to haste, and she swiftly shrugged off the last of the straps and snapped out the final connection.

Linya wriggled out of the impact harness and reached up to grab the metal rungs on the compartment walls.

She screamed as the skin was burned from her palms, and fell back into the harness-seat.

Fighting back tears of pain, Linya wrapped the fabric of her robe around her burned hand and tried again. She gritted her teeth and forced herself upwards, squeezing her body up through the compartment and feeling the onset of a sudden and almost overwhelming claustrophobia.

The hatch was numerically locked and in a single, terrifying second, Linya realised she had no idea of the code. As soon as the thought occurred, Linya gasped as the correct digits rammed into her mind, as forcefully as though they had been blasted into her cerebral cortex by a cranial shunt.

+Thank you, father,+ she said. +But you could have just spoken the code.+

+Don't thank me,+ said Vitali. +That was *Amarok*.+

Blinking away inload trauma, she tapped the code into the panel and the hatch's lock disengaged with a thudding series of ratcheting clangs.

'Thank you, great one,' she said, pressing a cloth-wrapped hand to the Mechanicus icon stamped into the metal collar of the hatch. Linya pushed up and slid the hatch aside, climbing into a space barely wide enough for a malnourished adolescent. Ribbed with bracing struts and complex nests of gyroscopic mechanisms, power relays and repercussive filters, the femoral companionway linked the Warhound's leg with the pilot's compartment, but she wouldn't have to climb that far.

Ruddy daylight poured in through an emergency hatch just below the complex arrangement of gears and gimbals at the Titan's pelvic joint. The air reeked of burning machinery, cooking lubricants and steaming oils. Linya squeezed through the tube, twisting her shoulders and forcing her body into all manner of strange contortions to push past protruding mechanisms and jutting outcrops of reinforcement spars.

Below her, the temperature gradient suddenly spiked and she knew the magma in the crevasse had melted through the floor of the compartment in which she had sat. The Titan sagged as its leg sank deeper, and Linya pulled in desperate fear as she felt the lower reaches of her robe burst into flames. Her shoulders were too wide, and she couldn't shift her body upwards.

+Linya!+ yelled Vitali.

'I can't get out!' she screamed, reaching blindly for the achingly close oblong of daylight just above her. Her feet were burning, the meat seared from her bones and sloughing from her legs like molten wax. Linya's cranial implants registered her pain and did their best to block the worst of it while still allowing her to function, but the sheer awful, intolerable, overwhelming force of it was too hideous for anything designed by the Mechanicus to overcome.

'I can't get out!' screamed Linya, before the heat scorched the words from her lungs.

ARCHMAGOS KOTOV HEARD the words echoing throughout the *Speranza* from Feeding Hall Eighty-Six, but couldn't believe they were real. Bondsmen did not speak out against their rightful masters, they accepted their role within the machine and were honoured to be part of such an interconnected hierarchy. So had it always been before, so would it be now.

'We will make the machine stop!' shouted the voice that had been positively identified as Bondsman Abrehem Locke. 'And together we will show Archmagos Kotov that unless we are free, his great machine will be prevented from working at all!'

As outraged as he had been by such presumption, it was nothing to the horror that followed as the bridge servitors sat bolt upright in unison and, in perfect synchrony, unplugged themselves from their duty stations. Those that could stand, rose from their bench seats and turned to face his command throne, and though he must surely be imagining it, Kotov felt the heat of their accusation.

'Ave Deus Mechanicus,' he said, stepping forwards and turning around to see that same look in every servitor's face.

The noospheric network surged with alarms and warning icons as previously maintained systems began to falter or shut down altogether. Forge control, engine stability, reactor core protocols, life-support... everything was shutting down or already lost. Only the most basic autonomous functions were still active, and even they would soon degrade without intervention.

Throughout the *Speranza*, tech-priests and lexmechanics rushed to every abandoned station in a desperate attempt to restore control, but as numerous as they were, the sheer number of duties undertaken by cybernetics far outweighed any hope of control by the Martian priests.

'What in the name of the Omnissiah has he done?' demanded Kotov.

Magos Blaylock was wired into a dozen systems, via every method of connection available to him. His entourage of stunted vat-creatures stood curiously inert, as though they had decided to no longer assist their master.

'Statement: unknown,' said Blaylock. 'Without exception, every servitor aboard the ship has ceased in its appointed task. They have either shut down their active systems connections or disconnected themselves... *voluntarily*...'

The last word was breathed as a whisper, as if by its very utterance, the evidence before their senses might be refuted. Kotov looked over at Blaylock, who, for the first time since he had been appointed Fabricatus Locum, looked utterly helpless.

'How has he done this?' asked Kotov, stepping down to the deck and dragging noospheric sheets of light to him. He saw the truth of Blaylock's words. Throughout the *Speranza*, the previously compliant servitor crew had ceased their functioning, standing as immobile as the flesh-statues in the cavernous cyberneticising-temples on Mars before the implantation of their encoded routines.

Kryptaestrex was a flaring beacon of angry noospheric code as his carefully structured resupply plans were hopelessly disrupted and the loading docks ceased operating. Across from the Master of Logistics, Azuramagelli struggled to reroute every avionics package previously controlled by a cadre of navigational servitors to his station. The sheer volume of computational data delegated to cybernetics was staggering, and Kotov winced at the data-burden crackling between Azuramagelli's brain fragments.

'We need to re-establish control,' said Kotov, extending a mechadendrite and hooking himself into the control web that oversaw the smooth running of the ship's servitors. 'Immediately. Send a restorative activation code to every servitor aboard the ship.'

No sooner were the words spoken than his mechadendrite surged with feedback. Kotov snatched the sinuous limb from the connection port, trailing a froth of belligerent code and golden sparks.

'The servitor networks are shutting themselves off from us,' said Blaylock. 'Locking themselves behind walls of binaric white noise. Even if we could establish a connection, they wouldn't hear us.'

'We need to get them back,' snapped Kotov. 'I will not be shut out of my own ship by a damned bondsman. A bondsman you have singularly failed to dig out from his wretched hiding place. This is your fault, Tarkis, you should have found and executed this man long before now.'

'Rebuttal: this bondsman all but vanished from the *Speranza*,' said Blaylock. 'No amount of armsmen or bio-signature survey sweeps revealed any trace of his presence. It is my belief he has had help from Mechanicus personnel in evading capture.'

Kotov forced a measure of calm into his floodstream, knowing that such recriminations were pointless. Accusations could be made once control had been re-established.

'How close are our armed forces to the feeding hall?' he asked. 'I want Abrehem Locke dead.'

'Cadians and armsmen are within four minutes,' answered Kryptaestrex. 'But we need this bondsman alive. What if he is the only one able to restore the servitors to their proper place?'

'It's not him,' said Azuramagelli. 'It's the damned servitor that had its memory restored.'

'Impossible,' snapped Kryptaestrex. 'That was just a rumour, a ridiculous farrago spread by the lower menials. I've heard its like a hundred times or more.'

'Then explain this,' said Azuramagelli.

Kotov shut them both up with a harsh blurt of binary.

'A servitor that had its memory restored?' he asked.

'So the lower-deck rumour mill has it,' answered Azuramagelli.

'Tell me everything you have heard,' ordered Kotov. 'Before I lose complete control of my ship.'

THE ENGINARIUM TEMPLUM of the *Speranza* was a place of miracles, where the power of the Omnissiah was at its most controlled and most violent. Forget the explosive death of munitions, forget the murderous power of the Life Eater. In the plasma containment chambers was where the raw, primal essence of the Machine-God and the genius of the Mechanicus were most sublimely combined.

Or so Magos Saiixek had thought until three minutes and fourteen seconds ago.

Now he realised he was standing at the heart of what was likely to be a colossal explosion of superheated plasma energy that would reduce the vast structure of the *Speranza* to vapour. Chiming alarm bells pealed from on high, drowning out the binary hymnals of appeasement as geysers of emergency venting spewed columns of superheated steam into the air. Moist banks of humid, chemically rich vapour gathered about the reactors like jungle-fog, refracting the scintillating illumination of the emergency lights in golden rainbows.

Each cylindrical reactor was five hundred metres in diameter and two kilometres in length – almost eighty-five per cent of their mass comprised layers of ceramite heat shielding and containment field generators. One reactor alone was capable of supplying the energy demands of a mid-sized hive for centuries, and Saiixek was looking at twelve such reactors stretching off towards a vanishing point at the far end of the chamber.

Entire cadres of servitors had been devoted to regulating the unimaginable core temperatures with mantras of prayer or ministering to the many hundreds of machine-spirits inhabiting the mechanisms empowering the reactors. The never-ending catechisms of maintenance and the continual ritualised workings were attended to by five hundred servitors for each reactor and, until three minutes and twenty-five seconds ago, they had been attending to their duties in perfect order.

Now those same servitors simply stood and watched the reactors to which they had been bound relentlessly and inevitably spiral to destruction. Every override code, every mastery file and every Servitudae Obligatus had been rejected, like a high-functioning data-engine ignoring the advances of a lowly technomat. Power was no longer being fed to the engines, and the *Speranza*'s orbital track, already far lower than was prudent, was decaying at a rate that would soon see the ship caught within the planet's gravity envelope beyond hope of escape.

Assuming Saiixek didn't lose control of the reactors before then.

Standing atop the latticed mezzanine, overlooking the array of runaway fusion reactors, Magos Saiixek now understood how perilously tenuous his grasp on their control had been. He had stood at this very station and issued orders to these monolithic machines and thought himself their master.

But what he had mistaken for mastery was little more than an illusion.

Every single mechadendrite Saiixek possessed, from thickly segmented cables like gleaming snakes to fibre-fine sensory wands, was engaged with the control stations to either side. Cold mist surrounded him, the cooling mechanisms of his upthrust backpack coating everything nearby in a veneer of hoarfrost. His black robes cracked in the frozen temperatures, though his metallic skull steamed with excess heat bleed from his monstrously overclocked cognitive processes.

Like a conductor before an impossibly vast and complex orchestra, Saiixek had subsumed the capacity of every magos within range to process the insanely complex hexamathics of uncontrolled fusion in an attempt to keep the reactions from achieving critical mass.

It was an impossible task, and the best he had managed was simply to keep the reactors from exploding. The geometric progression of the calculations' complexity would soon outstrip his borrowed capacity to process, making his efforts a holding action at best, one that would see him burn out large sections of irreplaceable brain matter.

But if his delaying tactic bought time for the archmagos to re-establish control of the *Speranza*'s servitors, it would be a price worth paying.

Saiixek gasped as he felt a sudden thrust of cold within his physical volume.

Such was the level of disconnect from his organic form, it took him several seconds to comprehend that his body had been injured. Saiixek looked down to see a length of white steel jutting from his body, a gracefully curved sword blade of non-Imperial design.

'How curious,' he said, as the blade was withdrawn and stabbed home three more times.

This time there was no ignoring the pain and Saiixek fell to his knees. Blood and oil spilled from the precision-cut wounds in his body, flooding from his internal structures at a rate that he had not the capacity to know was mortal with any sense other than his eyes.

He looked up as a woman circled around from behind him, clad in form-fitting armour of emerald plates. She wore a bone-coloured helmet with a long red plume and bulbous extrusions at the gorget like some form of stinger. Her cloak of gold and green billowed in the vortices of hot and cold air, and her ivory sword dripped oil-dark droplets of his blood to the mezzanine floor.

'Eldar?' asked Saiixek. 'Ridiculous. You cannot be here.'

'You destroyed our vessel,' said the eldar warrior-woman. 'Now we destroy yours.'

'Illogical,' said Saiixek. 'You will die too.'

'To prevent your master from acquiring such power, we would die a thousand deaths.'

'Outrageous hyperbole,' said Saiixek, slumping against a control panel as the life flooded out of him.

'WHAT DO YOU mean, you can't get any closer?' cried Vitali, his desperation clear even over the internal vox from the cargo deck.

'I can't say it any clearer,' replied Roboute. 'We're hooked on an e-mag tether and the *Speranza*'s not reeling us in. I can't raise anyone on the embarkation deck either.'

'Please, we have to get back aboard! Linya will die if we don't get her to a medicae.'

'I know that, damn you,' snapped Roboute, instantly regretting his outburst. 'But unless you can override this tether, we're not going anywhere. The shuttle's trying to link with the embarkation deck's data-engines, but so far no luck. We're not part of Azuramagelli and Kryptaestrex's shipping timetable, and there's no one answering who can override it.'

'The *Speranza* is in lockdown...' said Vitali. 'Something terrible must have happened, an accident or unexpected event.'

'So we're stuck here?'

'Until they bring us in, yes,' said Vitali, and Roboute heard a father's terror at the loss of his child.

It was a terror he shared.

The *Renard*'s shuttle was stuck in a holding pattern below the ventral fantail of the *Speranza*, kept a fixed distance from the Ark Mechanicus by the same e-mag tether that would normally pull them through the gravimetric turbulence surrounding the enormous vessel. Their lift-off had been unscheduled and would no doubt earn them a stern warning from Magos Azuramagelli, but this was an emergency and Roboute was willing to risk any censure to get Linya to a medicae quicker.

Tears rolled down Roboute's face at the thought of Linya Tychon's death.

He understood there was no prospect of a union between them; he'd accepted that. Instead, he'd been looking forward to a growing friendship, but even that looked unlikely.

The distress signal from *Amarok* had been a howling bray of agony, a shriek of unimaginable pain that was instantly recognisable as belonging to a god-machine. Following that brash cry for help came a plea from Vitali Tychon, begging Roboute to fly to their rescue. The signal had been abruptly cut off, and seeing that Legio Sirius recovery craft would not reach the planet's surface for over an hour, Roboute had immediately lifted off.

The *Renard*'s shuttle landed amid the devastation of a ruined city, but Roboute's myriad questions concerning the unexpected metropolis died in his throat as he saw the horrific injuries suffered by Linya.

Only Vitali Tychon had emerged from *Amarok*'s wreckage without significant injuries. With the exception of Princeps Vintras, the crew of the Warhound were dead and the war machine crippled, listing over a sealed crevasse with one leg sunk fully into the cracked ground. Though he still lived, Vintras had not emerged unscathed; Manifold feedback left him weeping and paralysed, his nervous system wracked with sympathetic agony at the mortal wounding of his engine.

But his injuries were nothing compared to what Linya Tychon had suffered.

Roboute barely recognised the young, vivacious girl he'd met at Colonel Anders's dinner, her flesh burned black and raw, with only her upper body having escaped the worst of the hellish inferno. Her father was keeping her alive, barely, with noospheric connections to her neuromatrix blocking the pain centres of her brain, but he was no medicae, and he could do nothing to treat the physical injuries that would undoubtedly kill her. They'd got her on board the shuttle as gently as they could and followed the most direct course for the *Speranza*. The shuttle's servitors were administering first aid as best they could with their limited knowledge of human physiology, but without specialised medicae treatment, Linya would soon be dead.

And now this...

Roboute had tried every trick in the book to break the *Speranza*'s tether, every risky evasion technique and downright dangerous manoeuvre he'd learned in the skies of Ultramar, but nothing had come close to even weakening its grip. They were trapped out here, hooked like a fish on a line, unable to close or break away from the Ark Mechanicus.

A warning light flickered to life on Roboute's avionics panel, and he checked the readout to make sure he was reading it correctly, but hoping he wasn't.

'Hell…' he said, standing and looking out through the shuttle's armourglass canopy. 'Oh, this is so very not good…'

No doubt about it. The shimmering blue-hot plasma glow within the *Speranza*'s containment fields was fading, which meant the engines were no longer supplying thrust.

Which meant its orbit was decaying.

The Ark Mechanicus was going down.

THE GATHERING TOOK place in the forward observatorium above the dorsal transit arrays, a central location that allowed the senior military forces the best options for deployment throughout the ship. From here the mag-lev transit trains were within easy reach, and the main internal teleporter array was in the process of being powered up by a chanting choir of tech-priests – with the accompanying ritual catechisms being voiced by carefully coached deck menials instead of servitors.

Starlight filtering through the upper reaches of Hypatia's atmosphere fell in glittering beams of umber and magenta, illuminating the terrazzo floor panels and reflecting across the multitude of stargazing optical machines that hung from the polished glass dome or stood on vast girder structures.

The commanders of the *Speranza*'s fighting forces gathered to hear Archmagos Kotov's briefing, each rapidly digesting hastily prepared dossiers on the mutiny's ringleaders. Magos Dahan and Sergeant Tanna waited for Kotov to begin, while Colonel Anders continued to peruse his briefing documents.

'What we have here is a full-scale mutiny,' said Kotov to the assembled warriors, wishing to incite in them the same righteous anger at events taking place below decks. 'A bondsman named Abrehem Locke has defied the legal and holy writ of the Mechanicus and incited rebellion throughout the *Speranza*. I want him and his cadre of supporters hunted down and killed.'

'How many targets are you talking about?' asked Tanna.

Magos Blaylock answered the Space Marine's question. 'Six that we know of. Bondsman Locke himself and three others who were collared along with him on Joura, Vannen Coyne, Julius Hawke and Ismael de Roeven.'

'De Roeven? Is he the servitor with the returned memories?' asked Anders.

'So below the waterline rumour would have it,' said Blaylock. 'Though such a thing has never been documented before, so must be viewed with suspicion. In addition, Bondsman Locke is accompanied by a rogue Mechanicus overseer, Totha Mu-32, and an imprinted arco-flagellant, Rasselas X-42. Both should be considered extremely dangerous.'

'An arco-flagellant?' asked Anders with a sudden intake of breath. 'I thought they were purely Inquisition weapons.'

'They are,' said Dahan, flexing the articulated joints of his multiple arms. 'But who do you think makes them for the inquisitors?'

'Where did it come from?' asked Anders.

'Does it matter?' replied Tanna. 'We do not need to know where it came from to kill it.'

'No, but if I'm going to put my men in harm's way, I want to know everything I can about this arco-flagellant. I saw one of them in action on Agripinaa. The thing went through a martyr-company of Bar-el penal troops who'd gone over to the enemy. It wasn't pretty. And if this bondsman has one, then I'm going to damn well know everything there is to know about it.'

'We do not have time for this, Colonel Anders,' said Kotov.

'If the servitors do not return to their stations within the next two hours and eleven minutes, the *Speranza*'s orbit will have decayed to a level that will mean a catastrophic re-entry is inevitable.'

'Then answer my question quickly.'

'Very well,' said Kotov. 'When I discovered the *Speranza*, it was unfinished, a buried skeleton of a starship that was virtually complete, but not entirely so. Many of its deeper structures and chambers were left unexplored or were inaccessible. It is likely this arco-flagellant was implanted with weaponry and pacification routines, but left as a tabula rasa for the designated inquisitor to imprint upon it.'

'So it's been sitting there like a bloody time bomb, just waiting for someone to stumble over it and set it loose?'

Kotov did not care for the Cadian colonel's tone, but recognised he had little time in which to take umbrage. 'Essentially, yes.'

Anders nodded. 'That was careless of you. It's like me forgetting where I parked my Baneblade squadrons and being surprised when someone drives them over me.'

'What information do you have on Bondsman Locke's current whereabouts?' asked Tanna, cutting off Kotov's bilious response. 'Give me his location and my men will use these internal teleporters to attack with a swift and merciless response.'

'For reasons I cannot explain, we are currently unable to track Bondsman Locke or his immediate co-conspirators via their sub-dermal fealty identifiers,' said Blaylock. 'It seems likely they have been removed or shorted out by Totha Mu-32. Which would explain why the regular snatch teams of armsmen and cyber-mastifs were unable to locate them after their initial display of mutinous behaviour.'

'This just gets better and better,' said Anders.

'The mutiny began in Feeding Hall Eighty-Six,' continued Kotov. 'In the short time since then, it appears to have spread to neighbouring decks. Every servitor aboard the *Speranza* is currently in an enforced dormancy state from which they refuse to be roused, but there are tens of thousands of bondsmen aboard this vessel. And every one of them heard Locke's broadcast.'

'So we could be looking at a ship-wide army of mutineers?' asked Tanna.

'You people,' said Anders with a shake of the head. 'You keep calling this a mutiny, but that's not what this is. I can't believe you don't see it.'

'If it is not a mutiny, then what would you call it, colonel?' demanded Magos Dahan.

'It's a strike,' said the Cadian colonel. 'Mutineers want to take over a vessel, but that's not what these men are doing. I've listened to what Bondsman Locke's saying, and I don't think he wants a starship of his own.'

'Then what *does* he want?' asked Kotov.

'You heard what he wants,' said Anders. 'He wants the men of this ship to be treated like human beings. Don't get me wrong, these bondsmen are legitimate servants of the Mechanicus, and they're here to do a job, just like every grunt that joins my regiment. But what every Cadian officer knows, and what the Mechanicus has forgotten, is that the way to get the best out of a man isn't to beat him to death with a stick, but to beat him just enough that he's grateful for a hint that the carrot even exists.'

'Such a thing is unheard of,' said Kotov, horrified at the idea of entering into negotiations with bonded servants. 'They are indentured workers, bound to the purpose of the Mechanicus and the will of the Omnissiah. To allow them to believe that their demands might be met is to break with thousands of years of tradition and precedent. It cannot be done. I refuse to entertain such a vile notion!'

'I don't think you have a choice,' replied Anders. 'In two hours this ship is going down unless you offer these men something that'll convince Abrehem Locke to put the servitors back to work.'

'You believe I should stand before these... *strikers* and address their so-called grievances?'

Anders shook his head and said, 'No, archmagos, I think these negotiations need a human face.'

Microcontent 16

ROBOUTE HAD SEEN and heard many bizarre things in his time as a rogue trader, but the looping recording coming over the vox from the *Speranza* had to rank as one of the strangest. Hearing a man called Abrehem Locke making a stand for the rights of his fellow men on a Mechanicus ship might, under different circumstances, have stirred the underdog in Roboute's heart.

Leaving the shuttle flying on its own autonomous systems, Roboute wound a path through the companionways and corridors of the shuttle to the cramped crew berth where his own servitors – which, thankfully, seemed free of whatever rebellious streak had overtaken those of the *Speranza* – had taken the wounded Linya.

Roboute smelled the stench of her burned flesh long before he reached the berth.

Trying to hide his horror as best he could, Roboute stood in the doorway and felt his fist clench in anger. He didn't know where to direct that anger, no one was to blame for this. According to Vitali, Princeps Vintras had worked miracles in keeping the Titan upright as long as he had. What god was there to rail against for sending the earthquake?

Linya lay encased in a counterseptic dermal wrap that kept contaminants from reaching her burned and exposed flesh, but did nothing to begin the healing process. A basic bio-monitor was hooked up to her arms and an oxygen mask was clamped over her mouth and nose. Her scalp was raw and red where her hair had burned away in clumps, and milky tears leaked from the corners of cracked augmetic eyes. The fire in the Titan had blinded her, but that was probably a good thing.

Concealed beneath the dermal wrap, Linya's legs were crooked lumps of fused meat and burned muscle, little more than ruined nubs of bone. They were fleshless below the shin, and even if she lived, Linya would never again walk as she had done before.

Vitali Tychon sat beside his daughter, resting a spindly mechanical hand next to her on the bed. A slender copper-jacketed wire ran from the back of Linya's skull to an identical port behind Vitali's ear. The old man looked to have aged a hundred years since Roboute had last seen him; no mean feat for a man centuries old.

Vitali didn't look up as Roboute rapped a knuckle against the doorframe, but nodded briefly in acknowledgement of his presence.

'I take it there is no change in the tether's status,' said Vitali, phrasing his words as a statement instead of a question. Vitali would likely know before Roboute if anything changed aboard the *Speranza*.

'No,' said Roboute. 'I'm afraid not.'

Vitali shrugged. 'I could almost admire this Locke fellow

were it not for the fact that his actions will in all likelihood see my daughter dead.'

'They're trying to get things settled, Vitali,' said Roboute.

'Yes, I heard that a parley has been arranged in the main port-side embarkation deck. Apparently the revolutionaries have seized it and are preventing any resupply vessels from docking.'

'Colonel Anders is en route to negotiate with Locke,' said Roboute. 'He's a good man, and if there's a way to sort this, he'll find it.'

'The outcome will not matter to us,' said Vitali sadly. 'The *Speranza*'s orbit is decaying too sharply, and since this shuttle is not as thickly hulled or shielded as the Ark Mechanicus, we will die long before it. We will be torn apart by gravitational stress forces or burned up by atmospheric friction, take your pick. Assuming, of course, the Cadians don't just gun everyone down and doom us all anyway.'

'I got the impression that Colonel Anders is too smart for that kind of gunboat diplomacy.'

'I hope you are right, captain,' sighed Vitali. 'In any case, it is clever of the archmagos to send a human to speak to Locke. A less inhuman face might make all the difference.'

Vitali reached out to place his hand gently on Linya's shoulder, the clicking fingers of his metallic hand clenching into a fist before they made contact.

'She always wanted to hold onto her baseline body-plan as long as possible,' said Vitali, and even with his back turned, the man's grief was entirely obvious. 'Seems like such a silly thing to have insisted on, but she was quite adamant.'

'I don't blame her,' said Roboute. 'It's easy to forget your humanity when you don't see it in the mirror every day.'

'That's the kind of thing she used to say.'

'She'll get through this,' said Roboute, 'She's a strong one. I hadn't got to know her well, but that much I could tell.'

'You are not wrong, young man,' said Vitali, finally turning to face him.

Nothing could have prepared Roboute for the deathly pallor and gaunt death mask of Vitali's face.

His eyes were sunken deep into their sockets; though the majority of his flesh was artificial, there was no disguising the suffering he was experiencing.

'Imperator, are you all right?' asked Roboute.

Vitali nodded, though he was clearly very far from all right.

'My daughter lies dying before my very eyes,' said Vitali. 'Within sight of one of the greatest technological marvels of the galaxy. There's an irony there somewhere.'

Roboute knelt beside Vitali and placed a hand on the venerable stargazer's shoulder. He felt vibrations running through Vitali's body, the micro-tremors of a man holding back an ocean of unimaginable, fiery agony.

'Pain has to go somewhere,' said Vitali, the muscles in his face tensing and twitching with the effort of keeping his daughter alive. 'And I couldn't let her last hours be filled with suffering.'

Roboute had heard that Vitali was managing Linya's pain, but seeing the traumatic reality of that process was horrifying. He felt his admiration at Vitali's devotion to his daughter soar – the Ultramarian core of him knew he could do no less.

He stood and used the vox-panel on the wall to open a channel to the *Renard*.

After a minute of clicking, static-filled growls, Emil Nader's voice barked from the augmitter.

'Roboute,' said Emil. 'Are you aboard yet? We can't get anything from the Mechanicus, all the internal systems are down. What in Konor's name is going on?'

'Shut up and listen, Emil,' snapped Roboute. 'We don't have much time. The *Speranza*'s on lockdown, and the shuttle's snagged on an e-mag tether.'

'Hell, and I guess you know the orbital track of the Ark's decaying?'

'Painfully aware,' replied Roboute. 'Now listen, we need to get back aboard right bloody now, and I'm going to need your help to do it.'

'Go ahead, whatever you need.'

'You remember that lunatic hauler pilot out of Cypra Mundi, the one with the ship that had those giant green eyes painted on its prow?'

'Rayner? The captain of *Infinite Terra*?'

'That's the one,' said Roboute. 'You remember how he died?'

'Of course I do,' said Emil. 'I still get nightmares thinking about the evacuation of Brontissa.'

'Yeah, tyranids do make things messy,' agreed Roboute. 'Now listen up, Emil. We're stuck out here, and unless Mistress Tychon gets to a proper medicae deck soon, she's going to die.'

'Shit! What do you need us to do?'

Roboute took a deep breath, knowing that what he was about to ask of his first mate was so dangerous that it might charitably be called suicidal.

But if there was one pilot in the galaxy Roboute would trust to pull this off, it was Emil Nader.

'I need you to do what Rayner tried,' said Roboute. 'But I need you to pull it off.'

IT FELT STRANGE going into a hostile situation without his ubiquitous Hellhound tanks at his back or the roaring form of a Leman Russ Conqueror beneath him. Colonel Ven Anders firmly believed that marching towards the enemy on foot was a tactic of last resort or a way for gloryhounds to get themselves killed trying to make a name for themselves.

Yet here he was, marching towards the towering shutters of the embarkation deck at the head of a command squad of twenty Cadian Guardsmen, and not a single battle tank to be seen. Archmagos Kotov wasn't about to let him negotiate with Abrehem Locke without a show of force from the Mechanicus, and thus Magos Dahan and three Cataphract battle robots marched with him.

Anders wished the archmagos had despatched someone else. Dahan was twitchy and full of blistering indignation at this strike, just the sort of mindset that could turn this negotiation into a full-blown firefight. Bringing three hulking battle robots didn't exactly display a willingness to reach a peaceful solution.

Sergeant Tanna and a warrior named Varda were also part of the detachment, but were at least keeping a low profile to the back of this detachment – or as low a profile as two Space Marines could keep. Anders's original plan of keeping a human face on the negotiations was starting to look less and less convincing, but he'd extracted oaths from both Dahan and Tanna that they would make no aggressive moves. Beside him, Captain Hawkins fought to keep his hands from reaching towards his pistol and sword.

'Steady, captain,' said Anders as they reached the embarkation deck. 'We don't want to upset the natives, now do we?'

'Sorry, sir,' replied Hawkins, conspicuously forcing his hands to his sides. 'Force of habit.'

'Understandable, but I want it absolutely clear that there is to be no weapon drawn without my express order. I don't even want bad language or unkind thoughts, you understand?'

'Absolutely, sir,' said Hawkins. 'I've passed the word, and

anyone that messes up will have Rae to answer to.'

'I think Lieutenant Rae will be the least of anyone's worries if this goes to hell.'

'Right enough, sir,' said Hawkins as the shutter began to grind its way aside, accompanied by the wheezing clatter of gears and protesting servos.

'Here we go,' whispered Anders, marching into the embarkation deck. 'Once more into the Eye.'

The cavernous space beyond the shutters should have been filled with industrious labour; with servitors, bondsmen and Mechanicus logisters coordinating deck operations to Kryptaestrex's detailed resupply plans. A dozen recently arrived cargo haulers sat before the shimmering integrity field at the opening to the void, their hulls icy and sealed shut. Stevedore-servitors stood dumbly at the cargo doors, unmoving and rendered uncooperative by whatever power Abrehem Locke's restored servitor had exercised over them.

Ready to meet them were around fifty men in the dirty red coveralls of Mechanicus bondsmen. Anders saw thousands more behind them, lounging on stacked crates, milling in conspiratorial groups or sprawled on the deck asleep. To see men asleep while the clock ticked down to extinction almost beggared belief, but Anders had long since learned that human beings were capable of the strangest behaviour in times of crisis.

Their welcoming committee had ripped the sleeves from their uniforms or otherwise disfigured them in an obvious attempt at visibly throwing off the shackles of their perceived oppressors. Every one of them was armed, either with a heavy length of steel piping or a buzzing power tool of some description. Anders recognised the leader of this group immediately: Julius Hawke, an ex-Guardsman and a die-hard malingerer according to his file. He carried a rusted laslock, and despite a long list of disciplinary infractions and poor performance evaluations, it was clear he knew how to use it.

'You Anders?' asked Hawke.

'I am Colonel Ven Horatiu Anders, Colonel of the 71st Cadian Regiment of Hellhounds. Why aren't you in uniform any more, Guardsman Hawke?'

'Been a long time since anyone's called me that,' laughed Hawke, a sour bark that spoke of years spent undermining authority and mocking his betters. Despite what he'd said to Hawkins, Anders felt a strong desire to draw his sabre and run this affront to soldiery through. 'I'm just Hawke now, and I *am* in uniform. This is the uniform of the ain't going to take any more shit regiment.'

'I am here to speak with Abrehem Locke,' said Anders. 'So I'd be obliged if you'd take me to him.'

Hawke shook his head. 'I don't think so.'

The man's tone was infuriating and Anders bit back an angry retort.

'I was told he would be here.'

'Yeah, he is, but we didn't say nothing about bringing three bloody battle robots and a couple of Space Marines hiding at the back,' said Hawke. 'You think we're stupid?'

Anders dearly wanted to give the answer he knew he shouldn't, but contented himself by saying, 'Every second of my time you waste brings this ship closer to destruction. You tell me if that's stupid.'

'I've seen your sort before,' said Hawke. 'Think they're better than the rest of us grunts. You know, I knew an officer called Anders once before. A cocksure bastard, that's for sure. Got himself killed on Hydra Cordatus.'

'Ah, yes,' said Anders. 'I read your statement on the way here.

During a supposed attack by Space Marines of the Archenemy, wasn't it?'

Hawke nodded. 'Yeah, that's the one.'

'On a dead world of no material or strategic significance,' said Anders. 'An attack both the Adeptus Mechanicus and Adeptus Astartes claim never happened.'

'That's what the Mechanicus *want* you to believe,' sneered Hawke, as though Anders were the very model of gullibility. 'Course they're not going to admit there was a fortress there and that the enemy came and took it off them like coins from a drunk.'

'Can you take me to Bondsman Locke or not?' asked Anders, tiring of Hawke's rambling.

'Yeah, I can, but just you.'

Captain Hawkins stepped forwards and said, 'That's not going to happen.'

'Now who's wasting time?' asked Hawke.

Anders waved Hawkins back. 'If that's what it takes to end this.'

'Sir, you can't just–'

'Captain, remain here with the men,' said Anders.

'Sir, I can't let you walk in there alone,' insisted Hawkins.

Anders ignored Hawkins's protests and said, 'I will be quite safe, I assure you. I need you to maintain discipline and keep the ranks straight. Oh, and if I'm not back in twenty minutes…'

'Sir?'

'You have my permission to kill everyone on this deck.'

Anders turned back to Hawke, whose face was a picture in stunned shock.

'Right then, Bondsman Hawke,' said Anders. 'Take me to your leader.'

Making her way through the guts of the humans' starship was childishly easy. Its gloomy corridors were draped in shadows and threaded with passageways even its crew appeared to have forgotten. The sepulchral gloom masked Bielanna's ascent from the depths of the ship as she slid through the shadows of towering machines that had not moved for centuries and along abandoned passageways ankle-deep in rat-infested water.

Towering metallic skull-on-cog icons stared down at her at every turn, nestling cheek by jowl with fretted stone gargoyles and gleaming machinery of brutish complexity: all pneumatic gears, clanking chains and smoke-belching pistons. The humans' starship was a mass of contradictions: a nightmarish temple where inhuman machinery was venerated and a breeding ground for the teeming masses of humanity who crewed it.

Bielanna would never understand the mon-keigh, a race so numerous and wantonly fecund that they outnumbered the stars. But the unimaginable scale of their species did not give them solace, but rather filled them with fear and drove them to stamp out any form of life and worship that did not match their own. Such unthinking hatred could only ever breed hatred in return, but the humans could not see that by their own actions were they damning themselves to an eternity of strife.

The more Bielanna saw of the humans aboard this ship, the less she thought of them as sentient beings at all. They were living grease in a grinding mechanical engine, corpuscles shunted from place to place in service of the great machine's continuance. How they could not see that they were little better than microbes crawling within the body of a larger beast was beyond her.

'They are not worshipping you,' she whispered, pausing beneath one of the half-machine, half-human skulls stamped on a sheet steel wall. 'You enslave them and they believe themselves blessed.'

The skull belched a gout of flame and smoke from its empty eye socket, and Bielanna slid away into the darkness, following the threads of fate that had led her to risk moving into the occupied areas of the ship.

The vision had come suddenly, staggering her with its potency.

A gathering of humans in one of the vast chambers used to bring their ugly cargo ships aboard.

The meeting of a warrior and a man reluctantly fated to be both a saviour and a destroyer.

Most human lives were so ephemeral that their influence on the skein was microscopic, so infinitesimal that they were virtually an irrelevance, but whoever these two men were, they were worthy of notice, men whose actions could actually have an impact on the future.

Ariganna's impatience had made the meeting of these men inevitable, a fixed locus upon the skein around which a million times a billion possibilities revolved. The exarch had grown tired of skulking in the depths of the starship and given in to her war-mask's urge to kill. Where she had previously confined her slayings to those mon-keigh that unwittingly entered their shadowy lair, now she actively hunted the upper decks as a lone predator of unparalleled savagery and limitless cruelty. Bielanna had seen Ariganna kill the magos controlling the lethally volatile engine reactors. A bewilderingly complex web of infinite possibility exploded before her eyes.

As Bielanna had hoped, her connection to the skein had become stronger with every passing day and every light year the ship travelled from the reborn star system. But instead of cohering her sight of the future, that strengthening had only made her interpretations more ambiguous. Entwined memories of the past and visions of the future's infinite variety filled her every waking moment, and Bielanna found it almost impossible to distinguish between what was real and what was imagined.

Yet the vision of these two men remained constant whenever she looked into the future.

She came at last to the place where the thread of fate she had been following now branched out beyond her ability to trace with any certainty: a towering stained-glass window depicting a grey-steel temple atop a red mountain that churned out armoured vehicles and smoke in equal measure. One of the window's lower panes was broken, and Bielanna eased herself through, emerging onto a stonework ledge overlooking a vast deck space with an enormous opening on its far wall that looked onto the void.

Thousands of the mon-keigh were gathered below her, flickering embers of life and fleeting existence. Some embers burned brighter than others, and she flinched at the radiance coming from two black-armoured giants, kin to the warrior the avatar of Kaela Mensha Khaine had killed. She had seen the fate-lines of Space Marines before, and they burned with a directness that was almost pitiable, but the fates of these warriors felt somehow familiar, as though she had flown the futures they too would walk.

Simmering aggression filled the deck like a sickness, and Bielanna needed no psychic sensitivity to feel the rippling undercurrents of fear and imminent violence oozing into the atmosphere.

That was good.

She could use one to provoke the other.

Leering cherubs with rebreathers instead of faces had been

carved on either side of the window, and as she knelt at the corner of the ledge, the metallic skull of the nearest rolled a mechanised eye in her direction. Bielanna ignored it, feeling her gaze drawn to the flickering energy field that kept the deck pressurised. She felt a momentary tremor of unease at the sight of unknown stars that should not exist.

She shook off the sensation of being watched by these ghoulish stars and took a breath of polluted air as her senses eased into the flickering fate-lines of the mon-keigh. She sought the one whose fear was the greatest and most easily moulded, finding him easily among the mass of slave workers and shrouding his mind with emanations of his darkest nightmares.

The future was bewilderingly complex and inconstant, but one thing was certain.

The humans known as Anders and Locke could not be allowed to settle their differences.

Anders sat on a shipping crate on the far side of the embarkation deck. He and Abrehem Locke sat opposite one another, ringed by a laager of tracked Mechanicus earth-moving machinery. Anders had to admit to feeling a little let down by the sight of the firebrand whose rhetoric of insurrection had echoed from one end of the *Speranza* to the other.

Hollow cheeked and shaven headed, with metallic glints at the corners of his eyes, Abrehem Locke did not look or sound like a revolutionary, and his augmetic arm wasn't particularly impressive either without weapons or any form of combat attachments. He looked exactly like what he was: a Mechanicus bondsman on the verge of starvation, exhaustion and mental breakdown.

Anders could almost sympathise.

The arco-flagellant, however, was another matter. The

cybernetic killer stared with an undisguised urge to kill him, but Anders dismissed it. If it attacked him, he would be dead before he even had a chance to react, so there was no point wasting time worrying about it.

'You realise that if we fail to reach agreement, we all die,' said Anders.

'I'm aware of that,' replied Locke.

'Then tell me what I can do to end this.'

'You can get Archmagos Kotov to release the bondsmen,' said Locke. 'I'd ask for the servitors to be reverse engineered if I didn't think the iatrogenic shock would kill them.'

Anders nodded. 'You know he's not going to agree to that. Especially after you had the Master of Engines killed.'

Locke's eyes narrowed and his shoulders squared in irritation. 'Saiixek is dead?'

'I believe that was his name, yes.'

'Saiixek was the first magos I saw when I came aboard the *Speranza*,' said Locke. 'He worked a hundred men to death before we'd even broken Joura's orbit, hundreds more just to reach the galactic edge. I won't shed a single tear for that bastard, but we didn't kill him. Unlike Magos Kotov, I don't have blood on my hands.'

'We *all* have blood on our hands, my friend,' said Anders, surprised to find that he believed Abrehem. 'All service to the Emperor requires sacrifice.'

'I'd prefer my own sacrifice in the Emperor's name to be a willing one,' said Locke, lifting his bionic arm by way of example. 'That's what Kotov fails to understand. This ship is a machine to him, and all we are to him is human fuel to keep it going, to be spent and used up at will.'

'You should try life in the Imperial Guard,' said Anders.

Locke shook his head. 'No, you misunderstand me, Colonel

Anders. I know the realities of life in the Imperium. Everyone serves, whether they want to or not. Sure, maybe we didn't all sign up for this, but we're here now and we have a job to do. Treat us like slaves and all he'll get is resentment and revolt. Treat us like human beings worthy of respect and everything changes.'

'Do you think the Mechanicus are capable of that?'

'They can learn,' said Locke, leaning forwards. 'After all, it's in their best interest. Which would you rather lead into battle, a regiment of willing soldiers who know you're going to do your damnedest to keep them alive, or a bunch of conscripts who couldn't give a shit for your war or who won it?'

'I'm Cadian, so you already know the answer to that, but rhetorical questions aren't going to solve this,' said Anders, nodding to the cyborg killer at Abrehem's shoulder. 'Since you seem keen to point out hypocrisy, isn't it a bit rich that you keep that arco-flagellant around? He's bio-imprinted to you now, a slave to your every command. Do you want him to be freed too? The archmagos tells me there's no file on who he was before his transmogrification, but he would have been a monster. A child murderer or rapist or a heretic. Or something even worse.'

Locke appeared genuinely disturbed at Anders's words, as though the provenance of the arco-flagellant had never occurred to him, or he knew something of the arco-flagellant's previous existence he wished he didn't. Given what was rumoured of Abrehem Locke's nature, the latter seemed a more likely explanation.

'You're right, of course,' said Abrehem with a fixed expression. 'But right now a little hypocrisy is a price I'm willing to pay to get what I want.'

'A little evil in service of a greater good, is that it?'

'That's a negative way of putting it.'

'I don't see another,' said Anders. 'Listen, Abrehem, you can't sit there on your high horse, demanding freedom and claiming to hold the moral high ground, then admit that you're willing to accept a little bit of slavery if it achieves your aims.'

'I don't have a choice, colonel,' said Locke, and once again Anders saw past the hectoring rebel to the desperately tired man whom circumstances had forced into the role of a leader; a role he was manifestly unsuited to filling. 'This is the only way.'

Anders folded his arms and said, 'You strike me as an intelligent man, Abrehem, not a suicidal one. You must have some level at which you're willing to compromise. We could sit here and haggle and posture till we reach that level, but as I'm sure you know, we don't have the luxury of time. With Saiixek's death and servitors refusing to work, the *Speranza*'s going down. Very soon, we'll all be dead unless you and I can agree.'

'At least this way it will be by our hand instead of the Mechanicus.'

'And what about everyone else?' asked Anders, letting a measure of his anger show. 'What about all my soldiers? The menials, the void-born, and all the other thousands of souls aboard this vessel? Are you willing to murder them all over a principle? I don't think so.'

Locke's eyes flashed defiance, but it was hollow bravado and the fire went out of him. He was angry, yes, but he wasn't willing to murder an entire ship to achieve his goals.

Anders knew he'd won and felt the knot of tension in his gut relax.

Before he could take solace in Locke's backing down, the sharp crack of a gunshot echoed from the other side of the laager of vehicles. Anders recognised the sound with a sinking heart.

M36 Kantrael-pattern lasrifle.

Cadian issue…

OF ALL THE manoeuvres Emil Nader had attempted in his long years spent at the helm of a starship, this had to rank as one of the stupidest. He'd made emergency warp jumps before he'd reached the Mandeville point, run the gauntlet of greenskin roks and navigated the heart of an asteroid belt, but this was just insane.

The panel in front of him was lit with repeated calls for him to return to the ship, calls that only served to highlight the bone-headed literalness of the Mechanicus perfectly.

'Demand: vessel *Renard*, your launch is unauthorised,' said a grating mechanical voice over the vox. 'You are to return to the *Speranza* immediately and shut down your engines.'

Emil didn't waste breath in replying, knowing there would be no point.

'Repeated demand: vessel *Renard*, your launch is unauthorised. You are to–'

Magos Pavelka interrupted. 'While it is true that we do not have clearance to depart the forward embarkation deck, we are of the opinion that remaining aboard is not the safest option since the *Speranza* is in imminent danger of breaking up in the planet's atmosphere.'

'Couldn't have put it better myself,' said Emil, shutting off the vox-feed from the *Speranza*'s deck magos. 'We'll make a scoundrel out of you yet, Ilanna.'

Pavelka sat across from him in the co-pilot's seat, while Sylkwood was down in the engine spaces, trying to keep the *Renard*'s engines hot enough to make the manoeuvre possible without turning the flanks of the *Speranza* to molten slag.

'I do not flout Mechanicus protocols lightly, Mister Nader,' said Pavelka, feeding as much navigational data as she could to Emil's station. 'The deck magos will enforce proper chastisement upon our return to the *Speranza*.'

'Seriously?'

'Of course,' said Pavelka. 'As is only right and proper.'

'Assuming we don't die out here.'

'Assuming we do not die,' agreed Pavelka. 'I calculate the odds of our success as–'

'No, no, no...' said Emil. 'I don't want to know, you'll jinx me.'

Pavelka looked as though she was about to rise to that particular morsel, but simply nodded and carried on feeding him information on the gravimetric field enveloping the Ark Mechanicus. The ancient machinery generating the *Speranza*'s internal gravity, coupled with its sheer mass, created a squalling region of turbulence that made just flying in a straight line a daunting challenge.

This was where the e-mag tether had stranded the *Renard's* shuttle.

'You are aware, of course, that the last captain to attempt a manoeuvre such as this was killed and his ship lost with all hands?' said Pavelka.

'Yeah, I'm aware of that,' he said. 'In fact I saw it, but Rayner was crazy and he had dozens of tyranid bio-parasites clamped to his hull. Even if he'd pulled it off, everyone on that ship would have died. Trust me, compared to what he tried, this'll be easy.'

'Then you and I differ on the definition of *easy*.'

Emil grinned and thumbed the brass-topped switch connecting him to the engineering spaces below. 'Sylkwood, you about ready?'

Even over the vox, the enginseer's abrasive tones were clear.

'Yeah, we're ready, but don't expect this to be a smooth ride.'

'Just so long as it's one we all survive.'

'I'm not promising anything,' said Sylkwood. 'We're going to lose some of the manoeuvring jets, and the structure's not rated for this tight a turn.'

'But the *Renard*'s a tough old bird, yeah? She'll hold together, won't she?'

'Tell her you love her, then promise you'll never make her fly like this again and she might.'

Emil nodded and flexed his fingers on the ship's control mechanisms. Ordinarily, a ship the size of the *Renard* would rarely be flown manually, operating instead via a series of inputted commands, moving between pre-configured waypoints and automated flight profiles.

'Is there anything I could say that would persuade you to let the onboard data-engine navigate us to the shuttle?' asked Pavelka. 'You cannot hope to process the sheer amount of variables in the *Speranza*'s gravitational envelope.'

'If you're not willing to trust your own skills over the onboard systems then you don't deserve to call yourself a pilot,' answered Emil. 'I learned everything about starships in the atmosphere of Espandor, and I know how to fly the *Renard* better than any machine. I know her ticks and her every quirk. She and I have been through more scrapes than I care to remember. She knows me and I know her. I take care of her, and she's looked after us all for years. She's not about to let us down now, not when Roboute's in trouble.'

Pavelka reached over and laid a hand on Emil's shoulder.

'The *Renard* is a fine ship, one of the best I have known,' she said. 'And for all that I believe you to be needlessly antagonistic towards my order, you are a fine pilot. You might not wish to know the odds of this venture succeeding, but I am fully aware of the likelihood of success.'

'Is that a good thing?'

'Of all the baseline humans I know, I would have no other piloting this ship right now, Emil.'

Pavelka's uncharacteristically human words touched him, as did her use of his given name.

'Then let's go get our captain,' said Emil.

Microcontent 17

Captain Hawkins threw himself at Guardsman Manos, knocking him to the deck before he could fire again, but the damage had already been done. The first bondsman died with a neat las-burn drilled through the centre of his skull and his brains flash-burned to vapour. No sooner had he collapsed than Manos switched targets, killing another seven bondsmen on full-auto before Hawkins reached him.

'Stand down!' shouted Hawkins, fighting to pin Manos down. 'That's an order, soldier!'

Manos screamed and thrashed in terror, his face twisted in horror.

'They're monsters, captain!' screamed Manos. 'Let me up or they'll kill us all!'

Hawkins locked his elbow around the struggling Guardsman's neck as the cries of outrage from the bondsmen intensified. Any moment they were going to look for payback.

'The monsters from the Eye!' shouted Manos. 'Can't you

see them? They're going to kill us!'

'Manos, shut the hell up,' ordered Hawkins, tightening his grip. 'You're not making any sense.'

'I saw them,' sobbed Manos, his words slurring as Hawkins's sleeper hold took effect. 'They look like people, but their disguises slipped and I saw them... They're beasts straight out of the Eye and we have to kill them all... please...'

The bondsmen were yelling for blood now and moving towards the Cadian line.

Manos's struggles ceased as he slipped into unconsciousness, and Hawkins sprang to his feet as the man Colonel Anders had identified as Hawke supplied the final push over the cliff to this situation.

'They came here to kill us, lads!' shouted Hawke. 'Get them before they get us!'

The bondsmen threw themselves at the Cadian line, brandishing power tools and heavy spars of metal. Hawkins didn't fail to notice that Hawke wasn't leading the charge, but hanging back behind some of the larger bondsmen.

'No shooting!' shouted Hawkins as the bondsmen slammed into the Cadian ranks.

A man with a full-facial tattoo of a spider came at him, swinging a heavy piece of iron pipework. Hawkins ducked the swing and slammed the heel of his palm into the man's solar plexus. He stepped back as the man dropped with a *whoosh* of expelled air and brought his own rifle around to use as a cudgel. Three men in faded red coveralls attacked and Hawkins staggered as a clubbing fist smashed into the side of his head.

Instinctive training responses took over and he swung his rifle out in a sweeping arc that connected with his attacker's stomach and doubled him over. He dropped the second man with a jab of the lasgun's butt to the head and shook off the dizziness of his own hurt. He felt hands dragging his shoulders and spun around, slamming his rifle into the chest of his attacker.

His rifle butt split along its length against Sergeant Tanna's breastplate.

The Space Marine didn't so much as flinch at the impact.

Tanna hauled him back into the line of fighting, lifting him as though he weighed no more than a child. Tanna swept his arms out, knocking back half a dozen bondsmen with every blow.

Many of the men fell with broken bones, but Hawkins knew they were lucky to be alive. Anyone that attacked a warrior of the Adeptus Astartes was courting death, and the restraint in Tanna's blows was clear.

'Staying here is futile,' said Tanna. 'We must withdraw.'

'We're not leaving without the colonel,' replied Hawkins.

'Then lethal force is our only option.'

'No, we're not killing any more of these men!'

'We may not have a choice,' said Tanna.

The bondsmen had them surrounded, punching, kicking and screaming at them in fury. Hawkins's Guardsmen had formed an impromptu shield wall, fighting to keep the bondsmen back with vicious blows of rifle butts. Dahan fought with the bulbous pod at the base of his halberd, which was thankfully deactivated. The battle robots were currently inactive, but it wouldn't take this situation long to escalate to a level where Dahan felt he had no choice but to bring their terrifyingly destructive guns to bear.

The Space Marines fought without weapons, bludgeoning the bondsmen back with blows that were delivered with a finesse that was as precise as it was bone-crunching. Wherever Hawkins looked, he saw Cadians and bondsmen locked in vicious brawls. Discipline was paying off against anger, as the raw fury of the bondsmen was no match for Cadian training. Every man in Hawkins's command was fighting as part of a unit, each defending their fellow soldiers' backs and expecting the same in return. Living in the shadow of the Eye of Terror demanded a dedication to martial brotherhood that few other regiments could match.

Hawkins struggled to see if there was any way they could reach the circle of earth-moving machines where the colonel had gone to negotiate with Abrehem Locke. The deck was awash with bondsmen – there was no way they could make headway through so many men. At least not without using their weapons, and even then it was doubtful. Getting to the colonel looked hopeless, but then Hawkins saw the ex-Guardsman, Hawke. The man was doing his best to avoid the fighting, but the sheer press of bodies had forced him to the front.

'You're mine,' said Hawkins, shouldering his way through the fighting.

Hawke saw him coming, but there was nowhere for him to go.

The two of them slammed together and Hawkins pistoned his fist into the man's face.

Hawke hadn't survived the Guard for years without learning how to take a punch, and he rolled with the blow, ducking and slamming his own fist up into Hawkins's gut. The ex-Guardsman was a brawler, and a dirty fighter to boot. The two of them scrapped and grappled each other without finesse, clawing, gouging and hammering at one another like drunken pugilists at a punchbag.

Hawke fought with every foul trick in the gutter-fighter's arsenal, but Cadians knew every below the belt trick. Hawkins saw the next blow coming, a knee to the groin, and lifted his own leg to block it. He dropped and swung his rifle around, slamming the cracked butt against the side of Hawke's thigh. The man howled in pain, but Hawkins wasn't about to let up his assault.

He slammed a right cross into Hawke's cheek and followed that up with the opposite elbow to the temple. The man collapsed and Hawkins dropped onto his chest, pummelling him with right and left hooks until his face was a mask of blood.

He hauled the man upright and shouted in his face.

'Stop this now before someone gets killed!' he shouted.

Hawke spat a mouthful of blood, and even through his mangled features, he was grinning.

'You bastards started this,' he coughed. 'Your man shot one of ours.'

'I don't know what that was about, but if you don't call your men off, people are going to die.'

'Too late for that,' said Hawke, as a figure clad in black and silver landed next to one of Dahan's battle robots. Silver threshing limbs swept out and the robot's right arm was severed cleanly from its chassis. Another whipping blow and its head spun away from its neck as though it had been punched off by an ogryn.

A second robot was felled as its left leg was sheared off at the hip, and it crashed to the deck with its motors screeching and its augmitters blaring in machine pain. Hawkins released Hawke and stared into the flickering red eyes of a cybernetic killer.

The arco-flagellant knelt in the ruin of the two Cataphracts, the gleaming silver electro-flails sparking with electrical discharge as the oily lifeblood of the robots burned away.

'Kill. Maim. Destroy,' it said.

THE RENARD'S KEEL measured just under three kilometres, which meant that its normal turning circle was correspondingly large. A starship's hull and internal structure was designed to withstand the stresses of the void and vast forces of acceleration, but no human shipwright had ever designed a vessel of such displacement to be nimble.

But that was just what Emil Nader was asking of it now.

They were clear of the *Speranza*, and with a last nod towards Ilanna Pavelka, he hauled the controls around and fired a sequenced burn of manoeuvring rockets along the length of the hull. Vectored thrust from the starboard prow jets fired at maximum thrust, while the port-side jets on the ship's rear and dorsal sections provided counter-thrust to complete the pivoting turn.

Emil felt himself pressed into his seat as local gravity within the *Renard* increased. The superstructure groaned as torsion forces tried to buckle structural ribs and twist the keel into unnatural shapes.

'Lambda deck breached,' said Pavelka. 'Hull stresses thirty per cent past recommended tolerances. Engine containment field strength diminishing.'

Emil didn't answer. What would be the point? He'd always known this manoeuvre wouldn't be possible without suffering. He could feel the ship's pain, but forced himself to ignore it. To halt their manoeuvre now would be just as dangerous. He fired another sequenced blast of thrust, rolling the *Renard* onto its back relative to the *Speranza*. He let the turn continue until the two vessels were facing one another, before firing the main engines with a corrective burn on the vectored thrusters to stabilise their yaw.

The *Renard* was shaking itself apart as conflicting thrusts placed intolerable loads on its superstructure. Steel girders the thickness of Titan legs were twisting like heated plastic, and precision-machined panels were bursting from their settings as the ship warped under stresses beyond what even the most exacting inspector might demand.

'Lateral distance to *Speranza* is closing,' said Pavelka. 'Remember, she's in a downward spiral and our closure rate is increasing.'

'Compensating,' said Emil, his fingertips dancing over the control panel to apply an insistent thrust to keep them a more or less constant distance from the Ark Mechanicus. The mountainous bulk of the *Speranza* began shifting over the *Renard* as the smaller ship slid past below. The controls were fighting him all the way as the rogue gravitational forces surrounding the mighty vessel slammed into the *Renard*.

Scads of the upper atmosphere shimmered around the *Renard*, evidence of the descending spiral track of the *Speranza*. Striated bands of gaseous colours were bleeding into the black of space and Emil read a sudden and alarming spike of heat on the *Renard*'s ventral surfaces as he was forced to factor atmospheric friction into his course corrections. Gravity had the *Speranza* in its grip, and it wouldn't be long before that grip became unbreakable.

Emil dragged his eyes from the view through the canopy. What he was seeing out there didn't matter for now. Instead, he kept his gaze focused on the slender route he had mapped towards the *Renard*'s shuttle, a hair-fine parabola that only a lunatic might think was possible. He wasn't even aware of the adjustments he was making to their course, an innate skill and feel for the motion of a starship informing his every action. The structure of the *Speranza* flew over them, titanic manufactories and enormous processing plants slipping past silently as the two ships passed at what was, in spatial terms, point-blank range.

The gravity fields sought to pull the two ships together, but Emil kept them apart with deft flares from the dorsal vectors and an unimaginably delicate hand on the controls. At such differential speeds and at such close range, even minute alterations in pitch meant kilometres of space between the two ships would vanish in seconds.

'There, up ahead,' said Pavelka.

Emil risked a quick glance through the canopy and saw a glint of reflected light from the shuttle's hull. The term shuttle was misleading, as that vessel was itself over two hundred metres long and thirty wide. The tether holding it in place was invisible, but that the shuttle wasn't being buffeted from side to side by the *Speranza*'s gravity envelope was enough to tell Emil it was there. Its perceived motion was caused by the *Renard*'s erratic movement, which – minute as it was in relative terms – was still hundreds of metres to either side.

All of which would make scooping the shuttle up in the *Renard*'s forward cargo bay… tricky.

'Captain,' said Emil. 'We see you and are closing on your position.'

'Understood,' came Roboute's voice over the vox. 'You still reckon you can make this work?'

'*Please*. This is me you're talking to. It'll be like threading a needle from the back of a racing land speeder while blindfolded,' said Emil. 'Easy money if you fancy a wager.'

'You think I'd bet against you?' asked Roboute. 'You're as insane as Rayner.'

'Rayner couldn't wipe his own arse without a map and a servitor,' said Emil. 'Now shut up and fire the rig's drives when I give you the word.'

The shuttle steadily grew in size through the canopy, becoming a vaguely rectangular smear of light, then an identifiable silhouette of a trans-orbital ship, and finally a unique vessel. Emil fought to keep the buffeting movement of the *Renard* to a minimum, knowing that even the tiniest movement out of place would see both ships torn apart by a collision at towering closure speeds.

'Emergency depressurisation of frontal cargo hold,' said Pavelka. 'Opening frontal cargo doors.'

Emil felt the change in the *Renard*'s flight profile instantly. Aerodynamic properties that were irrelevant in space were suddenly of vital importance now that they were skimming the upper atmosphere. A winking light chimed on the panel.

'Now, captain,' said Emil. 'Fire those engines for all they're worth.'

THE EVACUATION OF Brontissa had been a nightmarish race against time, a countdown to extinction faced by billions of people with no clue as to the horror of what awaited them. A trading hub in a prosperous arc of the Melenian Dust Belt, Brontissa squatted at a confluence of trade routes and military channels, supplying both staple and exotic goods to the surrounding sectors, as well as providing a haven for weary captains to rest and recuperate while seeking out fresh contracts as their fleets were refitted in the web of orbital dockyards.

The full horror of the tyranid race was not yet appreciated by the people of the Imperium. Few could believe that such an unimaginable threat could exist within the Emperor's dominion, and fewer still had heard anything more than scare stories told third or fourth hand. Only when planet after planet of the Dust Belt went dark was something of the terrifying nature of these extra-galactic predators understood.

System monitors sent to investigate were never heard from again, and only when a demi-fleet led by an ageing

Apocalypse-class battleship encountered the vanguard of the tyranids was the scale of the threat understood. Only two ships escaped to bring warning back to Brontissa, but by then it was already too late for the majority of the populace. Regiments of Imperial Guard from adjacent systems and in-transit forces of Space Marines from the Exorcists, Silver Spectres and Blood Angels were diverted to blunt the threat.

An entire Titan Legion walked the surface of Brontissa, and as the military might of the Imperium assembled, its populace fled in their billions as worldwide panic finally took hold. Every ship that could be lifted into orbit took flight, their holds and corridors packed with refugees, and thousands were killed in the stampede to flee their doomed world. Many more died as the skies above Brontissa filled with colliding ships attempting to thread a path through the orbital architecture without heed or care.

A screaming horde of starships blasted into high orbit, but the tyranids were not some mono-directional mass of unthinking drones. They had devoured Imperial worlds before and had learned from each slaughter. The volume of space around Brontissa was seeded with billions upon billions of bio-organisms. Some were lethally intelligent hunter-killer creatures as vast as Imperial battleships and formed like frond-mouthed conches. Others were little more than organic mines, billowing in dense, spore-like clouds to cripple fleeing craft to be devoured at leisure.

Space around Brontissa became an orbital graveyard, a spinning, metallic wasteland of crippled starships. The fortunate ones died swiftly when their ships lost atmosphere and oxygen, but some survived long enough to be boarded and overrun by chittering hosts of flesh-eating monsters.

Roboute had brought the *Renard* to Brontissa to refresh his contacts in one of the system cartels, a diverse organisation that ran everything from absurdly overpriced luxuries to illegal narcotics and underground relics of dubious provenance. He kept his dealings with its potentates to a minimum, but there had been a passing of a long-lived patriarch, and the proper obeisance needed to be made to the newly appointed scion.

It had been an excruciating week of enforced formality and overblown theatrics, but Roboute had endured it for the sake of the vast sums these particular clients brought to his coffers. But when rumours of the impending alien threat began circulating, Roboute knew better than anyone the truth of this rapacious xenos breed. Everyone in Ultramar knew of the tyranids and the unimaginable scale of the devastation they could wreak.

Warning everyone he knew to leave Brontissa, the *Renard* lifted from the planet's surface amid a panicked armada, surviving several near-misses and once being clipped by the void array of a system monitor in blatant contravention of shipping rights of way. It had been a dangerous escape requiring some deft flying from both Roboute and Emil, but they had broken into open space before the unsuspected englobement of the planet was complete.

Just before breaking through the closing trap of bio-organic ships and orbital spore mines, Roboute had witnessed Captain Makrus Rayner of the *Infinite Terra* attempt a rescue of a beleaguered vessel he believed was carrying his wife and daughter. Roboute knew Makrus only tangentially, as a conveyor of goods thrice removed, but he had liked the man's spirit and his willingness to fly anywhere.

Already trailing a hull's worth of parasitic polymer fronds from a detonated spore mine, the *Infinite Terra* was in no state to manoeuvre. Its vectored engines were clogged with frothing biomass, and its void arrays were snapped after the impact of dozens of burrowing beetle-creatures with teeth like underground drilling rigs. The ship Rayner believed his family to be aboard was much smaller, a cargo lighter that could just about break orbit, but little else. Without inter-system capability or warp engines, there was no way it could escape the darting, bullet-nosed devourer beasts on its tail – Rayner knew it.

With his forward cargo bay wide open, he'd flown through the upper reaches of Brontissa's atmosphere – already turbulent with insidious tyranid micro-organisms that were consuming the oxygen and nitrogen in the air – and attempted to scoop up the cargo lighter. With both ships moving at orbit-breaking speeds the resultant explosion was visible from the planet's surface, flaring briefly as a miniature sun before fading into the distorting colour spectrum of the atmosphere.

The shockwave had swatted away a number of organisms turning their rudimentary senses towards the *Renard*, and though Roboute had not known Rayner well, he owed his fellow spacefarer a debt of gratitude.

Roboute later learned that Rayner's family were on a different ship altogether, one that escaped the terror of the evacuation and had sought them out to pass on the heroic manner of the man's death. Rayner's daughter had returned to Anohkin with Roboute, entering into a mutually beneficial business arrangement that lasted until her ship brought back the *Tomioka*'s saviour pod and Roboute had seen the possibility of a life beyond the boundaries of the Imperium.

Thinking back to the moment he had seen the *Infinite Terra* vanish in a searing nuclear fireball and watching the approaching form of the *Renard*, he wondered if he'd made a grave error in having Emil attempt the same manoeuvre. Probably, but it was too late to change anything now.

Roboute flipped open the ship-wide vox.

'Everyone hold onto something,' he said. 'This might get a little rough…'

Watching his own ship approach at speed while he was tethered in place was like watching a vast mega-organism approaching through the depths of the darkest ocean, its jaws wide to devour the tiny morsel before it without even realising it was there. This was going to be like a bullet flying back down the barrel of a gun and was just as risky as that sounded.

Emil's voice came over the vox from the *Renard*, 'Now, captain. Fire those engines for all they're worth.'

Roboute slammed the thrust controls out to their maximum deployment, applying a dangerous amount of energy within such close proximity to another craft. The shuttle lurched and the internal gravity wallowed as brutal acceleration strained to throw off the e-mag tether holding it in place. Roboute looked back through the rear-facing hull picters and experienced a moment of bowel-churning terror as the vast maw of the *Renard* filled the distortion-hazed screen and the pummelling bow wave of displaced neutron flow slammed into the shuttle's hull.

The image vanished in a flurry of static as the *Renard* swallowed the shuttle in its forward hold.

Roboute fought to keep the controls steady as the vast bulk of the *Renard* snapped the shuttle's tether and sent a squalling burst of feedback into the *Speranza*'s hull. The resulting explosion was lost to sight almost instantly. The shuttle's engines filled the *Renard*'s cargo hold with a seething mass of plasma fire, and everything the servitor crews hadn't removed was instantly incinerated. Only the instantaneous deployment of fire suppression systems kept the fire from burning through the rear bulkheads and gutting the rest of the ship.

Those same systems were themselves incinerated by the plasma, but by then they had done their job. The shuttle slammed into the rear bulkhead of the cargo compartment, and the heat-softened metal buckled like melted wax before the forward momentum of the *Renard* crushed the engines and empty rear compartments of the shuttle, folding them up like a concertinaing bulkhead door. Flames billowed from ruptured fuel lines, and what little air hadn't already been vented from the systems caught light and pinprick fires burned phosphor bright for seconds until oxygen starvation killed them.

Roboute, pinned in place by the force of the impact, just barely managed to slam his fist down on the explosive release bolts holding the shuttle's crew compartment rig to the cargo spaces. The rig's manoeuvring boosters fired and the g-forces holding Roboute in place lessened as the absurdly powerful engines fired with short-burn force.

Ahead of him, Roboute saw the flame-wreathed outline of the *Renard*'s cargo bay and fought to keep the tapered prow of the rig aimed at its centre. Burning the boosters with such power was depleting their fuel cells at an alarming rate, but the mouth of the cargo bay was now racing towards Roboute and he let out a wild whoop as the smaller rig roared from inside the *Renard*, its forward velocity beginning to outstrip the larger vessel.

'The rig's loose!' shouted Roboute. 'Cut your speed, Emil!'

Suddenly all that was around Roboute was empty space and the whipping bands of vapour in the upper strata of the atmosphere. He kept the engines sun-hot until he estimated that any projecting portions of the *Renard*'s prow were now behind him before hauling the control column up and to the side.

'Come on, come on!' said Roboute through gritted teeth. Silent acres of azure steel and adamantium slid by beneath him as the *Renard* ploughed onwards, trailing a halo of fire from its battered frontal sections. His ship had never looked so beautiful.

'Holy Terra, I can't believe that worked!' shouted Emil. 'You're alive? Really? We didn't blow up and this is all just my last moments in slow motion?'

'We made it, Emil,' said Roboute, letting out what felt like ten lungfuls of breath and feeling his heart rate slow from its current triphammer speed. 'Wait. You didn't think we'd make it?'

'Sure, yeah, I always knew *I* could do it,' said Emil. 'I just didn't know if *you* could.'

'Your faith in my piloting skills is touching,' said Roboute, turning the rig back towards the *Speranza*. The sheer scarp of its hull loomed before Roboute and the small craft was slammed back and forth by rogue gravity waves thrown off by the enormous starship.

'I see why ships need an e-mag tether now,' he muttered, finding the nearest embarkation deck's lodestar signal. His vox and avionics panels lit up with warning sigils and blaring binary code waving him off, but Roboute shut them all down and angled his course towards the *Speranza*.

'Hold on, Linya,' whispered Roboute.

TANNA THREW HIMSELF at the arco-flagellant, his fist arcing towards its skull.

The blow connected, but instead of tearing the arco-flagellant's head from its shoulders, it merely rocked the cyborg killer back on its heels. Tanna followed up with a thunderous punch, but the arco-flagellant swayed aside and slashed out with its gleaming electro-flail arms. The strike would have cut Tanna in two, but Varda's black-bladed sword swept out and intercepted the lethal whips and sliced them from its wrist.

Varda fired his pistol at the arco-flagellant at point-blank range, the bolt blasting a chunk of meat from the killer's side, but, incredibly, it stayed upright as chem-stimms blocked out the pain and spurred its hyper-accelerated metabolism to heal itself. Fresh flails extruded from the arco-flagellant's gauntlets as it threw itself at the two Space Marines. The red circle at its forehead pulsed like a heartbeat, and its gleaming fangs were bared as though it was relishing this chance to fight opponents capable of harming it.

Varda backed away, using the Black Sword to keep the arco-flagellant from getting too close. Tanna drew his own sword now that he had a foe he could legitimately kill. He came at the cyborg killer from the opposite side to Varda, slashing low for its legs. The creature leaped over his blade, slamming a fist into the side of Tanna's helm. He felt bone crack and was driven to one knee by the force of the blow. He threw his left arm up in time to block another fist, but he was powerless to prevent the slamming head-butt crashing full into his visor. The impact was monstrous and would have caved the skull of a mortal man. Tanna rocked back, his nose shattered and one eye filled with blood as he toppled to the deck.

Tanna knew there was a scrum of desperate fighting going on all around him, but he could hear nothing beyond the ringing in his ears and his ragged breathing. His right eye lens was a cracked and static-filled mess. He felt the surge of power from his armour as the spinal plug blocked his pain receptors and released a burst of combat-enhancing stimms. He rolled, expecting a follow-up attack, but Varda was slashing his sword at the arco-flagellant's neck.

Except the killer was no longer there, moving with preter-natural speed thanks to the volatile concoction of potent and highly dangerous drugs coursing through its hyper-stimulated metabolism. The arco-flagellant ducked beneath Varda's blade and spun around him to ram suddenly ramrod-straight flail-talons into the Emperor's Champion's side. The energised spikes punched through Varda's plate and he loosed a guttural roar of pain.

But rather than let that pain master him, Varda turned in to the arco-flagellant and put a bolt-round straight into its chest at a range of centimetres. The bolt punched into the killer's chest and the explosive warhead detonated microseconds after, exploding from its back in a bloody exit wound.

But still it refused to die.

Its electro-flails crackled with power and Varda cried out as the shock was delivered straight to his nervous system. The Emperor's Champion dropped to his knees, and Tanna cried out as the Black Sword fell from his grip. The arco-flagellant wrenched its arm in Varda's side, but the Emperor's Champion had his hand wrapped around the writhing steel embedded in his body, holding it fast to his flesh.

Tanna then realised that Varda had not dropped his sword, but released it deliberately.

And now swung it on the fresh-forged chain Tanna had crafted.

The strike was as horrendous as it was unexpected, the blade slicing into the arco-flagellant's shoulder. It ricocheted from the bone and tore into the meat and steel of its skull. Sparks and oil-infused blood sprayed from the wound as the arco-flagellant staggered away from Varda. It howled in a mixture of rage and pain, one arm hanging limply at its side as though the synaptic connections to the limb had been severed.

'Finish it!' commanded Varda.

Tanna surged to his feet and swept his bolter from the mag-lock at his thigh.

The aiming reticule was useless in the smashed visor, but Tanna didn't need it.

But before he could squeeze the trigger, the integrity field at the opening of the embarkation deck blew inwards with the sudden passage of a damaged cargo rig. Given the unexpected and unauthorised arrival of this ship, none of the pressurisation differential protocols or energy damping generators had been initiated to receive an incoming vessel. Ice-cold air blew into the embarkation deck with hurricane force as the integrity field was breached for the briefest second and the battered rig slammed to the deck with a shriek of tearing metal.

It left a cascade of fat orange sparks in its wake as it skidded across the deck like a rampaging bull-grox, smashing cargo containers aside and ripping up a row of loader gurneys in its headlong rush across the deck space. Bondsmen and Cadians scattered like ants as they fought to get out of its pathway.

The violated integrity field snapped back into place, and a concussive e-mag pulse slammed through the deck and toppled those few men still standing like a fist to the guts.

Microcontent 18

THE *SPERANZA* PULLED out of its descending spiral into the atmosphere of Hypatia with less than thirteen minutes remaining before breaking orbit would have become impossible. The violent arrival of the *Renard*'s shuttle rig provided the necessary moment of calm for Colonel Anders and Abrehem Locke to impose a cessation of hostilities and restore a semblance of order.

It was a fragile ceasefire, one that could flare to violence in a heartbeat and might have done so had it not been for the sobering sight of Roboute Surcouf leading a sterile gurney from the crew compartment of the shuttle. Borne upon the gurney was the grievously injured Linya Tychon, and the sight of the horrifically wounded magos had instantly quelled every thought of conflict. Both sides withdrew to lick their wounds and, in Abrehem Locke's case, vanish once more into the labyrinthine structure of the Ark Mechanicus.

As a Mechanicus bio-trauma squad encased Linya in a

stasis-capsule, Roboute paused before leaving the embarkation deck, staring up at one of the vaulted chamber's towering lancet windows – a vividly stained-glass window depicting a sprawling Leman Russ manufactorum atop Olympus Mons. One of the window's lower panes was broken, and Roboute stared at it for several minutes with a curious expression on his face, like a man trying to recall a half-remembered dream, before following Linya and her father to the medicae decks.

Moments later, servitors throughout the *Speranza* returned to their normal working patterns, re-implanting themselves into the ship's vital systems and, more importantly, re-establishing control of the overloading reactors in the enginarium decks. With dedicated binaric choirs appeasing the enraged spirits of the plasma cores, the runaway reactions within their nuclear hearts were cooled and normal operation restored, allowing the *Speranza* to pull out of its self-destructive descent.

Mechanicus clean-up crews arrived to salvage Roboute Surcouf's shuttle and return the embarkation deck to functionality in time to receive the flotillas of cargo haulers from the surface of Hypatia. With orbit restored, the resupply operation continued as before, though at a substantially increased altitude and measured pace.

No trace could be found of the arco-flagellant; it had vanished as comprehensively as its master, though indications were that Brother-Sergeant Tanna and Emperor's Champion Varda had seriously damaged its biological components. Both Space Marines had suffered injury at the hands of the cyborgised destroyer, but without the ministrations of an Apothecary, they were forced to rely on basic medicae treatment intended for baseline humanoid anatomy, which could patch up the surface hurt, but do nothing for any underlying damage the arco-flagellant's flails had caused.

No one beyond the first victims of Guardsman Manos's opening salvo had been killed in the fighting, which in itself was something of a miracle, but the medicae decks were filled with bondsmen and Cadians sporting broken limbs, deep cuts, fractured skulls and hefty concussions. Manos himself was now confined to the *Speranza*'s brig, a broken man with no memory of what had driven him to open fire.

All the subsequent deep neural trawls could establish was that sometime around the shooting, synaptic activity in Manos's amygdala, the mass of nuclei buried deep in the temporal lobes of the brain, had increased tenfold. This section of the brain, often neutered during a senior adept's passage through the upper echelons of the Cult Mechanicus, housed the body's control mechanisms for fear and rage, which – together with the murder of Magos Saiixek – led some magi to speculate that an outside agency had exerted some form of psychic influence over the Guardsman. What that outside agency might be, no one was saying, but below the waterline speculation was rife, with talk of xenos boarders, warp creatures and a rogue psyker among the crew.

The coffin ships of Legio Sirius returned the mortally wounded carcass of *Amarok* to the *Speranza*, and though there was no love lost between Elias Härkin and Gunnar Vintras, *Vilka* had escorted the fallen remains of its fellow Warhound to Magos Turentek's repair cradles. A procession of Mechanicus mourners marched alongside the fallen engine, and spirit-singers encoded memories of its lost machine-soul within the Manifold to honour its sacrifice. The Omnissiah would reveal the Warhound's new spirit in good time, ready for when its physical form was ready to walk again.

With the current crisis averted, and to prevent another revolution below decks, Archmagos Kotov had been forced to agree to several of Abrehem's demands. At first he had demanded another military response, but after consultations with his senior magi and receiving counsel on mortal psychology from Ven Anders and Roboute Surcouf, he had been brought round to the idea of negotiation.

The end results of those negotiations were sweeping changes in the duty rosters of the bondsmen's shift patterns, implemented on a ship-wide basis, together with an improvement in the quality of nutritional foodstuffs served in the feeding halls. Retroactively applied maximum lengths of service were added to the servitude covenants between Archmagos Kotov and the *Speranza*'s bondsmen, and a charter of workers' rights was to be drawn up that better outlined the exact duties and responsibilities of the starship's crew.

All of which had served to enrage the master of the fleet to the point of apoplexy and a full system purge. Being dictated to by menials was unheard of in the annals of the Adeptus Mechanicus, and the thought of such present humiliation was only barely outweighed by the thought of future glory. Between them, Surcouf and Anders finally persuaded the archmagos to agree to the principles of Abrehem Locke's terms – though both harboured doubts as to how long he would abide by the agreement when the *Speranza* returned to Imperial space.

The Ark Mechanicus remained in orbit around Hypatia for another five days, ferrying fleets of haulers from the surface to restock the depleted supply holds and carrying out swathes of badly needed repair work. While Blaylock studied the temporal implications of the regressing world, both Kryptaestrex and Turentek petitioned for another week to fully replenish their stock of raw materials. Kotov refused these requests and ordered Azuramagelli to resume their course towards the unnamed forge world upon which he believed Archmagos Telok could be found.

As the *Speranza* set sail, Kotov sat upon his command throne and once more turned his gaze upon the geometric arrangement of stars at the heart of this quest into the unknown.

'You still believe this venture can succeed?' asked Galatea, easing into position at Kotov's side.

'I do,' replied Kotov, unwilling to waste words on the machine intelligence.

The silver-eyed proxy body waved an admonishing finger.

'We are not so sure,' it said with a throaty, augmetic laugh. 'You are a servant to lesser beings now. No longer master of your own vessel.'

'*My* vessel,' spat Kotov, shaking his head. 'You said so yourself – this is *your* vessel now.'

IT WAS COLD, always cold. Marko Koskinen shivered in the freezing chill, even though he was swathed in furs and thermal layers. The black and silver mountain was long behind him, its frigid winds and ice-locked slopes a distant memory, but here evoked in the freezing temperature of the pack-meet. Breath misted before every assembled crewman of the Legio, from its gun-servitors – temporarily removed from their weapon mounts – through its moderati and all the way to its princeps.

Magos Hyrdrith had emptied the space of heat, an easy task on a starship travelling the void, and crackling webs of frost patterned the glass and steel of the forgotten chamber. No one knew what purpose it had once served, and after today, no one would know what purpose it was serving now.

A hundred souls stood in two long ranks, facing each other across a central pathway to a raised rostrum upon which sat the life-support engines of the Legio's senior princeps.

The Wintersun occupied the centre of the rostrum, his bio-support cradle surrounded by grey-robed adepts with canine pelts of fur and claw draped around their shoulders and skull masks obscuring their half-human, half-machine faces. The princeps's truncated wraith-form drifted in the milky grey suspension, his sutured eyes and implant-plugged torso regarding proceedings like a withered monarch.

Beside him, the Moonsorrow occupied the position of *Tyrannos*, a rank of great significance that granted absolute authority in the absence of the alpha, a title recently bestowed upon Eryks Skálmöld in recognition of his honoured status and a clear symbol of his right of succession. Elias Härkin, encased in his wheezing, pneumatic exo-harness, stood at the base of the rostrum, honoured in his proximity to the senior princeps, but still subservient to their will.

Koskinen believed the Legio had been gifted a fresh start with the Wintersun re-establishing the proper hierarchy of dominance upon his and the Moonsorrow's return from the Manifold.

And now this.

Koskinen and Joakim Baldur flanked Gunnar Vintras as they stood at the opposite end of the chamber to the Wintersun. The Warhound princeps's shaven head was bowed and his shoulders were hunched, making him seem an utterly pathetic figure. Koskinen wanted to despise Vintras for what he had allowed to happen to *Amarok*, but the sight of the broken princeps told him that no rebuke he could offer would match the loathing the man had for himself.

Vintras wore his full Titanicus dress uniform: white and silver, with the twin canidae pins picked out in gold on the lapels of his crimson-edged frock coat. Without furs, Vintras would be chilled to the bone, but to his credit he let none of that discomfort show on his hollow-cheeked face.

'Let's get this over with,' said Vintras, looking over at Koskinen.

Koskinen didn't reply – it was forbidden to speak to an omega without the alpha's permission – and looked over at Joakim Baldur. His fellow moderati nodded, and they each took hold of Vintras by the upper arms and all but dragged him towards the rostrum. The two men marched between the paired ranks of Legio personnel, who turned away from the disgraced princeps as they passed, directing their attention towards the Wintersun.

The cold at the rostrum seemed sharper and more dangerous, like a sudden freeze was imminent.

He and Baldur presented Vintras to the Wintersun, who drifted to the front of his tank with his unseeing eyes fastened upon his disgraced pack-warrior. His elongated and bulbous skull nodded once and Elias Härkin took a clattering, mechanised step forwards.

'Gunnar Vintras, warrior of Lokabrenna and scion of the black and silver mountain, you come before us as princeps of Legio Sirius.'

The nasal distortion of Härkin's pathogen-ravaged vocal chords was unpleasant to hear, but what he had to say next was even more so.

'As princeps were you entrusted with the life and honour of the war-engine, *Amarok*?'

'I was,' answered Vintras.

'And have you failed in that duty?'

'I have,' said Vintras. 'My engine was mortally wounded and its machine-spirit extinguished. No one but I bears the shame of that.'

Härkin looked back to the Wintersun, who floated back into the occluding viscosity of his casket. This was a duty for the

Moonsorrow to perform, to fully cement his position as pack *Tyrannos*.

+A machine-spirit is never extinguished,+ said the Moonsorrow. +It returns to the Omnissiah's light. Bodies of flesh and blood can never outlive a body of steel and stone, a soul of iron and fire.+

'I accept whatever punishment you see fit to impose, Moonsorrow,' said Vintras.

+You do not get to call me Moonsorrow. Only pack uses that name and you are no longer pack. You are omega.+

Vintras nodded. 'So be it,' he said, lifting his head and baring his neck.

+Begin, Härkin,+ said the Moonsorrow. +Spill his blood.+

Härkin nodded and removed a long-bladed knife with a bone handle from a kidskin sheath attached to his leg calliper. Knowing what was required, Koskinen and Baldur once again held Vintras by his arms. Härkin took his knife and made two quick slashes, one across each of Vintras's cheeks. As droplets of blood ran down his face, Härkin placed the knife against the princeps's throat, drawing the blade over the skin; hard enough to draw blood, but not so deep as to end his life.

A princeps, even a disgraced one, was too valuable an individual to be so casually thrown away.

The required mental and physical demands of commanding a titanic war-engine were so enormous as to exclude virtually the entire human race. Only truly exceptional individuals could even train to become a Titan princeps, let alone become one. But censure had to be given and be seen to be given. Vintras would forever bear the ritual scar of failure upon his throat.

Härkin cleaned his blade on the fabric of Vintras's uniform

and sheathed it before reaching up to remove his canidae rank pins. He stepped back to his assigned position at the foot of the rostrum and nodded to Koskinen and Baldur.

Piece by piece, they stripped the Titanicus uniform from Vintras, letting each item of clothing fall at his feet like discarded rags until he stood naked before the Legio. His body was muscular and heavily tattooed, marked by honour scars and ritual branding marks indicating engine kills and campaign records. The skin beneath the inking was marble-pale and not even Vintras's stoic demeanour could prevent the cold from finally impacting on him. He shivered in the freezing temperature, naked and vulnerable and brought low before his Legio.

+Now you truly are the Skinwalker,+ said the Moonsorrow.

VITALI HAD BEEN advised against siring an heir. The likelihood of emotional attachment would be high, his fellow magi told him. The risk to his researches would be incalculable in the time it would take to raise an offspring, for surely he would wish to observe the development of his clone first-hand. He had ignored them all, desiring a willing apprentice to continue his work after he had gone. The arrangement was to be purely functional, for Vitali was a man obsessed with the workings of the universe and his concerns were cosmological, not biological.

But all that had changed when a one in ten trillion random fluctuation in the genetic sequencing of his clone had spontaneously mutated its code and transformed what should have been a genetic copy of Vitali into a distinct individual. A daughter.

Linya had surpassed his every expectation in ability and Vitali had grown to love her as much as any celestial phenomenon, even going as far as to name her after what many believed was the true name of the daughter – or sister, no one knew for certain – of the composer of Honovere. Invasive augmentation of developing brain cells during her hothoused gestation period in the iron womb had given her an enhanced intellect and growth speeds from birth.

Within her first year of life Linya was already acting as his assistant, her enhanced mind housed within the equivalent bodyshape of a six-year-old child. Her physical growth had assumed a more traditional pattern soon after, but her mind had never stopped developing, and soon she was outstripping magi with decades more experience in mapping the heavens.

Traditional education had proved too stultifying for her quickened intellect, and she had fled one Mechanicus scholam after another, always finding her way back to the orbital galleries to study with her father. And so he had trained her in the mysteries of the universe, and she took her place at his side as his apprentice as he had always hoped, though with a bond of mutual respect and love as opposed to the functional arrangement he had anticipated.

Many pitied him or shook their heads at his foolishness, lamenting what he might have discovered or otherwise turned his intellect towards were it not for the distracting influence of flesh-kin to keep him from his duty to the Omnissiah.

They were wrong, knew Vitali.

Any loss to the sum of knowledge held by the Mechanicus had been Vitali's gain.

Linya was going to surpass them all, she was going to rewrite human understanding of the stars and their aeons-long existence. The name of Linya Tychon would be mentioned in the same breath as those great pioneers who had championed the first transhumanism experiments – Fyodorov, Moravec, Haldayn and the vitrified enigma of FM-2030.

All this Vitali had *known* with a surety in his bones that he now understood was simple vanity.

Linya was his creation, and she was going to outlast him and exceed him in every way.

How very biological of him.

Sitting by his daughter's side as she lay unmoving within a sterile containment field, Vitali now saw how foolish he had been. The treatment Linya had received was second to none, the very best the *Speranza* had to offer. Senior medicae and Medicus Biologis had spent the last thirteen days bending their every effort into restoring her body, managing her pain with precisely modulated synaptic diversions and reclothing her surviving limbs with synth-grown skin.

They had done all that could be done. Winning the fight for life was now up to her.

Linya's future hung in the balance, and no one could predict on which side the coin of her life might turn.

Vitali's brain had been augmented, rewired and surgically conditioned in so many ways that its processes resembled those of a baseline human in only the most superficial ways. He thought faster and on multiple levels at once. His powers of lateral thinking and complex, multi-dimensional visualisation were beyond the abilities of even gifted human polymaths to comprehend.

Yet he was as crushed by guilt and grief as any father at the sight of his child in pain.

He knew he could have spared himself this pain had he not been too proud, too stubborn and too bloody-minded to listen to his peers and forego the siring of a successor. If he had been proper Mechanicus he could have neatly sidestepped this horror and simply chosen an apprentice from the most promising of his many acolytes.

But then he would have denied himself the joy of Linya's existence, the pleasure of her growth and learning, the wonder of her personality shining through, no matter how steeped in the ways of the Martian priesthood she became. Though Cult Mechanicus to her bones, Linya had a very rare, very bright spark of humanity that refused to be extinguished no matter what replacement cybernetics were implanted within her biological volume.

Archmagos Kotov and every one of the senior magi had come to pay their respects to his daughter, each expressing a measure of regret that was surprising in some, downright miraculous in others. Magos Blaylock had visited Linya's bedside on numerous occasions, each time displaying an empathy Vitali had hitherto not believed him capable of exhibiting.

Roboute Surcouf had been a regular visitor, and his grief was a depthless well of regret that reminded Vitali of the time he had spent with the eldar. Clearly something of that xenos species' capacity for extremes of emotion had been passed to the rogue trader during his time spent aboard their city-ship.

Vitali had no capacity with which to shed tears, having long ago sacrificed even that tiny space within his skull for extra ocular-cybernetic hardware. Instead, he extended a sterile mechadendrite into the counterseptic field surrounding Linya and rested its callipers on her shoulder, hoping that some measure of his presence would somehow be translated to her sedated body.

The augmented mind was a complex organ, and despite their lofty claims and interventions, not even the highest ranked genetors of the magi biologis truly understood the subtleties of its inner workings. Mechanicus records were replete with apocryphal accounts of the grievously wounded and those in supposedly vegetative comas being brought back from the brink of death by the words of a loved one. And right at this moment, Vitali was willing to clutch at any straw, no matter how slender or unsubstantiated.

He read from one of Linya's archaic books: a rare collection of poems from Old Earth, monographs on celestial mechanics and the biographies of many of the earliest astronomers ever to make the stars shine brighter by bringing them within reach of their earthbound brethren. The first stanzas he transmitted via the noosphere and binaric code blurts, but when he came to Linya's favourite passage, he switched to his flesh-voice.

'I am an instrument in the shape of a woman,
trying to translate pulsations
into images for the relief of the body
and the reconstruction of the mind.'

The poem was said to date from an epoch before the Age of Strife, though that seemed unlikely given the devastation wrought in that cataclysmic era; but it had not been its clear antiquity that Linya liked, rather the fact that it acknowledged the role of a woman in the earliest age of galactic exploration.

Vitali had no real appreciation for poetry, but he knew beauty when he saw it.

Space was a vast wonderland, a tapestry of universal magnificence that any with eyes to see could witness. It was the desire to breathe that wonder into others that had driven him to galactic telescopes, and that same wonder lay at the heart of Linya's creation.

He would not sacrifice the pain he was feeling now and forego the joy of having known his daughter and watched her grow.

'Do you believe she can hear you?'

Vitali turned, expecting to see another Mechanicus visitor, but his lip curled in contempt as he saw Galatea squatting at the arched entrance to the medicae chamber. Its squat body was lowered almost to floor level and is silver eyes were trained on Linya.

Vitali felt his loathing for this… *thing* reach new heights.

Why should this abomination get to exist while his daughter's life hung in the balance?

He forced back the venom in his throat and turned back to the bed.

'I do not know,' said Vitali. 'I hope so. Perhaps if she hears that I am with her it will give her the strength to fight for her life.'

'A very biological conceit,' said Galatea. 'We know of no empirical evidence to support the capacity for perception while in a medicated state.'

'I do not care what you know or do not know,' snapped Vitali. 'I am reading to my daughter, and nothing you can say will convince me I am wrong to do so.'

Galatea entered the medicae chamber, its mismatched limbs clattering on the tiled floor. The ozone stink of its body and the flickering light of its brain jars reflected from the brushed steel of the machinery keeping Linya alive.

'We do not wish to do so,' said Galatea, extending a manipulator arm and resting it on Vitali's shoulder. 'We come to offer you our sympathy, such as it can exist for a biological entity. We had grown fond of Mistress Tychon in the time we had known her.'

'My daughter is not dead,' said Vitali, fighting to hide his surprise at the machine's unexpected sentiment. 'She may yet recover. Linya is a fighter, and she will not let this finish her... I know it.'

Vitali's voice trailed off and Galatea moved to the other side of Linya's bed.

'We sincerely hope so,' it said. 'She is too precious to be taken away by such ill-fortune.'

'I didn't know you had interacted that much with Linya.'

'Indeed, yes,' said Galatea. 'When we took over the exload from the *Tomioka's* cogitators, we linked with her mind and saw just how exceptional a being she is.'

'Exceptional,' said Vitali with a hopeful smile. 'Yes, that's exactly what she is.'

ABREHEM SAT ON a metal-legged stool before Rasselas X-42 and folded his arms. The arco-flagellant reclined on its throne-gurney with the articulated arm and leg restraints splayed, rendering it like some ancient anatomical diagram. The wounds it had suffered at the hands of the Space Marines were extensive, enough to have slain a bondsman many times over. Only its superlative artificiality and accelerated metabolic augmentation had kept it alive, though those selfsame biological mechanisms had kept it in a state of regenerative dormancy since then.

The aftermath of the abortive revolution on the embarkation deck had given Abrehem a great deal to consider, particularly his continued usage of the arco-flagellant. In the confused days after the *Speranza* had pulled out of her death dive over Hypatia, his time had been spent in secretive and noospherically conducted negotiations with Archmagos Kotov, hammering out a means by which the fleet could continue its mission of exploration *and* treat its workers with respect.

It had been a protracted and often thorny maze to negotiate, but a peace of sorts had been achieved. The servitors and bondsmen went back to work and Abrehem had sent Hawke and Coyne with them. He too had been offered amnesty, but knowing how easily his capture might allow the archmagos to renege on his promises, Abrehem, Ismael and Totha Mu-32 had remained in hiding.

The overseer had patched Rasselas X-42's horrific injuries as best he could, but even with inloaded medicae databases to call upon, the sheer incomprehensibility and density of the biological hardware within X-42's body rendered every attempt to restore function akin to little more than educated guesswork.

The bolter wound in the arco-flagellant's side had healed itself, forming a gauze of synthetic skin that over time had bonded with his hardened skin shell to leave a glossy carapace of scar tissue. Totha Mu-32 had removed over eighty-seven individual shards of bolt casing from the arco-flagellant's back before packing that wound with synth-flesh and applying a counterseptic dressing.

As grievous as the bolter wounds were, it was the Black Templar's sword blow that was of greater concern. Numerous chem-shunts situated in the hollows between X-42's shoulder and collarbone had ruptured, spreading a distilled cocktail of potent drugs designed to initiate combat reflexes, states of dormancy, healing and self-immolation. Mixed together, the effect had been to plunge X-42 into a delirious state of feverish nightmares that only the immediate engagement of high-level devotion protocols in its pacifier helm could quell.

But even that was of lesser concern than the damage the

powered blade had caused as it ripped up the side of X-42's skull. The metallic cowl encasing the left side of its head had been cut away cleanly, exposing panels of circuitry that were beyond any living magi's ability to restore. What their function might have been was a mystery, but that they were, on some level, still operative – albeit in an aberrant way – was obvious from the twitches and convulsions wracking X-42's body.

Abrehem thought back to Ven Anders's words as they'd spoken in the moments before things turned bloody. He knew he had been manipulated by a man who could convince other men to walk into hails of gunfire and then thank him for the opportunity, but that didn't alter the fundamental truth of what he had said regarding Rasselas X-42.

Abrehem *was* as good as keeping a slave, just as Archmagos Kotov was keeping the bondsmen and servitors in bondage. How could he demand basic human rights for the enslaved workers throughout the *Speranza* if he wasn't willing to live up to the same standard?

That question had driven him to take this course of action, a course of action that Totha Mu-32 had roundly condemned as an act of illogical foolishness. Ismael had disagreed and both stood behind him ready to step in at a moment's notice should something go hideously wrong.

Ismael appeared at his side and took his organic hand.

Abrehem hardly recognised his former shift overseer any more. The vain, arrogant, self-entitled shit who'd made his life hell on Joura had vanished utterly and been replaced by a figure of such serenity and peace that it was like looking into the face of one of the Emperor's saints painted onto a templum fresco.

'You will see terrible things within X-42's mind, Abrehem,'

said Ismael, his metal-cowled head so like that of the arco-flagellant, and yet so different. 'This is a very brave thing you are doing.'

'It is a foolish act of self-indulgence,' said Totha Mu-32. 'You will find nothing within X-42's mind but vileness. Do you think that upstanding citizens who love their children and worship the Emperor every day are turned into arco-flagellants?'

Totha Mu-32 gestured towards the twitching arco-flagellant and said, 'They are the worst scum imaginable. The dregs of society, the maladjusted, the insane and the irredeemable. *That* is who this was, and to think otherwise would be a terrible mistake. He is now a servant of the Emperor and the Omnissiah, and that is all he will ever be.'

Abrehem nodded towards Ismael. 'Just as a mindless servitor was all Ismael could ever be?'

'That is very different,' said Totha Mu-32. 'What Ismael has become is a divine gift, but I cannot accept that the Omnissiah would work through a wretch like X-42.'

'That's pride speaking,' said Abrehem. 'Saiixek accused you of the same thing, remember? That you claimed to know the will of the Machine-God. You said it yourself, X-42 *was* a monster. *Now* he is a servant of the Emperor and the Omnissiah, and I need to know if there is any humanity left within him, any last shred of goodness we can salvage.'

Totha Mu-32 said nothing, his half-human features unreadable beneath his crimson hood.

'I'm doing this,' said Abrehem. 'So either help me or get out.'

Ismael took a step forwards, keeping hold of Abrehem's hand and reaching out to lift Rasselas X-42's scarred and callused hand.

'The moment of connection will be painful,' said Ismael.

'I remember the last time,' nodded Abrehem. 'I'm ready this time.'

'No,' said Ismael. 'Not for this you are not.'

Microcontent 19

ISMAEL WAS RIGHT. Abrehem wasn't ready for the sudden, wrenching dislocation of having his every sense ripped from his body and rammed into the mind of another living being. It was like having the innards of his skull scooped out and flash-burned before being pieced together again, flake of ash by flake of ash. Abrehem felt his sense of identity slough from whatever form of consciousness he was experiencing, like a serpent shedding its skin and being reborn.

One minute he was Abrehem Locke, bondsman aboard the Ark Mechanicus, *Speranza*, the next he was…

He was…

He had no idea who he was.

He was Abrehem Locke.

No, he was… no, he was not. He was. He was someone else.

He was someone whose thoughts were like a rabid dog in a cage of its own making, the physical manifestation of an unending scream that was only kept silent by the complex alchemy of numerous pharmacological inhibitors. He sat in the centre of a soulless room of bare stone, coffered steel and bottle-green ceramic tiles, facing a heavy cog-shaped doorway of bronzed steel. Leather restraints at his wrists, ankles and torso secured him to a cold steel throne-gurney.

Incense fogged the air and heavy machinery, more suited to the interior of a shipwright's assembly hangar, sat idle to either side of the throne. Feed lines pulsed like arteries, venting tiny puffs of oil-rich vapour that tasted of bile and hypocrisy.

He tried to move his head, but clamps drilled into the bone of his skull and jaw prevented any lateral rotation. In his peripheral vision, he could see twin icons stamped on opposite walls: one a steel-toothed cog of black and white with an iron skull at its centre, the other a two-headed eagle with one eye hooded and blind and the other ever-watchful.

Both icons stared at him with impassive and unforgiving eyes.

He – *no*, the mind he squatted within – felt nothing but contempt for everything they now represented to him.

Chem-shunts buried into the meat of his forearms pumped honeyed muscle relaxants through his bloodstream, and neurosynaptic blockers had been introduced to his spinal fluid. He knew this because the trembling adepts who'd strapped his drugged body into the throne-gurney had spared no detail in their descriptions of what was about to happen.

The door irised open and a chanting group of robed figures marched through.

Their leader read from a heavy book, its weight too enormous for any mortal man to bear. Instead, it was borne upon the back of a stunted figure with an exactingly contoured hunch to its spine. He saw this arrangement of bones had been surgically crafted simply to bear the book. The figure's legs were foreshortened stumps of ossified bone and muscle, and he had no doubt its brain had been reconditioned to occlude any thought but the bearing of the book. Every moment spent in so awkward a posture must have brought constant pain, but it believed it was honoured to be allowed to bear the book, which he saw with grim amusement was the *Scriptures of Sebastian Thor.*

He knew the volume on its back could not be the original, of course. That sat in a stasis-sealed vault on Ophelia VII, guarded by millions of Sororitas warriors and Ecclesiarchy troops, the likes of which he had once led into the fires of battle.

This was, at best, a tenth-generation copy, which still made it an insanely precious artefact.

The man reading from the book was dressed in a white and red chimere, with a cincture of tasselled gold securing it at his waist. He wore a *Pallium Pontifex* around his neck, and the silver skulls stitched along its draped length winked in the half-light. A porcelain skull mask of pure white veiled his face, its cheekbones exaggerated and its eyes bulging monstrously. The jaw was distended, the teeth gleaming in the half-light as though death wished to savour the mortal fear of the condemned man. He recognised the *lexiconi devotatus* the priest spoke – an ornate and complex argot of piety unknown beyond the higher echelons of the Adeptus Ministorum.

Behind the pontifex came three priests of the Machine-God, cowled in red and black. The outlines of their bodies were misshapen, rendered post-human by hulking augmetics and artificial limbs. They walked with unnatural, disjointed movements, each one having transcended humanity to become something more and less at the same time. They had achieved a form of mechanical apotheosis, meaning that their bodies were more metal than meat, yet that was considered an honour.

Finally, a warrior of flesh and bone entered, and where the pontifex's face was hidden and the Martians were objective in their hatred, this man made no secret of his loathing. A man of violence, he was clad in form-fitting black armour, glossy and well cared for, but old and hard-worn. A reflection of the man inside, he knew. Alone of the new arrivals, his face went unmasked. Its deep-cut lines and flinty eyes were without compromise, without remorse and utterly without pity.

He knew this man. This man was responsible for putting him in this chair.

The tech-priests surrounded him, and though his nervous system was all but paralysed and his bloodstream choked with soporifics, they were still wary of him.

What had he done to earn such enmity from these men?

The pontifex spoke first.

'Lukasz Król,' he said – *finally a name!* – his voice distorted behind the skull mask. 'You have been sentenced to arco-flagellation by the holy writ of the Ecclesiarchy you once served. Death alone would be insufficient punishment for the monstrous heresies you have committed in the guise of the Emperor's servant, thus you will atone for your wretchedness and unnatural acts in His holy armies until such time as death claims you. This, it is pronounced, is a true and just command of Ecclesiarchy Helican, enacted this third hour of the hundred and fiftieth day of the nine hundred and eighty-sixth year of the Thirty-Sixth Millennium.'

The pontifex stepped back and the Martians began their work. They plugged themselves into the control mechanisms surrounding him with snaking mechadendrites, and the machine arms to either side of the gurney jumped to life like sleepers suddenly roused to wakefulness. Surgical equipment unsheathed from metallic cowls – needles, arterial clamps and whining bolt-fitters – and nests of components rose from the floor to either side of him.

'Reduce the balms and begin,' said the pontifex. 'He has to feel every moment of this.'

Fear rose up in a smothering wave, blotting out all thought and reason.

This is not my body, this is not my mind.

But the sensations surging through him were no less real, no less indistinguishable from injuries done to his own distant flesh. He wanted to scream, but this was Lukasz Król's memory and he was not about to let these men see him beg or weep or scream.

Piezo-edged bone saws extruded from the arms of the throne and sliced through his wrists with ultra-rapid precision. Blood jetted explosively, but even as the agony cut through his diminishing chemical haze, cauterising heat was brought to bear, sealing the stumps with a single pulse of agonising heat. As horrifying as the removal of his hands had been, it was nothing compared to what came next.

Clicking machines with calliper hands like the nightmarish claws of a demented toymaker began stripping the skin, muscle and nerve tissue from his forearms all the way to the elbow. Surgical flesh-weavers layered replacement nerve-strands over the reinforced bone and grafted fibre-bundle muscle in place of the discarded organic tissue.

His chest heaved and his limbs thrashed against the restraints. They simply tightened in response. He couldn't move. He could only watch as his entire body was pared back and remade.

Sealed caskets rotated up from the floor and opened with pneumatic hisses of condensing air. The monotonous stream of binaric nonsense the tech-priests were chanting faltered fractionally as the caskets opened to reveal the weapons within.

Such awesome tools of destruction required reverence.

Through a haze of tears and hate, he watched two of the machine-priests step forwards and attach the devices to his arms using implanted bolt-drivers, neural shears, flesh grafts and sacred unguents. He felt every insertion, every bolt driving down into bone and every screaming horror of exposed nerves being spliced together. A burst of power surged through him, and telescoping carbon-steel electro-flails twitched and danced as ancient, barely understood circuitry meshed with his crude organic functionality.

The gurney tipped backwards, and the drills, excising machinery and clamps went to work on his skull. Trepanning picks bored through bone and the clicking, mechanised hands inserted neural control implants before finally removing the upper dome of his skull. He felt the lid of bone creaking upwards and the horror of his mind being exposed was almost too much to bear.

Sacred arrangements of sacred oil were dripped into his brain cavity, with each anointing accompanied by the sixteen names of the binary saints. Spinning orbs with mechanical blade limbs as thin as spider legs clicked into place before him, whirring with demented glee.

No, no, no, no, not my–

The whirring orbs stabbed forwards and plucked out his eyes.

This is not my body! This is not my body! This is not my body! This is not my body! This is not my body! This is not my body! This is not my body! This is not my body! This is not my body!

Delicate clamps kept his optic nerves taut as complex targeting arrays, broad-spectrum threat analysers and visio-cognitive orbs were attached in place of his eyes and implanted into his skull. A cranial cowl that was part devotional feed, part cortical inhibitor and part death-mask was slotted home, lowered over his slack features and wired to the frontal lobes of what remained of his brain as hymnals blared from unseen augmitters. Like the grinning skull faceplates of the Chaplains of the Adeptus Astartes, it was the rictus agony of the Emperor, and all those whose doomed fate it was to look upon him would know he had been punished by an agency beyond that of mere men. Detailed schematics of the body-plans of the men before him sprang up on the inner surfaces of his eyes, complete with endurable stresses, violation tolerances and a hundred other measures of how they could be ripped into screaming ruin.

The work continued for another hour, agony upon agony, horror upon horror, until there was little sign that a human being had once sat in the throne-gurney. The mortal meat of Lukasz Król had been scraped away and replaced with an instrument of death and annihilation. Only Abrehem remained and even he was a ravaged shell, cored out by the same processes that had made sport of this man's flesh.

Yet even as his consciousness wept and wished for extinction, he felt the soaring ecstasy of having the power of life and death. For all intents and purposes, he was no longer human, his body enhanced to lethal levels of killing power and stripped back to the most basic physiological functions.

Lukasz Król had effectively ceased to exist, and in his place sat something else.

Something altogether more dangerous and more appalling.

'It is done,' said the pontifex, with a solemn nod, stepping forwards and dipping his fingers in an inkhorn of sanctified pigment that a genuflecting tech-priest held out before him.

He drew four parallel lines of crimson down the skull mask.

'In Thor's Blood are ye anointed. In Thor's Blood shall ye awaken,' said the pontifex.

Rivulets of paint slid down the mask like tears of blood, dripping onto a chest that now bulged with cardio-pulmonary enhancers, adrenal-slammers and dormant steroidal compounds. Spinal implants snaked down his back in a chain of injectors, and stimm-reservoirs on his shoulders gave him a hulking, over-muscled proportion to his upper body.

He was a killer now, a render of flesh, a weapon and an act of retribution all in one.

Abrehem revelled in this new incarnation, a being of almost unlimited violent potential to whom no atrocity was beyond his capabilities, no loathsome act of utmost cruelty beneath him. With all need for moral pretence torn away, Abrehem saw the full horror of what Lukasz Król had done, the torture palaces, the rape gulags and the experimentation camps where he had personally overseen all manner of unimaginable affronts to the Emperor.

This was good.

They thought they had taken away his life and made him their own, but they were wrong.

The killer had *always* been in him.

All they had done was strip the mask of humanity away to rebuild him stronger and more lethal than ever.

'I take from you the name of Lukasz Król,' said the pontifex, dipping his hand in the pigment once more and drawing another series of four vertical lines down Król's chest. The ablative polymer coatings introduced to his dermal layers made the skin feel hard and plastic.

Abrehem watched the pontifex check the serial identifier codes on the requisition form held out by another of the tech-priests and verify them against the name the doctrinal abaci had generated. 'I dub thee Rasselas X-42, and may the Emperor have mercy on your soul.'

'Bastards like him don't have a soul,' said the man in black armour.

'We all have souls, chastener,' replied the pontifex. 'The words of the divine Thor teach us that a single man with faith can triumph over a legion of the faithless. We have restored this man's faith, and he will repay that gift in the blood of our enemies.'

The pontifex nodded towards what had once been a psychopathic mass murderer known as Cardinal Astral of Ophelia VII, Lukasz Król.

'Even the darkest soul can find redemption and salvation in death.'

'I couldn't give a ship-rat's fart about his salvation,' snapped the chastener. 'I just want him to suffer for what he did.'

'Have no fear of that,' said the pontifex. 'He will suffer like no other.'

THE WRENCH OF dislocation as Abrehem was dragged back to his own flesh was no less jarring, but where he had plunged headlong into an unknown body, this time he returned to his own. Though it scarcely felt like his, and the weakness that filled him after the sense of ultimate strength was almost as painful as the surgeries undergone by Lukasz Król.

He toppled from the stool, as helpless as an automaton with its power cell removed and fell into the combined grip of Ismael and Totha Mu-32. Abrehem screamed like a lunatic as a tide of unremitting horror washed over him. His cybernetic arm clawed at Totha Mu-32 and Ismael as though they were warp-spawned monsters from the bleakest depths of the immaterium. Abrehem fought with the strength of the demented, hysterical and desperate to escape the abhorrent presence of Rasselas X-42.

He relived stolen memories – decades of nightmarish, unthinkable abuses, sickened and revolted by every grisly detail. Unnumbered souls had been sent screaming into oblivion, and Abrehem pressed his hands to his ears as he heard their screams echoing within his skull.

To think that one man could conceive of such things was repellent enough, but to know that entire cadres of the Ecclesiarchy had been dragged into the maelstrom of his insanity by unquestioning devotion was almost too much to bear. How many billions had died at the hands of the very institution that proclaimed its mission was to protect them?

Abrehem bent over and vomited the meagre contents of his stomach over X-42's dormis chamber, retching and heaving in disgust. He closed his eyes, willing the scenes of torture, murder and degradation to fade from his thoughts.

'Abrehem,' said Totha Mu-32. 'Abrehem, are you hurt?'

He shook his head and wiped the sleeve of his robe over his dripping lips.

'No, I'm…'

He wanted to say *fine*, but knowing what he now knew of X-42's atrocities, he doubted he would ever be fine again. With Totha Mu-32 and Ismael's help, he climbed unsteadily to his feet, swiftly turning and making his way from the dormis chamber after checking the arco-flagellant's pacifier helm was securely in place.

'Did you see?' asked Ismael.

Abrehem nodded. 'I saw,' he gasped. 'You knew, didn't you? You knew who he was.'

'I did, but you had to see for yourself,' said Ismael. 'And

now you know who X-42 was, do you still think he should be released from his condition? Would you restore the man he was?'

'Thor's blood, no!' cried Abrehem. 'Lukasz Król was a monster.'

'He was indeed,' agreed Ismael, 'but Lukasz Król was once a good man, a man driven by faith in the Emperor to excesses of violence against the enemies of mankind. But he began to see deviance and heresy everywhere he looked, and his bloody pogroms soon turned on his own people.'

'Król?' asked Totha Mu-32. 'The Impaler Cardinal?'

Abrehem shrugged. 'I don't know, maybe. I've never heard of the Impaler Cardinal.'

'Few have,' said Totha Mu-32, as he and Ismael set Abrehem down on his cot bed. 'The Ecclesiarchy are understandably reluctant to admit to one of their own going insane. Some, like Vandire or Bucharis, are impossible to deny, but Król's reign of atrocity was mercifully short-lived and confined to a single system.'

'How do you know about him?' asked Abrehem.

'Król's actions were recorded by the Mechanicus personnel who oversaw the dismantling of his bloody regime after an army of Adeptus Arbites led by Chastener Marazion brought him down. It makes for unpleasant reading, even to those who can detach themselves from empathy and physiological responses to revulsion. Now do you accept that no good can come of X-42's emancipation?'

'Absolutely,' said Abrehem, pointing a shaking hand towards the dormis chamber. 'Check the pacifier helm and seal that monster in there again. We can't risk that any shred of Lukasz Król might still be in there.'

'There will *always* be something of him in there,' said Ismael, gently lowering Abrehem to the cot bed. 'And that is the greatest tragedy.'

A dreadful sadness and soul-crushing weariness settled upon Abrehem, but the memories of Król's atrocities were already receding. Abrehem just hoped that in time they would fade completely. No one needed horrors like that festering in their brain.

'Rest now,' said Ismael.

Abrehem nodded, already feeling his eyelids growing heavy. He felt a blanket being pulled over him and rolled onto his side. It had been foolish of him to venture into the psyche of a mind-altered killer, but at least he knew that Rasselas X-42 would never hurt anyone ever again.

'Shut it down,' he murmured as exhaustion smothered him. 'Shut it down forever and seal this place up so no one ever finds it again.'

'I will see to it,' Totha Mu-32 assured him.

ROBOUTE HAD ALWAYS known the *Speranza* was a vast starship, he'd seen it from space and its inhuman scale was hard to miss. He'd berthed his ship within its cavernous holds, and he knew four god-machines of the Titan Legions, as well as thousands of Imperial Guard and skitarii, were billeted aboard – together with their armoured inventories and vehicles. He knew all this and more, thanks to reams of statistics provided by Magos Pavelka in awed, reverent tones.

So why did he now feel claustrophobic, like a rat in a maze, desperately hunting for a way out?

Ever since he'd brought the shuttle back aboard the *Speranza* he'd had an unidentifiable sense of being watched, that tingling at the back of the neck that tells a soldier a sniper has a bead on them. He had no evidence of this, but in the weeks since they had left Hypatia he'd felt like a helpless mammal being stalked by an invisible predator that could pounce at any time, but delayed the moment of the kill for anticipation's sake.

He'd taken to carrying his pistol with him at all times, even going as far as to keep the safety off, which continually chafed at his Ultramarian training. He took Adara with him at all times, even when traversing well-populated areas of the ship. Much of his time was spent helping Sylkwood and Pavelka repair the damage done to the *Speranza* and the shuttle or visiting Linya Tychon on the medicae decks.

The *Speranza* had already passed the outer planets of the uncannily geometric system and would achieve orbit within another two days at most. No one had yet named their destination, for if the Lost Magos was indeed alive and well on the forge world's surface, it was likely he had already done so, and Archmagos Kotov was nothing if not a stickler for the proper taxonomy of planetary nomenclature.

His days were filled with reading the myth-cycles of Ultramar to Linya and being hectored by Ilanna Pavelka at the terrible damage he and Emil had wreaked on the ship. When armpit-deep in the guts of a non-functional machine or lost in tales of the young Primarch Guilliman, he could almost forget the lingering presence that flitted around him like a persistent swampfly.

Eventually, he tired of walking on brittle ice and decided he'd had enough of sitting in the cross-hairs. If there was someone watching him, it was high time he knew who it was. Roboute unbuckled his pistol belt and laid it on the rosewood surface of his desk before striding from the *Renard*. He randomly picked one of the embarkation deck's exit archways and began walking. Each time he came to a junction of passageways, a stairwell or a processional convergence templum, he took the pathway that looked the least inviting or which had been scrubbed of all locational identifiers.

Within minutes he was hopelessly lost within the warren of dimly lit passageways, mesh-walled and steel-floored. Steam gathered in the upper reaches of vaulted cloisters, and melt-water from ice filling the breaches between passageways and chambers partially open to the void ran in metallic gutters. He walked in darkness, in shadow and by the light of looming vent towers that belched flame into the heating systems.

He marvelled at vast chambers of cog-driven pistons, each larger than a Warlord's leg, roaring machines with connector rods and couplings that scissored back and forth like the arms of a threshing machine or the oars of an ancient trireme of Macragge. The few tech-priests he saw largely ignored him, or steered him away from areas of high radiation or some other danger of which he was clearly unaware.

Wandering through row upon row of titanic cylindrical towers like grain silos, he tasted the greasy tang of bulk foodstuffs, and realised he was looking at the *Speranza*'s food supplies. Roboute walked along a raised walkway between the towers, coming at last to a chamber filled with noxious smells and eye-watering caustic vapours. Three dozen enormous vats, two hundred metres across, stretched into the distance, each filled with a grey-brown sludge of reclaimed matter, meat substitutes, protein pastes and complex carbohydrate additives.

Servitors on repulsor discs floated over the viscous mulch, plunging sample staves into the deep strata or removing contaminants. The sight sickened Roboute and he left the chamber, taking turns at random and always picking a route that had no markings to indicate where it might lead.

The feeling that there was a target on his back or that a noose was slowly closing on him was getting stronger, and he had to fight the urge to spin around and try to catch a glimpse of his pursuer. Whoever or whatever had its eye on him would make itself known to him soon enough.

He passed shrines to the Omnissiah, to the Emperor and to things he couldn't identify. Some appeared to be little more than votive offerings to some avatar that might charitably be considered an aspect of the Machine-God, while others were too disturbing to be connected to the Cult Mechanicus.

Some were clearly intended as little more than petty rebellions, where others were of a more sinister appearance, with items hung from the ad-hoc arrangements that Roboute didn't want to look at too closely. Others appeared to be newly erected shrines to Abrehem Locke and his apostles: the Red Ruin, the Angel Return'd, Blessed Hawke and Coyne of the Wound.

Roboute shook his head at the ridiculousness of these latter shrines, having heard Ven Anders and Captain Hawkins tell him the truth about Abrehem Locke's compatriots. But wherever men and women were confined without hope, they would make their own. Even in the darkest times, the human mind was capable of fashioning its own light.

He passed beneath a towering lancet archway and entered a long processional nave filled with statuary: robed adepts of the Cult Mechanicus arranged in two facing rows running the length of the chamber. Each was around ten metres tall and their projecting surfaces were thick with dust, as were the interlinked hexagonal tiles of the floor. Roboute remembered when he had first come aboard the *Speranza*, and Magos Blaylock had escorted them to Archmagos Kotov in the Adamant Ciborium. The statues there had been toweringly magnificent, sculptural likenesses of the greatest minds of the Mechanicus.

Who were these figures?

Were they men and women whose contributions had been outmoded or surpassed?

A deep sadness filled Roboute as he walked slowly between the statues of the forgotten magi, wondering why this place was now unvisited and abandoned. He paused beside a robed priest of Mars and looked up into the shadows beneath the hood.

'Who were you?' asked Roboute, the echoes of his voice swallowed by the centuries of dust. 'And what did you do? *Someone* thought you were important enough to warrant a statue.'

The statue stared across the chamber impassively, and Roboute knelt beside the carved plaque on its plinth and wiped away the dust.

'Magos Vahihva of Pharses,' said Roboute. 'The rest of the ship may have forgotten you, but I'll remember you. I'll find out who you were and I'll make sure I remember it. I know the Mechanicus say they never delete anything, but not deleting something isn't the same as remembering it.'

Roboute stood and looked up at the unknowable face of Magos Vahihva as an overwhelming sense of calm spread through him. He smiled and ran a hand through his hair, before straightening his jacket and brushing stray particles of dust from his cuffs.

'About bloody time you showed yourself,' he said.

'You were aware of my presence?' said a voice with a breathy, lyrical quality he hadn't heard for many years. He closed his eyes as he turned around, savouring the cadences of the voice as it defied the chamber's acoustics and resonated throughout its length.

'I was, but only because I've been around your people before,' said Roboute, finally opening his eyes. 'I hope this encounter is as pleasant and non-violent as the last.'

A woman in armour that looked to have been crafted from ceramic and alabaster stood opposite him. She was tall, with a leanness to her frame that was both beguiling and somehow at odds with how his brain told him a woman's body ought to be proportioned. A helmet with horns like antlers sat on the plinth of the statue behind her, and he couldn't help but notice the polished pistol strapped to her thigh and the long, bejewelled sword sheathed at her shoulder.

'I am not going to kill you,' she said.

'That's reassuring,' replied Roboute with what he hoped was his most winning smile. He'd essentially engineered this meeting, though only now did he truly understand the tantalising sense of familiarity he'd felt on the embarkation deck.

The eldar woman's face was sculpturally perfect, a pleasingly proportioned oval with large eyes and a tousled mass of scarlet hair entwined with glittering stones and golden beads. Her lips were a pleasing shade of blue, but pursed together in a way that made her seem inordinately angry.

In fact, now that he looked closely, he saw her apparently expressionless face was in fact taut with suppressed rage, an icy fury that simmered just beneath the surface. Despite her earlier words, Roboute suddenly doubted the wisdom of this course of action. He took a faltering step back towards Magos Vahihva as she approached him with a liquid fluidity that left no trace of her passing in the dust.

'You are Roboute Surcouf,' she said, not posing the words as a question.

'Yes.'

'And you have spent time aboard an eldar craftworld.'

'Yes.'

She stopped in front of him as he backed up against Magos

Vahihva's plinth. Her breath was a contradictory mix of warm honey and sharp lemon. 'You understand how rare it is for one of your kind to set foot on a craftworld?'

Finally, a question.

'Yrlandriar of Alaitoc told me that, yes.'

'Alaitoc? Yes, that makes sense,' she said, cocking her head to the side and looking at him strangely, as though some part of a puzzle had just fallen into place for her. 'Its people have always been foolishly trusting. Too eager to seek the middle ground instead of choosing a direct course of action.'

'You know me,' said Roboute, daring a question of his own, 'but who are you?'

'Bielanna Faerelle, Farseer of Craftworld Biel-Tan,' she said, following that with what sounded like the opening bars of a song until Roboute realised she was saying the name in her native tongue. He ran the sounds in his head again and compared them to the human version of the name she'd said, dredging up memories of frustrating afternoons spent in a forest of crystal trees that looked oddly like humanoid figures.

'Fairest light of... distant suns?' he ventured.

Her eyes widened and he laughed at the surprise in her eyes.

'We're not all barbarians, you know,' he said. 'Some of us actually wash too.'

Bielanna ignored his sarcasm and said, 'Did the Alaitocii teach you our language?'

'Yrlandriar taught me a few words here and there,' said Roboute modestly. He was far from fluent, but nor was he ignorant of the rudiments of eldar language.

'Like an owner teaches his pet the commands to sit or beg,' said Bielanna.

Anger touched Roboute. 'More like a master instructing a novice,' he said in conversational eldar.

She laughed in derision and shook her head. 'None of your kind can master the eldar language beyond grunting a few basic phrases. And your analogy is flawed, it infers the novice could go on to become a master. That is not the case.'

'I've heard differently,' said Roboute, tiring of her condescension and deciding a change of tack was required. 'Why did you attack our fleet in the Halo Scar?'

Her face changed in an instant, her slender fingers curled into fists.

'What choice did I have?' she snarled, her porcelain doll features transforming from serene beauty to bilious anger in a heartbeat. 'I flew the paths of the skein and saw what harm your foolish quest might wreak.'

Roboute struggled to follow her internal logic. 'You're saying you killed our ships over something we *might* do?'

Bielanna shook her head and let out a vexed hiss. 'You mon-keigh are so terrifyingly ignorant of the nature of causality it is a wonder you have not already plunged into species-extinction. You blunder through space like a wilful child who screams and wails when the universe does not bend to his will, turning a blind eye to consequences that displease you.'

Glitter light built in her eyes and Roboute remembered Yrlandriar telling him that farseers were powerful war-psykers, as versed in the arts of death as they were in the arts of prognostication. Once again, Roboute realised he had let the appearance of a woman blind him to the truth that she was not what she seemed. In Linya's case that had cost him a little embarrassment and earned him a measure of humility. Here it could kill him.

'What is it you think we are going to do?' he asked.

She sighed and said, 'It would be like explaining a symphony to a ptera-squirrel.'

'Try me, I'm cleverer than I look.'

'This thing that you seek,' said Bielanna. 'It can reignite dying stars and shape entire star systems. Its power can unmake time and space and make a mockery of the universal dance. Do you really think your upstart race of savages is ready to be the custodians of such a thing?'

'Perhaps not,' said Roboute. 'But if it's so dangerous, why don't you just go and get it yourself or destroy it if it's too dangerous to exist?'

Her fractional hesitation was all the answer he needed.

'After the battle in the Halo Scar, the shipmasters thought you'd escaped, but you didn't, did you?' said Roboute. 'Your ship must have been destroyed and you had to board the *Speranza* to escape. You're the ones that have been killing the work crews below the waterline.'

'Your reckless quest into the unknown has cost eldar lives, so why should I care for the lives of their killers? Why should meaningless flicker-souls be of any consequence to me, when your kind are going to murder my children before they are born?'

Roboute endured her venom though he understood little save her anger. Much of it was the bitter spite attributed to the eldar in Imperial propaganda, but her last words stretched his understanding to breaking point.

'Kill your... what?' he asked. 'We haven't killed any children.'

'Nor will you, for the potential for their birth is fading,' said Bielanna. 'With every second you travel towards this *moraideiin* world, their life-thread from the future to the present grows ever fainter.'

'Moraideiin? I don't know what that means. You mean Telok's forge world?'

'Telok, is he one of your machine-men?'

'You don't know?'

Her face flickered, and on any human expression it would have been meaningless – a muscular spasm or a nervous tic – but in the face of an eldar it was tantamount to a murderer's inadvertent admission of guilt.

Suddenly it made sense to Roboute. 'You're a farseer, but you don't have any power, do you? It's this whole region of space and the Breath of the Gods. Something in what it did to Arcturus Ultra is stopping you from seeing the future, isn't it?'

She moved so quickly it was like a skipping image on a picter. One minute she was standing before him, the next he was pinned to Magos Vahihva's plinth with her hand at his chest and her sword at his neck. Phosphor-bright will-o'-the-wisp danced in her oval pupils, and Roboute tasted the bitter, ashen-cold taste of psychic energy in his mouth as it filled with coppery saliva.

'Will I show you what power I have?' she asked, her voice stripped of its previously lyrical quality and all the more terrifying for it. 'Shall I burn the primitive brain in your skull or curse your soul to wander the void for eternity? Will I melt the flesh from your bones with balefire or shall I simply cut your throat and watch you bleed to death? I can end your life in the blink of an eye, and you say I have no power?'

Roboute held his breath as Bielanna's eyes bored into him, the hypnotically bright sparks in her eyes swelling until they shone like twin pools of starlight.

'Reveal to me everything you know of this Telok,' commanded Bielanna, and Roboute felt her presence within his skull like a silk-gloved hand stroking the surface of his mind. 'You will tell me everything regarding this voyage. And then you will return to your fellow mon-keigh and forget that we ever spoke.'

Roboute nodded, as though this were the most sensible thing she had suggested.

'And when I have need of an *agaith*, you will be the hidden blade in my hand.'

'Yes,' he said. 'I will.'

Microcontent 20

ANY FEARS THAT, upon achieving his goal, Kotov would be disappointed by what he found at the end of his quest had been shattered utterly in the last three days. The final approach to Telok's forge world had been a sensory overload in unique celestial phenomena. Not only were the star systems around the forge world clustered tighter than any other system-grouping Kotov knew, but the Kuiper belt, planetary bodies and asteroid fields within the central system travelled in orbits as precise as any engineered by an atomic clockmaker.

The system – which Kotov still insisted on leaving unnamed – comprised twelve planets, each one equidistant from its inner and outer neighbour. All were of roughly Terran size and composition, with the exception of three gas giants in the system's central belt, between which vast fields of asteroid debris hung in glimmering curtains of ejected matter and ice.

The impression was of rocky fragments on the floor of a sculptor's workshop, of discarded components from some vast, and yet unfinished, engineering works. Such was the unnatural order imposed on the system that even Vitali Tychon had been coaxed from his daughter's sickbed to provide stellar analysis and plot new cartographae charts. Though every moment away from Linya chafed the venerable stargazer, even he was held mesmerised by the dizzying ramifications of this system.

The bridge of the *Speranza*, normally a place of continual binaric back and forth, coded hymnals and clattering servitor operation, was now draped in reverent hush. Though no one worthy of the rank of Cult Mechanicus gave any credence to the notions of any deity beyond the God of All Machines, it was hard not to imagine the hand of a divine creator in the celestial architecture of this star and its attendant worlds.

Even the solar wind was a thing of beauty.

The rush of electrons and protons flaring from the upper atmosphere of the star was being filtered through the *Speranza*'s augmitters, and the normally chaotic interaction of particles was rendered into a geomagnetic symphony. It was a cascade of perfectly modulated integers that to an unaugmented ear would sound like soft surf on a beach, but to the superior Mechanicus aural implant became a harmonious interaction of perfect numbers, helicoidal patterns and waveform sounds that were as beautiful as they were artificial.

Holographic projectors displayed the system's twelve worlds in floating veils of light, together with fleet deployment and the ongoing data inloads from the *Speranza*'s forward auspex arrays. The projectors encoded each of the system's worlds with differing colours representing the various atmospheric, geological and climatological systems at work.

At the astrogation plotters, Azuramagelli coordinated the manoeuvres of the Kotov fleet to bring the *Speranza* into a declining orbital track in a way that maximised its defensive posture without appearing to be overtly hostile. Every ship was pulled into close formation, with the fleet's three remaining warships tucked in close-defence positions. *Moonchild* and *Wrathchild* hugged the *Speranza*'s flanks, while *Mortis Voss* trailed in the tail gunner position. The rest of the Kotov fleet, fuel tenders, supply ships and refinery craft, were spread over its upper sections, ready to cluster in for defence at the first sign of trouble.

Vitali Tychon worked alongside Azuramagelli, and though his daughter had shown up an error in the Master of Astrogation's calculations upon their first meeting, he had expressed his deep regret at Mistress Tychon's wounding.

Across from Azuramagelli and Vitali, Kryptaestrex continued to oversee the ongoing ship-wide repair works from his Manifold link to Magos Turentek's prow forges. Despite Kotov's deep mistrust regarding the concessions he had been forced to make to Abrehem Locke, Kryptaestrex was reporting that the new working dynamic between the Mechanicus and its bondsmen was already paying dividends in terms of productivity and efficiency.

Magos Blaylock moved amongst the magi and servitors like an anxious scholar at proficiency examinations, assessing their work, offering suggestions on superior analytical technique or refining aspects of their binary. Kotov watched his Fabricatus Locum at work, seeing something more than simple devotion to duty in his observations.

Putting aside Blaylock's curious behaviour, Kotov turned his attention to the world occupying the central position in the viewing bay. Telok's forge world was bathed in a purple haze of borealis, beautiful in a way that only devotees of the Machine could truly appreciate. The shimmering corona was a by-product of inhumanly massive energy generation on a planetary scale.

Kotov had seen such hazes around forge worlds before, but never on so bright and consistent a level. The quantity of energy being generated was enough to empower the manufactories of at least six Exactis Prima-level production hubs.

The planet was roughly double the Martian mass and boasted an atmosphere capable of being processed by human lungs. Its geology was unknown, as was anything else of its surface conditions. Initial surveys had proved maddeningly inconclusive, with each sweep of the auspex revealing contradictory data-streams that on one pass revealed a planet undergoing traditional – if somewhat accelerated – ageing, while on another echoed Vitali Tychon's data from Hypatia, which appeared to indicate signs of geological regression. Yet, as impossible as such readings appeared to be, Kotov had almost become used to encountering the inexplicable. After all, had not the Breath of the Gods remade Arcturus Ultra and transformed it from a dead system into one that would eventually prove to be habitable?

The collateral effects of such dizzyingly complex stellar engineering were a mystery, and the space in which such an event had occurred was bound to throw up anomalies for centuries to come. Yet for all that his mind was just about able to reconcile the cognitive dissonance of physically impossible spatial anomalies, Kotov couldn't quite shake the feeling that something was, if not *wrong*, per se, at least not quite as right as he would like.

He pushed the nagging sentiment aside, feeling a mounting excitement in his floodstream as the noospheric range counter streamed closer to high orbit. No matter how Kotov conditioned the biological responses of his brain, he couldn't suppress the sense that fate had led him here. He remembered the darkest moments of his despair with shame, when the second of his forge worlds had been destroyed and he had cursed the Omnissiah for forsaking him. But out of that abject misery had come the discovery of the *Speranza.*

From the ashes of his broken hubris, Kotov had recognised a last lifeline to serve the Machine-God, that everything he had suffered was a test. Despair became hope and a newfound devotion to the Omnissiah.

This was where it had brought him, to impossible wonders beyond imagining, a reconnection with the past and a chance to rebuild the future.

All that spoiled this perfect moment was the presence of Galatea.

The hybrid machine intelligence prowled the bridge like a stalking arachnid, moving between the veils of light displaying the twelve worlds and studying each one. Each examination was cursory, saw Kotov, as though it was already aware of what was displayed. A tremor of unease passed through Kotov at the sight of Galatea's studied nonchalance, seeing an echo of Blaylock's peculiar behaviour in its perambulations.

Galatea said it wanted to kill Archmagos Telok, but Kotov no longer believed that. For all its pretensions to humanity and Kotov's increasing distance from his own, Galatea's lie no longer carried any conviction. Some other motive was at the heart of the machine intelligence's desire to be reunited with Telok, and that unknown variable gnawed at Kotov like pernicious scrapcode.

Magos Blaylock concluded his wanderings through the other magi and returned to his station beside Kotov's command throne. The gaggle of servitor dwarfs fussed around his train of pipework and hissing regulators.

'Is it all you hoped for, archmagos?' asked Blaylock.

Putting aside thoughts of Galatea, Kotov said, 'It is *more* than I could have hoped for, Tarkis.'

Blaylock nodded slowly. 'I must confess I doubted the wisdom of this quest. I believed your reasons for its undertaking to be motivated by pride and desperation, but now that we are here... I...'

Kotov turned to face his Fabricatus Locum, surprised by his uncharacteristic loss for words and candid admissions. He had long known that Blaylock harboured doubts, but had thought them put to rest after their walk in the Processional Way. Blaylock's features were no indicator of his mental status, having long since been submerged in mechanised implants, but the ripples in his noospheric aura were clear indicators of his conflicted status, like a machine stuck in an infinite loop attempting to reconcile two conflicting doctrina wafers.

'Is something the matter, Tarkis?'

Blaylock didn't answer, and Kotov was about to repeat the question – though he knew full well Tarkis must have heard him – when he received an answer it was the last answer he might have expected.

'I do not know,' said Blaylock with disarming honesty.

'You don't know? Here we are, surrounded by wonders no priest of Mars has seen in thousands of years, on the verge of reaching the quest's goal, and you don't know if something is the matter? You surprise me, Tarkis.'

'That is part of the problem,' said Blaylock, shaking his head, as though clearing it of some irritant code. 'No one from Mars has been here in thousands of years, yet I feel that this arrangement of stars and planets is somehow familiar.'

'You *feel* they are familiar?' asked Kotov.

'Apologies, archmagos, but there is no other word in my lexicon that fits the situation. I *feel* as though I have seen these stars before. And this is not the first time I have had this sensation.'

'When did you have it before?' said Vitali Tychon, approaching from the astrogation hub.

'Just before the energy emission from this planet reached the *Tomioka*,' answered Blaylock.

'Interesting,' said Vitali. 'As I am reading a great deal of similarity in this arrangement of planets and celestial/temporal interactions to an archived monograph on idealised stellar geometry inloaded by Magos Alhazen of Sinus Sabeus. Your former mentor and, if I am not mistaken, something of an evangelical devotee of Archmagos Telok.'

Blaylock paused as he accessed his internal database.

'No, you are mistaken, Magos Tychon,' he said. 'I am familiar with every submission made by Magos Alhazen to the Martian Tabularium Mons. He submitted no such monograph.'

Kotov shared Vitali's surprised expression.

As soon as Vitali mentioned the monograph, Kotov had retrieved it from the *Speranza*'s archives and instantly digested its contents. Sure enough, the postulations put forward by Alhazen were a close, and in some cases identical, match to the stellar data displayed on the command bridge.

That Blaylock seemed unaware of it was as close to impossible as Kotov could imagine.

Before he could pursue the matter, every single holographic display on the bridge flickered and was snuffed out by an incoming transmission from the planet below. The *Speranza* had been exloading generic hails and Mechanicus greeting protocols as soon as it had entered the system's edge, but they had all been ignored until now.

Each of the holographic hubs filled with a rotating icon of eight bodies seemingly issuing forth from molten bedrock or a swirling rush of what might represent flames. Kotov had never encountered the image, but he recognised a Mechanicus hand in its formation, the golden ratio tracing a line through each of the figures' elbows and giving the whole a pleasingly ordered form.

'Starship *Speranza*, this is forge world Exnihlio,' said an automated vox. 'Prepare for inload.'

'*From out of nothing*,' said Vitali, voicing the Low Gothic translation of the name.

'Exnihlio,' said Kotov, rising from his command throne. 'This is Archmagos Kotov, High Lord of Mars and Explorator General of this expedition. Do I have the honour of addressing Archmagos Vettius Telok?'

Kotov was about to repeat his question when the image of the writhing figures was replaced with complex navigational waypoints tracing a narrow transit corridor through the highly charged atmosphere. Only a vessel of sufficiently low displacement would be able to fly such a passage, and even a cursory parsing of the data indicated that deviating from the prescribed pathway would be extremely hazardous.

'Landing coordinates,' said Azuramagelli. 'An older format, but that is only to be expected from a world without hexamathic enhancements.'

Kotov nodded, feeling a potent sense of anticipation at the thought of setting foot on Telok's forge world. Travelling to the fiefdom of another magos was always a time of great importance, a chance to share data, pursue new directions in the interpretation of techno-arcana and barter services and information to further the Quest for Knowledge. What might he learn on the world of an archmagos unfettered from the censure of his peers and the restrictions of Universal Laws?

'Archmagos?' asked Blaylock. 'What are your orders?'

'Send word to Sergeant Tanna,' said Kotov. 'I am going to have need of the *Barisan*.'

All evidence that human beings had once occupied this space had been removed and the chamber returned to its former state of abandonment. The remains of Hawke's still had been removed, and its component parts placed in reclamation funnels. The lumen globes recessed in the coffers were dimmed and the images of the saintly figures wreathed in shadow. Ismael had taken Abrehem to a shrine below the waterline, leaving Totha Mu-32 to complete the internment of Rasselas X-42.

'Abrehem should never have found you,' he said, circling the slumbering killer.

Clad head to foot in black, the arco-flagellant sat with its ironclad head bowed, a flickering light stuttering like a malfunctioning strobe beneath the smooth inner face of its pacifier helm. Images of Imperial holy men and divine visions of harmony played out before X-42, keeping it locked in a state of perpetual bliss.

Given what Totha Mu-32 knew of the Impaler Cardinal's reign of blood, it was a more merciful fate than any he had accorded his victims. The arco-flagellant's muscles twitched as rogue synapses flared and sparked in its brain, the inevitable result of a sword to the skull.

'I wonder what effects the damage is having on the visions within your skull?' wondered Totha Mu-32. 'Whatever the repercussions, I hope they hurt. You deserve to suffer for the things you have done. And once this chamber is sealed, you will suffer them until the *Speranza* finally ends its days.'

Totha Mu-32 continued his circling of the arco-flagellant, checking that every restraint was as tight as it could be made and that every dormancy connector was firmly attached. He checked every spinal shunt, every cortical inhibitor and every neurological blocker.

Satisfied everything was in order, he ran a final diagnostic on the pacifier mechanisms, ensuring that the machinery was functioning within acceptable operating parameters. Hooked directly into the *Speranza*'s power grid and with multiple redundancies, the mechanism could keep an army of arco-flagellants sedated for longer than the Ark Mechanicus was likely to survive.

Totha Mu-32 backed out of the chamber, still, despite every precaution and check he had just made, unwilling to turn his back on the cyborg killer. He paused by the shutter to the dormis chamber as a cold wind sighed from within, like the last exhalation of a slumbering predator who is just waiting out the winter before emerging to hunt once more.

Rasselas X-42 remained unmoving, a hunched statue of caged murder and horror. Even dormant, it exuded dreadful danger. Though it should be impossible for the arco-flagellant to break the psycho-conditioning holding it fast, Totha Mu-32 half expected the creature to raise its head one last time.

The arco-flagellant twitched and the light beneath its helm flickered on.

Totha Mu-32 swept a hand over the hidden door mechanism and the heavy bulkhead shutter slammed down into the floor with a percussive boom of engaging locks. A handprint of dried blood was smeared in the centre of the door and Totha Mu-32 placed his own hand over the impression of what he knew was Abrehem's hand.

This, coupled with a trigger word, had caused the locks to disengage and begun X-42's reactivation sequence. Totha Mu-32 spat on the bloodstain and rubbed the sleeve of his robe over the flaked blood until nothing remained of it.

Taking a last look around the empty chamber, Totha Mu-32's gaze was met by the hundreds of iron black skulls set into the walls. Part temple, part prison, part sepulchre; each interpretation was apt for the monster entombed within.

A flicker of code squirmed through the walls, fragmentary binary debris from whatever conduits had once passed through this chamber en route to unknown destinations. Much of it was degraded to the point of simply becoming squalling gibberish, and soon it would be entirely reabsorbed back into the noosphere.

Totha Mu-32 turned and strode from the chamber, leaving the lumens to gutter and die as the code encircling the chamber finally faded out. The empty sockets of the grinning skulls set in the bleak walls glimmered with the dying code, as though they alone were custodians of a secret they wished to tell, but were forever sworn to keep.

Like Totha Mu-32, they knew that some doors were best left unopened.

But they also knew that some doors can never be shut entirely.

LIKE THE PHOENIX of myth, the *Barisan* had emerged from the flames of its rebirth stronger than ever. The damage it had suffered on Katen Venia had been almost entirely erased by the ritual ministrations of Magos Turentek and his army of artificers. The compression fractures in its hull plates were repaired, the impact trauma to its superstructure was undone and the torsion stresses in its spine had been unkinked.

For all intents and purposes, the craft was as good as new, as fine as the day its frame had been struck in the Tyrrhenus Mons forge-complex. Turentek had seen the seal of the Fabricator General and had bent his every effort into restoring the work of Mars's pre-eminent worker of metals and spirit. The *Barisan* had suffered greatly in the crash, and its machine-spirit was a vicious, cornered beast of a thing, but Turentek had eventually earned its trust with the quality of his workmanship and the devotion of his servants.

Tanna felt the gunship respond to his every command as though they had been flying together for centuries. It wasn't exactly compliant per se, and could still shrug him off like a tiny biological irritant, but at least there was a measure of respect between them now.

'The gunship has healed well,' said Archmagos Kotov, seated beside Tanna in the co-pilot's seat.

Tanna nodded tersely and said, 'Magos Turentek has my thanks.'

The view through the canopy was a tempestuous melange of lightning-shot cloud banks and flickering geomagnetic storms that clashed, burst and roared and blazed with tortured energies. Streamers of plasma and forking traceries of vertical lightning shot up from the surface, making it feel as though the *Barisan* was evading a thunderous barrage of anti-aircraft fire.

'It is like flying through a hundred thunderstorms at once,' said Tanna as a booming pressure wave slammed into the gunship's fuselage.

'This is not a thunderstorm,' said Kotov as Tanna corrected their flight path.

'Then what is it?'

'The inevitable consequence of planet-wide power generation,' said Kotov, gesturing through the streaked canopy to where a vast dirigible-like device hung motionless in the sky. The billowing hull of the object was englobed in arcs of purple and amber lightning that coruscated down a thick length of metallic cabling hung from its underside and vanished into the roiling banks of charged vapour like a trailing arrestor hook.

'What was that?' asked Tanna as the floating contraption was swallowed by the clouds and disappeared from sight.

'Some sort of energy collector, I imagine,' said Kotov admiringly. 'It seems virtually every machine and temple on the surface of this world is given over to power generation, and that amount of power creates all manner of distortion in the upper atmosphere. I suspect Telok has unlocked a means to harness what would normally be classified as waste by-products.'

'The Breath of the Gods requires such power?'

Kotov hesitated before answering. 'It is impossible to know the energy demands of something so far beyond our comprehension,' he said. 'In fact, it amazes me that one world can provide the power for something capable of such incredible reorganisation of matter and energy.'

Another energy discharge rocked the *Barisan*, and Tanna swung the prow back around as a pair of the giant dirigibles hove into view through the vapour-slick clouds. This time, the view was clearer, and Tanna saw they were little more than vast bladders of a rippling metallic fibre constrained by mesh netting and hung with copper and brass mechanisms that spun and crackled with activity.

Tanna brought the gunship lower, the altitude spiralling down as he followed the convoluted route to the surface. Had he not seen the atmospheric effects for himself, he would have believed they were being led down a deliberately circuitous flight path.

'There has to be an easier way to the surface,' he said, more to himself than Kotov.

'Are you following the waypoint coordinates correctly?'

Tanna didn't even spare him a withering glance. 'You would already know if I was not, because you would be screaming.'

'Point taken, brother-sergeant.'

'The waypoints are accurate, but it's what we will find at the end of this flight that worries me.'

'You suspect danger?'

'I always suspect danger, archmagos,' said Tanna. 'That's why I am still alive.'

'Had Telok wanted us dead, he could have found an easier method than guiding us into a thunderstorm.'

'Perhaps he has reasons to wish us alive when we reach the surface.'

'Such as?'

'I do not know,' said Tanna. 'You are the Mechanicus here. This is your expedition.'

'We are fellow crusaders, brother-sergeant, I thought you understood that,' Kotov said. 'Do you not think that I could have taken any number of Mechanicus transports down to the surface? I could have preloaded the route Telok sent us, but I chose you to fly me down to this historic meeting because I value what you represent. You are the Emperor, and I am the Mechanicus. Two facets of the Imperium working together. Our unity stands as testament to our sacred purpose in coming to this world.'

'And it is never a bad idea to have a squad of Black Templars at your back when venturing into the unknown.'

'That too,' agreed Kotov, and Tanna could almost share the master of the expedition's excitement.

Despite everything they had suffered, they had actually reached their destination alive.

The atmosphere grew thinner, and blocky shapes loomed from the clouds, vast cooling towers belching toxic fumes from the planet's surface and squat funnels that shot plumes of green fire into the sky. Arcing static crackled in the air like fireworks at a triumphal parade and virtually every auspex panel fizzed with distortion. More of the dirigibles drifted past the *Barisan*, hundreds of them floating like blooms of jellyfish in a turgid ocean. The gunship flew lower still, and more of the titanic buildings – if buildings they were – emerged from the banks of cloud.

Tanna saw towering steel structures wrapped in coils of energy, crackling pylons hundreds of metres in diameter and exosphere-scraping pyramids whose bases were thousand of miles wide. It was like flying over a gathering of hive-cities that had forsaken their individuality and simply merged into one continuous planetary crust of steel and caged fire. Tens of thousands of metres below the *Barisan*, tesla-coil skyscrapers jostled for space amid vast power domes and immense capacitor stacks.

The entire surface was a coruscating, reticulated grid of lightning that spat from raised copper orbs as large as kroot warspheres and arced from conical towers fringed with hundred-metre spines. Streamers of light flowed through the gnarled mass of enormous structures, as though the planet were an organism with illumination for blood. Warm rain streaked the canopy as Tanna brought the gunship down, following a newly appeared graphic of approach markers on the avionics slate. The margin for error was minimal, and Tanna realised his earlier suspicion that there existed an easier way to reach the surface was incorrect.

He gestured to vast, funnel-shaped towers rearing up to either side of their flight path like guide poles on a snow-locked runway. Each was topped with a flanged maw that drew in great lungfuls of the clouds and vapour banks.

'Are those atmospheric processors?' he asked.

Kotov could barely tear his gaze from the magnificent spectacle of the colossal, planet-wide city of industry and the inhumanly vast structures passing on either side, but he nodded curtly.

'Yes, I believe they are,' he said. 'They have the hallmark of early STC universal assemblers and are probably what makes the air breathable. What of them?'

'Those towers are creating a stable corridor of calmer air for the gunship to fly through.'

'Again I ask, what is your point?'

'That this route was specifically created for us,' said Tanna. 'Right now, this is the only way anyone is getting to the surface.'

'And?'

'If those machines are switched off, we will have no way to get off this planet.'

Microcontent 21

The Barisan set down in the rain on a landing platform of elevated stonework in the centre of an open plaza that resembled the civic square of an Imperial city. Steel and glasswork spires pierced the sky on every side, but dominating the eastern side of the plaza was a colossal hangar-structure with a vaulted silver-steel roof and glittering masts at its four corners. The sky was a painfully artificial shade of blue, striated with bands of deeper azure and pale streaks of cyan.

Lightning coursed up the sides of every structure, as though their only purpose was to create and channel energy, making the air taste like biting down hard on a copper rod. Kotov marched down the Thunderhawk's frontal assault ramp with a gaggle of scrivener savants in his wake. A pair of servo-skulls with iron-cog halos drifted in lazy orbits above him. His body was a part organic, part cybernetic hybrid in the fashion of an ancient order of theologic warriors from a now lost peninsula of Terra, with a flowing crimson robe whose every fibre was a fractal-formed binary equation.

He had come armed, as was his right as an archmagos, with the same gold-chased pistol with which he had fought Galatea's abominations aboard the Valette Manifold station. The volkite weapon was a relic of the deepest past, an artefact so precious it truly belonged in a stasis-sealed treasury case in one of the great Halls of Wonders within the Dao Vallis repositories. Two menials hastily robed in Mechanicus finery carried the remains of the *Tomioka*'s distress beacon taken from its saviour pod upon satin cushions – a symbolic gesture of the path that had led them to this place.

As befitting an archmagos of the Adeptus Mechanicus, he had come with an escort: eight skitarii in their black and gold armour bedecked with poisonous reptiles of Old Earth. Ven Anders had chosen a squad of his elite veterans, and Sergeant Tanna had come with his Space Marines. As the man who had brought him the locator beacon, Roboute Surcouf had, of course, been accorded a place in the landing party. He had brought young body-guard and his ship's magos, Pavelka, with him. Kotov read the censure brands in her noospheric aura with a note of vague curiosity. Surcouf was not the only one of the *Renard*'s crew to have flaunted authority, it seemed.

Kotov stepped from the ramp, setting foot on a forge world that had not known the tread of a representative of the Imperium of Man in thousands of years. He marched to the edge of the stone platform, where a set of wide steps led down to the plaza, and surveyed his surroundings for any sign of Archmagos Telok or his agents.

Kotov was not so vain as to have expected a triumphal welcome or a mass turnout of whatever workforce laboured in the power plants and forges of this world, but he had expected *something*. They had crossed the galaxy, endured all manner of hardships and indignities and suffered great loss to reach this world. A flicker of perturbation danced at the edge of his thoughts at the emptiness surrounding the *Barisan*.

His skitarii took up position to his right, while Colonel Anders formed the Cadians up in two ranks on the left. Tanna and his Space Marines stood like giants carved from basalt and ivory at the base of the assault ramp; Surcouf and his people joined him at the steps, while the menial took a subservient position on his right. Kotov carried a long sceptre of gold and bronze, topped with a jet and bone representation of the Icon Mechanicus. Trails of incense pleasing to the Omnissiah wafted from its coal-red eye sockets.

Putting aside the lack of any discernible form of greeting, Kotov instead turned his attention to the world itself, feeling the perpetual vibration in its bedrock that was common to planets entirely given over to the workings of the Adeptus Mechanicus.

But there was more to it than that.

Kotov felt the unmistakable presence of grand designs, of new and unimagined workings taking place here. Deep in the very essence of what made him an archmagos, he sensed that magnificent things were afoot on this world. Technologies as yet undreamed, research that had stagnated millennia ago and which was now resurgent, developments in arenas of sophistication that the magi of Mars could not even begin to imagine.

This was a world that was in the purest sense of the word, unique.

And it was empty.

Sergeant Tanna and Colonel Anders approached and stood to either side of him.

'Were we not expected?' asked Anders, clad in his dress uniform, regalia that only a Cadian would recognise as being any different from battledress.

'We are expected, of course,' replied Kotov, fighting down a mounting sense of unease. 'We received detailed instructions for our landing.'

'From an automated source,' pointed out Surcouf. 'That could be hundreds of years old or more.'

'No,' said Kotov. 'Had that been the case, the given waypoints would not have delivered us to the surface, but seen us torn apart in the geomagnetic storms on our descent. The coordinates we were given are only relevant at this precise moment.'

'Then where is Telok?' demanded Tanna.

'He will be here,' said Kotov. 'The authentic catechisms of first communion were exchanged with the binaric purity of genuine Mechanicus signifiers. We are expected and we will be met.'

'I think you might be right,' said Surcouf as previously invisible seams appeared in the facade of the enormous hangar-structure with the vaulted silver-steel roof. A titanic gateway was revealed, like one of the portals offering access to the vaults of arcana beneath Olympus Mons, and from it marched a glittering behemoth.

Easily the equal of an Imperator Titan in height, but as wide and long as the largest Mechanicus bulk lander, it was an impossibly huge scorpion-like creature of glass and crystal. Its segmented body was veined with shimmering lines of emerald light and low-slung between enormous legs like frozen stalactites hewn from the roof of a colossal cave. It moved with the sound of breaking glass and grinding stone, and no one could miss the similarity to the bio-mimetic crystal-forms they had fought on Katen Venia.

'Throne preserve us,' breathed Tanna.

'What in the name of Terra is that?' hissed Anders.

Kotov fought to hold back his own fear, but the sight of so monstrous a creation circumvented his rational neural pathways. Nothing could stand against such a towering war-engine, not the might of the Imperial Guard, not a Titan Legion, nor even the awesomely destructive war-engines of the Centurio Ordinatus. This was death in frozen, crystalline form.

'Now that *can't* be good…' said Surcouf, backing away towards the *Barisan*.

'We have been brought here to die,' said Tanna.

'No,' said Kotov, though the evidence was hard to deny. 'That makes no sense.'

'Believe what you want, archmagos, but we are leaving!'

'Is it even possible to get back?' cried Anders over the clashing din of the crystalline beast's stamping, seismic approach.

'It has to be,' said Tanna. 'We reverse our course to the surface and hope the stable corridor through the atmosphere is still open.'

'You're staking our lives on a forlorn hope,' said Anders.

'Better a forlorn hope than no hope,' pointed out Tanna.

'True enough,' nodded Anders, waving his own men back to the gunship.

Kotov alone did not move, nor did his skitarii or his aides. He watched the approach of the crystal leviathan with transfixed awe.

Tanna shouted at him to get to the *Barisan*, but Kotov ignored him.

Better death than to return in disgrace.

THOUGH HE HAD helped Kotov reach this world, Vitali Tychon had declined the chance to accompany the archmagos to the surface. It had been hard enough to leave his daughter under the care of the medicae staff for the time it took to begin the cartographae protocols on approach to Telok's forge world.

What if she were to wake while he was away?

With his work complete on the command bridge, Vitali had ridden the mag-lev to the medicae deck and now hurried towards the burns unit. The attending surgical adepts were quietly confident that Linya would survive and recover much of her former operational utility. Her legs had been amputated at mid-thigh, but augmetic replacements had already been fashioned by Magos Turentek that closely mimicked the appearance of human limbs.

The rest of the damage had been largely cosmetic, and the vat-grown skin patches were showing signs of renewed growth. It would never be the same as human skin, but it was as close as could be created without a clone donor – and Linya had always been adamant that she could never allow another life to be brought into being simply to act as a repository for spare organs.

The corridors of the medicae deck were deserted, which was unusual, but with the ship in orbit around Telok's forge world, Vitali was not entirely surprised. How often did an adept of Mars get to travel beyond the edges of the galaxy, let alone witness a forge world established in the depths of intergalactic space?

He hoped Linya would be awake. He wanted to speak to his daughter again, to hold her hand now that she was no longer at risk from infection and the counterseptic field was no longer required. He had no doubt that she would have insights into the nature of this world that had escaped the more traditionally minded magi.

Besides, he could use the help in cataloguing the many anomalous readings he was detecting from the world below. Much like Hypatia, Telok's forge world exhibited signs of aberrant senescence, appearing to experience periods of hyper-accelerated ageing balanced out by concomitant periods of renewal. Geological push and pull were all part and parcel of a planet's existence as its orbit traced an elliptical path around its star, but this was something more, something unexplained and, for now, beyond his ability to fathom.

Too many inexplicable anomalies that shared this same characteristic were mounting up for Vitali's liking: the reports of the robotic guardians on the *Tomioka* being in a state of decrepitude but yet still functional; the apparent planetary youth of Hypatia and the presence of a pre-Age of Strife metropolis; and now these nonsensical readings.

Whatever Telok had found in the wilderness space, it had effectively unravelled the fabric of space-time and made a mockery of the physical laws governing its operation. Vitali's thinking was too literal and methodical to make sense of such things; he needed Linya's ability to think in curves to galvanise their cogitations.

Vitali turned into the burns unit and followed the familiar route through its sterile corridors, still turning over the problems of trans-dimensional fractures in space-time and their collateral effects on universal chronometry.

So focused was Vitali on this largely theoretical and largely unknown branch of Mechanicus art that at first he didn't notice the bodies.

He stopped in his tracks and all thoughts of quantum theorems were forgotten.

The central hub chamber of the burns unit resembled an uprising in a slaughterhouse.

Corpses and severed limbs lay scattered throughout the space like offal, too many and in too much disarray to even begin to guess at how many dead bodies surrounded him. Horrified, Vitali saw one body cut in half at the waist, sitting in a lake of oil-sheened blood, another that was little more than a truncated slab of meat with metallic nubs of bone protruding from its torn flesh. Mechanical parts were strewn amongst the hacked up meat, and Vitali saw the robes of magi, servitors and menials.

The carnage had been indiscriminate, the exalted murdered alongside the enslaved.

Worse, there was clear relish taken in these killings, a savage joy in the reduction of human flesh and machine augmentation to ruin.

Prudence and logic dictated a retreat, but his daughter lay defenceless in one of this deck's treatment chambers. Whatever maniac had perpetrated this senseless massacre might still be here, might still have designs on killing anyone he came across.

Vitali was no warrior and had always eschewed the implantation of weaponry within his body-plan, but right now he would have gladly had an integral beam weapon or energy sword. Stepping around the worst of the blood and discarded body parts, Vitali picked his way towards the passage that led to Linya's room.

Scarlet droplets had sprayed the walls here, as though the murderer had swung his killing blade to spatter the lifeblood of his victims in some perverse act of vandalism. With a sinking heart, Vitali hurriedly followed the looping arcs like a trail of horrid breadcrumbs.

'No, please, no,' whispered Vitali as he saw the blood drops traced an unerring course to Linya's room. 'Ave Deus Mechanicus, please no.'

The door was ajar and Vitali heard sounds of movement from within.

Though he had no ability to fight beyond what innate human nature had gifted him, Vitali didn't hesitate and barged through the door.

'Get away from her!' he shouted without knowing who or what lay within.

The grisly tableau before him halted him in his tracks and he sank to his knees in abject horror.

Galatea squatted at the side of Linya's bed, the silver-eyed tech-priest body hunched over his daughter like some predatory vampire creature. Blood haloed Linya's head and Galatea's arachnid limbs were wet where it had hacked its victims apart in the medicae hub.

'Magos Tychon,' said Galatea. 'We are glad you could be here.'

The machine intelligence straightened up and Vitali recoiled in horror.

'Ave Deus Mechanicus!' wailed Vitali. 'What have you done? Omnissiah have mercy, what have you done to my Linya?'

'We said your daughter was exceptional,' said Galatea, as a web of micro-fine connector cables wormed their way inside a glass cylinder of bio-conductive gel to infest the newly implanted organ within. 'And now her mind will be exceptional within our neuromatrix.'

THE CRYSTALLINE LEVIATHAN moved with a hypnotic fluidity that should have been impossible for something so enormous. The sheer magnificence of its construction and very conception was astounding, beyond anything even the most crazed techno-heretics imprisoned beneath the Baphyras Catena dared to dream into existence.

It appeared to have no moving parts as any Mechanicus enginseer would understand the notion, its joints and segmented body parts seeming to move within and through one another in ways his ocular implants told him ought to be impossible; as though the bonds between the crystalline lattices within its body were fluid in ways no one had thought possible.

Tanna shouted at him once more, but again he ignored the Space Marine's words.

What fate would there be for an archmagos who returned empty handed from an expedition that had suffered such loss? He would be stripped of his last holdings and reduced to his component parts to be reclaimed into servitor implants. How would that serve the Omnissiah?

Better to die within sight of his goal than to flee towards disgrace.

The aching blue of the sky and the lightning arcing between the giant tesla-coil towers glittered from its multi-faceted form. It had a beauty all its own, a lethal majesty that had a perfect symmetry of form that struck Kotov as being ostensibly similar to Galatea's appearance. The comparison was a poor one; the hybrid machine intelligence's mismatched body-plan was at best a crude approximation of this magnificent creature's form.

No. Not an approximation.

A copy...

Three figures appeared at his side and Kotov nodded to Sergeant Tanna, Colonel Anders and Roboute Surcouf.

'You are not leaving?' he asked.

'I left Kul Gilad to die on the *Adytum*,' said Tanna. 'I will not leave you to die alone.'

'I've come this far,' said Surcouf. 'Seems a shame to leave without seeing how it all ends.'

Anders nodded in the direction of the leviathan as it loomed overhead, a titanic monster that could crush them underfoot without even noticing.

'And even if we got into the air, that thing would swat us down in seconds,' added Anders. 'And I'm mechanised infantry through and through, I'd much rather die on the ground than in a burning wreck of a Thunderhawk. No offence to your flying skills, Tanna.'

Kotov shook his head with an amused grin. 'No one is dying here today.'

Anders looked set to disagree when the vast plaza was suddenly filled with the sound of splintering glass. Every one of the landing party craned their necks upwards as a million spiderwebbing cracks zigzagged over the surface of the towering scorpion creature. Its entire body began coming apart, as though it had been struck by a precisely resonant hammer-blow at its most vulnerable point and its structure was revealed to be no more solid than grains of powdered glass.

Cascades of glittering shards fell in a razored deluge from its upper surfaces as the immense war-engine began disintegrating from the top down. First the swaying stinger tail fell apart, dropping thousands of crystalline fragments to the plaza. Its body collapsed into itself, shedding mass like a ruptured sandbag. Its legs followed seconds later, toppling inwards like a row of dying Titans. The entire crystalline machine was falling apart, as though whatever molecular structure had allowed it to retain its shape was suddenly and catastrophically undone. The noise was deafening, the sharp-edged sound echoing from the surrounding structures and buildings in a thunderous crescendo of breaking glass and splintering rock.

Vast drifts of crystalline debris slumped from the implosive ruin of the beast's dissolution, towering dunes of broken glass spreading out in a tidal wave of lethally edged shards. The rain of glassy fragments broke against the raised platform in a shattering tide, spreading around it with the fluidity of liquid. Such was the volume of the giant scorpion creature that the scale of its death filled the entire plaza with glittering debris.

Then Kotov saw it was not debris and not death.

It was deployment.

The matter shed from the giant creature began cracking and splitting further, reorganising itself into new arrangements. Thousands of crystal-forms were taking shape from the dune sea of crystal, swiftly acquiring mass from the expelled matter of the host creature. Instead of one creature, now tens of thousands of crystal-forms surrounded the raised landing platform.

'What in the Emperor's name...?' breathed Tanna, turning on the spot to see how thoroughly they were outnumbered. Like the vast army of statuary once assembled by a despotic ruler of Old Earth, the crystalline statues were arranged around the landing platform with perfect symmetry, their ranks as serried as any mass deployment of Imperial Guard on the muster fields.

Kotov studied the figures at the base of the platform's steps.

Humanoid in outline, they resembled unfinished sculpts of a race of powerfully built warriors hailing from one of the Imperium's primitive feral worlds. The crystalline warriors before them turned with robotic precision, parting like a crystal sea to form an avenue of approach like the triumphal route travelled by a victorious Lord General.

Emerging from the army of crystal-forms was a being of hulking proportions, a terrible meld of metal, glass and steel. Superficially it resembled a malformed penitent engine, bipedal and roughly humanoid, but its legs were brutish, elephantine stumps that displayed none of the unfinished simplicity of the crystal-forms.

Its movements were ungainly and awkward, as though its form was somehow misshapen and not at all what its creator had intended. Portions of its central mass were clearly formed from dark iron, and scraps of scarlet cloth draped arms that were spined with crystalline growths sprouting from every plane of its upper body. Arcs of heavy pipework looped over its shoulders like the cabling of an electromagnet, and an oil-streaked hood sat in the centre of its chest like the sarcophagus of a Dreadnought.

'What is that thing?' asked Anders, pulling his rifle tight to his shoulder.

It reached the base of the steps and began to climb with a hideous, lopsided motion, the crystallising necrosis of its limbs making each flex of a joint a splintering nightmare. It left powdered glass in its wake and the closer Kotov looked at the partially obscured iconography on the metallic portions of its body, the more he understood that this was not a thing to be feared, but revered.

Slithering metallic fronds drew back the scarlet hood at the creature's chest and Kotov fought to conceal his mounting excitement as he saw a human face revealed, albeit one ravaged by the effects of crystallisation and extreme juvenat treatments.

It was, nevertheless, a face he recognised.

A face that had stared back at him from the pages of crumbling manuscripts and degraded pict-captures for centuries of his life.

'Welcome to Exnihlio,' said the creature, its wasted features moving like a poorly operated flesh-puppet. 'We hope you will forgive the theatricality of our introduction, but we had all but given up hope of ever receiving emissaries from Mars.'

Kotov stepped forwards and said, 'Archmagos Telok, I presume?'

To be concluded in Gods of Mars.

About the author

Graham McNeill has written a host of novels for Black Library, including the ever popular Ultramarines and Iron Warriors series. His Horus Heresy novel, *A Thousand Sons*, was a *New York Times* bestseller and his Time of Legends novel, *Empire*, won the 2010 *David Gemmell Legend Award*. Originally hailing from Scotland, Graham now lives and works in Nottingham.